FELLING OF THE SONS

A Bonanza novel

DEDICATION

This book is dedicated to the memory of David Dortort;
for his faith in me and my work,
and for his vision of the four Cartwrights
that stands the test of time.

HUGE thanks to **Adam Reinhard**
for creating the cover for this edition.

CHAPTER 1

June, 1860

Bret Van Remus glanced at his father before staring back out the stagecoach window. "I can kill a Cartwright, Pa. Let me do it." The rocky hills and valleys, green with summer in the Sierra Mountains, blurred through his mind. The Overland coach bound from Sacramento to Virginia City, Nevada hit ruts and lingering mud puddles as though included in the fare. Dust had settled on his lips but Bret only tasted the blood of revenge that marked their dusty trail.

He and his pa had fought over their plans for vengeance on the Cartwrights for eighteen years, putting it off, finding flaws, making adjustments, and now at age 30 he felt still 12, with no future and no past, just anger. "We don't need to involve any outsiders."

Clete Van Remus brushed absently at the dirt on his chesterfield coat without looking up from his papers. "No. I've said this before. I want your hands clean in this." He'd seen to their privacy in the coach by paying the full fare for just the two of them.

Pa thought himself wise using those eighteen years to invest, barter and even steal wherever possible. And now, by throwing money around in Virginia City, they would remain above suspicion when things started to go wrong for one particular family of so-called noble citizens. But Bret couldn't get past his own need – no matter how remorseless a killer Clete eventually finds to do the proper harm to the right target.

"Nobody'd know it was me." Bret pulled his long blonde hair from his face, an unconscious game he played with the wind. He didn't share with his pa, whose nearsightedness affected not only his physical ability to see the present but often the future, too, that he felt capable of exploding into a million bits of uncontrolled rage just seeing one of those murdering Cartwrights.

The bumpy ride didn't keep Clete from studying the property claim papers he had legally drawn and notarized. For the 100th time, Bret thought, he checked them to make sure they'd fool any judge in the land. Clete put the papers down to study his son. "Bret, you sound just like you did when you were 12. Now quiet and let me think."

"You find a problem?"

"You talk like the adult you profess to be and we'll have a conversation." He hid behind the papers again to rub his eyes but Bret didn't miss the gesture. Pa got those headaches often but refused to get treated for them, saying they came from the same hate Bret carried around. But Bret's hate made him feel stimulated, not incapacitated.

"You had those papers verified by the best judge in the district."

"I'm not worried about these papers. Just planning the best strategy for presenting them." He sneezed again and adjusted his Derby, a habit of marked resignation to his balding head.

"But why'd it have to take so long?" Bret clenched his hands tight on his lap to control the rage. Ma would have been ready for revenge the day after the murder if she hadn't been the one murdered. Not Pa. Pat hated the idea of making a mistake, of being wrong or looking stupid. Bret once caught him trying on a pair of spectacles and thought his pa might buy them, until he caught sight of himself in a looking glass.

"Ben Cartwright will never expect us, not in a thousand years"

"Whatever you say." Bret peered ahead on the trail, wincing at the dust, and jerked back inside the coach. "Oh my God. Indians."

"Really?" Clete didn't put his papers down.

Bret pulled out his gun and tapped the barrel on his knee as he glanced nervously between the window and his father. "Thought I saw one. Don't take much to get Indians to attack." Clete kept reading. "Well, get yours out, too. One gun ain't much good against a whole tribe."

"Indians belong here, same as you and me." A few years back Clete rode the stage with one jumpy Swede who thought he heard someone yell "Indians." He had screamed, "Oh mine Gott, vere, vere?!" and started shooting out the window like crazy. Wouldn't have hit one even if they'd been surrounded. Damn foreigners. "Besides, that little Paiute war helped us get that mine real cheap. Sent miners running for the hills!" Clete chuckled as he carefully folded the papers back up and shut them up in his satchel. "Like I said, timing."

"I don't know why we gotta live here, Pa. We could just do the killing and move off again."

"I told you, if I'm going to get the Ponderosa, we need to settle. When Ben realizes who I am, he'll get suspicious, unless I have legitimate purpose." Clete sighed. The stage climbed hills slow, with their final destination, Virginia City, nearly at the peak. "We have to gain his confidence, get established, make friends. And when his sons . . ." Clete grabbed Bret's arm and lowered his voice as though the driver sitting up top might hear. "I want you to stop calling me Pa. Swear to me! If Ben Cartwright learns my son is still alive, you won't be safe. Not once his sons start dying. Swear you'll call me sir or Mr. van Remus from here on!"

Bret grinned. That part of the plan seemed easy enough to him. "I swear. I won't call you Pa."

***

September, 1860
Adam Cartwright tucked two letters in his pocket and stepped outside the stage express office in Virginia City, lips pressed with worry. He pulled his dusty black hat over deep brooding eyes—his form, as lean and dark as a panther, recognizable in his red shirt and black vest. Adam tended to worry more than his pa, certainly more serious about life than his younger brothers, but he found his worry nearly always had cause. He trusted his instincts and ability to act when needed. Letters tended to mean business, good or bad, and without opening them, just by noting the correspondent, this time he guessed bad.

By the posted marks Sutter's letter had been waiting a pickup for a week now, and this other letter appeared hand delivered. They didn't get to town enough lately to check their post. Adam always tensed when he saw any mail from Sutter. Not that he disliked Sutter, or that Sutter meant trouble. These days Sutter had enough trouble of his own just trying to hang on to a piece of land. This other letter had the name Van Remus on the outside. Adam heard the name earlier that summer but they'd had a tough year so he didn't think to mention his uneasiness over the name to Pa.

As Ben Cartwright's eldest son, natural heir to the richest logging and cattle baron west of the Mississippi, Adam opened all letters given him that were addressed to Ben Cartwright, a responsibility that today, for no reason he could yet name, felt like a burden. Adam jumped back up into the buckboard, ignoring women's glances his way. Normally he'd nod back, share some frivolities. He debated taking the letters home instead of going on with his errands. But Pa and his brothers were out readying the herd on the mesa for the fall beef drive up to Salem, the capital of the new state of Oregon, so one would be back at the ranch until after dark.

He'd likely not get another chance to visit the Paiutes until mid-November, and by then they'd be gone from the Truckee River back up to Lake Pyramid and snows would shut off his route until the February thaw. So Adam stopped at several grocers and mercantile stores to turn in the list of the supplies for the drive, determined to stick with his plans for the day. When he came back through, everything would be ready to load in back of the wagon. Normally he would have gone to Carson City for supplies but this route got him to the Truckee and back just as quickly. Still, it would be late before he returned to the ranch, so he could only hope these letters weren't as serious as his gut feeling indicated.

Adam had thought it a risky proposition, driving cattle up a new trail through northern California and into Oregon, until they found Val Blessing, who had trail-blazed the area back in '56. Adam guessed his Pa had another reason for going into Oregon, and that reason was John Augustus Sutter, the California rancher they had stayed with back in Sacramento for a year, until he was 12. Could this letter be about cattle and nothing more? Adam wouldn't know until he read it. At the livery where he put in his request for the iron supplies Jake noted Adam's distraction, but Adam only shrugged Jake's questioning concern aside.

Once his errands were finished, supplies ordered, Adam headed the team pulling the buckboard, newly laden with supplies for the Paiute tribe, down the hills of Virginia City and northwest to their camp on the Truckee River. A war broke out only a few months back because of the Indians' explosive rage over the mistreatment of their women by drunken white men. They avoided all contact with whites now on the advice of their agent, but did have permission to settle for a couple months around this section of the river. Adam had maintained a friendship with them after the war, especially with Kudwa, who had to give up his shaman training to his sister to be a warrior and struggled with identity problems since the war. Adam understood him and so their friendship bonded. Kudwa wanted his role of shaman back but the Paiutes still feared for their future. As Adam had watched and listened, and gave him information about the whites around them, Kudwa slowly came to terms with the awkward role of having visions both of peace and of war.

The treacherous hills going down Sun Mountain into the valley were hard even on his big draw horse, and the distance into the barren foothills where the Indians lived in the desert between Truckee Meadow and Pyramid Lake would have taken him two days to travel. The Paiutes were left with land not good for much; sparse sage and the scarce wild game fled through in a desperate search for food and water. So the time they spent at the river was like a holiday to them. There they would strengthen and gather what resources could help them get through the long winter ahead, along with the few supplies they would accept from him.

Once the horse reached a smoother part of the trail, curiosity won out and Adam pulled out the letters. He opened first the one from Sutter, and then, more quickly, with one eye on the horse's progress, the other from Van Remus. He felt the slim worry swell into extreme concern, the day suddenly short that a moment ago had been long and the sudden need to get too many things done with too little time.

After reading both letters, he didn't know what had him so worried. And that made both letters even more troublesome. He couldn't remember anything about that year living with Sutter in Sacramento.

***

Clete stepped out of Virginia City's limited excuse for a bank on that late September morning with a grin wider than the Sierra Nevada sky. The news he had waited for arrived, the assay of his latest rock that showed the makings of a rich vein opening up in the Golden Cross.

As he waited on the step for his son's return, the assay report flapped noisily in Virginia City's notable wind. Bret hated this high altitude living but Clete felt healthier than ever. Now, after only three months his mine was second in size only to the Yellow Jacket and he hasn't had a headache in weeks. Clete had earned the respect of the locals over the summer by giving out as many jobs as the Yellow Jacket, at a fairer wage. A good reputation was gold to a man's standing in town. Even his nearsightedness seemed improved — the world around him looked crystal clear.

Bret steered the buggy alongside him, getting him off the wooden walkway being constructed even as people walked on the sloping streets. Virginia City, growing at a rate to match the silver being dug, was yet a child, little more than a year old since the discovery of the silver lode and continually under construction. All the sawdust in the air added to the breathless anticipation in the eyes of miners.

Clete climbed in the buggy and waved Bret on. He leaned back to catch his breath, coughing up some granite dust that had settled in his throat. "We're closing in on it, Bret!" He waved the paper in Bret's face. "Didn't I tell you the Golden Cross would pay for us?"

"Yes, Mr. Van Remus, *sir*, but what about the rest of the plan?"

Clete sat back with a contented smirk. "I think we're ready."

"You found a gunman?" Bret veered the buggy off to the side as the Overland Stage ripped into town.

"It's interesting, looking for a gunman," Clete said. "You have to ask without asking."

"I could do it. I told you that. Sir."

"Not necessary. He followed a trail of bills leading him to Hawkin's boarding house, where he found an envelope of money and instructions."

"I can't believe their luck to go all summer without me seeing 'em."

"It's possible we didn't recognize them. And that Ben," Clete fairly spat his name whenever it came out of his mouth, "was tied up in some kind of legal hearing all summer over in Carson City. But we got the time we needed, Bret. Don't forget that."

"Time. Always more time." Bret pulled the buggy in front of the International House but neither felt inclined to move. Bret looked at his Pa, grinning like a choked canary, purely busting with news.

"A Cartwright went through this morning. I heard this over at Will's shop — he's preparing an order that needs to be picked up tonight."

"About time! Why didn't you tell me earlier? Which one, Pa?"

"Simmer down. If I had mentioned it earlier, he'd be dead in the street and you'd be in jail for murder."

"But which one?"

"Doesn't matter." Clete's lips were set firm in a cheerless grin.

"Think he got the letter you sent?"

"Oh, he got it. Now he'll not have a reason to suspect us at all."

"I'm not sure I'd care if they did."

Clete knew well the sound of pure hate in Bret's voice and could picture his son's face without looking — an 18-year mask of hate rooted in a 12-year-old heart. He looked back down at his assay report, one that encouraged him to believe they neared the main vein of silver. He felt just a trace of regret. Once they started the killing, he'd have to leave all this behind — the men, the excitement. Even though he planned it so that they could take over the Ponderosa, killing Ben's three sons had that element of risk. But Bret would rather kill his own father than give up on the revenge that ached inside him for so long.

***

Adam reached the Paiute camp just after the midday sun crossed high sky. He gave a hawk call before riding in, knowing their fears

9

remained since the War of the Summer Months when 160 of their tribe died and the rest left to disband and starve. Here on the Truckee they built only temporary shelters because they would move back to the desert before the end of the month. Adam visited them in the desert a few times but had always left there in an upset and angry mood. Only a few lodges had been rebuilt and most still slept on the cold hard desert ground at night. Every visit he made sure to bring them more clean blankets.

They tried hard to be self-sufficient but the desert gave them so little on which to live. Mr. Wasson, their agent, was doing all he could but help came slowly. In the desert they dug ditches for irrigation and learned to plant. On Adam's last visit there Kudwa had showed Adam their progress, but his fear for his people was clear visible on his face. Once they had been happy, thriving on their own terms in Truckee Meadow. Now they were forced against their own nature to live where nature discouraged life, to dig into the skin of Earth Mother and make grow what the Earth didn't already provide, while being assured that it would make them better people, better than living off gophers, mice and grasshoppers, things nature offered in plenty.

Kudwa, a slightly built, wide-faced Paiute with an in-your-face persona that Adam enjoyed, greeted Adam with an embrace and waved him in front of the fire. Kudwa was small for a Paiute but few could match his fierceness in battle. He also had a more somber outlook to life; Adam at times thought they mirrored each other.

They made their usual trades, Adam getting in return nice Indian handmade goods that he would give to the schoolteacher in Virginia City to distribute. The people gathered in a semi-circle around the fire, all except for Winnemucca and his daughter. Winnemucca had taken ill shortly after Sara had left to visit another tribe. Adam sat with deliberate solemnity across the fire from Numaga, a man he respected greatly for his efforts to keep the people peaceful – at least until the attack on Wilson Station.[1]

"What is it, Adam Cartwright, that you can share with us today?"

---

[1] Dan De Quille, *The Big Bonanza*, 1947, 131. The De Quille book appears to be a source of material used on the series. The episode "The Paiute War," that aired October 3, 1959, called it Wilson's Station but the attack was at William's Station.

Felling of the Sons

Using whatever native words he could muster, Adam told the Paiutes about the railroads that would come into Nevada from the direction of the rising sun. He explained how many more whites would come this way on this iron horse, more than 100 times the number now. He drew a demonstration of 100 times in the dirt, and explained how they would all have to adjust to many more people. Numaga asked how these railroads came, like horse or like wagon. Adam described the engine, but added that some things were better seen than explained, to which he saw nods of agreement.

"Standing beneath the engine all the way across the land will be rails," he drew in the dirt, "and these rails will be set on wooden ties to hold them in place." He drew ties to connect the rails. "From our land, the Ponderosa, men will want trees for..." After a pause, Adam jumped to his feet. Trees. That second letter, what Van Remus wanted?

Kudwa stood with him. "Dechende[2] if they want your trees." Kudwa's English wasn't as good as Numaga's, who acted as interpreter. Kudwa refused Numaga's help in talking with Adam, because they instead wanted to learn each other's language together.

"Say no?" Adam smiled sourly and shook his head. "We sell — nadewagahwa — some, but sometimes they want more."

Kudwa nodded. "We have met these men who always want more," he responded in Shoshone. Adam knew what he said more by the way he said it.

Adam looked around at those seated at the fire. The children with their open, eager eyes, and older children, a little less trustful. The women, not one without something working in her hands, painstakingly weaving the tiny strips of mice furs into a blanket. The men, a few who survived the war as warriors. Because he couldn't finish what he wanted to share with them, they were alerted to a danger that didn't even involve them, stilling all industrious hands and their eyes taking root on his face, many of them as skittish as a calf at branding season.

---

[2] Shoshone language words used are from the official website at http://www.shoshonidictionary.com/shoshonidictionary.asp, but I apologize to the people if they are not used very accurately.

11

Adam put a hand on Kudwa's shoulder. "I have many thoughts." He struggled to find the right word. There were a number of English words that couldn't translate, like thought and problem and worry. "Neetsiigwa — in my head today. I am sorry but I must go." He turned to the buckboard.

Kudwa stopped him, the pain in his eyes clear even when his words were not. "My people can help save your trees."

"You just take care of your people." Adam tossed a wave to those watching, climbed up and whipped the reins.

Kudwa watched Adam's back until he saw only dust. "Adam Cartwright is wrong." He turned to face the others. "Adam Cartwright worries about trees. I will make him understand that we can help him, as he has helped us."

When he received assent, he added a breastplate to his chest extending down to his breechcloth and took a bow with two arrows. He mounted the small mare the Cartwrights gave them and rode off on Adam's trail.

***

The air brought a chill in the dimming sun as Adam took the trail back up to Virginia City—the day seemed noticeably shorter than the day before. He took the first letter out of his saddlebag, the one delivered that day by Pony Express, to read again.

> "Ben. Sorry to be the bearer of bad tidings, but you should be aware that an old nemesis of ours from those early days has re-emerged, and from what I hear, now lives in Virginia City. Clete Van Remus is a lawyer with money and means. I fear for you, Ben, if there's any man who would try to destroy you, it is he. There is nothing more he can do to me. Forearm yourself, Ben. You will not be able to respond to this letter as I am embroiled in a drama of my own, trying to retain some of the great acreage I once had.[3] Pity us, Ben, for what we tried to do, and what we have endured. I wish you and your family

---

[3] By 1862 he had only a few hundred acres left. Oscar Lewis, *Sutter's Fort: Gateway to the Gold Fields*, (Englewood Cliffs: Prentice-Hall, 1966), 192.

well. If I'm wrong about him, I apologize for worrying you. As always, John Augustus Sutter."

Adam folded the letter up and tucked it in the saddlebag on the seat. Pa moved them from Sacramento without saying why, but stayed Lewis in touch with Sutter and often talked about how wonderful he made life in Sacramento Valley. Pa kept them so busy after the move to Nevada, working to lay claim to land and building a home, that Adam never stopped to consider why he couldn't remember Sacramento.

He remembered seeing Lake Tahoe for the first time, and until today thought perhaps it was his first real firm memory. An early explorer named it Lake Bigler but soon everyone came to call it "Tahoe," the Indian word for 'big water in the sky;' water with a depth of pure blue he'd never seen anywhere else. By the time Adam left for college they had a good homestead started, through sweat and fighting for food, their family growing as strong and flexible as nature itself.

Reading Sutter's letter made those early days on the Ponderosa feel like Pa had been hiding out. From Van Remus? What had happened between them? Pa talked about Sutter but never about anyone else from that time they spent there. Hearing Sutter's name always made him tense, but he never thought to ask why.

The move to Nevada, Adam thought, squinting at the tall hills leading up Sun Mountain, came in about the fall of '42, some 18 years ago. Much of his memory of those times seemed curiously blank. He had been 12 when they moved away, not all that young. He could remember other events from growing up, but, as he thought about it, those memories could be stories that Pa told them rather than anything he selected to remember himself.

With every leveling of the land under the teams' feet he pushed them hard again. At another slow upgrade he pulled out the Van Remus envelope. These two letters, coming at the same time, brought a sense of urgency that made other matters trifling. This time he read Van Remus's letter slowly, hoping with each word to remember the man.

"My dear Ben Cartwright. And I use that endearment in all sincerity. Sacramento is a buried past for us. Though we've had our problems, I mean you only the best now."

The handwriting appeared neat and legal. Problems in Sacramento? Of what nature? A business deal perhaps? Pa's interests were in construction, cattle and other livestock, farming, trading — a little of everything in the colony established by Sutter. Adam had met Sutter on several occasions since moving to Nevada, but couldn't remember him from living in California at all.

"Remember Juan Agosto?[4] The snake got what was coming to him. Remember how he came between us? Remember that? Oh, I'm sure you must. If not for him you and I would be richer men today and our friendship would never have severed."

Adam pursed his lips. Juan Agosto. He'd heard the name before. How would he and Van Remus be richer? Did Pa know about the gold before the gold rush? Sutter could have kept them from laying claim to some very rich land by knowing about the gold before anyone else and keeping it hidden. And Sutter did try to hide knowledge of the gold found at his mill in 1848. Strange that Van Remus hasn't realized that even if he got title to the land instead of Sutter, he wouldn't have held onto it any longer than Sutter did. Juan Agosto? Sutter obtained title from the Mexican governor, but even though Sutter had a burst of prosperity working with the U.S. government in the later years of the war, the Americans didn't respect his title after the discovery of gold. If Sutter knew about the gold, why did he end up so poor?

"I've been living in Virginia City for three months now, owner of the Golden Cross mine. Doing quite well with it."

With lumber so expensive, Van Remus could be after what most miners want — Ponderosa trees. A legitimate business deal with an old acquaintance—nothing more. Perhaps he thinks he can weasel

---

[4] It appears to be a Mexican derivative of John Augustus. Whether I found this in a source back in 1994 or made it up, I can't say now. But on August 29, 1840 Sutter was naturalized as a Mexican citizen. Richard Dillon, *Fools' Gold: Decline and Fall of Captain John Sutter of California* (New York: Coward-McCann, Inc., 1967), 105.

more out of Pa than he would otherwise. But Pa has never put old business connections ahead of land concerns. Unless...van Remus has something on him?

Adam remembered hearing about a new mine owner doing well, but thought nothing of it at the time. Mines and miners come and go so quickly around here. If Sheriff Roy Coffee knew of Van Remus's existence, he found no reason to mention it. They had a rough summer with the drought, logging contracts were demanding and the herd over-grazed wherever they were put. Miners and ranchers weren't always on the friendliest of terms, and the Paiute war took a lot of time and attention from other matters as well. Pa had to spend a lengthy time testifying on behalf of the Paiutes to keep them from being unduly blamed for that war. And they were more inclined to buy their supplies at Carson City, anyway, which was an easier trip on the horses.

> "Being owner of the Golden Cross kept me too busy to look you up. But I will. I promise you, we will have our chance to talk over old times."

Rumors ran about the Golden Cross all summer. They found quartz laden with gold and silver ore, but rumors were that a ledge of silver ran in its direction.

> "I look forward to seeing you and comparing the last 18 years. I tried once before, a few years back, but you had your boys on an extended vacation in New Orleans. Now we can hardly miss each other, can we? I hope you can see clear, as I have, to putting the past behind us. Fare well Ben, I'll be in touch."

Van Remus bought a mine and now he wanted trees. Trees — the lifeblood of the Ponderosa, all that timber needed for shoring wet and soft silver-laden walls. Odd timing, getting Sutter's letter the same day as this one, although it had been several weeks since the last post pickup. Without Sutter's warning, Adam would think nothing of Van Remus's letter at all.

Adam had heard a rumor that by the time of Marshall's gold discovery in '48 the Mexicans were already digging gold out of

California,[5] and that the American government went to war with Mexico so that U.S. settlers could fill the area before the Mexicans had all the gold. Easy enough for Mexicans to share knowledge of gold with certain Yankees well before the Mexican War, but as early as 1841? Fremont went to California in 1845 – Adam remembered the explorer Fremont got into trouble with Colonel Kearny during the war in 1847 for claiming himself as California's U.S. governor, and that the U.S. kept the takeover of the state secret until the army arrived. Pa told him Sutter related that story only a few years back. Kit Carson had told Kearny to go back, California already had been secured.[6] Was it over gold?

Adam knew well the U.S. government's need for mineral wealth and land. But rumors weren't worth anything; Adam only believed in good hard evidence.

Pa had enough on his mind without having to deal with this. He and Little Joe were short of men needed for the drive until they reached Green Bluff in Northern Sacramento Valley, where they could pick up some extra drovers. The lumber contract they had just finished took up more timber than Ben originally planned. They had to do some heavy re-seeding, fencing, and bouldering to strengthen up a section in the north 40 that had weakened.

Lousy timing, these letters — Sutter's accusations, Van Remus's friendly gestures. One thing for sure — Pa would remember Van Remus. Pa may just shrug it off and it'll be business as usual. Ever since Adam could remember, since he came home from college anyway, Pa let him do the worrying, believing in his eldest son's instincts and ability to be tough when necessary — although Pa still had a lot of fight in him, as well.

In Virginia City, Adam dropped off the Indian goods for the children at Miss Abigail's school. By the time he wiggled out of her company,

---

[5] Feliz Riesenberg, Jr., *The Golden Road* (New York: McGraw-Hill, 1962), 109. The Mexicans had a saying well before the gold rush – *no es oro todo que reluce* - "All that glitters is not gold." But gold, after all, was one of the driving forces of Coronado and other Spaniards who came north into what became the U.S. back in the mid-1500s.

[6] J. Patrick Hughes, *Fort Leavenworth: Gateway to the West*, (Topeka: Kansas State Historical Society, 2000), 38-43.

the sun had set. Adam didn't fear women — just Miss Abigail. There was a woman with marriage on the mind. He wanted to meet a woman the way his pa had, unexpectedly. Like one day he'll just turn around and she'll be there. Here all he had to do was drop his hat and he'd be surrounded by every available female, young and old. He didn't mind the attention. He just wanted to do the choosing.

Adam steered the team to Will's Grocery, which took him past the International House. This hotel with its San Francisco style finery sat in the middle of what could barely pass as a city, with its continual construction and general haze of deep diggings. Adam pulled back on the reins, hoping to catch sight of Van Remus. He didn't think he'd recognize the man and would not accomplish anything by confronting him. In renewed desire to find out what Pa remembers about Van Remus, he clicked the horses to get going.

***

From the lobby of the International House, two men watched Adam ride off. Vince, the hotel keep, happily accommodated Clete's questions. After all, Clete had rented an entire suite and paid six months in advance. Vince agreed a month earlier to point out any Cartwright he spotted in town because, as Clete explained, they had simply been too busy all summer to get re-acquainted. When Vince spotted Adam lingering outside the hotel, he called Clete out from the dining room.

"Adam is outside as we speak. Run out and meet him yourself."

Clete went to the door. He squinted as he watched the buckboard pull away, but didn't see the man clearly enough to recognize him. "Ah, that's the eldest, eh? He has grown up fine, hasn't he?" He glanced across the street where Joe Jolly sat waiting. Ever patient, like a vulture. When Jolly saw Clete nod in the doorway, he looked back at the Cartwright wagon and got to his feet. "I suspect there will be a time when I'll meet up with him. But I thank you."

"Right fine man," Vince continued. "Give you the shirt off his back and whatever's in his pockets besides. All those Cartwrights would. You say you knew Ben from before?" Vince continued with his ledger business even as he chatted.

"Back in Sacramento."

"Say, I remember him talking about Sacramento once or twice. Did you know John Sutter?" Vince turned the page on his ledger, missing Clete's sudden tight-lipped smile.

Clete couldn't tell if Jolly understood the message, so he stepped out onto the walkway in front of the hotel. Sure enough, Jolly watched Adam's back until the wagon took the first slope out of town. Clete walked to the mercantile and squinted in the window as though intent on a new pair of boots. He nodded at one fine pair, the gesture firm and deliberate. He didn't look at Jolly as Jolly stood next to him.

"Yeah?" Jolly's scowl gave the impression that he'd never learned the art of smiling.

"You see him? Black vest, on a buckboard. Just do it."

Jolly jumped on his horse. He placed a hand lightly on the butt of his rifle and headed out of town. Clete went into the mercantile and bought the boots, humming lightly.

CHAPTER 2

Kudwa rode with an anxious eye on the lingering light in the sky. He hoped not to be trapped too close to the city after the sun sank. He wanted to reason with Adam surrounded by the trees they wished to save, to use their spirit to convince Adam to accept his help. He skirted Virginia City, riding hard along the edges of the rocky hill. On the far side of the city where the road led to Tahoe, he got off his horse to wait for Adam to get ahead of him again. He could tell that Adam had not left the city by the lack of fresh wagon wheels on the road leading out of the city.

Kudwa felt Adam wanted his help even if he could not find the words to ask. He jumped down from his horse and knelt at the base of a tree to seek strong words of guidance. Trees were the Paiutes' friends long before the white man came. The roots, Earth Mother's many fingers, kept the ground they walked on from flaking into dust. If too many trees fall, the world will fall. This his grandfather and his grandfather's grandfather told as truth.

***

Adam eyed the slim glow from a half moon lighting his way. Their pace felt impossibly slow. He wished he had a day or two to think this over—bring up Van Remus's name casually and see how Pa reacts. But they were leaving on the drive and Van Remus could make some kind of tree-grabbing move before Pa gets back. And Pa could help him remember more about this early relationship. Not remembering was like a dark secret, and dark secrets made Adam uneasy.

Clete Van Remus. Sacramento. Juan Agosto was. . .John Sutter. John had used a Mexican name to obtain that land in California.

Clete Van Remus. Van . . . Remus. Tall . . . but Adam had been young, only a boy. Thin . . . beady cold eyes and a disruptive laugh. Adam let his eyes close as the horse continued its easy pace. Van Remus backed him into a corner — a shed — Van Remus cornered him, grabbed his arm, squeezing so tight the boy feared his arm would fall off.

"Your pa thinks it's over, thinks he's won. Well, I'll go, all right, boy. But you hear me. Someday your pa's gonna lose more than I ever had, boy, and I'm talking about your life now, do you understand? He thinks I don't know?" The shed could have been on fire and the shaking boy wouldn't have noticed. *"You're going to pay with your life! Not only you, but that little brat brother and any others he sires. I'll take care of all of you, so that he knows only the worst kind of suffering, as you've caused me. So fear for your life, boy. Fear for it! I'm coming back!"*

The buckboard hit a rock and Adam leaned back, eyes wide again. This wasn't his imagination, he knew, suddenly and surely, but a memory of a real event. "Hyah!" It no longer mattered what happened between Ben and Van Remus. He and his brothers were in danger now. Van Remus wasn't after trees at all!

"Hyah!" He cursed the slowness of the buckboard, the supplies and the nearness of night. Just yesterday he would have reveled in the beauty of the trees around him shimmering in the setting sun but now he felt too unstable. "Damn those letters and the faulty memory of childhood."

***

Kudwa called out to his friend but the wagon picked up speed before Kudwa could catch him. Kudwa sensed Adam's anger as he whipped the reins. It seems his friend couldn't ride fast enough to get where his anger led him. But the anger came from where — the stars? And then Kudwa saw another man pounding a fast horse down the road behind them, so he ducked deeper into the thicket to watch. Did Adam know that someone chased after him? But Adam did not look behind him. Kudwa loaded his bow but stayed hidden.

The man skirted along the trail, along the edge where the firm trampled dirt met the coarse and loose sand, like someone hoping to make less noise, and pulled his rifle out.

Kudwa felt his heart trying to burst out of his chest. He urged his horse out of the woods, readying his bow. His horse trotted and then cantered as Kudwa rode behind the galloping gunman. He tightened his body and pulled the string back---.

***

Felling of the Sons

The wagon rattled, wheels squeaking and hitting ruts, so Adam didn't hear the horse coming up behind him, didn't sense the rifle aimed at his back, and only realized someone had fired when he felt the sting and sharp exploding in his back.

His arms flew up as he thought to pull the sharpness away and the warmth flowing down his back distracted him, his mind fading into the dark. The buckboard hit another rock and he flew off the seat to the ground, rolling up against a thin pine. He fought the weakness, fought to get up. . .his hands felt the rough bark of the tree behind him but he couldn't grab hold. He had to get to Pa, tell him something—he wanted to tell Pa when he was 11 but didn't think Pa would believe him. . .and then blocked out. Pa has to know because his brothers are in danger now. . .and he was to blame.

Jolly jumped off his horse and cradled his rifle in his arm as he approached, grinning widely, the fallen man. "Hoped for a clean kill, first shot." He kicked Adam's leg with his foot. "Still alive? Now I gotta waste another bullet."

Adam struggled to get up. The man raised his barrel up but froze, eyes widening, and the rifle fell to the ground and he staggered, trying to get the arrow out of his back.

***

Kudwa let loose the string of the bow. When the man with the long barrel dropped it and fell, he ran forward to Adam and knelt at his side. The dying killer grabbed for Kudwa's foot but Kudwa kicked him away and quickly and silently slit his throat. When he turned back to Adam, a great wash flooded through him, choking his breath. His friend lay so still, blood seeping into the ground. Gently he picked Adam up. If his friend must die, he must die at his own lodge.

The horses and wagon had stopped, so Kudwa laid Adam across the bench on the buckboard. He removed the leather pouch from his waist and tucked it under Adam's back, against the bleeding wound. The medicines in the pouch were strong but untried on a wound. The clay bear, the bits of pine cone and needle, the medicine root, the wolf tooth and small pieces of rock Adam called sulfur and serpentine all had special meaning to Kudwa. Now they would save his friend's life or guide him on his spiritual quest into the next world.

Kudwa tied his horse behind the wagon and grabbed hold of the horse by the strap that held it secure to the wagon. A light fog rose up gently from the land to steal the light from the dying moon. He ran the wagon when he could, and slowed when he had to, yet as he inhaled the fog, he felt as though a great force filled his insides with the masterful souls of his many ancestors. He heard Adam stir and felt a calming certainty that his friend felt comforted by the night spirits as well.

Kudwa guided the buckboard to the front of the ranch house and hid in the trees to make sure they found his friend. When the door didn't open right away, Kudwa stood forward and gave a great piercing eagle cry. He disappeared into the trees that stood as silent and vigilant as Kudwa himself, hopeful for the life of a friend.

CHAPTER 3

Ben Cartwright sat down with his younger sons, Hoss and Little Joe, to a late supper of his favorite of Hop Sing's culinary arts, fried chicken and pan cooked taters. The smell of their servant's cooking was generally a soothing solicitation to a man's backbreaking day. This day, Hoss figured when he looked at Pa's face, must be an exception.

"I tell you, Pa, you'll be lower than fleas on a sidewinder if you don't find all them drovers you need in Californee." Hoss grabbed his usual helping thighs and legs before Ben or Joe could pick up a fork. "You might have to ride 'em yourself all the way over them foothills and up into Oregon. I hear it's a mite pretty up there anyhow." One look at Hoss gave an observer the idea that his size related directly to being aggressive when food plates were set before him. But even with his bear-like size Hoss believed early on what his Pa told him, that his kindly face atoned for his frightening stature. "Or you could hire them new trail hands that just come into Virginia City."

"I don't hire trail hands without credentials. And I'm not going to worry about what I do or don't find in California. If I end up going all the way to Oregon with Little Joe, I'll send word." Ben stared down at the lightly breaded chicken breast. He ran his fingers through his silver hair, dark eyebrows furled like storm clouds over his chiseled features. "And while I'm gone, you and Adam proceed on the bouldering in the north 40 like we discussed."

Hoss recognized Ben's stress over business matters was usual for this time of year. "Yeah, I cayn't wait to see old Adam's face when we tell him how we discussed him helping out — he wanted to go to Sacramento for a couple days, remember?"

Ben laughed with him. "Well, the theater can wait, he knows that. And I suspect Adam didn't have his heart as much set on it as he was just teasing *you*."

This made Hoss laugh even harder at Adam's joke on him.

"Hey, Pa, why don't you go all the way on this drive?" Joe asked, looking for a little fun of his own. "Then you'll see why we always complain when it's our turn."

Hoss frowned at his little brother and shook his head but few things stopped Joe's easy teasing. Some people said Joe's twinkling eyes and wide-open grin made him attractive to the girls. The girls would readily admit that his thick curly hair and impossibly quick boyish wit were just as engaging. That the three brothers each had different mothers was plain enough whenever they were in the same room together.

"Joseph, you know that I've driven enough cattle in my day."

"Yeah, in your day, Pa, but it's getting rough out there. There's more rustlers and more Indians taking what they can get---."

Ben slammed his fork down with a firm stare at his youngest. "Joseph!"

Joe grinned sheepishly and bent back over his plate.

"We don't blame Indians for trying to protect their food and water sources." After a pause Ben leaned back and chuckled. "I guess I can't blame you for complaining. Just remember, young man, I had sons so I don't have to go off on these drives. Did you think I would stay your age forever?" He winked at Hoss. "Now, if your brother would do us the favor of coming home, we could get the week finalized. Little Joe and I have an early enough day ahead---."

"The buckboard came in while you were talking, Pa," Hoss said between chews.

"Well, good." Ben bent back over his food. "I hope this food didn't get cold while you two had me jawing."

"And Hop Sing plum hates reheating," Hoss added. "It's why I learned to eat the way I do."

Joe laughed. "Sure, big brother. You just keep telling yourself that."

24

Felling of the Sons

"Wonder what's keeping Adam." Hoss stabbed another chicken thigh.

"Probably unloading." Ben stared at the door, looking like the food he chewed wouldn't go down. "Maybe he needs a hand. Hoss."

Hoss shrugged and stood. A sudden loud screech from outside stopped him. "That's Adam?" Ben followed Little Joe out behind Hoss.

"Pa!" Hoss yelled. "Looks like Adam's hurt!"

"What?!" Ben reached the buckboard where his son stretched awkwardly across the bench. "It's probably. . .just a head misery."

Adam blinked once and tried to look around but could only move his eyes. He shifted as though he might sit up, but his eyes squeezed tight in pain, face flushed and sweating. "Pa, I have to tell. . ."

"Easy, son, time enough to talk later. Hoss, grab his feet, easy now." As Ben and Hoss lifted him, Adam shuddered and passed out.

"Pa!" Joe yelled from the other side. "He's been shot in the back!"

"Joe, get the door and then run for the doctor. Easy now, Hoss." Ben linked his arms carefully under Adam's shoulders, waiting until Hoss got a grip under his knees. "We'll take him to the guest room."

Hop Sing wondered why so much food sat uneaten when he heard the commotion. He opened the guest room and turned the covers down.

"Will cook water now," he said, shuffling back out of the room.

"What do you suppose happened, Pa?" Hoss asked as Ben eased Adam on his side.

"We can only guess. We won't know until he tells us."

"If he gets the chance." Hoss regretted the words as he said them.

"I will not tolerate that notion." He carefully eased off Adam's black vest and peeled the black shirt up, exposing the raw and bleeding wound in his son's back. "He's bleeding, but it looks like it stopped for a while."

"Yeah, good thing or he'd be..." Hoss swallowed hard. "Shot in the back? Pa, Adam been feuding?" Hoss picked up Adam's cool hand and squeezed, hoping Adam would squeeze back.

"Not that I'm aware. Get Hop Sing. I need towels, a pitcher of cold water and one of hot." Ben pressed a corner of the bed's covering against the wound.

Hoss found Hop Sing in the kitchen with his arms wrapped around his head, standing over a pot of water not yet boiling. "Hop Sing! What you doin', reciting some new kind of prayer?"

Hop Sing jumped, rattling the pans hanging over his head. "Mr. Hoss! You walk too quiet. Yes. Prayer for Mr. Adam." The small Oriental servant looked down at the pot of water on the wood stove with deep consternation. "Should be hot." He stuck his finger in. When Hop Sing turned, he saw Hoss staring at towels in his hands. "Now you find prayer for Mr. Adam, too." Hop Sing nodded and got out the pitchers for water.

On his way back to Adam's room, hands full of towels and pitchers of water, Hoss kicked something on the floor. He stared at the odd lumpy thing, but Ben yelled again for the water so Hoss stepped gently over it and brought the water to Ben, who wet a towel with cold water and pressed it against the wound. After a moment he wetted another towel with hot water and wiped the wound clean, before reapplying the cold towel to stop the bleeding again. Hoss went back out of the room.

"Where is Joe with that doctor?" Ben yelled over his shoulder.

"Pa, it's only been minutes since he's been gone," Hoss shouted back from outside the door.

"Seems like hours."

When he came into the room Hoss put a hand on Ben's shoulder. "Adam will make it, Pa."

"How do you know that? You don't know that."

Hoss took a deep breath. "I believe it. Look it here." He showed Ben the leather pouch he held between two fingers. "I found it on the floor."

Ben turned the pouch over in his hands, the pouch streaking his fingers with his son's blood.

"Hoss, is this what stopped Adam from bleeding?"

"I reckon."

"How did it get there?"

"He had some help getting home."

"Indian help." Ben clutched the leather pouch tightly, blood oozing between his fingers. "It wasn't an Indian that shot him."

"You sure?" Hoss stared at his Pa's hand, at the blood, and bit back a shudder.

"If someone did this as a warning, it wouldn't have mattered if Adam died. This Indian deliberately kept Adam alive."

"Pa, he rode out to the Paiutes today. Are you sure he didn't make one of 'em mad somehow?"

"Well, we'll have to find out."

Ben put the pouch on the night table with the reverence Hoss felt it deserved. For whatever reason, it had saved Adam's life. Adam will want the chance to seek out his owner, when he's able. Hoss swallowed hard against the tiny 'if' crawling back into his thoughts.

CHAPTER 4

Ben settled into a semi-conscious state of awareness next to the bed, eyes steady on the wound and no thought in his mind but keeping his son alive. Hoss stretched out in the other chair, every now and again dozing before worry startled him back awake.

"Where is Joe with that doctor?" Ben rubbed Adam's shoulder gently until his breathing evened out again.

"Pa, it ain't been that long. Even if Little Joe took the short route, riding up and down hills that's crooked as..."

"I know how crooked it is!" Ben pressed the towel against the wound. "I'm sorry, Hoss, but for once I curse this wilderness we live in, the doctor so far away, and a man able to get away with shooting another man in the back."

"Maybe he didn't get away with it." Hoss stared at the medicine bag. "Adam's been seeing them Paiutes pretty regular since that war." He looked back at his brother's pale face and his massive shoulders shook off a shudder. "One of them...tried to..." His chin dropped as he fought to control the sobs in his chest.

"Hoss, he's going to be all right." Ben checked the wound. "As soon as this bullet is out and the doctor says he'll be fine, we'll find out who did this and why."

"Trail could be cold by then."

Ben leaned back, feeling as washed out and miserable as Hoss looked. "This was no random shooting. Whoever did this expects something from me. He's waiting for a response."

"What you reckon Adam was trying to say before?"

Ben pressed his lips together. "He'll tell us. As soon as he can."

28

At the sound of horse hooves Ben ran out and threw open the front door, his arms wide to greet the doctor. When Joe noted Pa's enthused reception of the doctor, he nodded with a near smile and took the horses to bed them down.

Dr. Jessup, a slender and normally jovial man, ambled in, stretching his back. "Gotta tell you, Ben, because of your boy I may never ride a horse again. Joe insisted my buggy would slow us down. That short way he took — I tell you, in the dark I felt for my own life several times. Joe sure knows his back trails."

"John, I really do appreciate it." Ben led Jessup into Adam's room.

The doctor lifted the wet towel on Adam's back.

"My son's got a bullet in his back, in deep. I'm afraid to try it."

"Nasty. And I don't like the position."

"The position?"

"Close to a lung. If the bullet's in deep, it could have punctured a lung. He may have trouble breathing after I get the bullet out, causing serious damage to other organs. Other organs shutting down, that's fatal." He pulled a couple of knives out of his bag. "Of course, you're lucky he's alive. Seems the gun fired from a far enough distance, anyhow, or he wouldn't be alive now." He shuffled supplies impatiently inside his case. "Damnation, thought I had enough chloroform. Your son didn't give me the time to go back to my office, he found me at the Walters' place, fixing a bad leg. Never mind, we'll make do. Bullet has to come out, or he has no chance. I wish those ideologists over in London and Edinburgh would come up with a way to prevent the inflammation this barbarous butchering does to the body. Joe, we need more hot water, and whiskey, we'll use it to kill the infection and in case the chloroform doesn't hold him down. The three of you help keep him steady."

"He's not conscious, doctor, hasn't been since we took him off the buckboard." The doctor took the moist towel off the wound and Adam groaned. Ben knelt next to the bed. "Adam, boy, listen...you're going to be fine. The doctor's going to take the bullet out."

"Pa." Adam's eyes squeezed tight in the lamplight. "Hoss. . .Joe. . ."

"Yes, they're here, son, we're all here."

"They take care. Van…ah…"

Joe brought the whiskey in. "He's talking? Did he say who did this?"

Ben shook his head. "I couldn't make it out. He seems to think you and Hoss are in danger, too,"

Dr. Jessup put the whiskey next to the bed on the night table. "He's in shock, Ben, he doesn't know what he's saying. We'll get the bullet out, let him rest, and then when he comes to, he'll talk clearer. The next 24 hours though, you'll need someone near him at all times." He dabbed a little whiskey over the wound. "That is, if with the grace of God, he survives my butchering."

He soaked a towel with the chloroform and placed it over Adam's face as the rest of the Cartwrights got in place for the surgery.

CHAPTER 5

Ben paced in front of the fire as Hoss and Joe sat melancholy in chairs. Except for the crackling fire and Hoss's foot tapping the floor, the stillness of a tomb permeated the walls. The doctor hadn't come out since shooing the three of them away after taking the bullet out, and until he did there would be no sleep for any of them. The surgery did them all in—the chloroform and whiskey never quite kept Adam still.

"I hope I ain't never gotta do that again," Hoss muttered.

Joe covered his eyes and shook his head. He sat so low in the chair that a mere sigh would land him on the floor.

Ben picked up the poker and lifted a log, sending a crackling flame with a stream of ash up into the flue of the broad stone chimney.

The guest room door opened and Dr. Jessup came out. He closed the door quietly behind him and looked at them with old and tired eyes. The great sitting room that Ben had so carefully filled with durable furniture from his travels seemed non-existent. The doctor only saw three hopeful faces.

Ben strode over to him. "Doctor? He'll be all right?"

"Bullet took a piece of the liver. Liver could heal or maybe not. Also nicked the lung. Important thing now is to keep the wound clean, keep him off his back. More men die after surgery from the irritation and suppuration of the wound. But you have to keep an eye on his breathing. If it seems his breathing quickens or stops, let him on his back for a little while. Delicate balance at best, Ben, which is why someone has to stay with him the next 24 hours."

"Isn't there…anything more you can do?"

"I've been working with some skin tonics and I've left a bottle with Hop Sing. It's a carbolic acid and oil dressing, but he'll still need close watching. If he lasts that long, then he should recover." John planted a warm, comforting hand on Ben's arm. "Take heart, Ben, he's made it this far." He read Ben's worried look. "Tell you what though, I know a young surgeon in Genoa, he's developed some new techniques. I've been thinking of getting him to pen a few out to me, so I'll write him. No time like today."

Ben followed Jessup to the door. "Would you like a ride back to town? Or spend the night?"

"Thanks, Ben, but I'm heading over to Carson City. I have an early call there in the morning." He slapped the hat Hoss handed him back on his head. "Stay close to him, Ben, keep him calm. Oh, and Ben, try and get some rest yourself." He allowed Hop Sing to lead him out, and the door closed softly behind them.

"Whelp," Hoss stared at the floor, his hands shoved deep in his rust-colored dungarees. "I'll take the first watch, you two go on to bed."

"No, Hoss, I'll do it." Ben stopped outside the door of the guest room to gather his thoughts.

"Pa, who did this to him?" Joe got to his feet behind Hoss. "We gotta find out, they can't get away with this."

"They already have! It doesn't matter what we do to them, Adam will still be hurt, may still..." he stepped in Adam's room and shut the door.

"That's not what I meant." Joe rubbed his sleeve across his forehead where the angry frown took hold.

"Yeah, well, he can't think no clearer now, little brother. Ain't none of us thinking clear. Come on, let's go to bed. We won't be no use to Pa or Adam if we sit up all night and stew."

Hoss headed up the stairs and Joe, after a moment's thought-filled pause, followed. At the top of the stairs Joe stopped short.

"Hey, Hoss? Who you suppose had a reason to shoot him in the back?"

"It's like Pa says, no use wondering now. We gotta wait 'til Adam's ready to tell us more."

"More?" Joe grabbed Hoss's arms and in worried exuberance swept his brother off balance against the painted plaster wall. "What do you mean, more?"

"He mumbled something 'bout you and me being careful and a Van something." Hoss glanced at his back pinned against the wall and grinned sheepishly. "You wanna let me go now, Little Joe?"

"Van something?" He turned away from Hoss, chewing on his lip.

"Yup. I got no notion what a Van is, but---."

Joe snapped his finger. "Adam named the guy who shot him."

"Awww, he was in shock, he didn't know what he's saying."

Joe looked back down the stairs. "Adam always knows what he's saying." His eyes glistened with a cold determination. "Hoss, you relieve Pa. It'll take me a little while to get to sleep tonight."

"Yeah." Hoss patted Joe's shoulder. "Nite, Little Joe."

***

Joe paced in his room, picturing his oldest brother maybe dying. Only a few days before him and Adam had some argument. Joe couldn't remember it now. Probably whether South Carolina had the right to keep slaves or secede. A sour topic between them — they were always arguing about it in some fashion, with the heated presidential election only months away. Joe argued with the blood of his Southern mother, a hard emotion to conquer. But then, Adam argued the same way, with the blood of his Yankee mother. Hoss, being part Swedish, stayed right in the middle of that argument like his Pa, a big wall of "knock-it-off-you-two"s.

When Joe heard Hoss's bed creak he waited five more minutes. He crept down the stairs with a cautious ear to noise, and as he neared bottom the step cracked. He froze but Pa didn't come out of Adam's room. When Adam gets better, they'll still argue.

Joe crept over to the front door and grabbed his coat, hat and gun belt, checking for ammunition. He glanced around and stepped outside, closing the door real slow. What he wouldn't give for one of their arguments right now.

He had bedded the buckboard horse down but the buckboard remained where it came to a stop, loaded with goods. With vague moonlight streaming down through the trees the smeared blood on the seat didn't appear as bad as Joe expected. Whoever shot his brother didn't count on Adam's remarkable power of will to make it home — probably expected him to die out there on the trail. Joe didn't know what he'd find riding back on the trail Adam took to get home but he wanted to get to it before someone else did.

He wouldn't let anyone get away with shooting his brother.

***

Kudwa dozed but the nearby screech of an owl startled him back awake. He had curled up on a patch of granite sand hidden from the road a short distance from where the man he killed fell. He knew enough of the white world to know that this man did not just decide to shoot another man in the back. This purpose had to do with trees because trees were the last worry on his friend's mind.

He sat up. Someone rode fast down the road on a black and white Pinto.

Joe saw the man dead in the road and drew the horse up short. Kudwa stepped out into the road behind him. With his hand on his gun, Joe alighted and walked to the man lying face down in the dirt, an arrow sticking out of the square center of his back. Joe stood over him, tense, fists clenching. As Kudwa watched, Joe checked the barrel of the rifle at the dead man's side.

Joe nodded at the rifle's chamber and sighed heavily before putting the rifle down. He turned to study the dead man a moment before reaching out. He touched the feather barb of the arrow gently, and took hold of the arrow with both hands to pull it out. He heard the snap of a dry twig and whirled around, his gun up and aiming just as fast.

Kudwa stood on the road, drawn to his full and ominous height in the shadow of night. He dropped the stick he had snapped and held up a hand to still Joe's gun finger.

Joe grinned, replacing his gun. "You did this?" He indicated the arrow.

"You brother of Adam Cartwright?"

"Yes." Joe walked to him, hand out. "Joe Cartwright." Kudwa put a hand over his chest. When he saw Joe's hand out at him, he met palms as Adam taught him. "You killed the man who shot my brother?"

"Binna'gwa Adam talk peace." He took a breath, English took effort, especially late at night. "Dedeegi trees. Baika," and he waved at the man on the ground.

Joe studied Kudwa's kind face. "And you brought Adam back home? Why did you come back here?" Joe used the sign language his brother taught him but didn't know any Shoshone.

"His spirit. . .duugu. . .peace." His hand waved at the dead man, and then skyward.

"Do you know who he is? A name?" Kudwa shook his head. "Did he say anything?" Again Kudwa shook his head. Joe smiled tearfully and clasped the man's arms. "We will always be grateful for your help in saving my brother's life."

"Adam is not dead?"

Joe made several mistakes in signing, and a couple times his hands got tangled up. "No, and we have great hope he'll be just fine."

Kudwa pulled Joe to him in a quick and exuberant bear hug. Joe laughed as he pulled away and slapped Kudwa's arm. He crouched down, knees on the dead man's back, jerked the arrow free and handed it reverently back to Kudwa.

"Help me get him on the back of my horse, will you?"

"Whites will hunt me?" Some English Kudwa knew only too well. Even in the dark night he could see where blood had pooled under the slit throat.

"No!" That came out louder than Joe wanted but Kudwa didn't seem to mind. "I'll tell the sheriff what you told me. The whole town will be calling you hero."

Together, he and Kudwa dropped the dead man behind the saddle on Cochise, his Pinto. Joe tied his weapon to his saddle and went through the man's pockets. He found oddities of the man's life—bits of wrapped taffy, a small bag of gunpowder, and two spent bullets.

"Adam worried about protecting the trees and I wanted to make him understand that Paiutes can help him."

Joe didn't understand Shoshone, so he shook Kudwa's hand warmly. "Thank you. I'm glad you waited here. Anytime you need a Cartwright's help, you just ask."

Kudwa stopped Joe from mounting and tried English again. "I come to see Adam?"

"Any time you want, Kudwa, any time you want."

CHAPTER 6

Ben sat at Adam's bedside, reading out loud from his favorite book, *Paradise Lost*. Talking aloud kept Ben from nodding off and might help Adam cling to life. Ben took a sip of the water sitting at the bedside. "Oh, remember this? This is where your mother and I found your name." He hadn't read these words to Adam since the boy was six years old and Ben told him that his mother had died giving birth to him. Adam had been such an alert, smart six-year-old and happy with Inger as his ma, so Ben guessed the boy could handle the truth. The question had been a favorite of his since the day he could talk— "Where's my ma?"

Intense agony rose in Adam's eyes hearing his birth brought her death. Having the two mothers he did know — Hoss's and Joe's — also die affected him in ways Adam's never shared. Ben tried not to chide himself for telling the lad the truth about Elizabeth. After all, he had known so little about raising a son.

He took another sip of water and cleared his throat. "Far otherwise the event, not Death, but Life Augmented, opened Eyes, new Hopes, new Joys, Taste so Divine, that what of sweet before Hath touched my sense, flat seems to this, and harsh. On my experience, Adam, freely taste, and fear of Death..."

Elizabeth made the decision weeks before giving birth what to name him, only to die before she could hold him. He paged to the end, her favorite part. "The world was all before them, where to choose their place of rest, and Providence their guide. They, hand in hand with wandering steps and slow, through Eden took their solitary way." He hadn't read this particular section out loud since she died as he read it to her. He closed the book. If Adam dies, this book goes in the fire.

Adam stirred slightly. He tried to roll on his back so Ben placed a gentle hand on his shoulder.

"Easy, son." Ben watched his chest closely for signs of rough breathing but after a moment Adam relaxed again. He almost lost his eldest son, still might, and he didn't have a clue as to why.

***

Hop Sing rose before dawn to unload the goods from the buckboard. Most of these he was expected to sort out for the drive — if there was to be one now. He grabbed a box and Adam's saddlebag. After dropping the box off in the kitchen, Hop Sing brought the saddlebag to the dining table. He unlatched the clasp and emptied Adam's usual gear — knife, matches, book, some money and two letters. Hop Sing looked at the front of each letter and considered bringing them to Ben but changed his mind.

He put the letters on Ben's desk and went back outside.

***

When Hoss relieved Ben, his Pa had nodded off clinging tight to Adam's hand. "Pa." Hoss shook him gently. Ben sat upright and looked over at Adam, expecting trouble. "Is he breathing okay?"

"A few bad moments but they passed. Did you get enough sleep, son?" Ben stood and stretched his back.

"Slept like a log, Pa. Don't know how though." Hoss sat in the chair warm with Ben's worry.

"Natural talent of yours, boy," Ben looked back at Adam with longing. "Wake me if there's any change."

They both looked up at the sound of a heavy box dropping to the floor. Ben glanced at Hoss. Neither of them cared what Hop Sing unpacked for. Ben reluctantly headed for the stairs, but stopped short. "The cattle drive. Noon today. All those men, cattle off on the range, waiting..." He looked over at the grandfather clock to assess the passage of time and went to his desk, ignoring letters to search for blank paper and ink. "Hop Sing!"

Hop Sing shuffled out. "Mr. Adam?"

"He's holding his own." Ben penned a note. "I need you to run this note to the western range. Have Val scribble an answer on this paper."

Hop Sing ran out the door. Val, the trail boss, will understand the situation and do as requested, Ben knew. With a final sigh cast at the door where Adam fought for his life, he climbed up the stairs to bed.

CHAPTER 7

Joe expected he'd be tired, but sheer determination kept him from feeling it. Still a few hours left to dawn, he turned off the road to Virginia City, heading for Sheriff Roy's ranch. At his age and suffering from sleeplessness, Roy won't like this early morning visit. But Joe needed his help, and needed to bunk for a few hours before they rode together to wake up the town.

Though still a good several hours until sunrise, the air around him already seemed brighter. The night air was cold but except for the tip of his nose and a couple fingers he couldn't feel it. Anger kept him both warm and awake.

Roy lived in a small square cabin with a shed and small barn for the two cows he kept most of the time grazing in his yard. This meager homestead nestled itself discreetly between two foothills as though trying to hide. Joe hoped to catch Roy at a sleepless moment but couldn't see a lantern burning. After hesitating — he had nowhere else to go — Joe alighted and pulled Cochise to the railing. He stepped up to the door and rubbed his hands on his canvas jeans, putting off the inevitable with thoughts of riding to town alone. Finally, after looking back over his shoulder to make sure the dead man across his horse hadn't disappeared, he knocked. He knocked harder as anger returned.

"All right, keep your pants on, I hear ya!" Roy's gruff voice sounded miserable through the heavy wood.

Joe backed up. Roy, a good and fair man, could be a might grumpy at times. As the footsteps stopped Joe heard the click of a gun. "Hey, Roy, it's me, Joe, Joe Cartwright!"

"Well, Little Joe..." Roy threw open the door, putting his gun aside. He had himself wrapped in a mangy old bear fur and what little gray hair he had left on his head was mussed. "Jimanelle, boy, what are you doing out here this time of night?" He looked past Joe at his horse. "Nothing's happened to Ben and the boys, has it?"

"Adam's been shot. Come on out here."

Halfway to Joe's horse Roy stopped. "Oh my, is that Adam?"

"No, Adam's home, doc's got the bullet out of his back but we don't know if he'll make it."

"Ah. Terrible thing." He shook his head and scratched at his gray mustache. "Shot in the back yet. Then who's this ya got here?"

"The man who shot him." Joe grabbed a fistful of the man's hair and yanked his head up. The slack jaw revealed a mouthful of decaying teeth. The eyes bulged open and the nose was covered with caked blood. Both avoided looking at the gaping hole in his neck. "Ever see him before?"

"I don't have my spectacles on, boy."

"Look close."

"The middle of the night and cloudy to boot." Roy held his breath as he squinted into the man's face. "Yeah, yeah, two days ago, a mean drifter, could be him. Told him to keep out of trouble, didn't see him again."

Joe dropped the head, startling Cochise. He stroked his horse's nose to calm Cochise down. "Remember his name?"

"I reckon I do, it was easy enough."

"Van?"

"No, Jolly, Joe Jolly."

"Not Van? You're sure?"

"I'm sure as I can think, anyhow. I always look for stranger in town in my wanteds. Why?"

"Then someone hired him. Adam named a man called Van something, or something Van. Anyone new in town with a name like that?"

"No, not real new. If they've been around more than a week I might not remember 'em, not off the top of my head. Sure Adam knew what he was saying, right after being shot and all?"

"He knew. Adam always knows." Joe turned away, shoulders slumping.

Roy squinted at Joe. "You get any sleep tonight, son?"

"No, but I don't feel…"

"Come on in here, and stretch out 'til dawn then." He led an unresisting Joe inside. "Don't have nothing for you to stretch out on, but I can get you a blanket for the floor."

"Didn't think to bring a bedroll."

Roy got the blanket from the bottom shelf of a well-stocked pantry. "Ben know you're out?"

"No, but I promised Hoss I'd be careful." Joe threw the blanket in a heap on the floor, stretched out and closed his eyes.

Roy left him alone. There'd be enough time come dawn to get the rest out of Joe about this whole sorry mess, he figured. The boy needed his sleep. For himself, Roy didn't expect to get any more. If only he had found a reason to kick that Jolly out of town, right off. That thought would lie with him the rest of his night – and longer, if Adam dies.

***

Hoss read from the Bible, every minute or so checking Adam's breathing. He stared until his brother's chest moved. The doctor didn't want him sleeping on his back unless his breathing got worse so the wound could heal.

He hoped Pa could sleep decent. He didn't remember ever seeing him this miserable. Here close to the middle of the morning and he hadn't even given that cattle drive a thought. Not that it mattered. The cows would get fatter, that's all. They could maybe send Joe on the drive without Pa, but Joe wouldn't go, Hoss felt pretty sure of that.

For this time of the morning the house should be pounding with noise. The inactivity would make Adam hopping mad. "You'll make it, brother. You're too stubborn not to. 'Sides, you'll want to get on that younger brother for sleeping late."

Hoss walked to the door. Joe's well off sleeping while he can. Hoss wondered if he should be doing something about the cattle drive. A low sharp gasp made him turn back. Adam was trying to lie flat. Hoss eased him back on his side. "Easy, Adam, better not move yet."

Adam blinked his eyes hard against opening. "Hoss? Where's Joe?"

"Adam, he's here, he's fine, it's okay, don't worry..."

"Hoss, listen," but his voice failed him. Hoss gave him a small sip of water that wet his lips but otherwise drooled down his chin. "Letters, read letters." He turned his face into the pillow with a low groan and slipped away again.

Hoss waited for him to catch his breath and checked the wound. It bled a little but held up. Letters? What could be so important about letters?

He opened the door in time to see Hop Sing run out of the kitchen. He looked windblown and dirty, like he'd run around the house chasing a stubborn goat. "Hop Sing! Where you been? What's that in your hand?"

'This letter for Mr. Ben."

Hoss grabbed the letter as he stepped out of the room and read quickly. "Oh, this is Pa telling the drovers to start tomorrow instead of today. You rode out to the drive?" Hop Sing nodded. "He took on those fellows with no credentials." He read further. "Hop Sing, Val's demanding more wages for all of 'em? Just coz Pa and Joe ain't going? That don't sound like Val."

"That's light, Mr. Hoss. Must show to Mr. Cartlight."

"We're better off pitching the herd down a well. Except those fellas would want their pay anyhow. Let Pa sleep. We'll give 'em their wages, we don't have a choice. Dadburnit. We'll have Little Joe run the message to the drovers, why don't ya wake him?"

"Like to, Mr. Hoss." Hop Sing enjoyed waking Joe up by pouring water in his hair. "Okay I see Mr. Adam first?"

"Sure, Hop Sing, he'd like that."

Hop Sing walked in shyly and stood transfixed, nodding when Adam's chest moved. Hop Sing's eyes closed and his face turned to the ceiling before he shuffled out again.

"Adam's gonna be just fine now, don't you worry. Did you unload the buckboard?"

"Yes, Mr. Hoss. Mr. Adam's saddlebag, too. He bling back two letter for Mr. Cartlight."

Hoss turned casually to the desk. He glanced down, sure enough, two opened letters he didn't see before. He grabbed them off the desk and ran back to sit next to his brother.

CHAPTER 8

Hop Sing ran down the stairs before Hoss could open the second letter, cursing loud enough to bring Hoss to his feet even with the discovery of the name *"van Remus."* Hoss stuck his head out the guest room door to come face to face with the Chinaman.

"Mr. Hoss! Mr. Joe not in loom," Hop Sing whispered hoarsely.

"Gone?" He looked up the stairs. "Dadburn that Joe's ornery hide. He snuck off?" Hoss carefully tucked the Van Remus letter into his vest pocket and fingered the other one, smoothing out the wrinkles from being clutched in his sweaty hand. "Ah, he probably just had some things to do early on." That van Remus didn't sound so bad. "Hop Sing, keep an eye on Adam. I gotta read this."

"Tlouble, Mr. Hoss?"

"I don't know yet." He turned away from Adam's room as Hop Sing slipped inside. Hoss made himself comfortable in the wingback in front of the fire. He poked the fire a minute and then pulled the letter out. It had been folded and refolded, signs of Adam's distress, same as the other one. Hoss read it slow and careful before putting it back down again. "Dadburnit." Hoss looked over at Adam's room. Sutter warned about this Van Remus. Something bad must have happened in Sacramento Valley. He was too young to remember but Adam mighta. With these two letters together, he mighta remembered something pretty bad.

Now Joe went out to find out who did this. And Hoss didn't have a clue what to do about it. He looked up at the stairs. Pa needed his sleep. *Dadburned that Little Joe anyhow.*

***

Clete Van Remus got himself a plush suite at the International about a month ago when the silver began to come in. He had enough money even before that, but he didn't need the nosy townsfolk to know that. Now he could afford to rent the whole house if he wanted it and not even hear a twinge of gossip about it. Champagne flowed in the evening, rich dark coffee in the morning, and a woman cleaned every hour and fluffed his pillow just before he retired. The furniture, thick as a hog about to be butchered, was done in blue and maroon velvet, so soft he could imagine himself floating off on a cloud.

Clete didn't think about comfort, not from the moment he stepped foot in Virginia City. He had business to finish, business that started nearly twenty years ago. He'd give the Ponderosa to his son and then get out of this hellhole of a town too new for itself and back to San Francisco, where he belonged. Or maybe they could call it even after just this one kill. As soon as the news breaks of a dead Cartwright, he'll get a glimpse of his boy's eyes. Maybe the hate will have burnt itself out. Out of both of them.

He stood staring out the window into the dirty, windblown street. San Francisco felt rich but here the silver strike felt like nothing more than digging in dirt and rock. He didn't like all the grubbing and scrounging, men as prairie dogs tunneling under their very feet. There were times when he walked outside that he thought he could feel the scraping of shovels underground against the soles of his thick leather boots.

Behind him, Bret ate breakfast like a young timber wolf. He complained that he never got to finish his meals, and as busy as they were, that complaint held true. If the logging foreman could be just a few minutes late Bret may get to finish this one.

Clete checked his watch. Sending loggers into the weakest section of timber on the Ponderosa, the north 40, would keep old Ben Cartwright off balance at the time when he's most vulnerable, after the death of his son. Even now his oldest lay dead in a granite dust pile somewhere, blood drying on the ground under the morning sun. Soon he'd be discovered, and the news would break all over town. No way to trace the killing back to him either. Jolly would be halfway to Sacramento by now, where he'd find the second half of his pay waiting – in the form of a man who owed Clete a favor.

Clete went to the safe to get the property claim papers, giving him legal right to the Ponderosa. Took a lot of work getting these papers ready, the part of the plan he liked best. Bret preferred the killing part, but Clete wanted the ranch and land, too. The joy of killing would fade, he reminded Bret, but land lasted. And owning a spread like the Ponderosa brought respect. People have been real obliging to him as an 'old friend of Cartwright.' When he asked questions like which section of Ponderosa land had been cut over most recently, no one thought twice about answering. He asked for leads on loggers, miners, just about anything and he got it, since mentioning Ben's name. Worked slicker than money.

He held the papers up to the sunlight as though inspecting them for flaws. He'd already put them through scrutiny in San Francisco by getting different judges to declare them legal and binding. But the timing – no, not after just one son's death. Ben will be off balance with Adam dead, but not destructible. Not yet. Clete turned away from the window to put the papers in the safe but gunfire turned him back.

A crowd gathered around two riders coming into town, and one of the riders had what looked to him like a big sack of grain on the back of his horse. Grain? That wouldn't make a crowd gather like that.

"Bret! Come here." Bret reluctantly joined his father at the window, munching on a muffin. "Your eyes are better. What's going on?"

"Hey, they got a dead body on that horse. Come on!"

Clete placed his papers back in the safe underneath his etchings and Bible and followed his son out the door. "And so it begins."

At the sheriff's office the riders alighted and tied their horses securely before turning back to the crowd they had roused. The young man, just a boy even in man's clothes, a short cut beige jacket and brown hat, his face pressed hard in anger, stood with his hands on his hips.

Bret nudged his father as they stepped out of the hotel. "Think they got that Cartwright on the back of that horse?"

"Could be." Clete glanced at Bret. He looked like a vulture, still hungry after the first meal.

They stood apart from the crowd as though distinguished visiting dignitary, while others pushed and shoved to get a closer look at the dead man hanging from Joe's horse.

"Who you got there, sheriff?" Someone yelled up at Roy.

"A man believed to be a hired gun. He was found dead after a shooting."

"He shoot somebody?" Another called.
Roy looked at Joe.

"My brother Adam," Joe answered quietly.

His brother? Hired gun dead? Did Jolly talk? Clete's mind raced as the first throbs of a headache started up.

"This is the other brother?" Bret spoke softly, lips barely moving.

"Has to be a third one. The second was bigger than that when he was five." Clete rubbed at the ache in his temples. He never considered marrying again. Ben's had three wives?

"Adam Cartwright dead?" came someone's incredulous question.

Roy broke the silence that followed this question. "Whoever hired this man to kill Adam is who we're looking for. I need each and every man in town, woman and child, too, if they can stand it, to look at his face and tell me anything you know, who you mighta seen him with, where he stayed, anything you know at all. Joe here believes this killing is part of a vendetta against Ben himself. So any help you can give is bound to come back to you, as Ben never lets a favor be forgotten."

"Never indeed," Clete muttered as he and Bret got in the growing line. Each took a gander at the dead man and found a question or two, but from their faces had no answers. They mighta seen him, some said, but not with whom.

Finally, Clete and Bret got a look. Clete stole a glance at the dead man and then watched Bret, who stared at the dead Jolly as though at a Sunday dinner cooling on his plate.

"How'd he die, sheriff?" Clete asked.

"Shot in the back by a Paiute," Joe answered.

"Do you know him?" Roy directed to Clete.

"Sorry, no." Clete wondered if the advance money was in his pockets. "Killed your brother, you say?" Joe didn't answer. "Terrible thing." Clete didn't like the way the sheriff stared at him.

"Say, we met when you first moved here, didn't we? It's a..." Roy puzzled over his lack of memory. "Carl Reem-something, innit?"

"It's Clete van Remus, owner of the Golden Cross mine. Don't feel bad not remembering, I've been in town near three months but no more than a few days of that above ground."

"That's right," Roy's face lit up. "Cletus *Van* Remus. What a name, eh, Little Joe?"

"*Van* Remus," Joe stuck out his hand. "Nice to welcome a new businessman to town. Name's Joe Cartwright."

"Cartwright?" Clete shook hands, grinning broadly. "My associate Bret." As Joe and Bret shook hands Clete saw a little of Ben in his face, mostly in the expression that something's got to be done and he's going to do it. "You related to Ben Cartwright who lives in these parts?"

"That's my Pa. You know him?"

"Sure, from the old days back in Sacramento Valley. New Helvetia, we called our settlement. I suppose that was before you were born?" Joe nodded, confirming Clete's third-wife theory. "Haven't seen him in years. How is he?"

Joe glanced back at his horse as he led Clete and Bret up on the walk, away from the crowd. "Torn up over my brother."

"Oh, I can imagine. Dead then, is he?"

"That important to know?" But Clete's expression didn't change. Joe rubbed his eyes. "Pa's heartsick, won't leave his room."

"Doesn't sound like the Ben Cartwright I knew. Why, I'd figure Ben would be out gunning for whoever." He caught Joe's odd, impassive stare. "But it's been awhile since I've seen him."

Joe leaned on a post holding the roof over the walk in front of Rusty Johnson's Saloon. "I'm doing the looking for Pa."

"Seems to me you already sandbagged the man who shot him."

"No, like Roy says, he was a hired gun, a stranger in town." Joe looked around. "Guess I'll walk around and ask some questions of my own."

Clete stopped him with a firm grip on his arm before Joe could turn to the door of the saloon. "You look plum exhausted, boy. Why don't you come up to my suite for some muffins and a cup of coffee? Fix you up right nice. Least I can do for the son of an old friend."

Joe looked up at the International. "No thanks. Trail's getting older every minute. Excuse me."

Clete watched his back, picturing a neat bullet hole between the shoulders. "Come on," he said to Bret standing behind him. "We got us some work to do."

***

Jon McManus was a big man with no particular love for logging in winter climes. Still, when the offer from Van Remus came through, the money tempted him even with the threat of early snow in the Sierras. Van Remus's wire mentioned two months' worth of work. With any luck, he would pocket the $10,000 and be on his way to Mexico before the snows — and before anyone caught up to him. Anyone, that is, who might still have an ax to grind over that 'misunderstanding' in northern California. Dead is dead, after all, self-defense or not.

He stood facing Van Remus in his suite with his black hat still firmly in place on his head, his face unshaven. His new boss may not approve but Jon never cared much for the opinion of land barons anyhow. Any man willing to pay that much money had a need stronger of his own.

"All right, McManus, out with it. I've got a busy day." Clete glanced out the window and turned back to face McManus with a smile.

"We all do," Jon growled.

"How many men did you bring?"

"They was still clinging like ticks to those big trees in Northern California, and you're better off without 'em."

"Offer came at a good time for you, though."

Jon stiffened. "What are you talking about?"

"I don't care what kind of unsavory deeds you've done, just that you've done them. Isn't that right, Bret?" But Bret had taken Clete's place at the window and stood transfixed by the street below. "We're offering the chance to make a lot of money for very little work."

"And I accepted."

"But you need a crew, I told you that."

"I looked. I do not care to fell a tree alone."

"And what did you find?" Clete rubbed at his temples.

"Brought a few from the California border, Truckee, Hangtown. No luck this side of California. Everyone expected me to work a different end of Cartwright property. What's the problem with this section, no one will work it?"

"Cartwright's got a loyalty." A sudden jolt of pain stabbed his head and he lashed out in response, knocking a chair over and nearly spilling the tea that sat on the table next to it.

"Mr. Van Remus, sir!" Bret barked from the window. "Don't let him get to you."

McManus waited with an innocent 'who me?' on his face while Clete took a deep breath and pressed both hands against his temples. He staggered over to the water pitcher and poured a glass. With water cooling his insides, he turned back to Jon. "Who'd you talk to?"

"Only them at logging camps."

"Kept my name out of it?"

"Your name didn't come up, and you told me to back down if they mentioned they knew Cartwright." He shrugged. "They may spread the word about us going up there. I got no guarantees."

"Risk is worth it, with board timber selling as high as $400 per hundred feet. Besides, rumors can be squelched. You got any problem having your reputation tarnished?"

Jon let out a bray of laughter. "What reputation?"

"So how many did you find?" Clete took a deep breath, made his way to a plush chair and sat, folding his arms as though to help slow down his breathing. McManus wondered if maybe he would die right there, and then he wouldn't get to see any money at all.

"Three men, scurvy mostly. Men that don't care what they have to do for a dollar."

"Enough to start. I'll round up more myself. If I have to, I'll offer a higher price. Got a gunman?"

"Sure. Not hard when you got the right 'suasion." Jon relished the look on his old buddy Carne's face when he found Carne in Truckee. There was still a rather tempting reward on that scourge's head and Carne knew it. And Carne knew Jon knew it.

"Get moving now, time is money. In another hour I'll meet you with supplies in front of the livery." Clete glanced out the window again, but didn't seem struck by anything interesting. "Wait. Take a long lunch and I'll see the five of you at 1:00. And McManus," the logger hoped he gave Van Remus the look of impatience he felt, that of his time being every bit as valuable. "You realize that I want that land destroyed. You understand that, don't you? Have any problems with it?"

Jon laughed. "Destroying land? Hell, that's no problem. There's always more land to walk on. Just don't ask me late to dinner." He left without saying goodbye. The boss can find him if he needs to.

***

When the door shut, Clete sank down in a chair. "Insolent Norwegian."

"A doctor could give you medicine for those headaches."

"Don't need medicine."

Bret strode to the door, brushing his long hair back before slipping his hat in place. "Yeah, well, the first time Ben Cartwright comes to town to stand you down he'll barely have to breathe hard." He left the suite, slamming the door behind him.

"Wait!" Clete staggered to his feet but the room swam in his eyes and he dropped back down.

***

After a couple of turns through town, Joe stopped with a bucket of hay and oats for Cochise. As the horse ate, he studied the streets but didn't get any new ideas. He led his horse to the water trough and retied him with a glance to the back of his saddle. The dead man had been laid out at the funeral parlor. Nobody remembered seeing the weasel, at least not with anyone who would have reason to murder Adam. The couple of names he picked up didn't pan out.

Roy was busy writing when Joe walked in. He sat on the corner of the desk and waited. Roy often joshed that he could create paperwork, but then what?

"Be with ya in a minute." Finally Roy looked up. "No luck?"

Joe shook his head. "How about you?"

Roy sat back and clasped his hands in front of his chest. "I think Van Remus is our man."

"I thought so, too, Roy, especially the way he kept asking if Adam was dead, but why would he do this to Pa?"

"That's what you have to find out. All I know is I went over all the documents we have with the town clerk and there just ain't no other Van among them that weren't here since he was a young'un, or can pay off a gunslinger like that. So if you're sure that's the word that Adam---."

"Hoss heard him, not me."

"I sent a letter right off this morning with Willie to Sacramento, he used to ride Pony Express, so he'll get 'er there quick. Might find out a thing or two about this Van Remus." Roy leaned forward and frowned over his reading glasses at Joe. "If I was you, Little Joe, I'd go on back home and get Ben's side of knowing Van Remus. Maybe he didn't and it's just a conjuring. But Joe, get yourself home fast and watch your back. In fact," he reached into his desk drawer and pulled out a deputy's badge. "I'll find someone to ride along with you."

Joe laughed. "Thanks, Roy. But I haven't needed a nursemaid since I was this high." He held a hand against his knee. "I will have another talk with Van Remus, like he invited me to."

Roy frowned. "Little Joe, I'm telling you you're better off just going home. Right now."

"You know, you worry too much, Roy. Adam got shot because he didn't know what to expect. I do." With a confidant smirk, Joe walked out of Roy's office.

CHAPTER 9

Bret went to the International's bar and ordered three whiskeys lined up. For the rest of the hotel's patronage the day was young, but Bret drank by emotion. He felt unwound after the third shot but tensed again when he felt his father's hot breath on his neck.

Clete grabbed his arm. "You know I can handle my ailment." When Bret jerked his arm back Clete whipped the empty glass out of Bret's hand.

Bret moved away and ordered another. "Pain makes you vulnerable and weak, *sir*. You always have a reason to put vengeance. If it weren't for me, we wouldn't even be here today. And you know it."

Clete grabbed his son's hair and jerked his head back, forcing him eye to eye. "You keep forgetting, don't you, boy?" He leaned close to Bret's ear as Bret couldn't move. "I do this all for you." He didn't let go so much as Bret pushed away from him.

Clete followed. "I decided to give you your chance."

Bret stopped. He resented the feeling of childishness that his Pa forced into him. "What chance?"

"Come back upstairs where we can talk."

Bret led the way back upstairs.

Inside their suite Clete reached awkwardly to embrace his son, but Bret walked to where the window was heavily draped and leaned toward the street. "I'm sorry I lost my temper, son."

"What chance?"

Clete poured himself a cup of coffee, relishing Bret's attention. "That young Cartwright is leaving town. I don't want to see him reach home."

Bret started toward him. "You're sending me---."

"I'm giving you enough money to find us another gunslinger. It needs to be done quickly."

"You want me to hire somebody?" Bret sat heavily, reliving the moment when he was 12 and his pa had grabbed the gun out of his hand and slapped him across the face. "Hell."

"And follow whoever you find. Make sure he doesn't make it back. But first, let me write a note."

"A note? You think I can't talk, either?"

"Tell the gunslinger to tuck this note into the dead Cartwright's pocket. Ben needs another hello from me to stew over, telling him I met his son and we had a fine conversation. Give me a minute to write."

Bret peered through the heavy curtain, shut to keep out morning sun. "If I'm gonna get this gunman out on the trail before this Cartwright kid heads on home you better hurry." Bret saw Joe walk of the sheriff's office, and a notion swept through him like a dust storm. When he turned back to Clete, he didn't bother to hide the smirk.

"Don't worry about timing." Clete refreshed his coffee and sipped on it as he walked to the desk. "That kid's not leaving town until he gets a word in with us, count on it."

"I'll feel better once you let me out of here. Coming up with a gunman won't be easy. He'll end up pounding leather to get into position, and that could destroy aim."

"You worry too much." Clete sat at the desk. "It won't take long to get the wording right."

Bret sat tense in the over-cushioned settee. "Pa, uh, sir, do you know why Ma went to see Mr. Cartwright that day she died?"

Clete paused before looking up. "Your mother was generally the sweetest thing around you, son, but with her sense of fair play assailed she could be the foulest thing you'd ever meet."

"You didn't answer my question." Bret's sudden realization that his father knew the truth all along prompted the question. This, at least, would explain his father's years of hesitation.

"She was on her way to threaten him! Cartwright had stopped me from making a deal with the Russians, did it himself, inserting himself where he had no concern. If I had known she was going I would have stopped her and gone myself!" His fist stamped the desk, making the ink bottle jump. "Cartwright claims he didn't know she was there, couldn't see her, and it was thunder that started the stampede."

"It wasn't thunder."

Clete ripped open a desk drawer and took out some writing paper. "Your ma, bless her, was cut off in her prime. We had a right to that land. Then Winnie was dead."

Bret heard the regretful sigh. "You coulda killed him right then and there. Killed them all."

"This way is better. Now, let me be to finish this note." Clete sat back and licked the end of his pen before putting it in ink.

In the silence the clock ticked loudly, mixing with Clete's heavy, sporadic breathing and the pen scribbling on paper. At the knock at the door Bret jumped, startled.

"Let him in," Clete said without a pause in his writing.

Bret walked to the door. A temper and some arrogance - maybe Pa developed a hard shell after all. Except for those head pains, he seemed as ruthless as his wife had been.

Bret opened the door.

***

Joe braced himself. When the door flung open, he found himself face to face with the young associate. Outside he had seemed older, but now Joe saw a vulnerability he didn't expect. He didn't seem like an associate, he seemed more like…

"What do you want?"

"I have business with Mr. van Remus."

"He's busy. Give him ten minutes." Bret started to shut the door but Joe fisted it open.

"Be with you shortly, young man," Clete called. Finally satisfied with what he wrote, he sealed it shut and called Bret over. "You remember what we discussed?"

Bret nodded, carefully tucking the note away.

Joe had stepped inside and watched them, his arms over his chest. He didn't plan to turn his back to either of them.

"I expect you to have this project complete by noon, so come back and report to me here."

Bret tucked the note away and left the room.

***

Hoss folded the second letter up and went back into Adam's room. Hop Sing's head hung low as he left Adam's side. Gently, Hoss touched the back of his hand to Adam's neck. Burning up with fever. At the sound of a distant knock, Hoss poked his head out and saw Hop Sing open the door. Ben stopped at the top of the stairs just as the doctor came in.

"John!" Ben ran down the stairs and grabbed Jessup's hand, pulling him to Adam's room. "Hoss, how's he doing?"

"He has some bad moments but then he's good again. He's got a bad fever now."

Ben went to Adam's side. He rewetted the clothe with some of Hop Sing's fresh cold water and dabbed at his son's sweating forehead as the doctor behind him opened his bag.

"I figured he would be, Ben, so I brought the medicine. I thought I had it with me last night." Dr. Jessup measured a dose and worked it into Adam's mouth. "See if he'll take a little water with that." Ben tried but got more water down his neck than in his mouth. "That's fine, Ben. I expect he'll start coming around soon now. Fever's good for the boy, means he's healing, he's fighting. We'll just keep it controlled."

"He already talked a little before. Pa---."

"Just a minute, Hoss. Doctor, is he out of danger, then?"

"His breathing seems steady enough. I'd venture a guess that the bad moments were shifts in position and reactions to pain. You say he talked already, Hoss? Most unusual so soon after surgery. I'm reserving my opinion though, Ben, until after we see how quickly the fever breaks and how he feels when he comes to. Problem with a deep wound like that, things can still go wrong."

"You can stay for a while?"

"For a little while. Have Hop Sing send in more cold water and towels."

"Pa, I got to show ya something." Hoss pulled Ben away from Adam's bedside. He held the letters out, but Ben was deep in thought until suddenly he grabbed Hoss's arm.

"Hoss! You said he talked earlier? What'd he say? Why didn't you wake me up?"

"I was gonna, Pa, then Dr. Jessup knocked. Pa, Adam said to read some letters, and I found 'em."

Ben took the letters, turning them over a few times to get a handle on them. His expression didn't change but Hoss had the feeling he couldn't look much lower than he already did. "Hop Sing!"

"Yes, Mr. Cartlight?" Hop Sing, more obliging than usual, came out on a second's notice whenever anyone called and without grumbling.

"See if the doctor needs anything." Ben walked to the settee and sat, absorbed in Sutter's letter. Hoss sat in the chair, unable to tear his eyes from his father's face. After what seemed an eternity, Ben folded up the second letter, the one from Van Remus. His hands shook so bad he seemed as though he had aged twenty years. "I was hoping this would never return to haunt me. God help me, I never thought I would ever see the day when I would — even for a second — believe it might have been better if one of my sons had died."

"Adam, Pa?"

"Before Adam's through remembering, he might just wish he was dead.

CHAPTER 10

Joe sat tense and alert in a hardback chair across from Clete's desk . . . *the only Van, Joe.* He watched the older man's face casually and eyed the surroundings as though on a pleasant social call. After Clete dismissed Bret with a note, he went back to writing, with the attitude that he had to take care of important things first.

"Were you and Pa good friends back in Sacramento Valley?"

"Good as you can find, boy. Why do you ask?"

"The person who killed my brother has a vendetta against Pa. I'm making sure it's not you before I ask for your help."

"Me? Do I look like a killer, boy?"

Yes! And stop calling me boy! Joe forced a smile. "You seemed interested in Adam's welfare."

"I knew your brother in Sacramento. I think he's about the same age as my associate, Bret." He crossed his arms on the desk and leaned forward, after pushing his writing materials out of his way. "Let me be honest with you. Bret is my associate, but also. . .my son."

"Ahhh." Joe stumbled over his sudden change of thought. Why drop this elaborate pretense now? "So he and Adam were friends?" Joe leaned forward in his chair.

"Well, you know boys."

"Yeah." The whole thing fell into place, sudden and sure. "You know, maybe a visit from an old friend might cheer Pa up. Why don't you and your son come out to our ranch for a few days? Get you out of this noisy city, enjoy the peace and scenery of our ranch, you know, talk over old times."

Clete slapped the desktop and stood. "That's very kind of you, but I'm too busy for social calls." He perched himself on the desk next to Joe.

"Why don't have your Pa come to me?" He replaced the cap to the ink bottle. "Or perhaps I'll pen him a note myself and invite him to dinner."

"He'd enjoy that. I don't think he even knows you're in town." Joe felt van Remus could be the one. "You're so honest with me I'll trust you with the truth." He watched Clete walk to the teapot. "My brother's not dead. I only said that to make whoever set up his shooting feel comfortable. I trust you'll keep the confidence."

"Certainly." Clete smiled broadly but without eye contact. His hands shook slightly as he poured his tea, so he filled his cup only half full. He strode to Joe with his hands out, beaming. "It is certainly good news to hear that Ben hasn't lost one of his own. But dear boy, where are my manners? Can I offer you a brandy?"

"Thanks but I have to get back on the trail." Joe worked hard to stay pleasant. "Whoever tried to kill him might try again."

Clete grabbed his arm. "Find out who hired that gun. Of course. Well, thank you for the gracious invite. I would enjoy the chance to meet with old Ben again. I'll see if I can't clear some time." He let Joe's arm go but kept his attention. "Tell me, are you the second son I remember him having back in Sacramento?"

"Who, me? Ho-no, that's---." But Joe stopped himself and finished lamely, "I wasn't born yet."

Joe turned to go but Clete grabbed his arm. "So your father married a third time? Your mother---."

"Why don't you and Pa catch up on old times yourself?" Joe tipped his hat at Clete and pulled away without giving Clete another chance.

Joe stood outside the door, sighed sharply in praise of his own self-control for not strangling the man on the spot, and headed for home.

***

Clete played with his tea and took a sip. The eldest still alive? Well, the youngest won't be for long. Clete went to the window and watched as Joe mounted up and rode off. He won't tell anyone else on the way out of town about Bret being a Van Remus, got too many other things on his mind. And when Bret gets done with him, he won't be telling anyone anything.

That young Joe Cartwright ought to learn that to win at chess you had to have a gullible opponent.

***

"Pa, I want to hear about Adam wishing he was dead but there ain't time. Joe's gone."

At once angry and afraid Ben looked up from the letter. "What?"

"He mighta left last night right off. Pa, we can't leave him out there. Adam said to be careful, and he mentioned a Van."

Ben prided himself on making quick decisive moves and the right ones. Now he faced a foe who may be innocent of any wrongdoing — or who may not. Whose only target may have been Adam — because why on earth would he bother with a boy he'd never met?

He went back into Adam's room. His eldest seemed calmer, his skin tone not so flushed. "Doctor?"

"It appears the fever's peaked out. He's strong, Ben. You're lucky."

Ben grabbed Hoss's arm and leaned on him in relief. Hoss could feel his own knees shake. "That is good news, John, because Hoss and I have to ride into Virginia City. We just got word on who may be connected with shooting Adam, and Little Joe is gone."

Adam jerked, his eyes blinking open. "Pa?"

Ben knelt down next to his son, glad to see his eyes again, flat and dull but seeing him back. "How are you feeling, son?"

"Ah...fine."

Ben laughed as he squeezed Adam's hand.

"Hey, welcome back, brother. You put up a durned good fight."

"Hoss," Adam's eyes squeezed shut. "Something."

"What, Adam?" Hoss knelt on the other side of the bed.

"Something to tell you." He licked at his dry lips. Dr. Jessup gently eased some water into his mouth. Adam had some trouble swallowing but got most of it down.

Hoss leaned forward. "You said something before, Adam, about me and Joe being careful, about Van and some letters."

"Yeah. . .careful. . .this was planned."

"Was it Van Remus, Adam? Can you be sure?" Ben spoke gently, underscoring his anger. Even Sutter only guessed, based on their past.

"I'm. . .it's. . .aaaahhh!" Adam's head jerked in frustration. "Can't. . .Pa, it was. . .can't." his eyes closed again as he drifted away.

Ben patted Adam's hand. "It's all right, son, it'll come back to you."

Dr. Jessup smiled at Ben's reluctance to leave. "Don't worry, Ben, I can stay a while. I still have several doses of this medicine to give him yet."

"Get Hop Sing to stay with him when you leave. I don't know how long we'll be, but no longer than we have to."

"Go take care of your business, Ben. Adam will be fine."

"Thank you, John. Come on, Hoss, we better ride hard."

CHAPTER 11

Bret left the International House with the note his father had written tucked into his jeans. Doing this killing behind Pa's back made the day, the time, the wait, even sweeter. The way Pa acted when Ma died kept Clete from thinking mean enough. Ma could have gotten them what they wanted back in New Helvetia, legal or otherwise. Ma would have killed Mr. Cartwright if she hadn't been trampled first, and then this youngest son wouldn't have been born at all.

"Ma, why you dressed up in Pa's clothes?" Young Bret had never seen a woman look so odd, and his own mother, besides.

Winnie carefully tucked her thick blonde hair under the heavy black felt hat before turning back to her son. Her deep-lidded eyes dropped almost to closing as she gazed down at Bret, who sat on the floor polishing the musket she gave him. In a very un-motherly fashion she sat on the floor next to him, crossing her legs Indian style. His mom told him that the Turks also sat this way, making Bret wonder how the Indians met the Turks. He thought about asking Pa because his pa knew a lot about immigrants, but kept forgetting. Bret realized he'd been staring at her woman part hidden inside his Pa's dungarees when she gently lifted his chin to look her in the eyes.

"You know how sad your Pa and me have been lately. We come out here to this great west because it was supposed to be freer here than in the Ohio valley, the way we was."

"I know, Ma."

"You know how poorly they treated us there."

"I know, Ma."

"Your father almost died from being beaten, would have if I hadn't showed up to shoot the varmint." She put a woolen, dirt-smelly arm

around his shoulder and hugged him. "Now I have to help him again." She jumped to her feet. "He can't get us what we want, so I will."

Bret followed her to the door. "But how, Ma?"

She cuffed him in the chin. "Now you don't really want to go through life knowing that."

He nodded, his eyes shining. "Sure I do, Ma!"

Winnie took the gun out of his hands. "Now you know."

"You gonna kill him dead, Ma, that Mr. Cartwright?"

She smiled sourly, eyes glistening with what he thought looked like tears. "It's the only way left. He beat your father up just as bad, only on the inside."

"Make Pa do it."

"Your father is a fine, wonderful man. When I married him, it's because I saw many gentle qualities in him. I thought I could learn to be like him. But I don't have his patience. He won't go out and kill Mr. Cartwright. I have to."

"Ma? You be careful?"

She laughed, not the fine light sound that he loved. "Just don't tell your father, he won't understand. If he finds out I did the shooting, well, Bret my boy, he just may not be able to look on me again, at least not in the same way as before. So don't tell him, do you understand?"

"Ma?" Bret threw his arms around her, feeling the sudden need to never let her go. "When I'm grown, will I be like you? Or like Pa?"

"Well," she said with a serious frown, "if you're like your father, prepare yourself. You will never get what you want out of life unless you marry well." She kissed his cheek. "Don't wait up for me. I may have to ride off into the night. Gone to fish, you tell everyone. I'll be

back, cooking your dinner same as ever noon tomorrow, I promise."
She winked at him. "Maybe we'll have sturgeon."

Bret headed for the blacksmith shop, but on the way stopped an old miner who directed him without any great detail the way to the Ponderosa. Sturgeon, indeed. At the blacksmith's Bret killed time waiting for fresh bullets to cool rather than picking up the week-old ones, mindful of the time he would need to stay ahead of the target. As he waited he saw a gleaming knife for sale. He made another purchase.

***

Joe knew as surely as the sun rose that he had to get out of Virginia City before Clete could plan anything on his back. He picked up supplies at the mercantile more out of habit than need. Hop Sing taught them never to ride home without goods. Joe kept the news about Bret being Clete's son to himself, not sure what to do with it.

Now that Clete knows Adam's still alive he's bound to show his hand. Joe figured he'd be so busy planning another attack on Adam that he'd forget about the other sons for a while, but then Joe remembered that Bret had gone out somewhere during his conversation with van Remus.

His senses tingled as Joe rode fast and hard to get home. Something foul drifted in the normally sweet-smelling air of the Sierras. Lingering hate in his mind for the one who shot Adam, Joe supposed, but it was more. It was people like van Remus who would lie and charm their way about the truth. If he has a vendetta against Pa, or Adam, he ought to 'fess up to it like a man and take his chances.

Joe felt a sting of embarrassment that he had almost been taken in by the man. Even if Adam was the only one he wanted dead, for whatever reason, that didn't mean he wouldn't try something against the rest of them. Something bad must have happened between Adam and Bret, was all Joe could figure.

Up another steep incline, Cochise slowed his pace. Joe tensed, knowing a bullet would probably hit him before he heard it, and yet he couldn't explain how he managed to fling himself off his horse so that the gunshot that tore past his ear only ripped off a piece of skin from his arm. He scrambled across rock and behind a pine, his heart pounding. He climbed to his left, skirting behind rocks, and another shot zinged, taking off a chip of rock in front of him.

"Why don't you show yourself, you coward?" he yelled. When the next shot fired, way off mark, Joe had a better idea of direction. With his grip tight on his gun he climbed the side of the foothill quickly, pulling himself up behind trees and using rocks as a shield whenever possible. With his knowledge of the area, Joe recognized the area where the ambusher would have a perfect shot, on a natural bluff overlooking the trail. Joe kept his approach quiet and heard a horse snorting. He tightened his grip on his gun and climbed up the side of the jutting granite cliff.

"Hold it," Joe said to the man who stood readying his horse to ride off.

Bret, strapping the rifle to his saddle, froze and glanced back over his shoulder. "All right. Go ahead and shoot. If you got the guts."

"Throw that rifle to the ground and turn around. Keep your hands where I can see them." With Bret facing him, Joe walked closer. "Did you have my brother Adam shot?"

Bret laughed. "That was us, all right. But there's something you don't know about your precious dead brother. He killed my ma!"

"Adam wouldn't kill nobody's ma. You don't know my brother."

"Oh, he killed her all right, came riding out of the woods like a wild Comanche, right into a herd of skittish cows and…"

"Shut your lying!" Joe waved the gun impatiently. "I told you my brother's no killer, any more than I am. And he's fighting for his life, because of your pa." He grabbed Bret's rifle and tossed it backward, listening as it rolled to a stop halfway down the rocky cliff. "And my brother isn't dead. He's going to be just---."

Bret screamed, "Noooooo!" catching Joe off guard long enough to knock Joe's gun away.

Joe tackled Bret, knocking him backward. He punched Bret solidly across the jaw, flattening him. Joe scrambled on the ground looking for his gun. Bret kicked out with a heavy booted foot, catching Joe hard alongside the ear and knocking him over.

Bret climbed to his knees and pulled the knife from its sheath inside his vest. Joe, on his knees, shook his dizzied head. His gun lay only a few feet from him. Joe dived for his gun just as Bret screamed and leaped. He pushed Joe backward and drove the knife up hard under Joe's rib, feeling the flesh rip, and hearing bone crack.

Joe dropped the gun and pushed his shoulder against Bret, his hands trying to take hold of the knife stuck in him. Bret pulled the knife back out, grinning as Joe cried out in pain. He flung the knife aside and delivered a blow to Joe's jaw that sent him rolling down the side of the rocky hill.

Bret waited until the body stopped rolling. He listened, panting, for a sound that meant Cartwright was coming back for more. After a few minutes of silence he got to his feet and packed up his gear, the rifle, and the bloodied knife.

He pulled out the letter that his pa had taken such care with. Using trees and brush to keep from falling, Bret slipped down the hillside to where Joe's body lay in the rocks. If the kid was still alive he would slowly lose his grip lying where nobody could find him. Bret tucked the letter inside Joe's jacket and climbed back up the hill, stopping halfway up to breathe deeply and calm his shaking limbs before mounting up to take a blind trail back to Virginia City.

**

Adam groaned, wanting to awaken, escape the unpleasant dream, but couldn't.

He was a boy again, or watching a boy holding a mother's hand. They seemed happy, walking out in the open meadows, laughing…but the ground began to shake, and the sky grew dark. Pounding hooves filled their ears, the stench of the cows in their nostrils and they were screaming, trying to run away, but they were surrounded, more cows, heavy hooves, fat and muscled bodies. He held his mother's hand tight, feeling her body jerk about as the cows ran over her, tearing her body to pieces, leaving him alone, leaving him to stand there, screaming her name over and over. In the next instant he sat astride a running horse. He held a gun in the air, and he yelled, yelling hard and firing, and then he fell off the horse screaming, like before, but this time an arrow stuck out of his back, except he couldn't feel it because he was not there. Pa stood over him in a bed with the arrow still in his back. Ben only shook his head sadly, saying, "Thunder, boy, only thunder, boy."

Doctor Jessup wetted the cloth with more cold water and put it back on Adam's forehead, but fever didn't make him shake and toss his head this way. From the way this dream distressed his sleep, those images could be as deadly as any bullet in the back. If Adam was lucky, he wouldn't remember them when he awoke.

CHAPTER 12

The loggers followed the main road from Virginia City down into Carson Valley. Lingering snowcaps peaked the high mountains of the Sierras, even though they'd just finished off one hot summer for the valley. Snow on those peaks made them look higher and fiercer than Jon McManus expected. He originally hailed from Colorado where mountains made men. He suspected these could be almost as trying.

Ahead of them loomed the steep climb to Ponderosa land where they'd be cutting. A dark shadow cast over the mountain, like a closed and locked door saying, 'keep out'. Jon himself never much believed in the property rights of others. If he saw something he wanted, he took it. He gathered his workers to have the same respect.

They cut off the main trail that led to the ranch to avoid the chance of being spotted, but lack of a solid path to follow made the slopes of the Sierras along Ben Cartwright's Ponderosa tricky to maneuver. Jon had worked this kind of uneven terrain before, and the men he found had enough experience not to whine over it. Because of Carne, they had to slow up when he grew fearful and got off his horse to walk. The man was a fool and an idiot - but he could kill without remorse.

"Carne! Get back on your horse. You ain't got the feet for climbing your horse has."

Carne looked back at him with surprise. After another couple of steps he mounted his horse. He lingered behind the rest, and rode slouched as though trying to melt into his horse.

The logging trail Van Remus sent them on gave Jon an uneasy feeling, a feeling he didn't take kindly to. Maybe he didn't care about destroying land in the comfort of a hotel room — out here, he could see how overcut it was. No decent logger would cut in here, let alone blast out the stumps after cutting. The flume was likely dismantled, as this area wouldn't be legitimate for cutting for another decade or more. Clete had said if necessary he'd shut down the mines and send a crew of men to construct another flume. Jon snorted at the thought — miners. Why, the fresh air alone would kill 'em. But if this Van

Remus wants stumps blown — well, what the hell. Trees can grow back anywhere. Trees were what he respected most in this world, after gold. Certainly not people like Van Remus or this Cartwright.

McManus looked for a tree close to the trail that was branded with the boss's sign, the upside down -C- hanging over the large -V-. That would tell him the proper location, but McManus knew he found the landslide waiting to happen already. When he spotted this particular tree, he halted his crew and pulled the loaded oxen to secure lofts. He and Louis unhooked the oxen from the drays, sent the stubborn beasts to a patch of grazing, and unloaded tools.

"Adolf, get over here and unload that third one. And remember, all of you, what I said from the start. Whatever tree you're working, make sure you mark it with the boss's notch. Like the first notch we saw. Van Remus wants it known he's been here."

"Doesn't that figure on getting him in trouble?" Petey's voice registered his surprise at his boss's audacity.

"He knows how to get himself out."

Adolf grunted as he unloaded the broad axes, hefting the one that felt good to him. "Sure, it's good ve can cut, good ve can chop, but where to take logs when ve're done? I like to see all the vurkings."

"Maybe he's just chopping and leaving." Petey grabbed his canteen for a swallow but the water was warm so he spit most on the ground after wetting his throat.

"No, that be vasteful." Adolf pulled out the kerosene cans, shaking one until he seemed satisfied with the sound.

"Quit the chatter. He plans to use the wood." Jon watched as Adolf held the kerosene in one hand and the box of gunpowder under his arm and looked around as though there couldn't possibly be any safe place to put them. "Put 'em over by the marked timber for now," Jon snapped at him. Sometimes that Adolf with his glassy little eyes and dopey expression could be so short. Only the bull of the woods had the right to question the one paying the wages, and that was Jon himself. "Besides, boss says for now cutting is good enough. He says we go ahead and start the cut, and he'll get us more men to move timber later this week."

"Now just a tall second," Louis stepped in. "Is that what you're butting your brains about? Why, I told ya I done worked this area for Cartwright till he fired me and there's a chute just beyond that next cropping there. These puny oxen can get the logs to it sure enough, if'n we cut small enough."

Jon grabbed his shirt. "You never mentioned working for the Cartwrights."

"Well," Louis stammered in the hot breath of the bull of the woods. "I reckon I did, but the way you swallowed them whiskeys when we first met I guess you didn't hear me a'tall."

"How good do you know 'em?"

"Well, only a day or two after I started the old one decided he didn't like my looks and cut me loose. Never did get an eyeful of any of the other Cartwrights. But I learned enough of this section, because it's where I spent two days cutting. Fact, I think he fired all of us for not abiding by his cutting restrictions."

Jon let him go, patting his shirt back down. "I 'spect that that's why I hired you." He handed Louis the stamp ax. "You cruise us some trees. Remember, I want some younger, finer ones along with the big ones that are left. Mark all of 'em unless you can feel your fingers around it. But we won't waste no time springboarding. With just four fallers we'll cut from the ground. Mark 'em in a trail to the flume. Rest of us will cut into these nasty pines to get them a'bleeding."

Louis nodded and moved away, putting the telltale notch in the tree marked with the brand.

A fine tree too, Jon thought, maybe 400 hundred years old. Maybe the oldest tree left in this section, but it could be felled as sure as the rest. "Watch you don't mark any toothpick timber, or I'll be marking you!"

Petey stepped up next to Jon, pulling on his second glove. "Think there'll be trouble?" He nodded over at Carne, who lifted a canteen from the mule.

"I know there will. But not today. Ole Cartwright's gonna find himself preoccupied for another two or so days yet, if Boss tells a clean story. If too many more trees are cut down in that section yonder, and we set about blasting out stumps, why, that'll open that whole area up to a landslide. Wouldn't that be something? Mmmmhmmm. That's when we'll likely see some smokin'."

"Landslide, eh? Say, we putting our own lives in danger?" Petey looked up the base of a Ponderosa and leaned against it as though checking its balance. When McManus seemed unconcerned about this last statement, he shrugged. "But if Van Remus doesn't expect trouble for another week, why tag the gunman along so soon?"

"You want to hire a fella like that and then tell him to wait around idle for a week?"

Carne spit out a wad of tobacco before taking another swallow of water. His face, tight and empty, turned their way and he gave them a black-toothed grin.

Petey went back to work.

***

Kudwa waited for the elders' decision outside the lodge of his wife. He had waited an entire day to get council so when they finally gave him their attention only moments earlier he had kept his words brief and plain. "It is not only for the Cartwrights that we must do this, but also for the sake of our people, for the trees hold the Earth in its place in the sky. If Adam Cartwright dies, if the bad whites succeed in driving his family off their land, then land would be lost for many, many days' ride to men who did not see the trees the way Adam and his family does, to protect the land the way the Cartwrights protect it. I wish two things - to stand vigil until my friend is well enough to watch his own back, and to learn more of the story from Adam. Then we will know if we need more weapons for another war with the whites."

Felling of the Sons

Perhaps that last had been his mistake, because at this the council members grew concerned. They were still unsettled from the War of the Summer Months and did not wish to stir more hatred. Kudwa had listened with a nod as many talked at once and then cleared his throat and stood, commanding further attention.

"Another war is not what I or Adam wish. But what is the alternative? What cost is peace? Do we lose all the trees and let the very ground we walk on crumble and fall away? Our lives will be no more when the trees are gone and the Earth floats to the sun."

All were silent as he sat back down again.

Finally Winnemucca stood. "We have heard you, Kudwa. Though you make the decision sound like a simple one, I am disturbed. We could reason with other whites, as we do with the Cartwrights. The time for war has ended."

"I agree with you," Kudwa told him. "But the time to protect the land has just begun. I ask only to be trusted to know and act on what is in all our hearts, for our children's future."

"Your voice hurts my head," Winnemucca said with a slight smile. "Go now, and let us talk this out. We will give an answer soon."

Kudwa went to his lodge but turned back to watch the council where the talk continued in low tones, where he stood worried that his words weren't right or his motives weren't true. How hard it was to stand somewhere between war and peace!

"Kudwa, come inside. You are wearing a hole in Earth Mother with your worry." His wife called to him. "All will be fine in the end."

He peered inside her lodge. She lay stretched out on deerskin, very appealing except that he had so many things on his mind. "The end? This is only the beginning, my wife, the beginning of a new and terrible day. Even Sun Father cannot foresee the end. How can you?"

"You will leave before a decision is made?" She sat up and put a hand out to him. "I can comfort you, and you will take my comfort on your long trip ahead."

"You think they will agree?"

"They will agree."

Kudwa glanced over his shoulder before crawling inside to lie down next to her, taking comfort in her strong and sure caresses. He allowed himself to feel only the smallest of pleasure, as pleasure in the midst of agony would bring a guilt hard to lose. Shortly after, he heard the stirring of voices outside and crawled away from his wife. He glanced back at her, sleeping peaceful, and allowed a brief longing to cross his face before walking to the elders standing outside the lodge.

"It is decided," Winnemucca said.

"Do I leave?"

The elder looked up into the sky at the direction of the sun path. "Soon it grows dark. It is perhaps good that you leave now. But before the Sun Father takes a third rest, you must return and share all you learn."

"This I will do." Kudwa put a hand on Winnemucca's shoulder. "I will be careful."

***

Slowly the light from the room opened his eyes. At first Adam couldn't focus, but when the room swam into view and he saw the doctor sitting there reading, some vague memory of riding home from Virginia City returned. "Ah..."

The doctor smiled broadly. "Adam, how are you feeling?"

"Thirsty."

Dr. Jessup held the glass steady to Adam's lips, and he drank easily.

Adam held the cool wet on his tongue, savoring it before swallowing. "What ah...day is this?"

"It's the afternoon, day after you were shot."

"After I was..."

"You had the bullet removed from your back last night – or, I should say, early this morning. You'll be okay, boy." He got to his feet. "I'll get Hop Sing in here to tend to you. I need to get back to town." He patted Adam's arm. "So I can take care of the really sick people." Adam grinned weakly. "I told Ben I'd stay until your fever broke. Looks like it did, ahead of schedule. I wish all my patients were as cooperative."

"Thanks. Where's Pa?"

"He had to head to town. Some kind of problem to settle." Jessup looked down.

"Hoss?"

Jessup paused. "Went with him."

"Joe?" Adam swallowed hard, the fear flooding down him worse than any pain. He rolled on his back as though getting ready to get out of bed and choked back the groan as the pain bit through him.

"Not yet. You're not ready to move. Tell you what, hold still a minute and I'll get Hop Sing to help me ease you onto your other side."

"Joe..."

But Dr. Jessup left the room.

Adam didn't need him to confirm it. Hoss and Pa had to leave because Joe left, Joe with his impetuous temper and need to right any wrong, Joe who couldn't sit still and think that there could be a better way. Joe left before anyone knew to stop him and now Hoss and Pa went looking for him.

He tried to move his legs but couldn't without doubling back in pain. "Damn," he said under his breath, eyes tearing. "Damn, damn, damn...."

CHAPTER 13

Clete climbed out of the mine, his wet feet precariously scaling the indents in stone. The climb angled a few feet to the surface, just enough to make him uncomfortable. Before long they'll dig lower and some other type of descent would have to be rigged. Once topside with fresh air in his lungs to replace the damp, he turned to view the trail leading down the side of Mount Davidson where he expected to see his son riding in with good news.

Above his mine, on top of the hill he dug into, sat a newer section of the city with saloons and a livery. If Clete had his way, those greedy merchants would move their businesses elsewhere. They only scoffed when he tried to tell them that the ground where they were building could be fragile. Cave-ins were frequent because they had no decent way of timbering to strengthen these gopher holes. Saloons built on top of mines didn't ease the ground tension any. One saloon owner jumped up and down on the floor of his business to demonstrate that Clete worried for nothing. And a city built on slopes like Virginia City needed to utilize every space to accommodate an ever-growing population. If he ran out of workers, he'd be the sorry one.

Clete stood to look for Bret but off in the distance saw two men riding hard into town, their speed impetuous, almost careless. As they closed in and slowed up, Clete, squinting hard, recognized the one sitting on the buckskin.

Ben Cartwright. Older, heavier, more intimidating than he remembered. The years had toughened them both.

He slunk back down into the mine. "Reeger," he called out to a miner who sloshed to a new spot, candle flame close to dying in the moist air, "I have a job for you."

Reeger was young, hefty, and not particularly bright but Clete could tell he understood the request made of him. He even kept himself from asking why, because even a simple man knew that questioning the boss that pays your wages just wasn't done. Van Remus's mine could hit bonanza. Any day now that legendary vein of silver would be found. For that reason and no more, Reeger was happy to do anything Mr. van Remus wanted.

Once Reeger rode out of sight, Clete leaned against the forward most progressive dig, ankle deep in water, contemplating a solution to the flooding. He heard Sutro's idea of extracting ore with a sideways shaft and wondered if that idea could be useful for draining water. Perhaps a quick letter to San Francisco?

Bret practically leaped down into the mine and his momentum didn't stop even knee-deep in water. "Clete. . .Mr. Van Remus, sir." Bret leaned on him, breathing heavily.

"You find a gunman?" Clete peered at a newly chipped area, pretending disinterest in Bret's hushed account.

"Did I … ah."

"Take care of young Cartwright?"

"Yeah! Sure did!" Laughing, he grabbed his father's lapels and yanked him nose to nose. "I didn't hire anybody — I took care of him myself."

Clete never saw Bret quite so nearly out of control, volatile as gunpowder ready to be torched. "Go on," he said calmly.

"I wanted to kill him myself. I rode on ahead and found a spot, but I…" he licked his lips as he laughed and his father pulled away.

"Did you shoot him?"

"No! I missed. I don't know how, I'm a good shot, you know I am."

"Sure, at tin cans." Clete turned back to the mine wall in disgust.

"I knifed him!"

"Say that again? Slower this time."

"He chased me!" Bret kicked the water on the mine floor as though demonstrating. "The fool chased me up the hill and found me, and he thought I gave up. Well, of course I made him think it. He jumped me and I stabbed him in the heart and pushed him off the cliff. And I left the note on his body."

"Well." Clete smiled. "At least you made up for a lousy shot. Now Cartwright will have to take me serious."

"Oh, he will." Bret slumped back against the wall, exhausted. "What about the murderer? He's still alive."

"I know. We have to do something about that."

"Maybe I could---."

"And soon. I'm tired of living at the International. I want the Ponderosa."

"I could do it."

"Do what?" Clete breathed deeply in the damp air, realizing he hadn't had a headache all day. Must have something to do with working underground, staying out of the sun and wind.

"Kill him."

"Now wait a minute, Bret, don't get carried away by the seat of your own pants. Killing someone out in the open is one thing, but going at him where he lives..."

"How about a fire?"

"Fire?"

"Sure, set the house on fire. Adam laid up, won't be able to get out."

"Not bad." Clete pondered this. "Not the whole house. But clean out the Cartwright stench before we move in. I'll think on it. You go on and check on the second shift, make sure they're staying out of that third tunnel like I say."

Clete watched his son sloshing away. But for Bret, Clete would never have learned the truth about why that herd stampeded.

After burying his wife Clete dived knee-deep into whiskey, but Bret was restless, anxious, and couldn't sit still. Clete had only weak words of consolation for his son, words he tried to believe, that the stampeding was an accident, a freak spring storm had spooked the cattle, nothing more. Not acceptable to Bret, just shy of 12 years, and becoming, as the hours grew long, less likely to him as well.

When Bret finally ran out of the house, Clete knew where he headed. Perhaps his son could learn what really happened. Freak storm? Hardly.

At the shack Cartwright called home for him and two sons, Bret had leaped off the horse and slunk inside a shed, just in case someone heard him ride in. His horse ran off, but it didn't worry him. When Bret felt safe, he snuck back outside. Some kind of a ruckus, lots of voices and carrying on came from inside the house. He crept over to a window and cautiously peeked in. They were all gathered around the bed where the Cartwright kid lay.

When they first came to Sutter's Fort, his pa expected that he and this kid, Adam, would be friends. Wasn't possible, Bret knew, because of the way the kid looked at him when they came upon each other in the open field — like Adam saw something in him that even Bret didn't know was there. Now they had this kid strapped into bed. Was he sick? Not that Bret cared.

"Easy, Adam, easy, boy." Ben dipped his rag back into the water and stroked his son's fevered brow. "John, when is he going to come out of this? It's been two days since the stampede."

Sutter sat on the other side of the bed. "It's like a fever, Ben, just got to work through his system. He had a nasty shock, seeing that woman go under like that."

Ben leaned close, his lips brushing his boy's cheek. "Adam, you couldn't help it." The old Cartwright practically bawled. "I don't know what made him come yelling like that, John. But he didn't know

Winnie rode in front dressed the way she was. None of us could have known."

Bret heard enough. The boy charged into a herd of beeves, making them run. That made it murder.

Clete wanted to kill Adam as soon as he heard Bret's story, but Bret wanted it worse. Fearing consequences of a violent act of his son's, he moved them to San Francisco with Bret shrieking for his mother.

During the gold rush San Francisco grew in spurts of hellfire, and Clete took advantage of opportunities to settle disputes. When he hung his shingle as a lawyer he did so legally, after years of clerking in a law office.[7] And the legal way to get back at Cartwright began to make its way into his hands. Gradually he learned how to plan for consequences. And slowly his son healed. Or so Clete thought.

He did try, several times, to get back at Ben in those eighteen years. He and Bret surrounded themselves with a gang that could be bought and rode out to the Ponderosa, and all the way there Clete imagined guns blazing and the Cartwrights going down without knowing what hit 'em. But no one had been home. He found out later that they had taken a long vacation in New Orleans.

He had another chance at revenge on a trip Ben took to San Francisco but held back. Ben had been alone. Clete realized then that he wanted the sons instead of Ben. How much sweeter could revenge be than taking away everything that Ben loved?

Timing was everything. Clete wanted to be beyond suspicion and he wanted to take everything Ben ever worked hard for in his life. Nothing less would satisfy him. Not anymore.

When he and Bret first came out here, he thought he could be happy just killing the eldest. Now he knows Ben married a third time. That made his anger, and his need for revenge, as hard to outrun as a tick on a deer. And he wouldn't try to run from it, not anymore.

---

[7] Dee Brown, *Bury My Heart at Wounded Knee,* (New York: Holt, Rinehart & Winston, 1970), 175.

CHAPTER 14

Reeger strolled along the wooden walk nodding at the people he knew, sharing bits of conversation when it struck him. When he reached the sheriff's office, he plastered a somber expression on his face and leaned against the outside wall. Those passing guessed he had business with Roy, who had his hands full at the moment.

"Roy, you just let him walk out of here?" Ben paced angrily as Hoss stood frowning.

"What did you want me to do, Ben, throw him in jail?"

"Joe was angry, he wasn't thinking, you shoulda seen that." Hoss folded his arms across his heavy chest like an ancient and angry Buddha.

Roy stood up behind his desk, shaking his head. He walked over to his door and looked outside. He didn't see Reeger, who leaned off to the side. "Angry? I could point out half a dozen people out there who look angrier right now than he did when he left here. Sure, he was mad that Adam got shot. But he behaved rational. Ben, when you gonna git it through your head that Joe is a grown man?"

"That doesn't mean that..."

"Well, innit he? Ain't he got the right to make decisions on his own?"

"Yeah, I guess so."

"He's grown, all right, Roy," Hoss said. "So's Adam."

"Perhaps Adam didn't know the danger like Joe does." If Roy waited for a backlash Ben disappointed him, from where Reeger stood, anyway. "How's Adam doing, Ben?"

"He was shot in the back, Roy!" Ben softened his voice, probably realizing his anger at Roy was misplaced. "Dr. Jessup was with him when we left, said he should make it."

"Good. Jessup's a good man." As Roy's naturally gruff expression relaxed Reeger sensed that was the end of this fun for one night. He figured he was starting to look a little too nosey to others so he backed off just a bit from his viewing. "Now Ben," Roy continued, "you oughta be grateful to Joe for coming out when he did and finding out what he did. If he hadn't, that man what did the shooting mighta been gone, mighta got picked up by coyotes or buried by that Indian and we'd know nothing right now."

"I know you're right, Roy."

"Pa, why don't we talk to that Van Remus feller?" Hoss eyed the door anxiously.

Ben nodded and picked up his hat.

"For the record, Ben, I did suggest that Joe ride with a deputy. I couldn't talk him into it, is all. Want I should get some deputies?"

Ben placed a heavy hand on Roy's sloped shoulder. "Thank you. I guess we can do as much as a deputy right now. Do you know which way he headed when he left here?"

"Well, he took care of the man what shot Adam. Jolly's over to the parlor if you want to see him." Reeger easily imagined Ben wincing at this with the soft "no" he gave in response. "We figured Van Remus to be the one who hired the gunslinger and Joe said he'd talk to him there. I reckon he headed on home after that."

"Van Remus is at the International?"

"That's right. But if Joe's missing, maybe you ought to look for him."

"We'll start with Van Remus. Show him what we think of someone shooting my brother in the back." Hoss beat a solid path to the door ahead of Ben.

Reeger watched Ben and Hoss walk to the International. There goes one mean and ugly Cartwright mood and he for one wouldn't get in their way. He ducked into Roy's office. "Roy! What's going on? Word's all over town that Adam Cartwright is dead!"

"Yeah, and a darn shame too. Bad things happen to good people. No accounting for it."

"What they gonna do?"

"I reckon what any family would do. I hope they stay within the law."
***

Ben and Hoss searched for Joe during a particularly hectic day in Virginia City. Two more mines were opening up with even more prospect than the Golden Cross, one being the Sierra Nevada that had been closed for a time and the other the Hale and Norcross. Men scrambled to be first in line for the jobs, and Ben recognized several as former drovers of his. Whenever a mine opened Ben had a devil of a time finding men to push beeves. At least that his own cattle drive made the trail without him or Joe, far from this new reach of trouble.

Ben thought to ask Hoss if he'd heard anything from Val about the drovers' demands, but they were kept busy stopping everyone they saw to ask about Joe for him to give cattle further thought. Several women shook their heads with appropriate words of sympathy and none of the miners took time to answer questions at all. A new saloon being built down the road had just collapsed into an abandoned mine. Abandoned mines were the worst. At least the worked mines had enough attention to shore up the timbering every couple of days or so. The workers salvaged what they could from the hole in the ground to use on a new site just a few yards away. The shouting at times was deafening.

Ben discovered to his vexation that most townsfolk thought well of Clete van Remus. Clete got his information by getting on everyone's good side, giving out jobs that were just a little higher paying than the rest, providing family benefits that others didn't provide, throwing money around and even giving free legal advice. Knowing these townsfolk all considered Van Remus a friend of Ben's made bile rise in his throat, even while he kept his conversation with them light and friendly. He recognized that he judged Van Remus even before talking to him, with Sutter's letter and a past to go by, nothing more. He needed an open and fair mind at a time like this. But right now that fair mind was pretty far out of reach.

No one at any of the saloons could say where Joe headed, although several remembered seeing him. Perhaps they didn't know, but with Van Remus's influence, perhaps they didn't care.

When they stopped outside the International to confront Van Remus, Ben grabbed Hoss's arm. "Let me do the talking. You're too dad-blamed hot tempered right now."
"Sure, Pa."

Ben strode inside, followed by Hoss. "And if I go for my gun, stop me." He leaned on Vince's desk. "What room is Van Remus in?"

Vince hesitated. "Is he expecting---?"

"Just tell me the room number, Vince. I'll see that you're not implicated if I murder him."

But Van Remus wasn't in his suite, and Vince had no idea where Ben could find him. He had a table reserved in the dining room but had already missed it by half an hour.

"Whelp," Hoss said, staring out into the street. "Time's wasting here."

"Yeah." Ben whipped his horse's reins off the rail. "Let's go."

"Where?"

"To find Joe."

"Where?" Hoss pulled his horse to him and climbed heavily, despondently up into the saddle.

"We only have two choices now. Head for home with the hope that Joe is home already. And watch on the way back for signs of a struggle."

***

Felling of the Sons

The trees sliced the rays of the setting sun, sending a peaceful, wistful romance down the hills of Mount Rose. Petey took a break from chopping into a pine to soak in the last of the day's sunshine, giving them only another hour before they break for the night. "You know, Adolf, mining is for gophers. Mining is like premature burying. I'll take the beauty of nature and cool fresh air." He laid the ax soundly into wood, causing the pine to tremble.

Petey and Adolf shared the bleeding process, making cuts in the base of trees to drain the pitch. There were few trees left standing in the area but Jon wanted them all bled, and insisted they work in pairs. He and Adolf worked opposite ends of their square, a total of only six hefty trees between them in the acre parcel. Petey didn't much care for his felling partner. The little German made him nervous by talking under his breath and jumping at every little noise.

"Petey. Could you come please?"

Petey threw his ax down. "Now what?"

Adolf's sleeve had stuck tight to a tree by its pitch and he couldn't reach the kerosene. As Petey loosened him, the little German gushed over how smart Jon was to make them work in pairs. When he was finally freed he examined his shirtsleeve and clicked his tongue over the pitch that would never come out. "Hey, let's break to nose bag."

"Hungry already?" Petey looked over his shoulder. "We can do one more before night."

"Expecting four of us to fell all trees here in a day?"

"Don't matter if we do. Sure Van Remus wants the lumber. What's most important is getting 'em down, filling them stumps with gunpowder and kaboom! Old Ben Cartwright won't know what's hit him till it's all over but the landsliding, that's the truth."

They hacked at the tree that Adolf had become attached to, finding a rhythm without hitting each other. They drew their broad axes up as the pitch started flowing, thudding sounds echoing off. For a moment, Adolf could only hear his breathing and then suddenly he whirled, the ax barely missing Petey's leg.

"Hey, watch it!" Petey jumped back.

"I hear some moving, didn't you hear some moving?"

"No, I didn't. Goddamn, you'd do anything to cut outta working. You may have experience but it's all from watching other people work."

"Oh, ha."

Real experience was hard to come by, and Petey knew it. When he came from Oregon down into California, Petey tried to get his two companions to start a logging camp in the midst of those tall red trees. They only laughed and called him 'that puny woodpecker'. He showed them all just by keeping at it, getting experience by learning everything the hard way.

Petey squinted through the growing darkness to locate the last unnotched tree and spotted the tough character halfway up the slope over some slippery rock. He reached for a large overhang rock and lifted himself up, his feet struggling for firm footing.

Adolf, behind him, suddenly screeched and dropped to the ground, the ppphhhhttttttt! buzzing past him in the still dry air.

"Will you stop being so jumpy!?" Petey thought to yell the second before the arrow sank deep in his leg. He screamed and fell backward down the slope, rolling past Adolf crouched on the ground.

Cautiously, Adolf opened his eyes and looked down. Petey was out cold. He had an arrow in his leg above the knee and a bruised forehead. Adolf froze, sure that an arrow with his name on it quivered on a drawn bowstring behind him. At the sound of a wolf baying in the distance, Adolf dropped to the ground in a dead faint.

***

Kudwa rode into the Cartwright yard. He never rode this close to his friend's lodge before, except to bring Adam home only a day ago. He had found the lodge out of necessity, sense, and the moon that night.

There were no other horses in the yard. Kudwa jumped down, remembering Joe's welcoming voice. He took a step, and then another, toward the front door. When he heard a loud bang from inside Kudwa scrambled around to the side of the house. After a moment the banging started up again, closer than before. Curiosity took hold of his fear and he peered inside the kitchen window.

An odd-looking person, small and with hair almost as long to the floor as his legs, chopped into some fresh greens with a knife. Something smelled good so he didn't duck quickly enough when the odd fellow looked up. "Ha!" Hop Sing yelled, startled. Kudwa hid beneath the window and listened as Hop Sing uttered odd explosive sounds. If that was English, Adam had more explaining to do. When Kudwa looked up, he saw Hop Sing staring out the window down at him. "You come see Mr. Adam?"

Kudwa's hand slipped down to his knife.

"You leave leather pouch, save Mr. Adam life? Come," Hop Sing pointed to the front door. "Come in, come." He ran out of the kitchen.

Kudwa scooted around and stood by his horse, waiting. When the door opened he tensed, but Hop Sing did not look threatening. Instead he waved, motioning Kudwa inside. Kudwa paused, but he had not come this far only to go back in failure. Adam often sat in Kudwa's lodging. Now Kudwa must sit in the lodging of his friend.

When he stepped inside the large house he stopped, staring up at the ceiling. He reached but could not touch the top. So much air space these whites needed for breathing! The floor must be evil — it appeared they did not trust ground but instead had seat things with legs to hold them up. A fire burned inside the lodge instead of outside, the flames dancing and talking but not causing all these other things inside to burn.

Hop Sing pulled him to Adam's room, where Kudwa saw his friend lying on his side, one arm half covering his face. "He rest. You sit quiet, until he wake. He glad you here. You wait." Hop Sing guided Kudwa to the chair and pushed him down.

At first Kudwa expected he would fall to the ground, but the soft chair caught him and an astonished smile crept over his face. He nodded at Hop Sing. "Good." Hop Sing put a finger to his lips, and Kudwa mimicked. "Ssssh."

Hop Sing nodded and left.

With a soft seat and a friend still alive, Kudwa felt himself relax. He had so little sleep since bringing Adam home and now, feeling warm and comfortable, his head kept trying to drop through his chest. At the sound of his name he looked up, startled. Sleep must have taken him for just a glancing thought.

"Good to see you, friend." Adam lay unmoving but his smile strengthened his weary face.

"You look well." Kudwa sat forward in the chair, concentrating.

"Ah, I wish I was. I sure need to get out of this bed right now."

Kudwa sprang to his feet. "I…will help."

Adam laughed. "I don't think I better try that yet, much as I want to." He nodded at the nightstand. "Your medicine pouch is here. My family must have found it."

Kudwa picked it up, now dry but stiff with blood. "Not me. You." He put it in Adam's hand.

Adam frowned as he fingered the bag. "You followed me home that day?"

"See you shot. I stop him but not in time." Kudwa gestured shooting bow and arrow.

"You killed him? And you put this medicine bag..." Adam put his head back, "to stop the bleeding." Kudwa stood, wondering what he said wrong. His friend spoke too much English, too quickly. "Or I would have died, because he was going to shoot again." Adam stared at the door that led to action in the outside world with hard and piercing eyes. "Van Remus said it and he meant it. What chance does Joe have now?"

"Adam, you sleep." In his confusion Kudwa edged toward the door and reverted to Shoshone. "I came because I needed to see that you're alive and to tell you I saw men on your land. I shot one who hurt your trees but you need rest so I will come back to tell you later." He disappeared out the door.

Adam tried to follow the Indian's tongue but with little success, so his friend's disappearance shocked him. "Wait, wait! Don't go!" Adam reached out to stop him and the pain threw him backward on the bed.

Hop Sing heard and pulled Kudwa back into the room. Together they eased Adam into a more comfortable position and Hop Sing gave him some water.

"Sorry, Hop Sing. Thanks. Kudwa, you have to tell me slowly what you said about trees."

As Hop Sing changed the bandage and applied tonic to the wound where the bleeding started up slightly, Kudwa walked to the other side of the bed and sat on the floor, preparing for council talk.

***

Ben and Hoss studied the trail on the ride home. The hope that Joe had arrived safely home didn't serve them well in their search for signs of trouble, so they both, without the exchange of words, found that worst of fears easily. With the setting sun playing tricks on their eyes, Ben or Hoss would alight and run off into the woods only to come back out shaking their heads. Both kept their eyes on the sun, knowing that darkness would be their worst enemy.

"Pa! Wait a minute." Hoss pulled up short and jumped down. At first Ben kept going, but this time Hoss was absorbed in more than a passing fancy. "Look at this." He bent forward. There were hoof prints jumbled in the gritty sand. He took a few steps up the incline that would take them up the side of the rocky hill. "Pa, did you hear that?"

"What?"

"I'm not sure. Sounded like a horse." He stared up at the rough terrain. "Up there?" Hoss forged up the hill.

Believing Hoss an easy target to spot Ben started to follow, but he didn't count on this particular incline, the size of the jumbled rocks or the bushes that were particularly tough to scramble around. In his haste he kept slipping as he worked up the hill. "Hoss!"

"Over here, Pa!"

His voice came from the left so Ben turned and had to climb over a heavy outcropping of rock before seeing Hoss — with Joe's horse. Ben grabbed the halter, fighting to keep from being paralyzed by alarm. "Cochise. He's waiting for Joe. Any sign of him?"

"No, but he ain't far, Pa."

Ben tied the horse to a tree, more from habit than need. "Joe! Joe!"

"There's no tracking to follow here, too much rock to climb over."

"We split up. Come on, move it. That way!"

They each went a different direction, spreading out by instinctively knowing how much land their eye range could scan in fading light. Hoss scaled the side of the cliff like a lumbering bear, until he came to a ledge. There, in plain sight, was Joe's hat. Hoss squatted down and picked it up, studying the ground. Sure enough, the ground was a little jumbled here, loose rocks and dirt, and flattened brush.

Hoss scrambled down, a moment or two losing his balance but then righting again, all the way seeing the same signs, and seeing rock with what could be splattered blood. "Pa! Pa, I found him!"

Joe lay motionless against the rock. Hoss gently turned him over. His jacket was half torn off and his dungarees ripped.

"Joe." Hoss wet his cheek with his spit and leaned down against Joe's nose, his hand on Joe's chest. Ben reached for his boy's head as he watched Hoss, disbelieving yet dying inside.

"Yeah, it's faint, but he's still in there." Hoss reached up to comfort Ben but his hand was covered with blood.

Ben ripped open Joe's shirt. "He's bleeding bad. Give me your shirt."

Hoss ripped off his shirt. He lifted Joe up gently so Ben could make a bandage around the wound to stop the bleeding. "We're lucky the air's cold, and the way I found him lying wedged in the rocks mighta slowed his bleeding."

"Lucky?" Ben bit at the word. "Go get your canteen, quick!" Hoss lumbered away as Ben turned back to Joe. "Joe." He patted his son's face gently. It would be better if the boy could swallow on his own. "Joe, come on, wake up, you can do it." No response. Ben pulled him close, tears rolling down his cheeks. Someone has to pay for this. And someone will.

CHAPTER 15

Kudwa paced as Adam again rejected his help, frustrated by his friend's strength even with the pain keeping him from moving. If only they could communicate better!

"You cannot... risk...gizhaan...another wa'aa'gi with your people. We can...subai'gaase. Already may be trouble...like wolves after children…with that arrow in one of them."

"Your people do not own the earth or trees! You are not the only one who needs to protect that which protects us!"

Adam tried to roll to his back but Kudwa gave him a gentle 'no' by putting a hand on his shoulder. He couldn't understand how his friend could be so stubborn when now, of all times, he needed help. His friend fought to stay awake as he sought new words to express himself. Kudwa wondered if he could go against his friend's wishes, go back into those woods, and make sure they all leave – one way or another.

"Please, Kudwa, friend, listen to me. This bad white we fight does this...because of what happened long ago between him and my father. It is our fight. We stop him, the rest…will stop." Adam closed his eyes.

Kudwa waited but his friend lost his fight to stay awake. Still Kudwa waited, until he heard horses outside. Kudwa ran out to the door, meeting Hop Sing half way. Hop Sing tried to explain that Adam's family had returned but Kudwa ignored him and bolted out the door. He paused long enough to see the boy who'd met him in the road had been injured. He jumped on his horse and ripped the reins loose, whipping the horse out of the yard even as Ben called out.

***

"Easy now, Hoss, easy." Ben had cradled Joe in his arms all the way home. His arms were numb and as he shifted to get off the horse his muscles filled with the itching of pine needles. The short diversion when the Paiute ran out of the yard faded as concern over his son again overwhelmed him. He hadn't regained consciousness, not once, and he'd lost so much blood!

Hoss eased Joe down into his arms and hurried inside the house. Ben followed, with just a moment's glance inside Adam's room.

"Hop Sing! We need you upstairs!" Ben's voice carried even when taking care not to shout. Hop Sing followed them up the stairs.

Hoss took Joe into his room and waited until Ben turned the covers back. Joe didn't look natural lying there. Hoss slipped his hand over Joe's heart again, as Ben watched anxiously. After what felt an eternity Hoss nodded. His little brother was fighting hard.

Hop Sing gave Ben a few towels from the cabinet.

"Pa, want me to run for the doctor?"

"No!" Ben's sharp response made Hoss step backward. "I'm sorry, son, but don't you see what's happening? I can't risk you, too!"

"But Pa, Joe's gotta have a doctor."

"I know." Ben clutched Hoss's shoulder for strength and sat down next to his youngest. He held Joe's hand tightly. "I'll go."

"What makes you think he ain't gunning for you, too?"

"Because he's found the perfect way to destroy me." Ben stood abruptly and walked to the top of the stairs. "I'd much rather he'd shoot me and he knows it."

Hoss grabbed his arm. "What happened 'tween you and Van Remus? And how was Adam involved? Pa, he was only a boy. Why would he rather be dead?"

Ben stared down the stairs where Adam lay. "Not now, Hoss." He met Hop Sing on the stairs carrying a steaming pot of water. "I'm going for the doctor. Make sure Hoss gets whatever he needs for Joe. And Hop Sing, keep checking on Adam too, all right?"

"Yes, Mr. Cartlight."

Ben pushed his buckskin hard to Virginia City, his mind reeling from Hoss's question. *What happened between you and van Remus?* This fight for land began long before he owned the Ponderosa. It began when he owed a debt to John Augustus Sutter. No matter how he tells it, Adam will accept a debt of responsibility for Winnie's death. Winnie had been coming to see him, Ben felt sure of that. But why dressed like a man? This was all so many years ago! He wasn't sure he even remembered half of what had happened back then, and yet memories were flooding him like a creek over a rotted beaver dam.

Did Van Remus find out how the stampede started? If Van Remus did know the cause of the stampede, Adam should be his only target. With this attack on Joe, the guilt landed back on Ben. Ben had accepted the blame for the cows getting out of hand. He thought Van Remus accepted that it had been an accident. He foolishly believed Van Remus would forget about it. Van Remus lost not only the land he wanted, but also the wife he adored.

When Adam finally remembers the part he played in it, the pain will be worse than that bullet in the back.

"Ben, he's already planning that trip west, leaving his wife here to make trouble." John Sutter put his pipe down as though it had developed a skunky odor. *"Do you have any better idea?"*

"Are you sure you want to do this, John? It might be easier to just sell him that strip of land and be done with it."

"It's one thing to let the Mexicans take the gold – they protect the secret well.[8] Let those settlers keep heading north and west, Ben, we don't need to be swarmed here. If Van Remus hits a strike, we'll be trampled. You know what scoundrels Clete and Winnie are. They'd never keep it a secret the way the Mexicans do. Besides, Ben, you know I've got that land tagged. Even if I could find a better site for a sawmill, I'd sell it to anyone over him. They're both lazy no-good scoundrels."

---

[8] Feliz Riesenberg, Jr., *The Golden Road* (New York: McGraw-Hill, 1962), 108. This story theme is fictional based on the idea that Sutter did try to keep Marshall's discovery a secret.

"I know you have a right not to sell. But his threat to go to the Russians is all talk – he can't hurt your dealings now that you've signed the purchase agreement. There's nothing he can do."

"Ben, there is one thing he can do. He can tell the Russians I've had Mexicans already taking gold out of here to Mexico. He can do that. I worked hard to get the payoff terms for all that property I bought on the coast.[9] They can make my life here hell, if they want. I've got it all now, Ben! I've got the lumber I need, the equipment, the---." Sutter stood and strode to the door. "I'll kill Clete, and his wife, too, if I can't think of anything else."

Sutter had a touch of what Ben called 'imperialism,' – the desire to rule an empire of his own. Ben couldn't reconcile the touch of madness he saw on occasion in Sutter's eyes when he talked about making California a republic with himself as its president. But he owed Sutter a great deal for giving them a home when he didn't know where else to go, and agreed with Sutter's vision for the valley; not outstripping the land but caring for it so that it retains its value in the years to come. Ben didn't know how Sutter kept such a strong hold on this area — maybe he supplied the Mexicans with gold to keep his settlement intact. Sutter also allowed Americans to settle in the valley, which didn't make Governor Alvarado too happy. He and Van Remus were two of those settlers.

So, unable to come up with any alternative, Ben left his sons in the care of one of Sutter's Indian nurses and made the trip to the coast where he knew the Russians were waiting for the weather to improve to travel home. It was a terrible journey, the late December wind and sleet rough on his horse, and he missed his sons fiercely at a time when they should be enjoying a quiet Christmas celebration. But he made the arrangements for much of the material to be delivered to the fort immediately, and at the same time convinced the Russians on Sutter's behalf that there was a man, Van Remus, willing to tell any lie necessary to discredit Sutter's work at the fort. Ben knew the description he gave of the little man would make the Russians laugh every time Van Remus opened his mouth. Ben hadn't known that he

---

[9] Oscar Lewis, *Sutter's Fort: Gateway to the Gold Fields*, (Englewood Cliffs: Prentice-Hall, 1966), 46-49. The deed of title to both Russian coastal properties was signed December 13, 1841.

would still be there when Van Remus showed up. Ben felt shame when he witnessed the degradation Van Remus felt over being laughed at.

By the time he had gotten back to Sutter's Fort Ben had felt an awful sinking guilt. But then he'd seen how peaceful, how beautiful, the Valley de Sacramento was and felt this guilt eased. The next time he'd seen Van Remus and his wife, they seemed resigned to the fact that they'd lost, that they would only remain land workers and not land owners. Ben figured they'd probably take gold out on the sly but unless Sutter wanted to run them off, they couldn't prevent that. Then winter settled in and no more was heard of them until spring, until just before they moved their herd to the branding pen.

And a month later, after the widowed Van Remus left for the coast, Ben moved his two sons to Nevada, with the well-intentioned need to get them far from bad memories.

Now he realized what a bad decision he had made running away. Though it hadn't felt like it at the time, that's what he'd done. He had run away. And he never ran from anyone again.

***

Like spiders testing the air to see if prey was nearby, Clete and Bret crawled out of the Golden Cross into the faded Virginia sunlight. Reeger followed them. "You say they left town, Reeger?" Clete asked as he brushed himself off.

"They were headed out of Virginia like I says, but I can't say they ain't doubled back by now." Reeger wiped the moisture off his face with the back of a dirty sleeve, streaking his face.

Clete squeezed water of out his pant leg as Bret walked into the road, oblivious to his soiled condition, and stared up C Street into the hills beyond the city as though trying to read its secrets.

"Let's get cleaned up and get that table at the hotel before they give it away. Join us, Reeger. We want to hear what you got to report after following Cartwright around. Should be worth the price of a meal."

***

"I don't know what you're doing to them Cartwrights but they're plenty mad," Reeger said as they sat at the dining table. The only grubby miner waiting to be served, Reeger was made discomforted by the stares of the other patrons. He didn't have any clothes to change into and Clete didn't offer any. He had been made to wait while Clete and Bret duded up and now sat feeling like a rat with a rash. "Think we ought to go somewhere else?" He dropped his eyes back to the bill of fare, wishing he could wipe the sweat off the back of his neck.

"What for?" Clete studied the menu. "Tell us what you learned."

"I better leave." Reeger stood and winced at the scraping of wooden chair on the stone floor.

"Sit down." Clete waited until Reeger slowly complied. "I hope by the tone of your voice," Clete put his menu down, "that you haven't decided to swap sides."

"Take up with the Cartwrights? Hell no, they don't have more than the time of day for the likes of me." Reeger frowned at some distant thought and shrugged. "You looking to take something from 'em?"

"Not just something, Reeger. Everything."

"Oh." Reeger almost said more but Clete leaned toward him with a look that could choke a Tahoe fish. Reeger leaned back. "No skin off my knuckles."

"Good to hear." Clete studied the menu. "Order anything you like — they got great chicken fixin's here. Me, I always take the bleeding beef, when I have the chance. You too, Bret?"

"Sure, Clete." Bret put his menu down. "About that idea of mine."

"Now's not a good time to talk *business*." Clete shot Reeger a look and Bret sat back. A comely and cooperative miss scripted their order with a flirt or two at Bret, then left. "What did you hear, Reeger?"

"They're steaming mad. Even with Adam dead, the Cartwrights are a powerful force to deal with. And they think you's responsible."

"What if I was?" Clete studied the young miner intently.

"What?" Reeger looked up startled from the beer he guzzled. "You done it?" When Clete didn't answer, Reeger nodded. "Well, I'll be damned. I'll be. . .damned. Guess you are serious, then."

Clete leaned forward. "I've watched you, Reeger, you got ambition. I'm thinking to make you shift boss, and before long, you would even buy stock, become a partner. I see that in you, Reeger." He brushed at dirt on Reeger's shoulder, making him tense. "But if you breathe one word of this, I'll kill you. I think you're smart enough to know that."

Reeger sucked in hot air. He saw it coming, and yet he didn't get up and run when he had the chance. His pa warned him rightly — his gut was always honest but when his gut talked food his ears went deaf. "I've been living here since before Comstock. Come with my pa, staking claims, losing out. It laid him under. Those Cartwrights, ever since I come, they always had things their way, packing a lot of weight. Now they got less to pack, is all."

"What else you hear, Reeger?"

"Followed them to your hotel, after finding out they're concerned about their youngest. They drilled ole Vince pretty hard. Ben made him know Van Remus is no friend of his. Could see an awful surprised look on Vince's face, lingered long after they were gone."

"Did Vince admit to Ben how he pointed Adam out to me?"

"He done that? Hey, I bet that's what scared ole' Vince!" He laughed but alone. "He could barely speak when Ben wanted to know when he seen Joe last. Vince didn't know nothing exceptin' that Joe seen you, and then they rode out of town."

"What about the sheriff? They find a way to pin me for the shooting?"

"They blame you, but there weren't nothing more there than suspicion."

"Now what do you suppose could have happened to the kid?" Bret asked as their suppers appeared in front of them.

Reeger sat back, a small whooomp of air against the chair accentuating his surprise. "Did you have something done to Joe, too?" Inside the whisper, a quivering of fear slipped through.

"Now do I look like a murderer to you?"

"But you killed him?"

"Reeger, I believe in justice. Adam got away with murder once."

"Murder?"

"He killed my wife."

"Killed your wife? Not a Cartwright, that's not---."

Clete leaned forward. "If you're on my payroll, there's one thing you have to do and that is NEVER distrust anything I tell you. Clear?" Reeger bent back over his food, after giving Clete a perfunctory nod. He started to have a very bad feeling, but then, he never got any breaks in life before. So he allowed the best meal he'd had in years turn the bad feeling to good.

CHAPTER 16

Clete and Bret left Reeger eating his crumb cake and drinking coffee and stepped out into the cool night air. Clete nodded at several who greeted him affectionately as he pulled Bret out into the street. The townsfolk were moving more quickly now, anxious to get where they were headed for the night. Few men rode the street at night and even fewer wagons went through. As long as they walked in the open street Clete felt them safe enough from being overheard.

"Bret, I've been thinking about what you said before."

"Pa, about that fire---."

"Shut up and call me Clete!" Clete's teeth clenched, a headache growing from the forced conversation with Reeger. "Pay attention and you'll see where I'm going with your idea. There's the doctor's office. I want you to feign a headache, a sore toe, a bellyache, whatever. Ask questions about the Cartwrights, get him to admit he's been treating Adam, keeping the scoundrel alive. Once you find out where in the house Adam's laid out, you can go on in with your matches."

Clete put a hand on Bret's arm and looked around. The activity around them had slowed nearly to dead, as though the mines swallowed the noise down at night, the perfect atmosphere for conspirators. He preferred the nights because then not seeing things too clearly didn't matter. "Remember, I don't want the house gutted. Just find out which room is his, and blaze it. By the time they get to him, he'll be gone."

"But if we do the whole house?"

"You heard me, Bret, we're only doing this to kill Adam, nothing more. I got my plans for Ben, and they don't include making him homeless. Except by us taking over the ranch."

"One of these days you're gonna see I'm right, *sir.*" Bret muttered with a scowl as he turned to cross the street.

Clete went back to Reeger at the International

"That was some good supper, Mr. Van Remus. I sure thank you for it. Where's Bret headed?" Reeger leaned forward, watching. "To the doc? Something wrong with him? Maybe supper didn't agree with him. I think meat oughta be cooked a little more myself. My ma used to---."

"My associate's fine," Clete snapped, temples pounding. "And it's not your concern."

Bret glanced back at Clete and stepped up the walk to Jessup's office.

***

Adam rolled on his back but the dream hurt more than the wound.

Animals of all kinds, screaming and crying in pain, ran after him as though he could help their hurt somehow, but there were too many, and he had to find his pa. Pa will know what to do, even though Pa told him again and again that he was old enough to face his fears like a man. He looked over his shoulder and the animals were gone but he saw eyes, human eyes this time, and feathers, and in human hands long spears. Clouds of dust flew up around him, blinding and choking him, but in his terror he rode on until he was surrounded by cows and shouting men and the cows were running, stampeding, and a woman screamed.

Adam woke with a start. Sighing angrily, he threw his arm over his face. Someone rode a horse fast out of the yard but he didn't concern himself over it. This wasn't just a dream. He wasn't sure what it all meant, but he knew that it happened. There had been a stampede and he had been there. Grimacing, he rolled slowly to his side and grabbed the edge of the blanket. With a jerk he threw the blanket back. His bare legs tingled as the cold air hit them, but at least he could feel them and move them, they worked.

"Mr. Adam! What you do?"

Adam looked up, the sudden action forcing him back against the pillow. "Hop Sing! You forget how to knock, huh?"

"Ah, Mr. Adam feel good now?"

"I was going to find out before you came in."

"Like I leave?" Hop Sing turned back to the door.

"No, no," Adam waved a steady hand to bring him back in. "Have you seen Pa?"

"Mr. Cartlight home."

"Good. Get him."

"Then he leave." Hop Sing watched with sad eyes as Adam fell back against the pillow. "He go for doctor."

"Doctor?"

"For Joe."

"Joe? Joe's hurt?" When Hop Sing nodded, Adam threw his legs out of bed, ignoring the pain. "Help me to him."

"No, Mr. Adam, not to get out---."

"Never mind, I can do this myself." He eased himself into a sitting position. "Nothing to it."

***

Hoss tenderly wrapped a clean bandage around Joe's wound after washing it the best he could. He didn't like the looks of it, not at all. The cut was raw and ragged, like a dull skinning knife could make, and from lying exposed to dirt for he couldn't guess how long, the discoloring signs of infection were already there. Pa has to hurry back with that doctor and medicine, he has to. At least the raggedness of the cut, the position he lay against the rock and the cold air kept him from bleeding to death. He still lost a lot of blood, and could still die from blood poisoning.

He eased some water into Joe's mouth the way Pa showed him, by gently tilting his head back to open his throat more. Joe coughed a second, but some of it went down. They couldn't give him much at a time, but he had to keep the liquids down or Joe would die of thirst after all that blood loss, which is what put him in this coma. Hoss wondered if it meant he might never wake up. The worst worry besides the poisoning was the angle of the wound. He stared at Joe so hard his eyes watered, sometimes it seemed only his concentration on Joe's chest kept his brother breathing.

"Hoss..." Adam had propped himself on the open doorway, his face a white mask of concern.

"Adam! What are you doing out of bed?"

Hop Sing stood alongside Adam, but not touching. "I try to say no."

"I'm fine, Hoss. Hop Sing got me started but he bounces too much. I'll be all right, Hop Sing. You go get some sleep."

Hop Sing muttered under his breath but left the room.

Adam walked to Joe's bedside. Hoss backed off but stayed within arm's reach. Adam lifted the bed covers to expose Joe's bandaged chest. Gingerly he touched the position of the wound. There was a big purple bruise on Joe's forehead and numerous scrapes on his face. Adam stroked Joe's hair just above the bruise. "What's this from?"

"Fell down the rocks after being stabbed."

"Fell? Or was pushed." Adam winced at some silent thought. "Lost a lot of blood?"

"Yup. Been like this ever since we found him."

"Pa?"

"Gone for the doctor."

"He holding up all right?"

"Well as he can, I reckon. Wouldn't let me go." He didn't want his injured brother sitting here but was glad for the company.

"I wonder why."

Hoss nodded at Adam's way of stating a question as a fact. "That's what he thinks, too."

Hoss gave up his chair for Adam, who sank into the moist warmth of the chair made comfortable by his brother's concern. "Ran off on his own, didn't he." Adam winced and Hoss nearly asked if he was paining too much to be here.
"'Fraid so. Adam, it's not your fault. You know how Joe is."

"Just keep telling me, Hoss." Adam tried to sit straighter. "How'd you find him?"

"Cochise hung around, waiting."

"Good horse. Joe takes fine care of that animal."

"Treats him like a brother. Better." Hoss wanted to make his brother smile but failed. "Want me to take you back down?"

"No."

Hoss pulled a chair over from the corner and sat next to him. "Anything else we can do for him, you think?"

"I think you're doing fine, Hoss." He patted his big brother on the leg. "Joe's gonna make it. He's even more stubborn than I am, you know."

"I know, Adam." Hoss sniffed. "But we gotta get whoever did this."

Adam bit back a shudder. "Listen, Hoss, Kudwa was here. He followed a trail on the North 40 and found loggers. Seems like Van Remus has more than just us to worry Pa with."
***

Bret hesitated outside Jessup's door. At this late hour the doctor could be in bed. He didn't know why he should care about an old man. Sometimes he felt like he hated the whole world, that he was old and crumpled up inside. Sometimes, when he woke up in the morning, he had to remember the hate to get his blood moving. He went from a kid to an old man when his ma died.

He knocked sharply as he opened the door, finding it unlocked. The doctor was writing at his desk and waved Bret to sit without stopping his pen. The house was small and comfortable, with a sharp tangy smell Bret never liked, the smell of someone who had recently died and there hadn't been time to bury her yet.

"You walked in of your accord, so I suspect you can wait another minute." Finally Jessup stopped writing and looked Bret over. "Well, you don't look injured, no bullet to take out. You sick? Maybe find yourself running outside to clear out your system a little too often? I hear that one a mite lately, what with the tainted water we've been..."

"No, it isn't me, sir, I'm fine. I...my boss suffers from headaches. I wonder if maybe you have something---."

"Why doesn't he come in? I don't dispense second hand."

"Oh. Well, I'll tell him." Bret stood. "Say, as long as I'm here, maybe you can answer something for me." He took a deep breath. "A friend of mine, I hear he's dead and I don't want to believe it. Maybe if you show me the death certificate I'll accept it."

"Well, it's a little unorthodox." He pulled open a drawer. "But it's a matter of public record. What's the name?"

"Adam Cartwright."

Jessup paused, replaced his file and sat back. "Guess I'll make your day then. I just left the Cartwrights this past afternoon and Adam's not only not dead, but since his fever broke he's not going to be dead either."

As he grabbed Jessup's hand and pumped it Bret's grin broke wide. "Say, that's great, that's just great. Good golly, I knew the rumors had to be wrong." He turned to leave, but hesitated. "Now you're sure we're talking about the same fellow?"

"Adam Cartwright, of the Ponderosa."

"He lives in a big ranch house, right? With lots of bedrooms on the top floor, right?"

"That's right."

Bret slapped his forehead. "Wow, this is great. I sure am glad I asked about him, I sure am." He walked to the door and opened it, but with a slight frown turned back. "I sure hope they didn't haul him up those stairs after he was shot, why, I think his room is way on the end, right of the stairs if I remember from the last time I visited."

"That may be so, but I've been treating him in a guest room downstairs."

"Ah! Of course they'd do that." Bret slapped his head again. "A right smart family, those Cartwrights. I even stayed in that guest room once or twice, just west of the front door, right?"

"Left side." Jessup stood. "If there's nothing else..."

"No, of course not. But say, would Adam be ready for visitors yet, do you think?"

"I'd give it another day or two. He still needs a lot of rest."

Bret grabbed his hand again, pumping it. "Well, I do thank you, sir."

On his way out he ran into a stern looking silver-haired man coming in. The man nodded vaguely at him and stepped aside. Bret slammed the door behind him.

***

Petey woke disoriented, knowing only that the pain in his leg was killing him. All around him on the sloping cliff the trees loomed like the ominous beasts of his nightmares. "Not good enough, Petteeeyyyy... how you gonna prove yourself now, Peeettttteeyyyyy." Waving their scraggly limbs toward him, pointing accusing branches.

He shifted, hoping to get up and run, and the arrow vibrated his bone, making him scream. Where was everybody? Had they all been killed?

"Adolf? Hey. Hey! Adolf!" Tears spilled onto his face but he didn't care because he was alone and going to die. Was everyone else already murdered and scalped? "MCMAANNNUS! HEEELLLP MEEEE!"

He backed up against a rock as something crawled toward him. . .Indians crawl, they creep up on their victims, was what he heard. The trees in his nightmare were really Indians and they had knives in their mouths for scalping. He squeezed his eyes shut, praying out loud. "Oh Lord, Lord, forgive my sins."

"Petey?"

Petey opened his eyes. The figure on its knees crawled toward him but more than that he couldn't tell. He could only see shadows, where every movement held new death. He squeezed his eyes shut again. "Adolf?"

"I'm still alive!" Adolf got to his feet and lurched over to Petey.

"Am I ever glad…" Petey grabbed Adolf's jacket sleeve and jerked him close. "What you mean leaving me like this?! Get this arrow outta me!"

"Doen yell! You got your arrow, I hide so mine vouldn't find me!"

"Till after sunset? Get it out!"

Adolf looked down at Petey's leg. "Pull it out, eh?" Adolf took off his black knitted cap and scratched at thin brown hair.

"Do you mind? Is it against your religion or something?"

"No, but it might hurt."

"What do you care? It won't hurt you!" Still Adolf hesitated. "Look, if you don't, I'll be stuck here. And if you walk away from me, I'll shoot ya! You know I will!" Petey clutched his gun tight against his chest as though Adolf would try and wrest it from him.

"All right." Adolf knelt on the ground and took hold of the arrow.

Petey screamed in pain. "Wait! Wait!"

"Change your mind?"

"No. Just..." Petey pulled a bandanna out of his jacket. "Just be sure and wrap it tight once it's out. My leg, not the arrow."

"Oh, sure." Adolf touched the tip of the shaft and Petey squirmed. "Why doen you vap your arms around tree in back ya?"

Petey looked up. "Okay." He did it, tensing his body. "Put a stick in my mouth."

"Oh." Adolf brushed off a stubby stick and stuck it in Petey's mouth. He grinned at Petey, his cupped hand poised near the shaft of the arrow. Gritting his teeth, he took hold of the arrow and pulled hard. Not hard enough. Petey squirmed so much that Adolf knelt on his leg to still him and jerked again. He felt the arrow loosen a little. Enthused, he jerked real hard and fell backward. "Yeah! Done it." He looked at the tip of the wooden stalk. "Except maybe I tink the point is still in your leg."

But Petey had passed out against the tree.

CHAPTER 17

After telling Hoss Kudwa's story about the loggers and adding a few deductions of his own, Adam lapsed into silence back against the chair.

Hoss didn't know what to say. He thought trying to kill them was the worst that could happen, but what good was any of their lives without the land? And he knew as well as Adam that they couldn't afford to lose any more trees in that section, but what could they do? They knew without saying it that their pa wouldn't be concerned over the trees, or the cattle, for that matter. Because of his sons, he could lose everything he worked so hard for. Pa would say he did everything for them anyhow, but he had dreams even before Adam was born.

Adam looked at Hoss with raised eyebrows. "You're starting to look like a grizzly bear. A thin grizzly bear. You give up eating and shaving in the same week?"

"Having two brothers who don't know how to duck can do that to a fella." Hoss's chuckle fell short. "Adam, what do you remember about Van Remus? I tried but I ain't coming up with nothing."

"You were too young. I can't remember much myself. When that letter came, I felt like a section of my life had been torn away."

"Huh." Hoss scratched his stubbly chin. "Well, Adam, you were kinda young, too."

"I was old enough. Anyway, since reading that letter, I figured out enough to ask Pa some questions. Problem is, there's not a lot of time for talking. Something has to be done."

"Maybe Pa kin get Roy and a posse together. Get those trespassers off our land."

"Maybe. But Van Remus may have some kind of document forged saying Ben gave him permission." Adam wiped the sweat off his forehead. "There must be something from his past that'll trip him up."

"Why did you warn me and Joe about going out?"

Adam shifted in his chair, wincing. He leaned over and squeezed Joe's hand, but got no response. "I wish he would have listened. Hoss, give him some water." Hoss stood and picked up the glass. "No, wait. Give me the glass and that clean towel." Adam dunked the towel in the glass, soaking it. "I can't reach. Hoss, take the dripping end and put it in his mouth. He might suck at the water, get more down this way."

Hoss worked open Joe's mouth and eased the dripping towel in. He used the dry end to wipe the water off Joe's chin and neck.

"Joe always worked extra hard to keep up to you and me. He always figured he could do everything we could, from the time he could walk."

"Yeah." Hoss watched Joe, unsure if the towel might gag his little brother. "Hey, hey look, Adam, he's sucking on it."

"We'll have to keep taking it out and re-soaking it, but it'll do until the doctor gets here. Any medicine left?"

"Don't think so. Pa checked." Hoss sat next to Adam. "You better get yourself some sleep, brother, or you'll need the doctor again, too."

"In a minute. Hoss, remember the time Joe got himself lost in the woods when he was young, right before I left for college?"

"Oh, yeah. Said he was hunting possum so's Pa could make supper for us before you left."

"I found him in the woods crying. Said he wasn't lost, only scared of seeing me leave. Said when somebody leaves they never come back."

Hoss rubbed his eyes with his fingers. "Just heard about how his ma died, didn't he?"

"There were times back east when I thought I'd stay there but then I'd remember Joe's face and I knew I couldn't. I couldn't do that to him."

"Or to me or Pa."

"That's right, Hoss." They watched the slow rise and fall of Joe's chest. Hoss wetted the towel. "But that's why he's going to be fine. Because he can't stand the thought of anyone leaving and never coming back. Adam's head dropped as he struggled with tears. Hoss slipped an arm around his brother's shoulder, allowing his own tears to fall unchecked. When finally Adam took a breath and looked back at Joe, Hoss saw how white his face was. "Come on, let me help you back down."

"You asked me why I warned you and Joe not to go out. When we lived in Sacramento, just as Pa was getting enough money and supplies together to come out here, he ran into trouble with Van Remus."

"What kind of trouble?"

"You'll have to ask Pa. I think. . .I remember a stampede." He swallowed hard against a thick taste in his throat. "But not much else. Somehow Van Remus's wife got killed on our land. I don't remember how." He grabbed Joe's water glass and took a hard swallow.

"Pa said. . .he said he hoped you wouldn't remember any of it."

"He did?" Adam frowned.

"Maybe. . .it don't matter why Van Remus is doing this."

Adam's hand shook as he rubbed his eyes. "It matters. When I read that letter, one very vivid memory came to me. It didn't seem real at first."

"What?"

"He cornered me in a shed by the house where we were living and threatened me. Said he'd be back to destroy Ben by killing me, and you, and anyone else Pa sires." He sighed heavily. "Joe announced himself as the third son when he went into town."

"Why, that dirty, no good. . .you were just a boy! And Joe wasn't even born!" Hoss gripped his hands together. "I'd like to get his neck right here. Did you ever tell Pa?"

"I'm not sure. I don't think so."

"But Adam, if he blames Pa for the stampede, or even for how his wife died, why go after you or Joe? It don't figure."

"I suppose he wants Pa to suffer the way he did."

Hoss grunted, nodding. "Did you see the stampede?"

Adam wiped his mouth, his voice only a whisper. "I've been thinking and I can only believe that I had something to do with."

Hoss jumped to his feet. "You talked enough. I'll take you downstairs."

Adam allowed Hoss to help him to the door. "At least you don't bounce." He looked back at Joe. "Hoss, take good care of him. We're used to having him around."

Hoss looked back at his younger brother's placid, lifeless face. "Yeah."

"Listen, tomorrow I'll be ready to help watch Joe. You and Pa have to sleep, too." Adam leaned gratefully against his bigger brother as they went down the stairs.

CHAPTER 18

Dr. Jessup sensed a different atmosphere at the Ponderosa when he stepped in the front door. Where before with Adam an almost visible wind of shock coursed through the house, now he sensed a more settled end-of-the-rope feeling. The Cartwrights were ready to strike back. After glancing in on Adam Jessup hurried up the stairs after Ben. Joe, youngest and liveliest, now pale and still, was carefully watched over by a grizzled Hoss.

"You look terrible, Hoss." Ben slapped his big son's back. "Go get some sleep. John agreed to stay the night."

"Pa, I'm gonna watch a minute. Then I'll let Adam know how he is."

"Adam knows about this?"

"He was up here sitting with me before."

Jessup nodded as he checked Joe's vitals. "Adam is making good, steady progress. Climbing stairs didn't hurt him. If it did he wouldn't have made it. Nothing more strenuous for him than stairs for the next few weeks and you'll have no further trouble with that son." He glanced up at Hoss with a warning frown.

"What do you think?" Ben knelt down by Joe and felt his forehead.

"Pulse and heart are very slow." He peered into Joe's eyes and turned down the covers to reveal the blood-soaked bandage. "Lost a lot of blood."

"Happened a while before we found him."

The doctor unwrapped the wound and grimaced. "Cleaned it up?"

Ben's voice caught. "Best we could."

"We have to fight the infection after I stitch up the wound. If we're successful there, it's a matter of waiting for him to come out of the coma. I'll tell you, Ben, I've seen it happen, men finally wake up after losing so much blood and they're not quite the same. Still, it's preferable to not waking at all."

"Not quite the same?" Hoss scratched at the new beard he had no inkling to shave.

"Could be lack of coordination, blindness, memory loss, no sense of humor..."

"No sense of humor? Ha! That'll be the day." Hoss wiped at his eyes.

"Hoss, go see if Adam has any more of that medicine left."

Ben put up a hand. "None left, John." He squeezed his eyes shut, his hand brushing his face. "Couldn't anticipate this."

Hoss headed for the door. "I'll go check anyhow."

"Hoss!" Jessup called him back. "Send Hop Sing up with more hot water and towels."

***

As Hop Sing ran up the stairs behind him, Hoss walked into Adam's room where his brother slept uneasy, tossed by a dream. Hoss put a hand on his shoulder to steady him, and waited as his brother gradually came out of it. He used to wake up so quickly and now he seemed like he fought even being awake. "You okay?"

"Yeah." Adam looked around, disoriented, and then back at Hoss, eyes focusing. "Joe! Is he...?"

Hoss jammed his hands in his pockets and slumped against the wall. "They gotta fight the infection. And if he comes out of the coma, he could be different."

"Different. Huh. I don't think any of us will be the same after this."

"Nope. I reckon not." Hoss looked up at Adam. "You want me to send Pa down so you can talk to him?"

116

Adam frowned. "No. We have to move against Van Remus, but Pa needs to be with Joe right now. The loggers won't be cutting at night." He shifted with a grimace. "Getting stuffy in here." Hoss stared at the floor. "Something on your mind?"

"How can we stop those loggers? Dadburnit, I feel so doggoned helpless in here. I want to get that Van Remus and squish him like a tick. I can't do nothing here to help Joe get better. But what if---."

"Got you watching your back now, huh?"

"It's not that. Dadburnit!" Hoss turned back to the door. "You say he sent loggers out to the north 40. Supposing we send another logger up there, someone who kin cause trouble, make 'em shut down without realizing what's happening?"

"You mean like what Kudwa did?"

"Yeah, like that, only. . .I'm not saying shoot them, but mebbe make it too hard for them to work. Find Van Remus's weak spot somehow."

"Weak spot? Huh. If he has one." Adam pursed his lips. "Wait a minute. He has a son. About my age. Could be mixed up in this as well. After all, it was his mother." Adam slunk down and closed his eyes. "Not necessarily a weak spot."

"What about my notion of stopping the loggers?"

Adam peered narrowly at him. "As long as it's anyone but you. If you send a fellow who can keep suspicion from himself, he could do things like busting equipment, wedging the flume, things like that. Have to do it gradual enough so they think they're jinxed." He closed his eyes again. "Kudwa started it with that arrow of his, could follow him up. But who?"

Hoss went to the door before turning back. Quite somberly he nodded. "I think I know just the feller."

Adam had already fallen back asleep.

Joe had his first dose of medicine just before Hoss stepped back in. The smell of medicine in the room was strong but heady when Hoss realized it would help save Joe's life, making it as sweet as the nectar of sage after a rain. The doctor re-bandaged Joe's chest using fresh towels while Ben and Hoss watched intently. The wound after being stitched appeared a little less ugly. Hoss bit back a shudder, but Joe probably didn't feel a thing.

"I'm having Hop Sing cook up some sugar water for him. It'll give him some extra nutrients, build up his blood quicker."

Hoss couldn't take his eyes off his brother. "Pa, go lie down. Then you kin relieve the doctor when he's tired."

"No, Hoss, I---."

"It's fine, Ben, I'm good for another couple hours. I'll wake you when I'm tired."

Ben squeezed Joe's hand tightly. "Joe, you hear me? You fight to get better and wake up." He closed his eyes briefly, as though concentrating to make Joe hear him. "I'll be back, son." After lightly leaning on Hoss's shoulder, he left the room.

"I'll be heading to bed myself, Dr. Jessup. Anything I can get ya?"

"No, when Hop Sing comes up with the sugar water he can show me where I'll sleep. Don't fret none, Hoss, we'll do all we can for Joe." Hoss turned away but Jessup stopped him. "Hoss? You just see to it that I don't have to be tending you next."

"Don't you worry none about me, doc. I'm too dadburned ornery." As he headed to bed the anger faded to misery.

Could he go through with this? He hadn't shaved for days, and he knew he looked a little drawn and lank from not having an appetite. If he wears odd-looking clothes like those loggers, even people in Virginia City might not recognize him. After all, they hadn't been in the city much all summer and people come and go like rain in the high hills. He could change horses at the livery, tell Roy to watch his

118

back and head into those hills, not using the main roads but some back trails.

Hoss didn't remember ever having a harder decision. Leaving meant not being here to see Joe, not having enough people to help so everyone could get their sleep, having Pa worry about him, and even just a little, he'd worry about himself, too. But that was the good thing, because he would be more alert than either Joe or Adam were.

He could relieve Pa for a couple hours before dawn, and then get Hop Sing up. Somehow he had to keep Pa from getting worried about him being gone. He needed to do some more thinking on that.

CHAPTER 19

Val Blessing had the stern no-nonsense look of an able drover with a voice the men paid attention to over the thunder of cattle hooves. Not a handsome man in the saddle, but a firm, strong one, Val felt somehow at a loss knowing how to handle those three scruffers from town. They showed up while Val waited for Ben and Joe. They told Val that the Cartwrights couldn't come along on the drive for some odd reason, and that they were sent to be hired on at a higher wage. Lucky the Chinaman showed up when he did to verify moving on without them. Val appeased his own men by sending a note back asking for the same wages for the rest of them.

But a whole day had passed without word and they couldn't stall up the drive any longer. They drove up into Sacramento Valley that day, but slowly, waiting for word. Val kept watch behind him, thinking the Celestial Skygazer would catch up somehow. They bedded the cattle for the night and trouble started up again. All during night chow drovers cussed about the scruff not working hard enough for what they were making.

Val threw the butt end of his smoke into the campfire and stood. He looked off into the distance at the setting sun as drovers sprawled around the fire watched him quietly. Their arguments had gained a pause, the tension intimating that blows would follow the next word. How Val handled the next few minutes, he knew, would make the difference on this drive.

Butch and Chet, one of the new drovers, stood beside him.

"Can't expect a reply from Cartwright out here, boss. If he was gonna send an answer, he woulda sent it already." Butch, Val's ramrod, looked over at the drovers smoking and finishing coffee, tensed and ready to brawl. "All of us are antsy to know - do we cut or ride on? I vote we ride on. I think the Cartwrights will come through."

Val rubbed his wrists. "Yeah. You keep thinking that, because we have to placate the men somehow. If we cut, we lose a lot of cattle."

"Do you care?" Chet shrugged at their impassive stares. "Not like they're your cows." He looked at the herd, some grazing, most chewing cud, behind them. "Could be though."

Val crossed his arms over his chest. "You're the one what got the drovers riled. I don't know why I would listen to anything you say."

"If your choices are to cut or to herd 'em, seems to me you could do both and get away with it. Cut because the owner doesn't give a hoot's holler in a cave-in about the beef or he woulda sent word. And then double back and round 'em up as strays. They're yours to drive in."

Butch lifted his hat and scratched into his tousled brown hair. "That's plum crazy!"

"They're branded, means even a rep has the responsibility to return them to the owner of the brand." Val looked down at his boots.

"Maybe so. But brands have a way of being smudged, and no one to prove who did the smudging." Chet was tall and hungry looking, heavy black brows under a broad brown hat, his worn clothes accentuating his intent. He spit a wad into the fire, making it sizzle. "They gotta be driven anyhow."

"He's got you there, Val." Butch looked to the sun, a dull glow low in the sky. "We can't just cut. We drive for the Cartwrights or for ourselves." Butch was the nervous sort, thin and wiry, always ready for stampeding. "Don't see why Cartwright didn't respond to your note. Of course I hear Chinamen ain't too trustworthy, though I always liked Hop Sing well enough. Maybe he's right about Cartwright. It don't set right with me, though. None of this."

"Gotta be a reason," Val said, staring at the dim yellow sunset as though willing it to stay til the issue was settled. "Ain't like you to doubt the Cartwrights, Butch. You're wrong about Chinamen, too."

Butch shrugged. "Only trying to see things both ways."

"He doesn't care about beeves." Chet broke into the silence that followed. "Old Cartwright is shook over his eldest being kilt."

121

"What?" Val, not a big man but strong-tempered when riled, grabbed Chet by the vest. "What do you mean about his eldest being killed?" His firm flat features took on a bad mean with his teeth clenched.

"Yeah, it's all over town. Shot in the back." Chet pulled away, looking instantly sorrowful that he mentioned it.

Val turned, slouching. Adam — why, only last month Adam invited him along to the Sunday social, knowing Val wouldn't go without a proper invite. That's where he met Miss Sally, who agreed to cook him a fine meal when he has the time to stop over. Adam joshed him about being 'shy' of time — just last week!

He turned back, raising his voice for all the men to hear. "We'll finish the drive, whether Ben means to pay us those extra wages or not." When one of the men started to complain, he held up a hand. "All right, extra pay, guaranteed. If Ben doesn't pay it, you'll get my wages. We ride at dawn."

Chet turned to Val in a fury. He took off his hat, revealing sparse black hair, and whipped the hat against his leg. "You mean just like that? Only 'coz old Cartwright's lost a son?"

"If you got a problem with it, stow your gear and ride out. I don't want any troublemakers on this drive. You'll get the pay Cartwright promised if you herd with us."

Chet exchanged a low converse with the other two drovers he brought to camp before turning back to Val. "We'll stay. Hell, we got nothing to do for a week or so anyway."

"All right!" Val stood with fists tight against his hips and raised his voice a notch, relieved that no guns would be drawn. "We're up before the day breaks to move 'em, so let's finish the night's inventory and roll out the beds. Spuds and Pete, you have the first watch singin' to 'em."

With Val conferring over the morning victuals with Cookie, others off checking the remuda and the herd, Chet pulled his men in close. "We'll finish the drive. But old Ben won't see any of it." He laughed. "One cattle drive, two payrolls. Get some sleep, boys."

Felling of the Sons

***

Doctor Jessup nodded off briefly and jerked himself upright, fighting dizziness. Another half hour and he'd have to get Ben up. Joe still needed constant care. He was flushed in fever, made worse by the difficulty in taking proper liquid nutrients.

He re-wetted the cloth for Joe's head and checked his pocket watch. Another few minutes before the next dose. If his fever doesn't break soon, the boy didn't stand a chance. Adam only had a bullet in him that needed to come out. With this loss of blood there wasn't a whole lot a doctor could do. Fight the infection and hope his constitution was strong enough to bring him around. At least with Adam improved Ben didn't have two sons to worry over.

Jessup stood to keep himself from dozing and walked to the window. No sign of moon or stars but the light of sky at night meant a moon was out there somewhere. When he's right under the sky high up here in Tahoe, stars seem so close, but from this angle they couldn't be seen for the trees. The Cartwrights valued their trees even more than the stars, so he supposed the tradeoff was fair. For himself he preferred a view where he could see into eternity. He figured when a doctor played God, that was a common enough feeling.

Jessup looked back at Joe, his boyish face pale and sweating in the lamp's flickering light. He and Adam were brothers, maybe only half-brothers, but brothers. Joe's odds of making it were better because of who he was. Being a Cartwright, instilled with a strong sense of belonging, improved his odds.

He turned back to the window. If Joe was going to show signs of improvement, it should happen by late tomorrow afternoon. Should. He won't put it that way to Ben, though, or Ben will hover and fret if it doesn't happen. After all, there was also a bad head bruise to consider.

Dark though the night, Jessup thought he saw a shadow darting between trees down below him. He leaned close, face pressed against glass, and held his breath. No, nothing. Overtired, that was all.

***

Bret saw the doctor's face in the window and hid quickly. What was Jessup doing up there? Damn, they found that young Cartwright! How? That white-haired man—that was old man Cartwright! He probably dragged the doctor right on out of there after Bret left. And of course Bret traveled a mite slower than a pa who figured his young brat was dying, while Bret took his time to make sure the house had quieted before starting the fire. All along the way Bret debated going against his father's wishes and torching the whole house. That would take care of all of them.

After some further thought, he decided against it. Seeing them go down one by one would sweeten the taste of revenge. They may be hard to kill, but they were not invincible. And if the whole house goes up because he spills a little too much kerosene, oops! So sorry, Pa. Not like he ever appreciated any of his son's efforts. Bret already felt bound to take a real ego beating when he tells his Pa that Joe didn't die. Damn Cartwright — how'd he find the kid? These Cartwrights were almost spooky. Like they had a direct link to heaven or something.

Bret crept to the corner of the house between the kitchen and front entrance where the spare room would be. He dumped half the kerosene from his lantern into a puddle right in the corner on top the wooden porch. He pulled the satchel of splintered wood off his back and piled it on top the kerosene, and finished dumping.

Only one thing left to do. Light the match.

CHAPTER 20

Ben tossed restlessly, knowing he needed sleep, unable to close his mind down as the reality of the past few days took hold. Since waking up from his first four hours of sleep after Adam was shot, he'd not distracted himself from Adam's care to think. When Hoss told him Joe was missing, thinking with his gut was all he had time for.

He knew he had to settle with Van Remus, but how? Turn him over to the sheriff? He had a letter and a past, but no real proof. They had the man who shot Adam, but with him dead the trail stopped. Adam named Van Remus, but he did it solely on the basis of the letter. Or did he? Even though Adam had no contact with Van Remus since he was a boy, there might be something he knew or remembered.

John Jessup was a good friend to stay the night. He pulled Adam through, and now the doctor's magic would work on Joe. It had to. If one of his boys dies, Ben couldn't even begin to think about revenge on Van Remus because nothing would bring a dead son back. Just like nothing could bring a dead wife back. He used to think he should hate Indians after Inger died, but to what purpose? His anger at Van Remus for his attempts at killing them knows no bounds, but if a son dies…

Why is it, he wondered, forcing his muscles to relax, that when we need sleep most it's hardest to find? After a couple of hours of sleep, he'd have to fight back. . .stop Van Remus somehow.

Someone pounded on his door. Ben's mind sprang awake, but at first he couldn't move. He felt groggy, his muscles lingered behind in dreams.

"Ben, it's John. Come out here, quick!"

Joe! Ben threw his legs out of the bed and stood, still fighting sleep. He got the door open but before John could say anything, Ben smelled it.

"Something's on fire downstairs, Ben."

At the edge of the stairs Ben saw thick angry smoke billowed out of the cracks of the door to the guest room. Adam's room. "NO!" Ben ran down the stairs, followed closely by Dr. Jessup. He threw the door open but the room was so filled with billowing waves of smoke that they couldn't see. He heard a low rushing sound and the crackling of fire.

"John! Get Hop Sing! Tell him to get the water pumping and start hitting the flames from the outside!" His eyes watered and he could barely breathe. "Hoss! Get down here!"

Fighting smoke with flailing arms, Ben lurched into the room. "Adam," He fell forward on the bed as flames shot out at him, licking and consuming the headboard. "Adam!" Using arms he could tell the bed was empty. Ben couldn't breathe or open his eyes. He fell to the floor, the heat burning at him, dangerously close to catching fire himself, but he had to find his son. Adam must've gotten out of bed.

Hoss grabbed him by the feet and pulled him from the room. Hoss had a wet towel over his face, and put one over his pa's face as well. Ben, coughing, fought to breathe as he kept the towel clamped over his face.

"Where's Adam?" Hoss tried to see into a room filled with angry swirling smoke.

"Couldn't find." Ben gasped. "Not in bed, must be. . .on floor, somewhere. . .find him."

Water hit the side of the house at rapid intervals and the smoke increased as the fire started to die out, the acrid smell of wood tar stinging his chest.

Hoss threw himself into the room on his hands and knees. Ben could hear him scrambling about like some wild buffalo, but could Adam have survived in that smoke? Maybe he made it to the study and passed out. Ben tried to get to his feet, but couldn't. "Adam!?" The entire lower level had filled with smoke in drifting waves. If Adam crawled out after the fire started, where was he? Had he been taken outside to be killed, execution-style? New fear forced Ben to his feet.

Hoss crawled out of Adam's room, gasping. "He's not in there, Pa."

Ben leaned against the door. "Have to look outside, Hoss."

They heard the back kitchen door slam. Hop Sing and John came back in, soiled, wet, exhausted and grinning, until they saw Ben and Hoss.

"Fire's out, Ben. You must have this lumber well treated to keep it from burning fast. It was contained in that one corner. Smoked something fierce, though."

"Hop Sing kitchen still usabow," Hop Sing added.

John looked around. "Did you find Adam?"

Ben shook his head. "You didn't see anything outside?"

"No, nothing."

"He's got to be in the house somewhere, Pa."

John looked up the stairs. "Wait. I heard a noise earlier, when I was dozing." He ran, more of a fast saunter, up the stairs.

Ben stood, his red, tearing eyes glued to the fired-out room. His house. The Ponderosa. Crumbling down around him. None of it worth anything without his sons. They built this dream so many years ago, the four of them together. They cut down trees, planted more, gathered their herd a cow at a time. They suffered, sweated, went hungry, but through it all they laughed, loved, they lived. They lived.

"Ben!" John leaned over the rail. "He's up here, in one of the rooms. Sound asleep. I'll go check on Joe."

Hoss laughed in relief as he helped Ben up the stairs. "That Adam, he'll be bragging tomorrow about how smart he is."

Ben grinned broadly at Hoss but his throat tightened and his knees were weak. He leaned heavily against his large son.

"Mr. Cartlight."

Ben looked back down the stairs at Hop Sing waiting patiently. "Hop Sing, sorry. Open a few windows and ah, cover those holes in the wall, if you can." He looked back at the now abandoned guest room. "And go to bed, you need sleep, too."

"I'll sit with Joe," Hoss said as they reached the top of the stairs.

"No, I slept some. I'll stay with Joe. I'll get Hop Sing to relieve me in a few hours and you'll relieve him. And when he gets you up, son, shave that beard." They reached Joe's room but Hoss couldn't leave. "Go on to bed, Hoss." Ben went to Jessup, who was giving Joe some medicine.

Hoss followed him into the room and stood at Joe's bedside watching the doctor.

"No change?" Ben asked as John finished checking his heart.

"No. Not too much smoke up here, at least."

"Is Adam all right? You sure?"

"I went in and checked his vitals. He's sleeping more soundly than I expected but there's nothing wrong. Go on and see him, Ben. But come right back. I'm an old man who needs some sleep."

"I'll be right back."

After Ben left, Hoss stood by the doctor. "I'm worried about Pa. I don't think he can hold up much longer. That fire was set deliberate."

"I know." Jessup frowned as if trying to retrieve a distant thought.

"Is there anyone you kin send out who can stay with us? That would sure help Pa and Hop Sing."

"Good idea, Hoss. I'll ask Norma Jacobs. I've often called on her to do some in-home care. She's very agreeable."

Hoss winced. "You cayn't think of no one else?"

"She's the perfect one, Hoss."

"She's got. . .a hankering for Pa." Hoss blushed and looked at his feet.

"All the better."

"But Pa don't need---."

"Sure he does." Jessup laughed, and Hoss couldn't help but smile back.

Hoss looked down at his brother sweating and restless with fever and the pain returned, just as deep as a knife. Or hot as a fire. They weren't even safe at home. When Ben came up behind him and put a hand on his shoulder, he had to fight the tears. Leaving here would be harder than anything he's ever done — like leaving them defenseless. "Adam okay, Pa?"

"Amazing how he moved back to his own room in time. As though he knew." Ben shook his head.

"Pa, Adam told me, well, you ain't talked to him since reading those letters. Do you reckon tomorrow, well, maybe you could tell him more about. . .dadgumit, you know, what this is about."

"I know, Hoss, and I'll talk to Adam first thing in the morning. Go to bed. We'll wake you when it's your turn."

"And give yourself a good shave in the morning," Ben said absently to Hoss' back. "John, I really appreciate you being here tonight."

"Ben, you can't keep going on this way. Little sleep last night, hardly any tonight. I have to go back to town tomorrow morning first thing, but I'll tell you what. I'll send Norma Jacobs back, you know Norma, I get her to help me from time to time. She'll be more than happy to stay with you while your boys recover."

Ben only half listened. He stared at his boy's face as though hoping to absorb his fever. "Fine, John, that will be fine."

John patted Ben's shoulder on his way out. "In ten minutes he'll be ready for another dose."

Ben held his son's hand, hoping to help him to sleep, but Hoss's face was slow to leave his mind. *Adam was telling me earlier...tell him more...what this was all about.*

Maybe someone else did this. According to Sheriff Coffee, Joe told everyone, including Van Remus, that Adam had died. Could there be another vendetta against them? No, no one else. Ben hoped, long ago, that Adam would never remember anything. Now he would look to his father to fill in the rest. It could prove to be the hardest thing he's ever done. A feeling, Ben could imagine, not unlike burying a child alive.

CHAPTER 21

Council talk went on far into the night. Inside the lodge the flaming stick passed from talker to talker. Resolution evaded them but the elders felt no weariness to rest. Much of the time they sat in silent deliberation, a re-sharpening of the vision and a contemplation of what might go right and wrong with any of their choices.

Kudwa was convincing but still the talk went in circles. Not too long ago they waged war against the whites and had been horribly defeated. After the first strike had been won in retaliation for an attack on their women, it seemed the whites would leave them be. Then the soldiers came from across the mountains, the "milisha," Adam called them, and there were too many, all crying to put the red man back where they say he belonged, with the dogs of the desert.

To the white man, an attack in justice for an attack does not end the matter. They must have justice for the attack of the attack of the attack – justice, then, never ends. Kudwa reminded them, with heavy thoughts since his friend's last visit to their village, that survival was the land, the water, the trees. Nothing could be simpler than this.

This night was the first time since that war that Kudwa could remember seeing so many of his men mourn at once, and it was a good thing, a cleansing thing.

"You say this Adam Cartwright, the one who visits us and brings us food, is still alive?" Pawuana, once a brave warrior, now with an arm blown off by cannon fire, struggled to grasp the intensity of the action Kudwa requested.

"He lives, but refuses our help."

"If he refuses, who is there to accept?"

Susqwa reached out for the fire stick, for only those whose faces could be seen in the night were allowed to talk. "Now we are little and no longer as strong as many of us can still remember we once were, but even that strength we once had was little enough compared to the whites that number as stars."

Kudwa couldn't hide a smile, even in the dark. "One would think," Kudwa said, "that the lateness in the hour would not bring out such a busy tongue."

Others laughed with him, for Susqwa generally had an aversion to using more than three words together at once. The two men exchanged a grin as the fire stick passed to Winnemucca.

Winnemucca held out the stick. "I am anxious for my warm wife and the night's wise vision before a decision is made. We will talk again in the morning. Once we all agree the decision will be made."

In the silence, Kudwa slowly got to his feet again, his head grazing the top of the council tent. He refused the flaming fire stick, as his next words had a different intent. "When you sleep, let this vision guide you. We are worth less than the land. We can only walk if the land remains under our feet. We do not do this for the whites or Adam Cartwright. We do this for our children. And their children. We can scrap food off the ground to feed our children. But we cannot put the ground back together that comes apart beneath us. Remember the tales told of the cracking earth."

Kudwa left them, taking his brisk, controlled anger to his wife's lodge for the night. She slept deeply, he could tell by her breathing, so he took care to lay gently beside her. He closed his eyes and pictured the ground below him, trembling, shaking in fear for what lie ahead.

Sleep did take him away, but to another land where the trees disappeared into the ground like snakes into their winter homes, leaving a bare empty ground of rocks and dried thorny brush. Kudwa ran from one tree to the next and hugged each as though to protect it, but the ground sucked it hungrily down even as his arms were wrapped tight, the angry tearing of wood from his bosom agonizing him. And when the last tree was gone and he stood wailing up into the blackened sky, a hole opened up beneath his feet and sucked him down as well.

When he awoke, the sun had risen but he was not refreshed. He held his wife close and trembled.

***

Roy Coffee unlocked the door to his office unusually early but he hoped to be visited by the Pony Express at any time. When Little Joe explained what was going on, Roy sensed a fear that Joe couldn't name. Ben's past went deep and beyond most people's imaginings, and long-lasting enemies could be expected. Many times Roy envied him his sons, but not the land that brought grief with its security. Children *were* the earth, maybe because he and his wife had never been blessed. They adopted a little orphan once, but she died of typhoid at barely a year of age. So he adopted whole towns as sheriff, and Mary aided unwed mothers through the church until her own death some years back. There were times when he thought of Ben's boys as his own, so the thought of Adam dying, perhaps dead, helped him word the letter he sent by Pony Express shortly after he and Joe brought the dead gunslinger to town. Any reply taking longer than two days would be a disappointment.

Shortly after the sun rose that morning a Pony rider came in at full speed with a letter for him from the Sacramento sheriff. The letter was rapidly scrawled.

> Roy, you sounded most distressed and, old friend, that made me curious about this Cartwright you talk about. Sure enough I remember Van Remus, and though I can't say I like what I remember, I can't give you any news to hold against him. I did not yet check with San Francisco authorities, where he lived after leaving here, but if you like, I can do this. That will take some time, so here's a quick response.
>
> I found records mentioning Van Remus back in the early 40s. Van Remus filed a complaint in April of 1842 against John Sutter and Ben Cartwright for preventing him from laying claim to a parcel of land the year previous, and this I found in Sutter's own records left behind in the land office. These assessments are not on file, only copies of some Mexican property rights to Sutter that our government has since overturned. In this complaint Van Remus accused Ben of killing his wife when some cows he herded stampeded over

her. If Van Remus believed Cartwright deliberately murdered his wife, he didn't pursue it legally.

There's nothing else. The matter just seemed to have died away. It's interesting that Sutter himself, being the law back then, kept all this material against himself. This area, as you know, was later found to be highly charged with gold.

"There may have been more material once, Roy, but there was a major fire in Sacramento in '52, destroying a lot of official paperwork. Don't know if this helped. If you want to give me another week, I can come up with some people in this area who used to know him, who may have different stories to tell. Let me know. Yours, Sheriff Sam Sterney"

Roy folded the letter up and tucked it inside his vest pocket. Ben never once mentioned anything about a woman being trampled. Roy had a feeling this was very important indeed. Not only that a woman was trampled, but also that Ben never thought to mention it. Not that it would ever come up in conversation. Still and all …

Maybe there are things he needed to know about Ben Cartwright.
***

Hoss couldn't find much appetite that morning but forced the food down. "Hop Sing, that was a mighty fine breakfast, and I do thank you."

"You still not eat good, Mr. Hoss. Now shave. Then sit with Mr. Joe."

"Ah, no, sorry. Hop Sing. I have to run an errand. I need you to pack me a big lunch, because I won't be back for some time. Maybe. . .all day." He walked to the stairs. "I'll sit with Joe while you pack it."

Hop Sing grabbed his arm. "Where you go, Mr. Hoss? You stay here, or you be like Mr. Adam and Mr. Joe."

"Now Hop Sing, where'd you get that notion? My brothers run into a peck of trouble you think someone's after all of us? We got a ranch to run, ya know, and with Pa worried and my brothers laid up, I'm all that's left to do the work."

134

"But what Mr. Cartlight say when he find you gone?"

"Well, nothing, 'coz here's what you're gonna tell him."

***

Hoss rode quietly out of the yard in the direction of Virginia City with a big lunch in a burlap sack hung over his saddle horn and his bedroll secured behind him. If Hop Sing noticed his odd dress, he didn't mention it. Good thing Pa kept old clothes like this laying around for employees to furnish them with change of dress if they needed it.

They were threatened at their home last night, and Hoss couldn't sit by any longer. He could get himself legally hired by Van Remus, a better plan than just showing up at the logging camp. That way he could meet the scoundrel and get Roy to watch his back at the same time.

Halfway to the city Bill Ferguson, from a ranch off toward Carson City, stopped him. "Hoss? By golly, it rightly is you! Doggone if I never woulda recognized you if it weren't for your horse! Why you growing a beard? Looks like you turned logger instead of rancher, by golly." Bill was a homesteader with two children who occasionally called on the Cartwrights sociably.

"I reckon I can trust you, Bill. Don't tell no one you saw me. My family is threatened and I've a notion how to stop it but I can't have them knowing it's me while I do what I gotta do."

"Oh, say, I heard about your brother Adam. And I don't blame you a'tall. But if you want to be somebody other than Hoss, well, then you better get off that horse, everyone knows him because you haven't changed him any."

Hoss looked down. "Dadgumit! Do you suppose you could trade with me, Bill?"

Bill scratched his thick crop of curly brown hair. "Well now, Hoss, this spindly little horse of mine won't do for a body like yours." His narrow eyes widened as he smiled. "I've got a better idea. Come to my spread and I'll fix you up with a bigger horse. That way we won't chance no one coming along and seeing us out here."

Hoss rubbed his palm against his itchy beard. He couldn't afford to take chances. As he followed Bill to his ranch, he started to feel a little less comfortable. If it weren't for Bill, he would have ridden into town on his own horse. Someone would have pointed him out to Van Remus as a Cartwright. What else might he have forgotten?

CHAPTER 22

Clete woke earlier than usual, feeling a fire in his veins as hot as the rising sun. After eighteen years, missing his wife should get easier, but even that vivid and very physical dream he'd had of her lately didn't usually awaken him with muscles tensed and screaming. He heard Bret snoring in the sitting room. Clete allowed himself the brief hope that the fire cleansed his son of the hate given him by his parents. Only if all the Cartwrights were dead they could get on with their lives, Winnie reminded him in his sleep.

Bret slept soundly in a chair, his legs stretched out in front of him and his head held up by a hand, elbow propped on the chair's arm. He slept covered in granite dust head to foot, his blonde hair gnarled and dirty, looking like he carried his horse instead of the other way around.

Clete pushed his elbow and Bret begrudgingly awoke. "Where you been, boy?"

"Oh, uh." Bret put his head back against the chair and shut his eyes. "Long night." He seemed inclined to go back to sleep.

Clete poured himself a cup of coffee from the pot delivered by the house staff and stared disgruntled from the steaming liquid to his unkempt son. "Bret, you let the hotel staff see you like that?" When Bret didn't answer, Clete kicked his foot. "I asked where you been, boy. And I want you to answer with the official statement."

Bret's eyes slit open. "Official? Oh," he struggled to sit up. "I was out hunting, got myself a shot at a cougar, too, but missed. You know what a lousy shot I am."

"Good." Clete took a careful sip of the strong, hot brew. "Now the truth." Bret's eyes shut again. "If you don't feel like talking, I got better things to do than watch you sleep."

Slowly Bret pulled himself out of the chair and stood to his full height, towering over Clete just like Winnie always did. He worked the kinks out of his back before grabbing some coffee. "I done it, sir, for what good it did."

"Call me Pa here if you want," Clete smiled gently. "What did you do?"

"Set the Cartwrights on fire. But it didn't go up fast and then they had it put out. Smoked an awful lot, though. I watched and waited, but couldn't hear anything. Maybe got him, maybe not."

"Anybody see you?"

"No sir. I was careful." He took a gulp of steaming coffee and winced.

"And if you didn't succeed in killing Adam then we showed our hand knowing he's still alive."

"Yeah." Bret looked lower than a rattler on a bed of pine needles. "I think the youngest Cartwright is still alive, too. The doctor was there, sitting upstairs in a room. I ran into old man Cartwright at the doc's last night."

"Did he know you?"

"Nope. I didn't know him either. Or I woulda stopped him somehow."

Clete slammed his cup down. In a fury he swept the pot off the table. Hot coffee hit the wall and spilled to the floor in a brown torrent. "Hell's fire! Those Cartwrights have a million lives! What in blazes does it take?" Stabbing needles pierced his brain, blinding him. He collapsed in a chair, pressing his fists against pounding temples.

"We can try again. We're making Cartwright's life hell, at least." Bret turned from the sight of his father's whimpering. "See a doctor for some pills or learn to live with it."

"Leave me be!" Clete forced himself to his feet, gasping and pale but steady. "We're making Cartwright's life hell..." He poured a glass of water and drank noisily, then took several deep breaths. "I'm not giving up on killing the sons. But we've got other fat in the fry pan. I

138

want to speed up the destruction of the land. We need to find more fellers to send up there."

Bret rubbed his jaw. "If we draw that Ben Cartwright out of his fortress to save his land, we can get at those two injured sons even better."

"And don't forget the third. I want him, too."

"Just show 'em to me. I'll take care of him."

Clete put a heavy hand on Bret's shoulder and squeezed. "You're hardly two for two. No, I'll handle this. I have---."

At an insistent rap on the door Clete gave Bret a puzzled look. He opened the door to see the frowning countenance of Sheriff Coffee.

"Good morning, gentlemen. Mind if I come in? I don't need much of your time, I know you're busy and all."

"Well, sure, Sheriff, come right on in."

Roy stopped when he saw the coffee mess on the wall. "Oh my, that's a shame. But I heard the coffee here wasn't too good."

Clete laughed. "Sheriff, you got that right! Sorry I don't have any to offer you."

Roy grunted. "I'm not." He peered at Bret. "Young fella, you look like you been hard to work already this morning."

Bret looked down at his clothes but kept his face expressionless.

"Forgive my associate. He was out all night hunting. Gets it in his head to have fresh kill once in a while. So what brings you to our door so early?" Clete gave Roy's shoulder a sociable pat. "Just a howdy from the local law?"

"Nope. I got a letter that I am quite frankly disturbed over and I hope you can help me figure it out."

"I will surely try, Sheriff. Have a seat here."

"Thanks, this won't take long. Mr. Van Remus, you were married once, weren't ya? How did your wife die?"

"How? Why, sheriff, if you know that much about me, I imagine you know how she died. What did you say this letter was about?" Clete backed away from the sheriff as he talked.

"She was stampeded, I know that. What was she doing over to the Sutter and Cartwright holdings, and how did the stampede start?"

"What do you want to hear? My version or the official one?"

"The truth."

"Ah yes, Sheriff, man of virtue, the truth and only the truth." He ignored the worried look Bret cast him. "Sheriff, I get the feeling you want to hold me responsible for what happened to Cartwright's son. Sure, Ben and I had a past. We bashed heads together a few times. And yes, his herd did kill my wife. But it was only an accident. Maybe at first I didn't believe so, but you have to understand how I felt when I found my wife dead. Once I simmered down I realized there was nothing they could have done. Why my wife approached a stampeding herd I do not to this day know."

"So you did threaten the Cartwrights? You admit it?"

"Sheriff, words said in anger are only words. You can't pin anything on them, even if they're written, because words don't kill."

"Not like cow feet, eh?"

Clete stiffened. "Was that necessary, sheriff?"

"You accused Ben of murder and but never charged him with it. Why?"

Clete fingered his empty cup. "I can't remember if I had a reason or not. This was all so long ago, and I've tried hard to forget."

"Adam have something to do with it?"

"Do? He was only a boy." Clete walked over to his favorite chair and sat, letting his hands rest easy on his lap, concentrating on not clenching his fists or wrapping them around the sheriff's neck. "Why all the suspicion, sheriff? Have I earned it?"

Roy crossed his arms. "I always thought I knew Ben Cartwright. But I don't know much about his life in the Sacramento valley. If there is a murder in his past and you can prove he was guilty, didn't you owe it to your wife?" He looked over at Bret who was staring sullenly at his feet. "Do you know any of this story, son?"

"You leave him out of this!"

Roy turned to Clete. "Is that right? He's your boy, is he?"

Clete looked down at his hands tightening and forced them to relax. "No, he's---."

"I'm not his *boy*!" Bret ignored the startled look Clete cast at him. "I suggest you do your research a little more thoroughly, sir. Mr. Van Remus discovered some months after the stampede that a thunderstorm in the mountain spooked those cows. That's all, pure and simple."

Clete and Bret locked eyes. "That's right," Clete said, noting the cold deadness in his son's eyes. "That's right."

Bret turned back to Roy, who kept his eye on Clete for another moment. "The woman, Van Remus's wife, wanted to earn a living but as a man because the only other place that would hire her was a saloon, and she was no saloon gal. She never herded cattle before and couldn't get out of the way."

"Bret---."

"I suggest if you want to find a murderer you look into the past of the man you found dead. Or better yet, run a check on your friend Ben Cartwright. A man who let a woman die, a woman who had a family."

Clete stood. "Bret! Let me handle this." Bret shook his head and turned away. Clete sighed. "Are there any other questions, Sheriff Coffee?"

Roy was put off only for a moment. "Out of curiosity I wired to a friend of mine and he tells me you and Ben had a past. He couldn't tell me much, but he's ready to give me more help if I ask him."

"So you came to see if it's necessary." Clete smiled. "Sheriff, I assure you, I am only a businessman here to run a mine."

"And you hired loggers who vanished into thin air. But I think I could find 'em if I look on the Ponderosa, couldn't I? I know a particular section of wooded area to start looking, too."

"I'm a lawyer as well as a businessman. If I have loggers on the Ponderosa it's because I have a legally drawn contract."

Roy eyed him incredulously. "I have seen enough here to send a letter back to Sacramento. In the meantime, I expect you to watch your step. If I hear any more trouble with the Cartwrights, I'm likely to throw you in jail out of pure cussedness." Roy nodded at them. "Good day to you." The door slammed shut behind him.

Bret charged at the door but Clete sprang up and grabbed his arm. "What are you, foolish? He's guessed who you are now!"

"I'm tired of pretending! I want the world to know what Cartwright did to my ma."

"Not yet!" Clete looked out the window. "We are in big trouble if he finds anyone to talk against us in Sacramento." He watched the sheriff walking down the street, and started to chuckle.

Bret stood beside him to look into the street. Clete kept chuckling as he watched Roy walk back to his office.

Bret nodded. No, they don't have to worry over Sheriff Coffee.

CHAPTER 23

Ben walked Dr. Jessup past the grandfather clock that softly chimed the morning hour. The smell of acrid smoke and charred wood burnt their noses. "I can't tell you how grateful I am you stayed the night, John."

"I know. Get some rest, Ben, or I'll be coming back for you."

"I'll rest easier now that Joe's heart is stronger. You think he'll be fine, that's what you said? I can expect him to open his eyes soon?"

"I think he's passed danger of dying, the fever has gone down considerably. But I can't say when he'll come to." He checked his bag again, sensing Ben's disgruntled look. "I have faith in you, Ben. You brought Adam back; you can do the same for Joe." He snapped the bag shut and reached for the door.

Ben followed him out. The morning was dull and cold as the autumn chill took good hold on the Sierras, a haze covering the rising sun as warm air was pulled from the earth by the cool. Jessup feared they were in for a bad storm, an early snow by the crisp feel to the air.

"Ben, I mean to make good on my promise, sending someone out here to help so you can take care of business."

Ben helped Jessup saddle his horse. "I wish I could ride into town with you, John."

"You'd never make it - you're too old." A groan slipped into Jessup's chuckle as he mounted. "I might be in need of a good strong liniment bath myself. Except I might fall asleep and drown." He followed Ben's stare to the charred corner of the house. "Something about that fire bothers me. Wish I could figure out what."

"Let me know if you do." Ben raised a hand in return of Jessup's as he rode off.

***

143

In the daze of a wearily wounded, Ben checked on Joe, reminded Hop Sing to wake Hoss, found his bed waiting and promptly fell asleep. When he woke again it was mid-morning and he felt much improved. He went in to check on Joe and found Hop Sing at Joe's bedside writing a letter home in his cryptic style.

"Thanks, Hop Sing, I'll take over for a while. After lunch I'll need to go to town, so I'll want you back. Did Hoss go back to bed?"

Hop Sing got up without answering and scurried to the door. Finally he turned back. "Mr. Jessup, he send help out, he say."

"Yes, he did, so we'll all be able to get more sleep."

"And you, Mr. Cartlight, find who did this to boys."

"That's right. That's why I'm heading to town this afternoon." He watched Hop Sing run out of the room. "Hop Sing!" He waited until he saw the Chinaman's worried face again. "Where's Hoss?"

"He. . .busy. Velly busy." Hop Sing disappeared again.

"Not sleeping?" Hoss couldn't let chores go, now that he had to do them for everybody. Ben sighed as his hand drifted down to take gentle hold of Joe's arm. Hoss took too much on himself sometimes.

Joe looked a little more like himself, some color returning to his face. He stirred briefly, sighed heavily and was still again. That sound he made, so Joe-like, meant he was still there. Ben grabbed the straw of hope and held tight — Joe would be just fine. At a thump in the doorway he looked up.

Adam leaned on the doorframe, a tan shirt on but not buttoned, revealing his hairy, partially bandaged chest, and his pants on but not buckled. He stared at Joe as he tucked in his shirt and fastened his pants before trying to straighten. "How is he?"

Ben stood. "Why are you dressed?"

Adam walked past Ben and sat in the chair next to the bed. "He looks better." He felt Joe's head. "Fever's down."

144

"Doctor says his heart is sound. He'll be fine." Ben frowned. "You thinking about going out?"

"I get restless lying around. Thought I'd help you with Joe. Maybe check the stock. Maybe Hop Sing needs to go to town."

"Don't worry about that, you've got another couple of days of bed rest ahead of you." Adam didn't answer but his jaw clenched. Ben could see he might get an argument but he couldn't lose this one. "Hoss said you need to talk."

"I can remember Van Remus, but only enough to make me crazy for the rest. I have to know everything, Pa."

Ben realized Adam already knew too much. Adam stared at Joe with that look of impassioned impatience. Ben sighed. "All right." He pulled up a chair, with a terrible sinking in his gut that nothing would be the same once the story was done.

"Van Remus' wife," Adam started. "I need the truth on how she died."

Ben took a deep breath, rubbing his forehead. "She was wearing men's clothes, armed with rifle and rode to our ranch, uninvited and unexpected."

"Do you know why?"

"No, I don't. My memory on this is hazy, too, but I remember being in the midst of a struggle over land rights. They were angry with us for rejecting their claim. She had a temper on her, Winnie did. I seem to remember Clete actually apologizing for her anger once or twice. Still, whatever she wanted, he felt she should have."

Adam frowned. "Then...after she died?"

Ben stared at his hands fisted on his lap. He straightened his fingers slowly, feeling the ache from the tension. "I stood him down and he moved on."

"Or so you thought." Adam paused. "Pa, he cornered me once, alone, after she died."

Ben looked up. "He did?" Adam related the story of the threat to kill all he sired. "Well. If I had known this back then, he wouldn't be alive today, I'll tell you *that*."

"Maybe I feared you would kill him, or maybe I was too terrified of him to tell you. After a while, I thought I'd had just a vivid nightmare. I only remembered it again after reading that letter."

Ben walked to the window. "He knew the truth all along." He turned back, seeing his still pale, still injured eldest son with that expression of innocent ignorance, demanding the truth. "That memory of yours may be enough to convict him of having you shot and trying to kill Joe. I'm going to bring Roy here, have you tell him, have him see what's been happening." Ben walked to the door.

"Pa, wait." Adam stood, face and stance determined to butt his father's hesitancy. "Was I at the stampeding where she died?"

Ben hesitated. "Are you sure you have to know, son?"

"You always said truth counts, no matter how it hurts."

Ben turned away. "I'm just an old fool who forgets the exceptions."

"Pa!"

"All right!" Ben regretted his anger but in a moment Adam will understand. "Tell me what you remember."

"I came riding out of the woods. Terrified. I don't remember why. And I saw the stampeding, heard the screaming. These are mostly dreams I've had, but they feel real." He wiped his forehead with his shirtsleeve. "I need the whole memory, Pa."

"I know, son. But it's painful." Ben could see his boy trembling and crying in his bed. "Damn that Van Remus! Why didn't he understand?" Ben walked to the window. When he looked out he could see Sutter's Fort, as though the past was unraveling in front of him. "You were running an errand to deliver a calf to one of the settlers in exchange for produce. You were an invaluable help to me, Adam, you took on more responsibility for a boy your age than I had the right to expect." He rubbed his stinging eyes, taking a breath.

"We were having some problems between the settlers and the Indians. Sutter employed a number of friendly Indians, several he brought over from the islands off the Pacific coast, and he also made friendlies out of some of the local tribes. He had a charm about him, Sutter did. You became accustomed to these natives, ate with them, and played with their children.

"But not all the tribes were willing to work for Sutter. Some believed we should trade freely with them, though they had little to give in return. They believed that those with a lot shared with those who had little, but very few whites I know cotton to that idea. White man's goods seemed extravagant to the Indians, while settlers saw them as beggars, wanting us to give and keep on giving. To the Indian one cannot be rich if your neighbor is poor."

Ben met Adam's eyes. He was listening, but impatiently. "I'm stalling, I guess. You weren't afraid of the Indians we worked with, when they dressed and acted like you and me, but you were terrified of those in the wild who ran raids on the settlers. After Hoss's mother caught that arrow, you were terrified of the Indians others call savages. Sometimes you woke in the night screaming that they were coming for us. I tried to explain to you that those who had attacked us and killed Inger were only protecting their rights, but Hoss's ma was the only ma you knew.

"As you got older, I thought you accepted it. I even brought you to one of those so-called savage tribes so you could watch one of their ceremonies, meet some of their people." Adam had slouched down in the chair. "Well, the day of the stampede, you came back from running your errand." Ben could see by the look on Adam's face that he was remembering.

It had been a beautiful late April afternoon and Adam was full of himself for following all of his Pa's directions, for herding that calf like an expert. Now he was free to ride, free as the wind, as fast as his pony would go. He took a different way home instead of following the usual bluff route. He urged his horse up a rocky canyon and through a thicket of pine and underbrush. He had often looked up this cliff on the way home, and this was a fine day to explore. The cliff ended in a natural incline and then it was a straight run to home.

Inside the heavy pine Adam reined his horse to breathe the cool pungent breezes. He didn't have to hurry home. Hoss would be engrossed in the wooden blocks Adam had made for him and Pa didn't want him helping with the stock that had to be moved from the north field to the branding pen. 'Another year,' Pa says, 'and you'll be ready.' Adam showed him today though. Adam puzzled over this, one man with two names. He brought that calf right to Sal's pen and got him to sign.

But Sutter had signed Juan's name earlier.

He sensed eyes on him, more a feeling of being watched than any sound of presence. Slowly he turned. Eight Indians, painted and armed with spears and arrows, sat on horses behind him. As he stared at them, one raised a spear and shouted, a horrible shout, a scream.

Adam urged his horse into a run, afraid to look over his shoulder, sure they would catch him, the sound of horse hooves echoing in the canyon like a million chasing him. He ran his horse faster than he ever dared before. He could see Hoss's ma giving him her 'don't you worry, little man' smile just before leaping to her feet to shoot at Indians like a man to protect him and baby Hoss. She took an arrow in the back and he didn't get to say goodbye.

Now they've come for him, and he suddenly felt like a bigger target than even his ma. "Paaaaa!" They were right behind him, swallowing his voice with their shouts and their horses and the thunder they caused. He couldn't outrun them but he had to! He couldn't let Pa lose the son Elizabeth died giving birth to!

Adam rode into the cattle herd screaming for his Pa. He was halfway down the length of the herd before he realized the thundering was cows running with him, but his horse was faster and he was going to find Pa at the front of the herd and then everything would be all right, because no one else was gonna die, Pa suffered enough, he wasn't going to lose his sons too.

He rode faster than even the thundering cows, getting quickly to the head where he saw Pa, sitting on that horse. . . No, not Pa, Pa wouldn't sit there staring at the herd, Pa knows stampeding cattle are dangerous and if he doesn't give his horse some rein he would get run over. . .Someone wearing a hat tilted down over the face turned suddenly – that wasn't Pa's hat neither – and then Adam saw the rifle that person had raised, aiming at. . ..

Adam's horse, finally exhausted, came to a rolling stop safe from the thundering herd but Adam couldn't tear his eyes from the person as the cattle swarmed, bumping and jostling the horse, the horse that tried to back away but didn't have enough rein so it reared up, clouds of dust surrounding them and then one rambunctious steer butted the horse, gouging its chest. The horse lost balance and fell, the rifle flew and the person fell between the cows' thundering hooves. Adam watched this body being kicked and stomped, cattle trying to run around but some pushed into and over the body, the body jerking, skin torn and ripped, and Adam could only watch as the hat fell off, revealing long, deep blonde hair. A woman, the cattle were trampling a woman. . .to death.

Adam felt Ben's hands on his shoulders but reality lingered miles away and apart from everything he used to be. He had just seen a woman die, trampled, bloodied, because of him. He took a deep breath and wiped his eyes clear but the vision didn't fade, like a fiendish devil in his mind stabbing him over and over.

"Why?" he stood, but couldn't seem to find any way to understand it. He collapsed back into the chair, hands pressed against his eyes.

"Why did you block it out? Well, Adam, it was too hard for you to accept. You went into shock, son. You were unresponsive for days. Hoss finally brought you around. He kept hanging around your bed and one day started bouncing on your chest." Ben laughed, trying to lighten the mood. "I remember how relieved I felt to hear you laugh."

"Were the Indians ever found? Were they even there?"

"Adam, I don't believe for a minute you imagined seeing Indians."

Adam touched Joe's stilled hand and squeezed it briefly. He couldn't stop shaking, couldn't control the memory that threatened to take away everything he ever thought about himself. "Van Remus has a right to be angry, to be bitter. I killed his wife. Men are hung for less."

"Now, Adam, it was an accident---."

"I've always known how Hoss's ma died." He'd sunk his head so deep into his hands Ben could barely hear him. "I don't remember fearing Indians."

After a minute Ben walked to the other side of the bed and sat heavily, voice unsteady. "After you came out of the shock, you changed. You remembered how Inger died but you convinced yourself you were never afraid of Indians. I couldn't understand it but the doctor said, considering the shock, your reaction was very normal."

His brother almost died because of him, Adam realized, staring at his still brother in bed. Almost died. Trembling, he got to his feet and tucked in his shirt. "Then it's up to me to set things right."

                                        ***

Adam had nearly reached the door before Ben could get to his feet.

"Now Adam, you aren't healed yet, you can't go riding off." Ben stopped Adam at the door and what he saw in Adam's face terrified him. Despair and determination made frightening companions.

"If I don't set things right, do you think I can go on living with myself? Pa, Joe almost died because of me!"

"It wasn't your fault! That woman didn't belong there."

Adam's teeth gritted. "I won't blame a dead woman." He cocked his head suddenly to the door. "Where's Hoss?"

"Out doing chores. Why?" As Ben watched, dumbfounded, a transformation took hold of his eldest. Dark anger and desperation replaced cool logic. "Adam, I don't think he'll leave the ranch."

150

Adam ran off toward the stairs.

"Adam! Settle down, you're not healed yet!" Ben ran after him. Adam leaned against the rail and stared at the scorched guest room. Ben started down the stairs. "Hop Sing! Come up and sit with Joe for a while."

CHAPTER 24

Ben told Adam what he could about the fire.

"Because I was afraid. All this." Adam faced the front door, fists clenching.

"Why don't you go back to bed, son?" The worst of all possible timing. Ben could see Adam forcing his body to heal, to get rid of the feeling of helplessness so that he could get out there and stop "all this." Adam's normal impatience with being injured now had a franticness to it, and with his strong will to act, lingering pain will be ignored. "You need rest. You haven't been---."

"I should have died, Pa! Now he won't quit until he's destroyed all of us. I won't let that happen." Adam grabbed his coat from the rack. As he went for his gun belt, Ben grabbed his arm.

"Adam, this is my problem. You were just a boy caught in the middle. Don't bear the guilt for this."

"How can I help it, Pa? If Winnie hadn't died---."

"Mr. Ben! Little Joe, he open eyes! Come qlick!"

Ben jumped up the stairs and Adam followed. Ben ran into Joe's room, crouched down next to his boy, and grabbed his hand.

Joe's eyes flickered and his lips moved, as though trying to speak. After a few moments he relaxed back into deep sleep again.

"Joe." Ben squeezed his hand. "Joe, can you hear me?"

"Pa, is he coming to?" Adam stood in the doorway.

Ben waited for a response but finally sat back. "No, no, just a spasm. It doesn't mean consciousness." He stood, his strong countenance pressed in defeat. "It doesn't mean anything." He slapped a heavy hand on Hop Sing's shoulder. "Thanks, Hop Sing, you can go now, I'll stay."

Hop Sing shuffled past Adam to the stairs.

"Hop Sing! Wait." Adam stopped him before he got down the stairs. "Do you know where Hoss is?"

"He leave early this morning." Hop Sing glanced at Ben and fled down the stairs.

Ben stormed after him. "Confound it, Hop Sing, you're hiding something."

Hop Sing's face paled. "Mr. Hoss say you worry."

"Then he shouldn't have gone," Adam thundered from the stairs. "Where'd he go?"

"He say someone need to take care of things. He only one left."

Ben rubbed his forehead. "Hop Sing, a straight answer, please."

"Mr. Hoss gone to California, check on cattle driving. Afraid they in big mess."

"Ah. The cattle drive." Ben wrapped his arms around himself, scratching his shoulders. "Well, that's probably the only direction he could head to stay out of trouble."

"He should've stayed here." Adam went back into Joe's room. He caught his breath, speaking low but aloud. "Dammit, Hoss, did you?"

"What's wrong?" Ben stood at Adam's side. "Did Hoss say something to you?"

Adam stared at Joe. "No." More firmly, "It's nothing."

Ben sat at Joe's side and felt his forehead.

As he watched Ben with his youngest, a sudden dizziness passed through Adam. "How can you forgive me for this?" He grabbed onto the bed frame for support. "I can't. . .forgive. . .."

Ben jumped up and held onto Adam as he collapsed, sobbing. "Let it go, Adam. You are not responsible, son." Ben felt with great and unnerving force the fragile condition of his eldest son as he helped Adam to his room. Adam couldn't stop shaking, his once proud, firm body hunched over, his breathing harsh and staggered. How could he survive this? How could any of them?

Adam sat gratefully on his bed but refused to lie down. Instead he took a deep breath and swallowed hard. "Pa. I have to stop him somehow."

"No. Don't you see what he's doing? He wants to see me destroyed and knows that killing one of my sons will do it. I'll stop him. I only have to figure out where to start."

"You could start by getting the loggers out of the north 40."

It was Ben's turn to listen.

***

Roy walked out of the Sugarloaf Cafe after a pleasing pork and dumpling pie lunch. He looked forward to kicking his feet up on his desk for an hour before digging into a heavy load of paperwork. He stood outside his office jiggling his keys. Usually he grabbed the one he needed right off but this time it kept evading his fingers.

At the sound of a gunshot he looked up. "Now who's fiddling around with their gun?"

Between the sheriff's office and the saloon next door was a gap of about four feet of empty space. Sometimes a drunk would get lost and crawl back there, ending up in the debris behind the building and making a nuisance of himself. Or he'd end up getting hurt in the loose rock where the ground took a sudden dip before sloping up into the hills again.

Felling of the Sons

As he looked down the alleyway toward the sloping hills, Roy pulled out his gun. He didn't see anyone, but as he took a few steps in could smell the gunpowder. "Hey! Who's back here? This here's the sheriff, and I want to make sure you're not hurt. So speak up!"

"Yeah, yeah, I'm hurt, couldja give me a hand back here?"

Roy tightened his grip. He'd been at the receiving end of tricks a time or two as sheriff, and wouldn't put anything past anybody. When he got to where the back sides of both buildings ended, he looked first in the opposite direction of the voice, and saw only empty barrels from the saloon and smashed crates.

He turned to the back of the building that housed his office and saw a young fellow leaning against the corner of the wooden frame, clutching at his arm with his hand.

"Oh, it's you, Gopher." Roy kept his gun ready. "What the devil you doing back here?"

"Hiya, sheriff, I was feeling a mite restless today so I wandered back here to see if there was a chance of developing a strike strike!"

Roy saw Gopher's eyes go up, his brows making a quizzical 'v' on his face. Roy caught only a glimpse of the man behind him before a painful blow to his head blackened him.

***

Chubby had a steady, reliable gait but this horse of Ferguson's was a plugger. After what seemed an eternity of riding Hoss stopped at Roy's office. If he could fool Roy into thinking he was someone else, he could fool anyone. Then once he tells Roy who he was, Roy will be sure to have someone watch his backside without revealing his disguise.

Hoss cleared his throat as he stood outside the office. He'd been practicing the accent all the way over but felt suddenly uneasy. He forced a goofy smile on his face and opened the door.

Standing there at Roy's desk was Byron Clem, one of Roy's deputies. "Can I help you?" he asked when Hoss hesitated.

"Look'n for da sheriff, dat be you?" If his Uncle Gunar could hear Hoss now, he'd be on the floor laughing. So would Joe.

"Sheriff Coffee you looking for? Nope, can't say as I know where he is. Something I can help you with?" Clem wiped his hand on his pants and walked over to him. "Name's Deputy Clem. There ain't much the sheriff can do that I can't in his place." Clem squinted at him. "You look familiar, you been in town long?"

"Naw, naw, jest a day. Look'n fer work, you know me find'n work?" Inwardly Hoss scrambled for an adjustment to his plan. Tell Clem? He couldn't trust Clem as well as Roy to keep a confidence.

"Well, depends on what kind of work you do. You look like you could handle quite a bit," he slapped Hoss on the arm, and Hoss, off time a beat, staggered sideways. "Easy, fella, gotta work on your stamina there."

"I goot and strong chopp'n on da trees, you know where tree work is?"

"Well, there's that Van Remus, word's around town that he's hiring out for loggers, but I don't reckon you'd care to work for him, if what Roy says is likely. You'd be better off going into the mines, although someone your size might just get stuck." He peered close at Hoss again. "You sure we ain't met before?"

Hoss backed up toward the door. "I tank you. I find this Remos and maybe get work. I tank you." He ducked outside, away from Clem's curious eyes. He stood on the porch, catching his breath. He barely fooled Clem. Maybe he only did because Clem wasn't expecting Hoss to fool him. But even without Roy's help, he couldn't quit. No one would know him by name in that logging camp, anyway. All he has to do is get through town with his eyes down so no one points him out.

He concentrated on a non-Hoss-like disagreeable expression and strode down the walk, keeping his eyes down, his mouth tight and lips pursed in a tight half-grin. The three-day growth of beard on his face made him feel like a stranger besides. When he reached the International's good food smells, his stomach rolled. Missing good food was the least of his problems. Worst thing was missing the look on Joe's face when he wakes up.

He missed Joe something fierce, missed his laugh, the way he could get in and out of mischief, the way his face got sappy and lost when he was sad, and fierce like a little tiger cub when he was angry.

Thinking about him fueled Hoss to storm inside the International to find and maybe even strangle this van Remus with his bare hands.

CHAPTER 25

Ben stroked Joe's forehead as Adam stared out the 2nd story window into the afternoon sky. Life used to be so simple, Adam thought as he looked out over the Ponderosa. They had their share of problems over the years but so far had come out on top, with luck along with sweat, fast thinking and plain common sense. Now it felt like they were running in slow motion, unable to think or act.

Adam couldn't feel the pain in his back, just a dull, listless ache that told him to do something or die. He killed a woman, a mother, and maybe she didn't belong there but knowing that didn't bring her back or ease Joe's pain. And now they were stuck inside, wondering when the next blow would be dealt and would they see it in time to duck. Adam rubbed the back of his neck. All because of boy's fear.

Pa hadn't said a word since hearing that over forty acres of timberland was in danger of being over-timbered, leading to erosion and even of the worst disaster, a landslide — making land an eyesore and an inhuman waste of God's good nature for as long as a decade, or more. He couldn't stand seeing Pa looking whipped. He has always strong, standing off crowds of angry people with nothing more than words, counter-moving the cleverest enemy with barely a glancing thought, not getting ruffled, riled but not loose-headed.

Pa never made a secret that he did everything for them, but now his sons could end up being the undoing of the land they all worked so hard for. Now Hoss was out there trying to save the land and would end up dead in the process. Why did Pa just sit there? Has he realized that having three sons was two or even three sons too many?

Adam remembered his pa making a wrong choice when sheepherders tried to cross their land. He admitted to Adam later what the right path had been and made his apologies easily. He knew he had another thing or two to learn and taught his sons to admit their shortcomings as well. Now Pa was neither wrong nor right—he was stymied. Ben had tried to take the guilt from his son to himself, even while realizing it couldn't be done. Pa's guilt in this—the reason Winnie had been

158

there that day—he would have to deal with on his own. But Adam had to keep Hoss from getting hurt or die trying.

Adam suddenly understood the feeling—like everything he ever thought of himself had been tossed down a deep dank well, and he either had to crawl down there and get it back or live the rest of his life as less than human. He could admit his mistakes. He could also do something about them. "Pa, I'm going to stop him." Adam strode away from the window.

"You're not going anywhere." Ben grabbed his arm. "You can't."

"Oh yeah? And how are you going to stop me, huh? Forbid me? Send me to my room? How about putting a bullet to my back?"

"Now Adam, that was uncalled for."

"There's no other way to deal with this, to help Hoss, to save the land. You just sit here like a whipped pup! That doesn't settle anything."

"We can't just run into this, Adam, it has to be planned---."

"What did you do to van Remus, huh? What kind of claim did he have that you kept from him? Gold? Did he find gold?"

"It seems so inconsequential now. You know how Sutter felt about life he established in the valley. Van Remus's claim of gold would have ruined everything, as Marshall's discovery did. People were streaming up the Oregon Trail to the Northwest and Sutter wanted to keep them headed that way instead of to California. He was happy with just a trickle of settlers."

"He ruined everything himself, didn't he?"

Ben thought about this, and grunted. "Sutter felt every reason to believe his secret would be kept, as it has been as Mexican territory for decades, even centuries.[10] Yes, he simply forgot his land was now American territory."

---

[10] Tales abound of gold being taken out by first the Spanish and then the Mexicans. For an example see J. Frank Dobie, Coronado's Children (Reprint Services Corp., 1930).

Adam staggered, suddenly tired, to the settee and sat. "Conquering a nation can be nasty business."

"I can still remember the last time I saw Sutter, just before the war ended in '48. New Helvetia was starting to thrive, with more laborers, more trade goods, and he still had control of it all. Sutter earned what he had honestly. He valued what he had, and he lost a lot."

"More valued than family?" Adam saw Ben's quizzical look. "You told me he left his family behind in Europe to come here and start over.[11] Maybe if you didn't have your sons, you'd be better off now."

"Now that's nonsense and you know it. That land that we kept from van Remus---."

"Was full of gold. Was it the land Marshall later built the sawmill on?" In the long silence between them Ben only nodded. "So now I know how you got the money for all this land here, huh?"

"You know better than that, son."

With shaking hands Adam reached out to stand. "I only know that because of me---."

"Mr. Cartlight!" Hop Sing ran out of the kitchen waving a letter. "I found note in pants of Mr. Joe. You lead. You lead light now."

Ben grabbed the paper and looked up at Adam. "It's from him." He looked at Hop Sing. "You found this in what Joe was wearing when he was stabbed?"

"Getting leady to clean. Mr. Joe allays leave things in pocket."

"This could be the break we're looking for, Adam. Something to pin on van Remus." Ben read quickly.

"He seems too clever to make a mistake like that." Adam watched Ben's hopes diminish as he read, and took the letter to read himself.

---

[11] "Sutter's Fort," State Historic Monument, State of California Division of Beaches and Parks, May 1968, 5-7.

"Out loud, Adam. I want to see if it sounds as bad when you read it."

Dear Ben. I am sorry to hear about the accident your son Adam suffered. As you know I'm living in Virginia City, and wanted to ride out personally to extend my condolences but my health has been poor of late. I suffer from headaches that prevent me from doing anything too strenuous, so I remain here in the city, mostly secluded in my room unless business draws me out. Your kind son Joe here has offered to arrange a get-together for the two of us at your ranch but I regret I must decline.

However, I would enjoy having dinner with you, say this Friday evening? I will make reservations for the two of us at the International for 6 p.m., and we'll be able to catch up on old times. I know our old times weren't always good, but I believe in water under the bridge. I'm going to send this letter off with your son to take home, and I would hate to see anything **happen** to him, so I will send him off with a hasty **adieu** so that he may get home before an **accident** befalls him as well.

Ben, you and I are both prospering, and time will tell which of us will come out ahead of the game, but I wish you only the best of all. Sincerely, Clete van Remus.

Adam took another moment to study the letter. "Seems some of the words are darker. Still, there's nothing here but what we read into it." He folded the letter back up.

"You're right. He is too clever to be caught that way." Ben paused. "Say, isn't today Friday? I think I'll keep that dinner appointment."

Adam waved the letter at Ben. "This letter is a trick. Be on your guard."

"Count on it." Ben hesitated. "Adam, promise me you won't do anything foolish. Wait until you hear from me."

Adam pursed his lips. "What about Hoss?"

"Hoss knows the danger, and I don't think Clete expects to see him out yet. He does expect me tonight." Ben grabbed his hat but his frown deepened as he looked back at Adam, still dissatisfied. "I'll get Roy to send deputies out to that section to rescue Hoss as soon as I get to town. Now you rest!"

"I don't know if I can. It hurts to stay here, Pa."

"Joe needs you."

"So does Hoss." Adam collapsed back onto the settee, hiding his face with his hand but not the trembling he couldn't control.

Ben ached to pull the pain from inside Adam's chest but felt as helpless as his boy did to do anything more than re-live it. "You had a reasonable fear, Adam. When you came out of the shock after the stampede, you were no longer afraid. There is one thing you might not remember about the day Inger was shot."

Adam took a deep breath and looked up, nodding. "Go on."

"That day Inger died. They came after us because one of ours killed one of theirs. Vengeance. I won't try to condone it, not in them or in Van Remus. We had to defend our own, whether we wanted to or not. After Inger died, the fellow they wanted gave himself up to them. Walked out there alone and let them kill him. Bravest thing I ever saw. Adam, her death, like her life, stood for something special. And it taught me the value of doing the right thing right off. Instead of hiding behind some kind of misguided loyalty."

"Like with Sutter?"

Ben looked at Adam, surprised. "My loyalty to Sutter. Hmmmph. Did you know he wanted to treaty with the Indians himself for the land his gold was on, without involving the government?[12] He knew what would happen to them, what wouldn't happen if he kept the land. We had a common interest, that of protecting the land. I still have that, and you do too, son."

---

[12] Lewis, 150-151.

After a moment of silence Adam drew himself to full height as though he'd never been shot and stared at the door. "You better go."

Ben put his hat on and left. As he mounted, he looked back at the house. Adam has been through hell and back. But was he back? Ben had the eerie feeling he may have lost a son after all.

CHAPTER 26

As Hoss knocked on Van Remus's door the alarm sounded, a piercing pipe whistle followed by the shouts of men running through the streets of Virginia City.

Hoss knew what it meant. Cave-in.

Hoss turned back toward the stairs just as Van Remus burst through his door and ran down ahead of him. After a moment's hesitation, Hoss followed. He didn't appear as villainous as Hoss expected. Hoss didn't know him by sight but there was something familiar about his smell and about the way he stumbled down the stairs, like a bat that nearly bumps into things to find his way around but just misses, by sense rather than sight.

In the street alarmed voices announced the collapse. "Cave-in at the Golden Cross!"

"Damn those spindly pine timbers!" Clete stumbled into his buggy as he missed the step-up, finally righted himself and rode off.

Hoss leaped on Ferguson's horse and followed. Word was Clete had been asking for trouble. The Golden Cross had become the deepest in the Comstock, the most ambitious, and also one of the wettest. Hoss heard about a man over in California who worked on strengthening the timbering in the mines and wondered if the man had ever been sent for. The fellow's name was something long and complicated, reminding Hoss of the way safely timbering the mines would be if they ever wanted to go deep enough to find that bonanza they keep talking about. From what he heard about mining, the pay streak had them going in circles, each owner finding a streak of the vein and believing he would find the mother lode, only to hit another dead end.

Clete stood outside the mineshaft watching the rescue activity as Hoss rode up. Hoss jumped off his horse and strode up to him. "Scus'em me, but you be need'n a hand? I got me a strong one, ya, and can lend."

Still frowning, Clete glanced his way. "I'm sure you do, immigrant, but it's dangerous down there. Think you can handle it?"

"I been told you hiring loggers, and I was gonna ask you for hiring me, when you dashed out. I help you, perhaps you hire me, yah?"

Clete cocked an eyebrow. "See if they got room for more diggers."

The entryway to the shaft was cleared again as two more men were pulled out. One was exhausted from the digging and the other, handled with more care, seemed dead until they laid him on the ground and he coughed.

"Easy with him, boys." Clete went to the injured man's side, speaking soft.

Hoss went to the shaft to go down. Could they be wrong about Van Remus? Maybe there was a different quarrel against them that they didn't know about. That memory of Adam's could be just that, with no more meaning than the dreams that ran through his mind at night. Hoss descended into the depths of the dark mine shaft.

Many men have soft spots in one section of their heads and tough ones in another. Van Remus must be like that. Adam was shot and Little Joe knifed. All trails ended here, that felt as sure to him as his feet touching the wet floor of the mine. They needed proof, and Hoss planned to find it as well as causing a shut-down to the logging camp.

Voices came from somewhere below him. His face grew moist and cool as he kept his head low through the candlelit mine, his feet sloshing through the ankle-deep river running through the tunnels. The line of wet running up higher on the walls meant an erratic water level. These poor fellows never knew what to expect.

As his hand scraped the wall, soft crumbling stone gave way under his fingers. The soft rock did not hold up well under the digging and blasting, making cave-ins a regular occurrence. He heard shovels scraping ahead as men tried to rescue others, the sound a sad melody to trapped miners. More lights flickered ahead and the shadows of arms throwing rocks reflected on the walls as men dug over the collapsed area.

"You use strong arm here, ya?" When Hoss got down on his knees, he recognized Jake, a former Ponderosa drover. He concentrated to force a dopey expression back on his face.

"Yeah, hurry on and dig in, we got three more miners missing yet, maybe more. Put those big arms and shoulders of yours to work." Jake stared at Hoss before sticking the tip of his own shovel back in. They dug faster and finally found a booted foot.

***

Jake took the body of Al Fister up with the help of Lem, busted up on one side but able to hold himself up. Jake laid Al to the ground as Lem just fell sideways, dropping Al, but it didn't matter to Al anymore because he was dead.

Clete ran over to them. Al had been the best friend he'd made since coming to this overblown, dirty city. He fell to his knees, straddling the dead man. Just last week he and Al were trading stories of back east and drinking beer in the Silver Dollar. Now Al was dead, in a cave-in he never expected to happen.

"Where is that Dutchman from California anyway?" Clete shouted as he looked around. "I thought McEnroy sent for him."

"They hadn't even been working in the weaker section," Jake said.

"It is now." Clete watched as the two boys who worked for the undertaker covered Al and put him in their makeshift wagon. "Take it easy, boys. He deserves respect!"

"Mr. Van Remus, who's the new fellow you sent down?" Jake knelt to help Jim tie a splint on to Stu's leg.

"The big Swede? He's looking for work as a logger." Clete watched old Stu get his leg tended. He had thought about firing old Stu. Now Al's dead and he still has Stu to fire. Yankees, he loses. Those immigrants never die.

"Well, he's good, I'll give him that. He seems familiar, that's all."

166

Clete squinted up at Jake, his pounding head blurring his already poor vision. Were they talking about Stu? Or Al? "Oh, the Swede. Forget about using him, I'm needing loggers."

When Hoss made it top ground he had a job waiting for him. He shook Clete's hand with as much vigor as he could muster, being as drenched and tired as the rest of them. "I do tank you! You send me where you want. I work hard, sir!"

"I won't be sending you off until we're finished here." Clete ignored the way Jake stared hard at Hoss as he went back down. Now this Swede he could work to death without any qualms, and he nearly told Jake so, but then Jake seemed to lose all interest.

As the last to leave the Golden Cross for the day, Clete took stock. Three dead, seven injured, one not accounted for, four able to walk. Work had ceased and all of this would come out of his pocketbook. The third shift offered to come in but Clete thought of a new purpose for the unstable section. Gopher left word where he could be found when Clete figured out what to do with the sheriff. He just figured it out.

CHAPTER 27

Ben felt itchy in the saddle. No matter how fast he got his buckskin going, he couldn't get it going fast enough. Sometimes Hoss seemed invincible, but he could be felled — and maybe even more easily because of his trusting nature. One thing Ben knew for sure, though. Hoss wouldn't let Van Remus know he was a Cartwright. Had to be what Joe did, not knowing what he was up against.

Clouds lingered in the sky that spoke of snow, a cool tone of regret for the passing season, but Ben didn't notice the chill. His sons lingered strong in his mind. Adam, for the pain in his mind worse than his back; Hoss, who felt he alone could save the trees; and Joe, who may never wake again and if he does, his mind may be partially lost.

Even as a youngster, Joe always had a quick mind. Life hasn't been dull from the moment he was born screaming and kicking. He wouldn't settle down much after being born, no matter how much talking Ben and Marie did to soothe him. When Hoss was born, he cried lustily but when he heard Inger's voice quieted right down. And Adam, Ben remembered the boy seemed able even as an infant to quiet himself down, as though all he had to do even as a baby was think through his problems. Could he have sensed, even then, that his mother was dying? Ben didn't put anything past the strong mind his eldest was born with.

Joe has been making noise in one way or another ever since, until now. Once when Joe was about nine and his brothers went off to bring in the young beef from the hill to be branded, Joe insisted he was old enough to bring in cows, too. Ben told him no, but Joe snuck off anyway. An hour after his brothers got back, Joe showed up leading a small stray with a sloppy rope around its neck. He stayed hidden from Hoss and Adam and got one of the cows that had strayed from their herding. He was late, he reasoned to his Pa, because he had to let the scrawny calf eat. Later in bed he admitted he was scared when he got a rope around the calf and looked up to find no sign of his brothers anywhere. He mostly let the calf lead him back.

And Ben realized, with a sharp inhale of breath, what had bothered him about the stampede being caused by his son. Adam knew full well, even at that age, how to instinctively behave around cattle. Could something else have caused the stampede? But what?

A buggy bounced down the trail from the city. When the woman sitting next to the driver stood and waved, Ben sighed impatiently and pulled up rein. "Good afternoon, Mrs. Jacobs, nice to see you." Inwardly he groaned. Everyone in town except maybe one or two newcomers knew her friendliness toward Ben. As the town's most prominent widow, as well as active church volunteer, townsfolk figured that she planned to get Ben to the altar sooner or later.

"Mr. Cartwright, what a coincidence. I'm having Charlie drive me to your ranch."

"I'm not there, so perhaps we could take up our business in town."

"No, no, Mr. Cartwright, going to your ranch is my business."

Ben frowned. "It is? Oh! Did John. . .Dr. Jessup send you out?"

"That's right. Ben, when I heard about your troubles I just wept. I am only too glad to help out your boys so you can get out there and settle things." She leaned toward him. "I knew you'd want me to hurry before that Miss Bulette came out here. You know how she is when she catches wind of something." She winked. "Are you going to town now? Of all times?"

"Yes, I really do have to. . .to settle things. But you have Charlie get you to the house, and Hop Sing will help you. . .ah. . .settle in."

"I'll be fine, Ben, you just go ahead. But you will be back for supper, won't you? I brought all the ingredients for a nice custard pie." Her large face spread out in an enormous grin as she reached back to show him the box she packed.

"Oh no, I have a dinner engagement. I might stay the night in town."

"Oh, I hope it won't come to that." Her small brown eyes wrinkled even more as she sent a toothy smile at him. "I'll plan on seeing you

169

tonight. And don't you worry about your boys. They're in good hands now." She put her hand on her bonnet, flattening it some as Charlie nodded at Ben and flicked the reins to the horse.

Ben waved as the buggy rode past. "Thank you, John," he said to the peaked afternoon sky.

He kicked the horse fast as he dared to reach the top of Sun Mountain and Virginia City, bringing thoughts of the coming confrontation back into his mind. Gut instinct was fine most times. But having a sound scheme made him less edgy. He needed every advantage now to stay on the right side of the law in smoking out the truth from a vengeful varmint. This time staying on the right side didn't feel possible. He wondered, however, if Adam would agree.

***

Hoss met Van Remus outside the Silver Dollar where three other loggers waited. A livery boy brought four fresh horses and hitched them to the rail. Goods for the camp and extra supplies were strewn on the ground. Hoss watched, still saddled, as the men followed orders to pack the saddlebags. As Hoss eyed them he knew he wouldn't trust any of them further than he could reach his arm without leaning. A combination of seeing his brothers nearly dead and these clothes, he knew, made him feel pretty nasty toward his fellow man right now.

Van Remus gestured for him to come get a horse but Hoss shook his head. "Mine goot horse," he said, pointing to his mount. Van Remus took some money back out of the livery boy's hand and sent him back with one horse and money enough for the other three.

Hoss listened carefully to the instructions Van Remus dished out. Pa and his brothers at times made fun of what they called his concentrating powers. When it came to something like this, he had no problem following along. Van Remus sent them to Cartwright land like he had the perfect right. He stepped forward at one point, a gut reaction to anger but kept his voice low. "This land gots lot of strong timber and rights to wood yours so, yah?"

Clete squinted at Hoss. "Now why would you ask a question like that, immigrant? Maybe you should just take your good horse and go back the way you came."

"Ah no, forgive, boss, I been in trouble with hang'n law, don't want no trouble on no account getting in wrong, is all." Hoss paused, scratching his chin. "Less'n of course da money is gooder dan what you say before."

Clete laughed loudly. "Spoken like a true Swede. Don't worry, I've got our ground covered." He waved to the horses. "Day is getting short. Go off with you, you'll get the rest of the instructions from the four already cutting."

The most amiable-looking fellow of the bunch in the heavy black shirt appeared to have been given the lead of the four as he jumped on the sprightliest horse and took off. A couple miles from Virginia City they turned off the main road. They were going to cross onto Ponderosa land the back way, the cheating, lying thieves.

Hoss adjusted in the saddle and really forced the happy stupid grin back on his face. Anger will come in handy soon enough.

***

Ben rode up into the city, images of Norma chasing through his mind. Norma with a rag dusting off the rifles, Norma knocking Hop Sing aside to make her pies, Norma rearranging his desk while watching the clock tick the hours until Ben would ride back to the ranch. He wondered how Adam was handling her. His eldest was usually levelheaded, but a romantic whirlwind like her could knock the steam out of a jackrabbit. And in Adam's present mood, any disturbance could set him off. If it weren't for the need to meet up with Van Remus.

When he alighted in front of the International, Ben strapped his gun belt to his leg and walked inside. Hoss's best protection would be in getting Van Remus in jail.

"Ah, Ben, good to see you." Vince stepped away from the counter as though Ben might lunge for his neck, as he nearly did last time.

171

"Where's Van Remus?"

"Uh, Ben, if you're looking to start something---."

"Where is he, Vince?" Ben planted his fists on the counter.

"Did something happen to Little Joe?"

"You could say that. You know where Van Remus is or don't you?"

"Was at the Silver Dollar, but probably back over to the Golden Cross cleaning up. They had a collapse."

"A collapse." Bent felt his impatience cave as his anger grew. Nothing like a disaster for a town to rally around a fella. "Serious?"

"Serious enough as they go."

Ben stepped back outside in the fading Nevada sunshine. Cave-ins wait for no man's dinner. Ben could almost believe that Van Remus would collapse a mine deliberately just to gain town sympathy.

That meant playing this dinner close and careful, just when he was ready to draw some blood himself.

CHAPTER 28

Adam slept on the settee, legs on the floor and arm over his face. He fell asleep nearly immediately after Ben rode off. The buggy rattled and squeaked as it pulled up outside, but Adam didn't wake until Hop Sing came down from tending Joe and shook his shoulder. "Mr. Adam?" He had to shake for a good minute before getting a stir. "Mr. Adam!?"

Finally Adam grunted and frowned. "Huh? What?"

"Sorry, Mr. Adam. Buggy in yard."

"Ah, Pa?"

"No. I go see who. You go up to loom to bed."

"It's okay, I can handle this." He sat up, his eyes still shut. As Hop Sing watched, Adam pressed his hand against his temple, forcing himself awake. He stood as if drawn by a sudden thought to instant alertness.

Outside he saw Charlie from the livery in town helping Norma Jacobs down from the buggy. "Adam! My goodness, what are you doing out of bed?"

"What do you want here?" His head throbbed but his back felt surprisingly numb.

"My goodness, Mr. Cartwright, such a greeting. Dr. Jessup sent me to help out. Perhaps you don't approve but your father does, and I'm sure your little brother might not mind either."

"Of course. I apologize." Adam turned to Charlie. "Leave your bill at our box in town, Charlie, Pa will take care of it there. He may be staying in town until he gets matters settled." After waving Charlie off, he picked up her satchel.

Norma grabbed his arm and her bag and guided him to the door. "Don't worry about my things. Dr. Jessup didn't send me out here to be a frail female."

"I don't want to be rude," Adam gently removed her hand from his arm. "But I don't need smothering. Save your fussing for Little Joe." He opened the door and guided her inside.

"My, you are not a very good patient. Ah, it is so good to be back in this lovely house."

"I'll show you to a room."

Norma hesitated when she saw the fire-damaged guest room. "Not there, I hope." She shook her head as she examined the damage. "I'll bet there's a story here." She looked hopefully at Adam.

"We have a small spare upstairs you can use. It's not as comfortable as that one. Well, more now, I guess." He received a light tittering laugh in return and winced.

Hop Sing appeared at the top of the stairs and Adam waved him back. Hop Sing shrugged and went back to sit with Joe.

"You should be bedridden, young man, from what John told me. Your face is pale."

Adam stormed to the stairs. "I told you I'm fine." He glanced back over his shoulder. "Are you coming or not?" He slowly climbed the stairs.

"I'd ask you to change your tone, young man, if I thought you'd mind me." Resigned, she followed him up the stairs.

She put her bag in the room he showed her and followed him inside Joe's room. "Oh, look at him, sleeping so peaceful. It just isn't natural for him to be so still, is it?"

Adam took Joe's hand, squeezing hard. "Joe, it's me. Can you hear me? Come on now, you can wake up. Come on, try hard."

"Oh, Adam," Norma sighed heavily and smoothed bed linen around Joe's feet. "I know how you feel, but he can't hear you. My, he just doesn't look natural lying there, does he? Why don't you lie down? I'll call you if there's a change."

Hop Sing got to his feet. "Nice to see you, Miss Norma. Must go to cook now."

"Hop Sing? Would you be so kind as to not use that weird spice I taste on everything when I come to parties? It's the only thing I ask, normal cooking while I'm here."

Hop Sing stared at her a moment. As he shuffled down the stairs he let loose a row of Chinese admonishments, and Adam dropped his head, hiding the first laugh he'd felt in a while.

"Adam?" Joe, groggy, squinted up at him. "Adam?"

Startled and alarmingly thrilled, Adam leaned close. "Joe, doggone it, boy, how you feeling? You're gonna be okay now."

"You're...alive. You...didn't die."

Adam laughed, squeezing Joe's hand. "I'm too stubborn and so are you. Damn, it's good to see you again, Joe." His heart pounded wild in his chest and his back felt like fire, but Joe was okay.

Joe looked at Norma smiling down at him, her grin as wide as Lake Tahoe. She can take all the credit she wanted, Adam thought, that was fine with him. "Who's that?"

"It's Norma, Joe, you remember her, don't you?" Adam frowned. Joe took reading lessons from her for several months.

"Oh, it's all right, sweetie," Norma said, patting his hand. "Give yourself a day or two. Seeing you bright-eyed is enough for now."

"Where's Pa?"

Adam cleared his throat. "He's gone to town to meet with Van Remus."

"Don't know why he tried to kill me. It's you they want. He said you killed his ma."

"His ma? Bret did this to you? Bret's in town with Van Remus?"

"Bret is worse than his father. Did this." He touched his bandage. "We fought fair until he pulled out the knife."

"I wonder if Pa remembers Bret. When boys are twelve, you don't see them as much of a threat." His words seared his throat. He knew one twelve-year-old who should have been tried and hung for murder.

"Clete kept his son secret. Told me because…because…"

"He had already planned this for you."

Joe swallowed hard, his eyes closing in pain. Adam sat him up gently and helped him swallow a little water. Joe looked up at him, eyes shining and mouth dripping water. "Adam? It's not true, is it? You didn't kill his ma. I told Bret you'd never do that."

Adam helped Joe get more comfortable, and looked over at Norma. "Could you leave us alone please?"

"Oh," she rubbed her hands, staring at the ceiling as though looking for an excuse to stay. "I could give Hop Sing a hand in the kitchen. He could use a woman's touch." She left but hesitantly, with a lingering look back at the two of them.

"Are you tired, Joe? Do you want to rest for a while?"

But Joe seemed even more alert. "Don't leave me, Adam."

"I don't want to wear you out, so let me know when you need to rest."

"Sure. Adam, you look bad. What happened?"

"I'm not sure. . .where to begin. I used to fear Indians."

"Oh. It's okay, Adam, a lot of people do. You'll get over it."

176

"No, Joe, I don't anymore." Adam hesitated. Joe's forgotten more than just faces. "I caused a stampede because I ran into the herd thinking Indians were chasing me. No one else saw them."

"Hooo, bet that made Pa mad."

Adam sat down. "The woman, Bret's mother, stood between the cattle and the holding pen and no one knows why. The cows. . .killed her." He leaned back. "Bret rightly blames me for her death."

"Sounds like an accident, Adam. We don't deserve to be killed on account of it."

Adam smoothed out Joe's messy hair. "Well, you don't, anyway." He frowned as he sat back. "I don't know how to make up for all this, but I have to, somehow."

"You'll figure it out, Adam. You always do. Where's Hoss?"

"Hoss." Adam peered out the window into the yard but the answer he hoped for wasn't there. "He's doing your chores. You get some more sleep." Adam turned for the door.

"Where's Pa?"

"You're awful nosey for just coming out of a coma." He smiled. "Pa has a dinner engagement. With Mr. van Remus."

"Is he gonna be all right, Adam?"

Adam strode to the door. "Of course he will, younger brother. They're just going to talk. Pa isn't sure of anything yet. He will be though, when he talks to you. I'm going to send Norma up, all right? There are some things I have to tend to. You take care and get your rest."

"Adam? They still want to kill you, they don't care it was an accident."

Adam nodded. "I know. But Pa and I are going to make sure they don't get any more chances. You can bet on that."

Joe saw the firmness of Adam's jaw as he left the room. "Oh, I do, brother. I always bet on a Cartwright." His eyes closed again.

At the bottom of the stairs Adam saw Norma and Hop Sing conferring at the dining table but turned his attention to the burning embers in the fireplace, his mind racing. Pa could send a bunch of men out after Hoss, but they don't know the land like he does. Or Kudwa. Kudwa knows where those men are.

He picked up a poker but just as suddenly put it down again. "Norma, would you go look in on Joe?"

"My pleasure, Adam." She scurried up the stairs.

Adam cleared any etchings of pain from his face with angry impatience before turning to Hop Sing. "Pack me some food, Hop Sing."

"Mr. Adam not foolish, Mr. Adam know better than to leave with pain in back."

"You reading the stars again, Hop Sing? Maybe you can tell me why you let Hoss go, huh?"

Hop Sing waved a ladle at him, speaking rapid Chinese anxiously.

"Look, Hop Sing, I know trying to stop Hoss is like trying to stop a runaway steer. But you won't have any more luck with me. So either pack some food for me or let me go hungry."

"Mr. Adam not thinking. Not like Mr. Adam."

"I don't want to argue with you!" He took a heavy breath. "Make enough food for two. I'll get Kudwa to help me." He put a hand on the small man's shoulder. "I have to help Hoss. You know that, right?" Hop Sing's eyes glistened. He shook his head and shuffled off to the kitchen. Adam watched as he picked up his chopping blade and whacked away at an onion. "You know, for a house servant, you're not very obedient."

Hop Sing whirled on him, cursing loudly in Chinese, waving his knife.

Adam held up a hand to ward off the Chinaman and rubbed his temple. "Wait. You know I don't mean that. I'm not. . .I'm just angry right now, Hop Sing. You understand?"

"Mr. Adam always control anger. Not like Mr. Adam."

"Will you stop?!" He pressed his hand over his eyes briefly. "Joe told me some things that Pa doesn't know yet. If I don't get out there and warn him, Pa and Hoss could end up even worse off than me or Joe."

"Little Joe wake?"

"That's right. Two people are gunning for us, Hop Sing, not just one. That puts Hoss in even bigger trouble. You see now?"

Hop Sing clasped his hands together and lifted them skyward, muttering a Chinese prayer. "Mr. Hoss only say cattle drive. I not believe."

"Don't be hard on yourself, Hop Sing. Hoss and I both have to do what we feel is right. You've always trusted our instincts. Hoss has gone to stop men from destroying some prime timber country on the Ponderosa. I told him. . ." he swallowed hard. "It was a good idea. I'll find him, Hop Sing. I have to keep one very big tree from being felled."

"You be all right, Mr. Adam? You sure?"

Adam took a deep breath and affected a deep reassuring tone despite the stinging in his head. "I'm fine, Hop Sing. You know I heal quick."

Within ten minutes Adam was ready to go with the food Hop Sing prepared.

"When Mr. Cartlight come, what I say?"

"You won't have to say anything. Pa will know." Adam belted on his gun and went out into the fresh pine air, just as the sun kissed the tops of the Sierras overlooking Lake Tahoe on its way to bed for the night.

CHAPTER 29

"Ben! Nice to see you in town! How's Joe?"

Ben stepped out of the International in time to see John Jessup's buggy heading up the street. Jessup veered toward him and Ben could see he was out on another call, his doctoring bag on the seat.

Ben shook Jessup's hand warmly. "Are you catching up on calls?"

"Been a mild autumn so far, 'til today. Joe come around?"

"No, but ah, Adam and I had a disagreement so I felt it best to get away for a while. Thanks for sending the help, by the way. You couldn't find anyone besides Norma, I suppose."

Jessup laughed. "I knew Norma would drop everything for you." He leaned forward, looking more tired than Ben expected. "Did you hear about the cave-in? I got to get to the social hall, there's injured miners, a couple dead, rest with some broken bones, from what they said. Take care of yourself, Ben. I got my prayers in for Little Joe."

"Thanks, John." Ben watched the buggy kicking dust down the road. He recognized an odd feeling of jealousy, of not wanting Dr. Jessup to wear himself out on others, and scolded himself.

But sight of the doctor stirred up new and immediate concern for his sons. He practically ran to the sheriff's office. "Roy!" he bellowed as he threw open the door.

Clem finished washing mine dirt off his face in the bowl Roy kept in the back. He grabbed a towel and went into the office. "Ben! I hear Little Joe's ailing and Adam's dead!"

"No, they'll both be. . .I mean, he's. . .they're. . .Let's keep it between us until we corner whoever's causing the trouble. Little Joe, too."

"Little Joe's dead? Now I never heard---."

"No, it's better people thinking he's. . ." At Clem's puzzled expression Ben grimaced. "Sorry, Clem, I don't have time to relate a three-day saga. Where's Roy?"

"Don't know, I was gonna ask you if you'd seen him."

"You don't know where Roy is!?"

Clem puffed up his chest like a cock. "Now, Mr. Cartwright, you know Roy has plenty of capable deputies to look out for the town and I'm one of them. If Roy has business elsewhere, I suspect it's his business. Not mine, or yours."

"Roy would never take off without leaving word with someone."

"Well, maybe. Truth is, I came to see him early this afternoon and he was already gone. So I just put my badge on myself. Don't know what to do though. I'm getting kinda hungry for supper."

Ben leaned on Roy's desk, his knuckles white as he gripped the wood. He felt quite ready to grab someone's neck, and it could be nearly anyone about now. "I gotta find him."

"Tell you what, Ben, I'll leave a message that you need to see him, in case he stops back in yet tonight."

Ben stepped back outside. Clem was a good man, but heaven help the town if something happened to Roy. He had a half hour before 6:00. With a resolve weakened by fear for Hoss's life, he jumped on his horse and rode through town, stopping everyone to ask after a missing sheriff.

***

Bret made himself comfortable in the lobby of the International as the clock chimed 6:00. Ben walked through, his gaze falling on Bret briefly and passing over. Eighteen years can do wonders, Bret thought, to a child's appearance as well as a man's disposition. He waited until Ben was comfortably seated at a table with a beer.

"Excuse me, are you waiting for Mr. van Remus? He sent me to send his apologies as he's been delayed a few minutes. Trouble in the mine, you know."

"Thank you." Ben's eyes narrowed as he studied Bret. "I heard."
"He asked me to tell you he hoped you checked your firearm at the front desk. Though I didn't ask him why." Bret remained cool under Ben's harsh scrutiny. "If you'll excuse me---."

"Well, he can forget it. As if I'd trust him past yesterday."

Bret took a deep breath and sat, facing him straight. "Excuse me, I know it's wrong to question a man's business, but you seem angry. I am Clete's business associate only so he doesn't fill me in on his personal affairs, but you look like a man holding a grudge. Mr. Van Remus is a decent man, a good employer."

Ben leaned toward Bret, studying him. "Decent? That's a good one." Ben finished his assessment of the young man and sat back. "You don't fit the image of a business associate."

Bret got to his feet. "Never pays to hold preconceived images of people. Came straight from San Francisco where I studied law like my pa …" He coughed. "…always wanted me to."

Ben held up a hand. "No offense intended. Answer me a question, since you have legal knowledge." He drained his beer. "A man can't be charged with murder if there was no proof he did the killing or paid to have it done, even if everyone in town knew that he had it in for the dead man, am I right?"

"That's pretty straight. I'd say words don't kill, or even emotion. Without a witness or statement of fact or some other hard evidence, you don't have much case. You being accused?"

"No."

"You're Mr. Cartwright, aren't you? I'm only thinking you must be because of what I been hearing in town. Seems they've been saying two sons have been killed. This true?"

"I wouldn't know. You've got me confused with someone else."

After a pause Bret left him alone. He walked into the lobby and kicked the richly upholstered bench seat. Vince looked up with a frown so Bret walked outside. "Cartwright thinks he's so smart. Just wait til I show him." He stopped when he saw his father coming down the walk. "Cartwright is in an ugly temper. He won't check his gun."

Clete pulled Bret away from door, his voice low. "You introduced yourself?"

"Yeah, you should know better than to hire a stupid associate!" He jerked his arm away. "Seems to think he's going to trip you up somehow. You better watch your step."

"Go amuse yourself, Bret. I've got work to do." Clete strode inside the hotel.

"Oh yeah? Well, I just might not be around when you get done."

Clete stopped at the sound of Bret's voice and turned around but he couldn't see his son's face much beyond a blur. He walked back to Bret and spoke with his voice low. "Now, look, son, you know what we've worked for."

"I'm not your son!"

"What?" Clete glanced around but didn't see anyone close enough to hear them. "Now, son, we don't always have to---."

"I'm not your son." Bret walked into the street. "You'll have to hire yourself someone else to do the job. I'm only your associate."

Clete followed him into the street. "Bret, wait. Let's talk about this."

Bret didn't stop. Clete watched as the son he knew, the only family he had, the boy who became a man almost overnight, disappeared into the saloon. He wondered if the boy knew how his father really felt about him, how all those nights when the boy cried himself to sleep for his mother Clete cried with him. How he ached when the boy was at school and only felt safe when he knew Bret was close by. Did he ever tell him those things? They've been disassociating each other now for so long, they've forgotten what being a father and son felt like. He'll take Bret away from here, make them into a family again.

First, he had some business to attend to. Clete walked into the International, with every step regaining the nerve he needed to get the job done.

CHAPTER 30

On the trail from Virginia City east into Ponderosa territory the four loggers steered clear of each other. Hoss would admit to either of his brothers or his Pa at this moment how scared he was. There were a number of sections for timbering they could end up at on the north 40, any one of them already overcut from a recent contract. If this Van Remus wanted to destroy Pa in every way possible, like Adam says, then they're here for nothing more than to ruin the land, not because they need the timber but to make the area prime for landsliding.

Now he was set to stop them alone. He often felt he could stop several men at once, and was even put to the test once or twice, but seven men — with axes?

Hoss stopped briefly to gaze down the side of the cliff they skirted. Looking down into a crisscross of half fallen trees he could see the rocky terrain take another leap upward and divide off. Casting its light through this rocky divide the sun was nearly gone, giving a shine to the dullest granite rock and shadows to the pine needles.

As much as he loved the countryside, Hoss couldn't lose sight of his goal. He had to prove that Van Remus was behind this illegal lumbering, and that he wanted his brothers dead. Stopping the lumbering could be as hard as the proving. Above them the ground already showed signs of loosening, roots bursting through the hillsides and rocks tumbling down. Just a little push would shove this whole side of the mountain to tumbling down, tumbling until it rolled right over their ranch, with Adam and Joe unable to get out of the way.

"Hey, you, Swede! You def or sumptin?"

Hoss looked up at Claude pulling back on the reins to wait for him. "No, naw, fine ears, just tinking away."

"What's your name, anyhow?"

Felling of the Sons

"Name — aww, just call me Swede, I go by dis too."

"Ah-ha." Claude — Hoss wondered if that was his real name — peered suspiciously at him. "What you wanted for?"

"Not. . .huh?" Hoss scratched at his itchy beard.

"You talked about almost getting hanged before. If you got sumptin dishonest up your sleeve like a gun to rob us, you better just turn tail and git before we make the rope stick."

Hoss held up a hand. "Only here to make dollar for self any way I kin and to go on to Californee. No trouble dis one want."

"Yeah, sure."

Hoss let his horse drift behind them again. He'll cause 'em trouble, all right. But he'd better be dad-burned careful how he goes about it.

***

Ben looked up from his beer to see Clete van Remus standing in the dining room, still wearing the clothes he'd crawled from the mine in. Clete surveyed the room with his arms folded across his chest, his eyes narrow and his mouth set in a damnable tight-lipped grin, a grin Ben had seen years ago in his nightmares. Ben had stood Van Remus down the day he charged at the house with a gun after finding out the truth about the stampede, ready to take the bullet for Adam. Clete had pulled the trigger, not caring who he killed, but his aim had been way off. The way Clete handled the rifle that day made Ben think that he'd never handled one before and couldn't even see his target. And now there he was, squinting as he looked around the room.

When Ben caught Clete's eye and nodded, Clete walked closer before grinning broadly. He held out a hand. "Ben Cartwright! You old scoundrel! After all these years. I wasn't sure I would believe it even when I saw you."

Ben hesitated but shook Clete's hand. He let it go quickly, distaste crawling into his mouth. "It's been a long time, Clete. Sit down. We've got some catching up to do."

187

Clete's smile vanished as he sat across from Ben. "Catching up? Is that what we're calling it?" He looked into Ben's face, remembering the man from years back.

"What is this, Mr. Cartwright, the Inquisition? I merely staked my claim on a parcel of land, is all. I mean to homestead it and make a living." Clete backed up into his freshly painted doorway and felt the soothing presence of his wife Winnie behind him.

"Sutter has the right to sell or not sell any parcel to anyone as it pleases him. We've been watching you and we know what you plan to do. You're going to tell everyone about the gold here and see to it that the Americans take this land right out from under Sutter – you'll ruin all of Sutter's hard work by starting a stampede!"

"You have no right telling us what we plan to do, Mr. Cartwright." Winnie stepped in front of her husband and crossed her beauteous arms in front of her chest. "Is there something else on your mind?"

"Yes, there is." Ben thundered. "You two want to take everything Mr. Sutter worked for and turn it into dust."

"You've no proof of that," Clete whispered. "Why would we---."

"I don't know!" Ben shouted. "But I intend to stop you." He mounted his horse. "Even if I have to kill all of you to do it!"

Clete shook off his reverie. "You intend to accuse me of trying to kill your sons."

"Let's get one thing straight. This is your dinner party, not mine." Ben folded his napkin on his lap. "Why don't we order? I hate to talk business without some hot food in me."

Clete looked at the bill of fare in front of him. "I've had a tough day, Ben, let's forget business and keep this little meeting to the amenities, how are you, how has life treated you all these years, which from what I've heard, is damn well."

"Damn well." Ben didn't look up from the menu. "I've heard the same about you."

188

"Did you think you had that much influence over me in the old days?"

"What happened between the two of us was your doing." Ben let his finger trail down the list of items on the menu. "And for the record, we were never friends." Two of his sons almost died, the red blood oozing from their wounds filling his mind, and he wondered how he could have changed what happened so long ago.

"John, I don't know what more we can do, short of having them thrown in jail. They'll take that gold and tell everyone whether you give them the land or not." Ben faced Sutter at the small wooden table they ate at together after a morning in the field. They heard the galloping hooves of two horses and went outside.

Winnie van Remus rode up ahead of her husband Clete, a more cautious rider. "How dare you tell us we have no right?"

"Ma'am," John began, "this is my settlement by right of deed---."

"To a foolish Mexican name of Juan who doesn't exist! How long do you think that will stand up?"

"I am a Mexican citizen, Mrs. Van Remus, so it stands for today." Sutter sat back. "Is that what this is? A takeover by the American government? If you get title to that land you'll---."

"Don't you even try to accuse US of anything!" she screeched.

Ben caught Clete's eye as he rode up, and recognized the look on his face, the same as when the Russians laughed at him. "If that particular piece of land is set aside for another purpose, John has every right to deny you title."

"That's the piece we want!"

"What Winnie means," Clete began, "is that we have our heart set---."

"They heard me." She turned back to Ben. "Have you appointed yourself Mr. Sutter's bodyguard? Or should I say Senor Agosto?"

Sutter stepped forward. "I don't need protection, my dear. And Ben's right, I do have other plans for---."

"You let the Mexicans pan! What are you, anti-American? You, Ben? You denying your Yankee roots now? He's an immigrant but I would expect more from you."

"This is Mexican land, my dear. I answer to them here, not to the Americans. And you're forgetting that I allow anyone to settle here, regardless of their roots or how the Mexicans feel about it. I've given you the land I want you to farm."

"Think you can have everything your way, don't you? Dear gentlemen, watch your backs. I'm not easily crossed." She whipped her horse away, and after a moment, Clete followed.

"Do you know what it cost me?" Clete's voice broke into Ben's reverie.

"You could have backed off when you had the chance." Ben lowered his voice. "The land you had was prime property." To his ears their voices reverberated through the dining hall.

Clete lowered his menu. "We wanted that parcel and you killed Winnie to stop us from getting it."

"It was an accident!" Ben bit off the words, keeping his voice low. "Roast pork looks good to me. How about you?"

Clete threw his bill of fare down. "Cow meat, raw and throbbing, barely dead. Still kicking, as a matter of fact. Maybe just needs another bullet, this time to the head."

Ben looked up, his heavy brows furled. "Don't rile me, Clete. In my temper I could take you down in a second, right here, right now."

Clete smiled as Betsy came over to take their order. "The rawest meat you can find, my dear. With hot black coffee and plenty of sourdough. And a bottle or your best red wine so I can toast my old friend here."

Felling of the Sons

Ben gave his order and swallowed the rest of his beer. His throat had gone terribly dry. His sons lying in the ground covered with dirt was an overwhelming image that played with the strength he needed to stand on. "What do you want, Clete? After all these years?"

"I want what you took from me — my land and my wife. I want those 18 years back."

"You blamed fool. Make your demands within the reason of the day and the hour."

"Make me an offer. Say, the Ponderosa."

"For my sons' lives? You admit you tried to kill them?" Ben leaned back when Clete only smiled. "Do you know why Winnie came to see me the day of the stampede?"

The server girl delivered the wine and Clete poured them both a glass, the rich red liquid not pleasing to Ben's eye. Ben picked up his glass and studied the liquid, waiting for Clete's response.

"No. Do you?"

"Why don't I believe you?"

Clete took a heavy swallow of wine. "How did the stampede start?"

"It was an accident." Ben stared down into the wine, seeing the life of his boys in his hands. "I told you then and I'll tell you now. If you know more than that, then tell me. You think I stampeded the cows deliberate because I knew she was too foolish to get out of the way?"

"My wife was not foolish! She was intent. . ." Clete clamped his mouth shut and sat back.

"Intent on what?" Ben smiled as Clete looked away. "If she hadn't been foolish enough to think she was safe on that big horse of hers, we wouldn't be here now. So let's put the blame where it belongs. On foolish Winnie."

Clete stood, furious, heart pounding. "On your eldest brat cub!" With a furtive glance around the restaurant he sat again.

"Well. Now we both know. You knew all along how the stampede started and the attacks on my boys is vengeance for an *accident* eighteen years old."

"You can't prove that."

"Adam told me you threatened him when he was only twelve years old. He remembers, Clete, and he can convince the sheriff and even a jury how real that memory is."

"Won't stand up as evidence of anything."

"Evidence. You're clever with the law now, aren't you? But not clever enough. Because I know one more thing now than before. Before I only suspected you. Now I know it. And I'll tell you this. No one threatens my family and gets away with it."

The men plastered aching smiles on their faces as their platters of food were placed in front of them. The smell of Clete's red cow meat made Ben dizzy, freshening the image of newly dug graves in his mind. He tried to eat his well-cooked pork but the smell made him nauseous. Finally he leaned back and held his coffee in front of him. Clete ate like a vulture over a rotted corpse, like a wolf with no guilt over the killing of innocent life.

"Have you seen the sheriff today?"

Clete stopped in mid-bite and looked up. "No. Why would I? I'm not causing any trouble. I had a rough day, saving lives." He put a slow drawl on those last few words. He chewed hard and swallowed fast, punctuating his words with his fork after every bite. "You don't scare me, you know. I have the town's support and I have nothing more to lose. But you. . .you have plenty. You can try and kill me but I'll be sure to take at least one of your sons down with me. And that third wife of yours as a bonus." Clete shoved his last piece of red meat in his mouth, swallowing it almost whole. "In fact, maybe I should go after her next. I'm in a playful mood."

Felling of the Sons

Ben narrowed his eyes, studying his prey. He knew he should admit that Joe's wife has long since passed, but a sudden realization hit him. "Where's your son, Clete?" That young lawyer, Clete's associate …

"Took ill with the typhoid and died two years after my wife." Clete paused, staring down at his plate. "Damn near destroyed me."

Ben couldn't tell if this man was capable of telling the truth. "You have no right to take your grief out on my sons." He felt put off, just the same. He had been sure Clete did not know how the loss of a son felt.

"You want the truth, just between us?" Clete lowered his voice to a whisper. "I've hated you from the moment you set foot on my claim in Sacramento Valley to tell me I was trespassing. I've hated you and Sutter since you thought you had the right to keep it all to yourself. I've hated you, and those bastards you sired, and now it's a disease eating away my insides."

Ben leaned forward, stabbing his finger at Clete. "A moral man controls his hate and recognizes his own responsibility. I'll be watching you every minute, Clete. Step out of line, just once, and you'll be nailed faster than a squatter on a porcupine!"

"Without the sheriff?"

Ben sat back. "What do you know about Roy?"

Clete pushed his plate aside. "Only that you say he's missing. I practice law now, Ben. After I moved to San Francisco in '41, I vowed to get back at you one way or another. I've got you both ways, legally, because there is nothing you can prove against me, and I know it. And unethically, because you're still going to see every one of your sons die. They're sturdy, I'll give them that. But even a redwood can be felled. You will never take a safe breath again. Not until you're alone and the Ponderosa is mine. And not a soul overheard me say that to you." He stood, threw several coins down on the table, and left the dining room.

As Clete reached the door that led into the street, Ben grabbed his shoulder and turned him around. Clete's eyes went wide but he couldn't stop the blow aimed for his face, and on skin-splitting impact went flying through the door, over the walk and out into the street. As he struggled on his back in the dirt, he saw Ben charge at him. He reached inside his jacket and pulled out a gun too big for his inexperienced hands. He fumbled and aimed up at Ben, squinting.

Ben drew and shot it from his hand. "Still can't handle a gun, can you? Get up here and fight me, you coward. Or do you prefer men's backs? Come on!"

Clete got to his feet, swaying, holding the hand nicked by Ben's bullet. "You know I'm no match for you." He glanced around at the crowd that gathered. "Why don't you tell me straight what's eating you so we can talk civilized?"

"Civilized?!" Ben stormed over to Clete and delivered a clean right to his gut.

Clete dropped to his knees and vomited. The sight of the red meat coming back up eased Ben's temper a bit, as though Clete's loss of dinner loosened his grip on his sons.

Clem and another man grabbed Ben from behind. "That's enough, Ben, or I'll have to lock you up. You been drinking?"
 "Clem, you don't know him, he tried to kill two of my sons!"

Clem let him go. "You pressing charges, Ben? I'll throw him in jail."

Ben straightened his vest as sweat dripped into his eyebrows. "Not yet, Clem. I got to find Roy. You seen him yet?" Ben wanted to get Clete behind bars but without Roy, he wouldn't be there long.

"No, but I came across a note that says he's taken to his bed with the ague."

"I'll come have a look at it." They turned to walk to the sheriff's office.

"Hold on, deputy!" Clete's voice was gravely, thick with bile. "I'm pressing charges."

"For what?" Clem looked curiously between the two men.

Ben faced Clete down, his silence stronger than anything Clete could think of to say.

Clete sat back. "Ah, what the hell. Just a friendly quarrel, that's all. Ain't that right, Ben?"

Ignoring him, Ben followed Clem to the sheriff's office.

CHAPTER 31

Clete saw Ben walk away, like a cowboy who'd just squashed a snake with his horse's hoof. He rolled in the dusty street and grabbed the gun Ben had shot from his hand. He aimed it at Ben's back but the figure swayed and blurred until all Clete could see was Bret saying, "I'm not your son!" Clete squinted, forcing hate back into his veins, and squeezed the trigger but Ben seemed to dissolve into thin air, white and throbbing, and a stabbing bolt of lightning pain shot through his head. He screamed and fell backward and the shot fired harmlessly skyward. He tore at his hair as though hoping to pull the pain out by the roots.

Several drunken miners from the saloon ran over to Clete, including Reeger. Reeger stayed behind as two of the more ambitious helped Clete up.

"Mr. Van Remus, sir? Are you all right?"

With pain and the hate that engulfed him, Clete fought to get away, vaguely aware that employees of his were trying to help him instead of killing Cartwrights. "NO!" Clete jerked away. "Leave me be. Mind your own affairs." He staggered to the walk and collapsed in front of the International. When he saw Reeger Clete waved him over. "Got another task for you."

Reeger walked over, hesitant but respectful. "Whatever you say, boss. I count my blessings not being on the shift that got rocks on the head."

"I need you to follow Ben Cartwright."

"Now, sir? Follow him where?"

"Wherever. To his house if you have to. Find out his next move and report to me."

At first Clete thought that Reeger, that lowlife German, might argue with him. Finally, after Reeger's mouth worked soundlessly and he appeared to be guessing the time, he nodded, walked over to the sheriff's office and sat on the walk outside.

Clete noticed that the fervor around him had died down, although busy eyes in the street still paid their own business less mind than his. The International was only a few feet behind him, but with eyes on him, it might take him days to get back inside.

That gun. . .that gun in his hand, and he couldn't shoot Ben down.

"You have to let me do it, Winnie, you're a woman."

"You can't see more than two feet in front of you, Clete! How are you going to shoot Ben off a horse? He'll see you way before you see him." Clete had followed Winnie out to the horse's stall where she tried to brush him off by brushing her horse down. *"Those spectacles back east would have made a difference, but you were too stubborn. Vanity, thy name is Cletus."*

"I would recognize his horse."

"We can't take that chance. Besides, I've been practicing. I've been killing rabbits while riding at a gallop, haven't I?"

"But you're a---."

"If you're worried about me taking the blame, don't be. I've planned it perfectly. They'll be busy with the cattle and won't see me until after the shooting, which should cause those lousy cows to run and by the time everything settles down, I'll be long gone. No one will believe a woman did the shooting and you will establish yourself as somewhere else the whole time, so no one can blame you either."

Though the scheme was brilliant, Clete felt a trembling that entire day that he spent in the fields with the other farmers. He had never offered to help on the common potato field before. When one gruff old fellow asked him what made him show up that day, he merely replied that he felt a cool touch of autumn in the air. He realized now that if Winnie had been successful, the plan had been flawed by this stupidity.

But Winnie did not expect the cows to stampede before she fired the gun and she paid attention to nothing except her aim. When her horse became skittish, she tightened her grip on the reins, which made the horse rear in fright and flip her off under the cattle's feet.

Clete and the others in the potato fields looked up as the earth shook under them. One merely muttered, "Quaking," and bent back down again, but Clete wondered why he hadn't heard the distant retort of gunpowder that got the cows running. Only minutes later, it seemed, one of the drovers from the herd came running hard into the potato field. "Mr. Van Remus, sir, you better come with me."

As he ran behind the smelly field hand Clete's head pounded. They grabbed Winnie after the shooting – she didn't get away and now he was going to see his wife hang for something he never should have let her do. How was he going to tell Bret?

At the long corral where the young beef were penned but restless and flaring, men gathered around a heap on the ground. One fellow saw Clete coming, and tapped another fellow on the shoulder. That fellow looked up. Ben Cartwright.

Clete squinted at the man alive who was supposed to be dead. "What's going on?"

On the ground, her long blonde hair streaming, Winnie lay staring up at the sky, her face battered and bloody, man's clothes half ripped from her body.

"Winnie!" Clete dropped to the ground next to her. "Winnie, my God, what were you. . . Winnie, tell me you're not. . ." He touched her shoulder and gently shook her. "Winnie!"

"I'm sorry, Clete," Ben's deep voice behind him rang with sympathy. "She was in the path of the cows and her horse reared." A woman ran out from a house nearby and grabbed Ben's attention with words meant only for him. Ben ran to the house, concern for Clete forgotten.

Clete pulled Winnie up in his arms and held her tight. "You weren't supposed to die."

Felling of the Sons

How could he tell Bret? Cartwright's fault, that's what he told Bret. Cartwright did this deliberately. He never told his son why Winnie went to the herd that day.

Clete stumbled up the steps of the International, shrugging off Vince's offers of assistance. Time to take control of the Ponderosa.

***

Angry, drunken arguments, arm wrestling that ended up with men on the floor, and gambling, where a man would go angrily for his gun before realizing he left it with the bartender, all marked a typical night at the Bucket of Blood Saloon. But when the fighting between Cartwright and Van Remus started up in the street, they all stopped to watch. Except Bret, sitting in a corner alone. When it was over, the men ambled back to sit again.

"I've never seen old Ben so furious. What you suppose set him off?"

"Ain't you heard? His son Adam was kilt, shot in the back. I hear tell that Joe is dead as well, so says Clem over to the sheriff's office."

"And he thinks that Van Remus is the one what did it? He seems straight to me. You see him care for those miners today in the collapse? Ain't no owner ever cared that much."

"That's straight enough, but they do go back aways. From the way I hear Vince talking, he's my sister's mister, you know, he works over where Van Remus stays and he says he even pointed Adam out the very day he was shot."

"That don't mean nothing."

"Maybe not. Mighty big coincidence. Adam and Joe Cartwright are about as decent as they come."

"If I was Hoss, I'd sure be cautious of my back."

"I expect Ben will see that justice is done him. See how he got Van Remus to back down on pressing charges? Most men would be throwed in jail for coming at a fellow that way, but not Cartwright."

Not by my father, Bret thought sullenly. He turned to face the men behind him. "They ain't dead. Don't go giving Cartwrights sympathy they ain't got coming."

Jimmer, a young miner, jumped to his feet. "Bret is right! Old Ben said it himself in the street! He said Clete van Remus *tried* to kill his sons! Not that he actually done it. I knew something bothered me about that."

An old ranch hand with a stove-up back gave Jimmer a crooked look. "Why would Cartwright lie about his sons?"

"To draw out the ones what done the shooting." Bret got his whiskey refilled.

"You got any ideas who?"

Bret stared at the golden liquid in his glass. "Nah." He swallowed hard and looked out the saloon door into the street. All he could see of the ruckus was a small mound of dark red in the street that a mangy brown dog chewed on. About time old Cartwright showed some spark. Clete will to have to fight hard now. He will have to show more guts than what's laying out there in the street.

Clete let his wife do the yelling and pushing that got them anywhere. Ma would have killed Ben Cartwright if it weren't for the damned cows. His father passed up a chance to have Ben Cartwright thrown in jail. That would have given Bret the chance to torch the house the way he wanted to in the first place. "I couldn't be born of the likes of him," Bret muttered under his breath. He pushed away from the table suddenly and stood. "He's not my pa."

Outside of the saloon Bret saw, after a moment of puzzled inspection, Reeger in the street, staring at nothing in particular. Bret walked over to him, uneasy by the man's stance.

"What you up to, Reeger?"

Reeger started at the sound of Bret's voice behind him. "Ah, just planning how to carry out Mr. van Remus's newest orders, that's all."

Felling of the Sons

"What'd he say to do?"

"Follow Ben Cartwright home, find out his next move. Report back."

"So what's the problem?"

"Is it true what they're saying about Joe Cartwright?" Reeger clutched at Bret's shirt, more for support than threat. "Is he dead now, too?"

"They were asking that back there in the saloon, too. Ben's got everyone believing it." Bret looked around for sign of Cartwright and his father going at it again, but Clete had slunk away, a coward. Nothing more. "What if he *is* dead? You got a problem with it?"

"I didn't mind helping before. But I ain't getting mixed up in no murdering. I accepted what you told me about why you kilt Adam. Maybe I shouldn'ta."

"You losing your gut now, too, Reeger? Maybe I oughta feed you to the dog, too!" He pointed to the street.

"Don't think I ever had it to lose." He walked back to the saloon.

Bret grabbed his arm and jerked him back. "You try to walk out on your boss now, Reeger, you try, and you watch your back the rest of your short life."

"You saying you own me now?" Reeger swallowed hard. "I didn't say I'd let Mr. van Remus down. I only said I wanted no more to do with killing. Maybe someone else did kill Little Joe, ain't for me to say." He looked down at Bret's hand on his jacket. "You gonna let me go? I figure I got time for another beer before Cartwright leaves town."

Bret patted Reeger's arm and let him walk into the saloon. As he watched the door of the saloon where Reeger disappeared, the wind picked up, flapping the front of his vest lightly against his chest. The streets were empty except for a few drunks stumbling about. Bret imagined the whole town a'flame and nobody around to care. The sun had set a while ago, but traveling in the dark didn't bother him any. He did it last night, and felt like a bat stealing hell.

Bret turned to mount his bay, but had a sudden thought and doubled back into the Bucket of Blood. He eyed up the four corners of the whiskey-soaked walls, saw where Reeger tried to hide himself, and walked over to a table in the far corner where Juce sat, spinning his gun lazily in one hand and belting the whiskeys down with the other. Juce was considered a fast gun — fastest miner around he was called, until the whiskey weakened his gut. The last time he tried to draw down he passed out on the ground and the bullet from his opponent just missed creasing his scalp. No one's felt the need to try him since.

"Juicy, got a question for you." Bret stood in front of him, maintaining the posture that Juce answered to, both hands on gun belt and legs slightly apart.

Juce grinned at him with bloodshot eyes. "Yeah? Oh, it's you. I 'spect I got a minute to spare. You know, I do appreciate you and Clete giving us all the work and the fine wages. I do believe I would do anything for you, yes sir." Juce grinned wide enough to swallow the mountain they stood on.

"Is that the truth?" Bret waited while Juce thought about it but not long enough for him to change his mind. "Then do you suppose since you're so big on us that you could do us a turn?" He took out the writing pad he kept in his vest pocket and sat. "I need you to give Clete this message." He scribbled quickly. "All you have to do is find him and see that he reads it right away. He might be in his room at the International. Think you can handle it?"

"Well, I'll go right now, Bret. You don't worry about me. I'll find him." He watched Bret scrawling, shrugged lazily and went back to his drinking. He twirled his gun in his other hand and, after finishing his shot, held the cool metal against his cheek, caressing it.

"There you go."

Juce tucked the note in his pocket and leaned forward. "Why can't you see 'em yourself?" He asked, spitting warmly into Bret's face.

"I got work to do." Bret walked outside into the chilling night air.

Juce followed him out. "This real important, huh."

"He might even give you another job to do. Something that could earn you a week's mining wages. You tell him I say so." Maybe Juce couldn't shoot straight. But he can make Reeger real worried about his life in the attempt.

"I surely will, Mr. Bret!" Juce fell off the wooden walk, into the street. "I surely will."

***

"Clem, this is not Roy's handwriting." Ben stared at the note. "It's not his way of writing, anyway, even if I couldn't swear to the scribbling."

"Oh, I don't know, Ben, it don't say much." Clem took it back. "Not a good day, retiring early." He put it back down on the desk where he found it, tucked under some posters. "Seems pretty straightforward to me. Tell you what I think you should do, Ben. Go home and get some sleep before Van Remus decides to press charges. Probably will, you know, and might have a right to. Early in the morning, if Roy's not at his house or here, I will tear this town apart." Ben stared at Roy's desk as though trying to read its secrets. "Go on, Ben, there's nothing more you can do."

Ben allowed himself to be guided to the door. "I do want to check on Joe---."

"Joe? You mean he's not dead?"

Ben clamped a hand on Clem's shoulder. "Clem, I appreciate your concern and kind words." Ben left Clem scratching his head.

When he was out on the walk Clem called him back. "Ben! What about Hoss?"

"Hoss? Have you seen him?"

"I think so." Clem related his encounter with a familiar Swede, and had them both laughing, Ben more in relief than anything else.

"So he *is* taking precautions." Ben scratched his chin. "Hoss should be safe enough tonight, but Clem, listen, if you run across Roy, tell him that Hoss is out there and see if he can't get some men together and ride out there to arrest the whole bunch for trespassing. I've got two injured sons that still need tending, but if I can't find Roy tomorrow, I'll go looking for Hoss myself."

"Sure, Ben. I think you're right, too, that Van Remus, he's out for the night. Oh, and Ben?" Clem stopped him again. "I'll do what I can to keep Van Remus from pressing charges." Ben only stared blankly at him. "You know, for beating on him in the street."

Clem looked so serious that Ben nearly grinned. "Thanks, I was worried about that, too." He tipped his hat at Clem, jumped on his horse and rode off.

CHAPTER 32

Ben pulled his horse up when he saw Jessup outside his office enjoying his evening smoke. He should be hard out on the mattress after his long and tough day. Jessup waved and stood as Ben came over to him. "John, I'm surprised to see you out on a cold night."

"And I'm surprised to see you still in town. You heading on home to see Joe?"

"I thought about staying in town but I need to see how my boy's doing."

"Let me know if there's any more I can do for you, Ben. Would you like another supply of that medicine?"

"Won't be necessary, will it? Adam's up and around now, and Joe's fever's broke, you said he was healing up fine."

"Say, about Adam being up and around, I hope you're encouraging him to take it easy."

Ben looked down where his hands tensed on the saddle. "I have, but Adam's gotten so restless, John."

"He's at the most frustrating part of the healing, where he feels good enough to be up and about but where the healing inside isn't complete yet. It's important, Ben, that he rest. There's no way of telling when a fella is bleeding loose on the inside until he keels over dead from it."

"Thanks for the word, John, I better get back." Ben kicked his horse off into the hills. Hoss was strong and in disguise and Ben understood his need to help. He had to make Adam see that, too. Ben wasn't easy with Hoss being out there, and now had a missing sheriff to worry about. At least now he's made that scoundrel Van Remus a little more nervous for his own life. That should buy him enough time to go home and make sure both his sons are still there.

***

Jessup sat back and watched Ben ride off. Those Cartwrights had a natural hard-headedness about them. In that respect Joe was lucky, because the wound under the rib cage will be painful until he's mostly recovered. But if Adam gets to believing he's fine, there's no telling what he'll do.

The chill got under his skin, but he didn't like the smell of his pipe in the house so he bore it out. He had sent that letter off to Genoa right after Adam got hurt but maybe not in enough time to do Adam any good. He's known Adam for years and maybe even better sometimes than his own Pa knew him. He never met a man so able to hide pain and push himself to the very threshold of existence as Adam could.

Jessup had stressed the urgency to his colleague of sending him some new procedures for surgery. Old as John knew he was, he would hang up his bag if he couldn't learn a new technique. Maybe another letter would help.

Jessup went inside to his desk, the only piece of furniture he brought from the east, bought with his first doctoring money. It was a little wobbly from one leg shrunk up but still had a smooth writing surface. He penned another letter, brief but direct.

The hour was late but the Pony office stayed open for such emergencies as the doctor might need – one of the benefits of his position that Jessup didn't take lightly. The boy on duty took the letter with the reverence owed it and rode off, knowing the trail to Genoa well enough to follow it in the dark. Dr. Jessup made sure of his speed and diligence by watching. Ben Cartwright's trouble could mean none of his boys would sit very still for long – not if they could help it.

He wasn't sure he blamed them. All he could do was try to keep them alive.

***

Kudwa mounted his small sturdy animal. His wife held out an eagle feather to him. "This was my father's. He told me to wait until I saw the right moment to give it to the man who is in my heart at a time when he most needs it. That is you, and the time is now."

Felling of the Sons

He reached down, hesitant, trembling. Kudwa had never before held such a rare and precious item, for the eagle represented a wide, free and strong creature that sees and knows all. "My wife, with this feather, and to you, I will make the land safe and return to you."

He held the feather high, shouted a war cry of peace and the horse jumped off through the dry foothills of the high Nevada desert. The people had made a quick return to the desert from the Truckee River because of what he had to do. Here, at least, they were safe, should trouble start.

The scenery went on for miles as hilly and dry in one direction as in another. With little to watch for in hunt, Kudwa found his mind easily distracted back to a time before the Paiute War, when he trained to become Shaman. There were other shamans, older than him, but he grew very adept at hearing the voices of their ancestors through Sky Father and their descendants through Earth Mother, reassuring him and his people that they would survive, no matter what the whites did to them. Then came the war and his visions stopped, because one vision had told him that through war and justice they would get their land back and instead they were pushed farther away. His sister now trained as Shaman as other women had in the tribe's ancient times. He felt now that helping the whites, through Adam and his family, was the new trail his people must follow and if this vision was true, perhaps other visions would follow.

Kudwa found a small pool of water and watched his horse drink before dipping his own hands down into the water placed there for them to pause and reflect. After two dips with his hands to quench his aching throat, he sat back. An overwhelming vision of falling trees swept through him. Adam saying, "I sure need to get out of this bed right now," and Kudwa offering to help him. Adam saying, "Yes, it is time, it is time." Trees falling, many trees falling, collapsing on top of each other as though someone had stolen all their roots.

Kudwa stood, his limbs shaky. After a brief prayer in the six directions and a request for inner sight, he jumped back on the horse and rode off.

***

Riding took much of the stamina Adam hoped to reserve for what lay ahead. A northern wind whistled through the snow-tipped Sierras and through his skin, attempting to push him from the saddle. Every few minutes he shifted forward again, leaning down to butt the wind. If not for the tall Ponderosa pines surrounding him, the wind would have made the ride intolerable. Already his back throbbed like a drum. At each pounding he clenched the reins of the horse until his nails dug into his palms, and with his jaw and mind set on the task ahead, the back pain gradually disappeared.

When Adam found the Indian camp at the Truckee River had been abandoned, he nearly lost the hope that he'd found along the way. But he remembered Hoss - as a small child bouncing on his chest one day when he was ill to make him better, chasing down an old steer when he was only 13 to keep it from getting out of the pen, the look he gave Adam the first time he had to talk to a girl. Hoss was out there alone trying to save all of them, and the land, too. Hoss needed to know what he was up against. If Adam could do that much, he would feel all of this was worth it.

At least in desert country the wind was high above him. The night was long dark by the time he made the village and he felt chilled through. He gave a hawk call and waited. When he heard the owl cry in return, he urged his horse on over the rock.

Kudwa wouldn't turn him down, but Adam remembered rejecting Kudwa's offer of help earlier. Now Adam had to save Hoss's life. That made it all so tangible and certain, physical and real, rather than something tucked away cautiously in his mind. Taking care of Van Remus and his son would be next – but first he had to make sure Hoss was safe.

Paiute women and men stood in front of the campfire as he approached. Adam lifted a hand in greeting and several lifted theirs in return. He took a deep breath and straightened, threw his right leg up to alight.

And couldn't figure out how suddenly he was flat on the ground, with Old Situha rubbing his face with her cool wet hand. He blinked hard and struggled to sit up, though Indian hands were holding him down. "Adam Cartwright is not well."

"Kudwa?"

Numaga squatted by them. "Kudwa rode to the Shoshone camp. He will be back before the sun comes up again. He will find men to help you, Adam Cartwright. Stay here and rest."

"No," Adam rolled to his knees and stood shakily. "I spent much time getting here. Must rescue my brother." He grabbed onto his horse's saddle horn and blinked hard. Even in the little light from the fading campfires blurred. "Someone...help me up." A pair of hands pulled him away from the horse to a lean-to where he collapsed again. As they made him comfortable, Adam fought not to give in to exhaustion. "Hoss, I've got to help him, he'll be killed."

The Indians tried to reassure him as he passed out.

CHAPTER 33

Reeger watched Ben haul up in front of the doctor's. When Ben started off again Reeger followed, almost running a fellow miner over in the street. "Hey, you better stay on the walk, fella. In the dark, it's hard to see drunks that can't see themselves." Reeger tipped his hat at the drunk and continued on.

Juce rubbed the back of his hand against his mouth as he watched the sloppy rider disappear. He patted his jacket to check on his supply of bible papers and touched some paper that crinkled noisily. He put the paper to his nose and sniffed, and in recognition a wet grin lit up his face. He turned and quickened his pace to the International House.

He found Clete in the International's bar, soaking up wine.

At one glance of the note, Clete swore bitterly under his breath. He pulled the drunk's attention away from a whiskey bottle. "Can you sober up quickly for say, one thousand dollars?"

***

Hoss and the loggers reached camp just before sunset. Hoss saw distressing signs of activity. Bleeding cuts were made in every tree he saw, no one caring about the conserving of the soil or the prevention of landsliding. It seemed like they were trying to encourage it. They weren't loggers—they were set to destroy, nothing more. Hoss got off his horse and wandered from tree to tree for closer inspection as others watched him. "De do good work. Maybe we show dem even more, eh?" He chuckled with humor he didn't feel and mounted.

They had followed a dark trail that led to bedding for the night, the air soaked with the smell of fresh pine sap that awakened the senses. At the bedding area leveled out of the slopes, three men sat huddled around the fire and looked up from their silent eating at the approach of the riders. A fourth man approached them, bread in one hand, gun tight and threatening in the other. Hoss saw a fifth man propped against a tree a distance away.

Felling of the Sons

"Light and state your business," Carne growled, waving the gun.

"Easy," Claude said, alighting. "Clete Van Remus sent us to join your crew. Seems you ain't getting the work done fast enough."

Carne looked over at the campfire where Jon McManus got to his feet. "As long as you brought your own grub and gear and you ain't miners. I'm McManus, this here's Carne the watchdog, over there's Adolf and Louis, and back by the tree, Petey."

"I'm Claude, this here's the Swede, Bart, and Bob."

Hoss walked over to Petey, who didn't care to look up. In the dying light of day Hoss could see his face sweating, and he had to force himself to eat. "Someting bothering ya der?"

"Just let me be!"

McManus stood next to Hoss. "I'm worried about him. He insists on working and he's a damn good feller too, but he took an arrow to the leg and we got nothing but some bandages and balsam pitch to treat 'em with. I told him to get hisself to a sawbones but he ain't listened."

Hoss found the bandage to mark the location of the wound and looked from there to check the veins in the man's leg. No mistaking, even under the dark sky, that the vein that had begun to turn green. The man's insistence on working was costing him his life. "Gotta come off."

"What?" Petey looked up at the heavy and bearded face hovering over him. "WHAT?!"

"The leg, it's gotta come off. Or you're dead."

CHAPTER 34

The cattle drive reached the edge of the Cascade Range in northern California. After watering the herd in Shasta Lake, Val pushed them on around to the east of the lake, settling them in just before dark. When Butch, Val's second, asked him about it, Val explained that Pit River, only five miles ahead, couldn't be reached traveling at dusk and beyond and cattle spooked too easily. High foothills surrounded them and they were all worn to the bone already from pushing it.

Val held his boys back as Chet and his two men bullied their way ahead in the chow line of beans, hog fat and biscuits. Butch could see Val had little patience for bad tempers. Tension mounted as Chet said something derogatory about trail bosses to make the others laugh, and then stared hard and deliberate at Val. Even through the night sky the challenge was readable.

After several attempts to converse with Val, Butch got to his feet and walked over to where Cookie tossed supplies back into crates.

"Don't like the feel of this drive at all," Cookie grumbled.

"I got ya there." Butch scratched at his sparse hair that matched his build. He was small but not too many challenged his gun. He reasoned those were his main offerings to Val that got him hired on as second. His wiry build helped him stay mounted easily, and made him invaluable in circling the cattle during a stampede.

"Think Mr. Cartwright ought to be let in on this?" Cookie towered over him, a powerful man who had a gentle way with biscuits.

Butch shrugged as he held his cup out for more coffee. "Maybe. Let's see if anything happens here first. If we have to, we kin always send Pony from the next town."

They heard a shout and moved in closer to the fire to see Val and Chet squaring off, angry words spoken once the business of eating had been set aside. "You've questioned my orders ever since you rode out here. Now I don't know what kind of burr you got stuck in your craw but we better have it out right now," came Val's admonition.

"You don't know what you're doing, that's all." Chet spit into the fire. "If you had one pea for sense you'da bedded these animals back at the lake where they could water both at night and in the morn."

"Bedding by water is only one way of thinking and it's not my way. Cows spook easier by water and are injured easier. They're harder to herd away the next day, getting too cozy as they are."

"For a trail boss you got no smarts at all. I'm challenging you for this job." Chet spread his legs, his right hand slipping down to his side.

Val groaned, dropping his hands. Butch heard he wore his guns light, never drawing against a man. That didn't make him a coward, only temperate. "Have you gone plum loco?"

"I'm challenging ya, Val."

"You ain't worth the money Ben's paying ya. And now we're looking to cross the orneriest trail yet, over Pit River through the Cascades. Do you know the route?" Chet didn't answer. "But hell," Val shrugged. "If you're that dead set on running the show, I got nothing against it." Val spread his arms wide and bowed.

Butch remembered him talking about that play he saw once with Adam and realized that Val was planning something in honor of his dead friend. But why was he turn-tailing, giving Chet the drive?

"Now, that's more like it!" Chet turned to Cookie, who stood to the side eyeing the dirty plates strewn on the ground. "Cookie, turn your wagon tongue to the south."

"South? Hold on, we're heading 'em north to Oregon."

Chet turned back. "You all heard him, didn't you? Putting me in charge? And I'm turning the trail because I'm working for Van Remus."

"Why, you mangy, no good..." Val glanced over at Butch.

Butch only nodded. He knew these fellows meant trouble all along. Val, Butch came to figure later, took his nod to mean he'd stand behind any decision Val called on this one.

"We're heading these cows south to a ranch outside of San Francisco. You'll get plenty more money this way, because old Cartwright don't have money to pay you with anyhow."

Val stepped forward. The campfire was all the light they could see by since the sun set, the flickering light not quite reaching the pierce of Val's eyes. His somber face, half lit in the campfire, was a mask of anger. "You're a liar and a thief."

Chet laughed. "You're all with me, men, ain't ya?"

Jim threw his butt into the fire before looking up. "Ya did make him boss, Val."

"Then I'm canceling it. My name is still in that cattle ledger."

Chet shook his head. "Too late. Turn that wagon, Cookie."

"You're no cattleman," Val said in a sudden low voice.

"What?"

Val pulled his gun, aiming it at the dirt. "You don't know the ass from the horns."

Chet slapped his hand to his holster but Val had his pointed at Chet's gut. "You planning on using that? You got witnesses here to say you didn't give me a chance to draw."

"I could let you steal the cattle," Val's gun slowly rose up to aim at Chet's head. "But within a day you'd have us so worn out the cows would have no meat left. They'd be worthless."

"Butch! Make him holster that thing before he does something crazy!"

The gun continued to rise in the air until it pointed at the sky. "I'd sure hate to see you in a hard rush."

Butch couldn't believe what Val could be thinking. Cattle spook easy at night, he knew that.

"Hell, he's just crazy. You can see why he can't be boss!" Chet relaxed and turned back to the business of getting the chuck wagon turned, to where Cookie stood, arms folded, ready to continue the fight.

Men around the campfire rose slowly to their feet, their eyes as they stood in the flickering fire showing their amazement and growing horror. They realized what Val was up to just as he fired the gun three times. The response began with lowly bellows as several cows jumped to their feet, and quickly the sound of scrambling and bellowing and jumping grew louder and harder until it seemed the Earth itself shook enough to open wide, as the angry bellowing of frightened steers scorched their nerves.

"Stampede!" Jim yelled, and everyone ran for the remuda, for the night horses that weren't saddled.

***

Reeger lost track of Ben a few miles out of Virginia City but he knew the way to the ranch.

Reeger always thought Ben a pompous old rich man, the way he threw his weight around, getting his own way. Same with Adam and Hoss. He'd forgotten about Joe until he heard Joe was attacked. Once he and Joe were after the same girl, Rosalie her name was, a shy little beauty. He and Joe fought over her as anxious, love-struck boys do. One day, without any kind of warning, Joe stopped by where Reeger was shoeing a horse and told him that he didn't want to see Rosalie anymore and could Reeger keep her busy for a while so she wouldn't notice him not showing up. And oh, how Reeger kept her busy. He and Joe never became friends but Reeger never forgot.

Now old Ben Cartwright had worse than his share of grief but he still handled things. Reeger found himself admiring the old man despite himself. With every plodding step his horse took, he was less and less sure of why he had listened to van Remus in the first place.

***

Butch felt a horror unlike ever before. He'd been in many a stampeding, always the one to chase down the lead cow and start the circling, but only a few times at night and always in those times losing a drover or two. Two miles the hastily saddled horses pounded through dark, uneven terrain before they caught up to the tail end of the stampeding herd going back over the trail they had trampled during the day. Butch could barely keep his own senses but somehow remained aware of the other drovers struggling to control the herd same as he was. At least he wasn't alone. His worst nightmare was trying to control a herd alone.

Chet and his men pulled up the tail end of the hard riding drovers, barely able to keep up, but Butch could make out Chet's white mare pushing hard, as he headed in Val's direction, Val on his pinto, as though Val's trail was the trail of Chet's salvation. Or maybe he only wanted to kill the man for putting them in this pickle barrel. Nothing Butch could do about that now. They were about on the tail end of the stampeders and the cows were turning so if they weren't extra careful, soon the drovers would be at the cattle's head. Val knew that.

Chet about reached Val too, Butch could see Val's off-white hat bobbing as he shouted barely audible orders, his pinto kicking its feet up high in spirited excitement, and he could see Chet gaining. And then Chet's horse stumbled on maybe a prairie dog hole and he went flying. Chet screamed for his life, his lungs caving in to be heard, but only Val turned. Butch couldn't reach him and wasn't sure he'd bother even if he could. Val turned, Val who knew and directed the way the cows were running, Val who knew that if he let Chet die he'd feel himself guilty of murder for starting the stampede. Chet cowered on the ground, getting kicked by stampeding hooves, screaming, not knowing which way to move. Val, who only wanted to prove Chet incapable, reached down to pull Chet up, but in the dark, the ground uneven and the cattle turning again, Chet half hanging on Val's horse, screaming — Val had no chance, not one.

***

Joe woke lazily to see Norma reading at his bedside, her lips moving in intense concentration. He let his eyes wander around the hazy room until he remembered where he was. That picture on the wall of the Indian — Adam picked that out for him. Norma kept reading. He

216

liked the way her lips moved, and wondered if Pa had married again. He didn't think so, but his mind felt so cloudy he couldn't be sure. And he didn't want to risk looking foolish.

"Ma?"

Norma's head jerked up. "Oh my, you're awake. How are you feeling?"

"Where's Pa?"

"Well, I certainly hope he'll be home soon. After all, he did promise."

His headache had lessened but Joe couldn't shake the fuzziness that he felt when he tried to concentrate. He braced his arms on the bed and pushed up into a sitting position with a groan. She didn't say she wasn't his ma, so she must be. Why couldn't he remember it? She was familiar enough—he could remember her reading to him when he was younger. But doggonnit, he couldn't remember them getting hitched.

Norma jumped up when Joe let slip an involuntary groan. "Let me fix that pillow for you. Still sore? That must have been some knife they used on you."

The intensity of that blade slicing his skin right to his rib bone seared through his mind. The look in that fellow's eyes was of sheer hatred, craziness. He was the one to fear. Not the father, but the son. "When Pa comes home, I gotta see him." He threw his blanket off but Norma slapped his hand lightly and tucked him back up.

"I only have one of you boys left to care for and I'm not letting you get away."

He killed my ma! "Where's Adam and Hoss?"

"I would have stopped him. Anyone could see by his face that he wasn't healed except that Chinaman of yours."

"Adam not healed?" Joe didn't have a clue what day this was.

"Oh, don't you worry now. They probably rode over to a neighbor's to recruit some fighting power. They'll be back."

Joe believed her. He wondered vaguely if there was a fourth son around someplace. "I'm...hungry." Although a sister would be nice.

"Oh, that's wonderful! I'll go see what Hop Sing has for us to eat!"

After she left the room, Joe kicked off his covers. The exertion made him pant in exhaustion and he had to lay back to fight the dizziness. He worked his legs toward the edge of the bed, and the wound reacted, making him feel freshly stabbed all over again. He forced himself to slide off the bed until his feet touched the floor. He couldn't stand yet, but in another day, with some good food in him, he'll be ready to go after that son.

CHAPTER 35

Petey stared up at the stranger called Swede like he was some kind of crazy man. He tried to speak but his throat felt like he had swallowed pinesap. When the Swede knelt down next to him, Petey tried to push him away but the Swede was harder to discourage than granite rock.

Hoss felt his forehead. "I know dis horrible news. But otherwise you die horrible death sure." He gripped Petey's bad leg firmly.

"The pain's almost gone," Petey managed hoarsely as he tried to shift his position but failed. "I'll work hard. . .put balsam on it."

The Swede shook his head. "Not dis time."

"You can't cut off my leg," he blubbered. "The pain's going away, I hardly feel it."

"Going dead, leg is. Gonna put your whole body dat way, if it don't come off."

"You want axe? Or saw?" Adolf stood behind Hoss, holding up tools.

Petey looked up at the axe and fainted.

                          ***

Hoss swallowed hard. Pa always told him he was a sucker for a lost cause. "Maybe me yust take him to town, yah?"

McManus shook his head. "That would take hours, maybe all day, the way these things go, and I can't spare one man, let alone two. Anyway, it's too dark for you to be traveling with a sick man."

"Yeah," Louis said, staring hungrily at Petey's leg. "Let's hack it off and by morning he'll be ready to work again."

Feeling ill at what he'd started, Hoss held out his hand. "Give me de ax." With the smooth wood handle firm in his hand, he held his other

219

arm out. "Everyone step back." He swallowed hard, his stomach churning in the mounting fervor. "Who's doing the holdin'?"

Jon and Bart dropped down on either side of Petey and grabbed his arms. Petey squirmed violently, screaming, trying to draw his leg up under him. Louis dropped one knee down on Petey's stomach, eyes fixed on the spot of the chopping. Adolf sat on his foot, his eyes squeezed shut.

Hoss took careful aim and swung down hard, using the distorted reality of night to imagine a tree trunk instead of a leg, to force away the image that would come when the ax cleared through the tissue and bone. . .not much different than chopping through a sapling except for all the blood. After one excruciating scream Petey passed out. Hoss threw the ax aside and grabbed the bandages offered by Louis. He folded the bloodied excess skin flaps down over the heavily bleeding stump as well as he could before clumsily affixing the bandages to stop the bleeding.

"Sit there, hold tight, once all the bad blood out, we'll stop blood flowing with these bandages. I'll come back in a---." Hoss stumbled up the hill and fell to his knees, sick. He's had to shoot horses, destroy cattle. But this. . .there was nothing more horrible than this. Perhaps Petey would prefer to die, but Hoss never could let a man die with slow poison in his veins. This way, either he'll recover or the shock will kill him quick.

Petey was made comfortable and a quick grave dug for his leg. Hoss told them to change the bandage once the bleeding stopped and bury the bloodied bandage as well. They didn't need the scent to attract a coyote or wolf pack. The new crew was told where to bed for the night and no more words were exchanged as they all settled in. Hoss chose the spot furthest from anyone and no one questioned him, the weight of what they'd just done silencing all complaints for the night.

After what seemed a hell's eternity fighting to stay awake, Hoss heard snores loud enough to cover Petey's groans. He sat up. Joe often said ten men sounded like one Hoss, but he would change his mind if he heard these six sky-rattlers. He realized that once or twice during the leg chopping he lost conscious use of his dialect but no one else

220

noticed either and should have no reason to think of it now. He could only hope, because he couldn't back out now.

Hoss went over to where the oxen were tied and bedded. He saved his relieving to use as a cover in case someone woke and saw him. The loggers can pull the lumber to the flume if they still insist on cutting down his trees. His trees. He wished a couple of those boys would wake up. He would relish having them feel how hard a standing tree could be when a body is flung at it. They'd know what it felt like to be felled, right quick.

The biggest ox, a black and white, snorted lightly as Hoss worked on the rope. Once untied, he gave the leader a shove. Unlike cattle, they had little inclination to be frightened off. The ox bleated, an uncommon sound, and as Hoss looked around he wondered uneasily if he could pull this off. He didn't have much love for these bruts and less experience. The beast, well fed, wouldn't budge. In quiet desperation Hoss stood at its side and grabbed a front leg to encourage it to take a step. He finally got the animal's leg off the ground, and before he knew what was happening, the beast fell sideways on top of him.

"NNNNNnnnnnyeeeahhhhh!" Hoss's arms flailed underneath the beast as he fought to remove it and remain quiet enough not to wake anyone. The animal brayed softly but wasn't making much effort to stand. Hoss pushed against it, easing slowly out from beneath the beast, like the cork from a bottle of wine except the cork had to pull itself free. How does a logger explain he doesn't know oxen can't stand on three feet? This was the worst of fixes, made better only slightly by the sound of Joe's laughter when he hears about it.

Hoss finally pulled himself out, aching, probably bruised, and finally, like a cow, the damn thing got to its feet again. Hoss waved his arms wildly behind it, and perhaps the thought of falling again made it walk off. The other three oxen followed like obedient sheep. They might still be close by in the morning, but he wasn't about to bother with them further. He crawled to his bedroll and waited but no one stirred, so he turned his attention to a box he had stumbled over earlier.

Gunpowder. Enough to blow off a mountainside, and all they had to say was that they planned to blow out some stumps. Hoss went back for his saddlebag and stuffed it with as many bags as he could. That only took care of half. He dug at the base of a dead tree, one he figured they wouldn't bother with. He buried the rest as deep as he dared dig, and stoked the dwindling campfire with the empty wooden crate.

***

Bret had helped Clete plan the landsliding, including the amount of gunpowder they'd need. So he figured he'd find the loggers' camp with no trouble. But night fell darker in the hills than in the city. Bret found himself wandering for most of the night and caught whiff of campfire smoke by chance. He alighted and tied his horse, sensing movement ahead. He crept through the woods toward the low smoking ash, feeling like an owl in the night closing in on prey.

A big fellow half-sat and half-lay over the fire, pushing at something with a stick to get it to burn faster. Something about him being up and burning something this time of night didn't set right. Bret walked casually into his camp and the man looked up, his face whimsical in the campfire. "Hello. Seems like everyone's settled in for the night. I thought you'd all still be chopping."

"Nah, some sleeping make us strong for da morn, I just woke to stoke da fire." Hoss stuck his hand out and they shook briefly before Bret jerked away. "Is you a boss, like dat Van Remus?"

"That's right." Bret walked to the fire, staring at the charred box but feeling the big man at his back. "With all the natural firewood around here, you shouldn't need to burn a box."

"Ha! Dis is so!" Hoss slapped Bret on the back. "But dat empty box now one less ting we need to haul wit us."

"You got a point there." A low howl sent Bret's spine crawling. "Wolves?"

"No, a fella needed leg off. Bad shape. You bring medicine, yah?"

Bret shrugged. "Sorry. So you came out with the second group Clete sent?"

"Dat's so."

"Where you from?"

"HO! Not too many need ask me dat."

"Well, I am." Bret crossed his arms and leaned back against a tree.

"Is sad, leaving me home land after papa died and momma, she got kilt falling down de well trying to get us five young'uns some water. I found home for young'uns and come out here, tinkin' money be easier to find. Not so. Work hard, do anyting."

Bret laughed. "Then we better get some sleeping in because I plan to help out, first thing in the morning." Bret got his bedroll down and made himself comfortable close to the Swede. If there was foul play afoot, he was just in time to catch it.

***

Ben wasn't sure when he'd felt so exhausted. Several times during his ride back to the ranch he had to force himself upright in the saddle. After checking on Joe, he'd sleep fast but heavy. Only when he got the door open and the woman rose to her feet in front of the fire did he remember Norma.

"Norma. Sorry. It's so late. Did Hop Sing ready a room for you?" He took off his gun and hat, hoping she wasn't in the mood to talk.

"Ben, it is good to have you home," she said with a coo in her voice. She drew him to the fire. "Warm up some and I'll bring you upstairs to see your son."

Ben had to admit, in one of his more vulnerable moments, that coming home to a warm, smiling female dressed in a soft floating gown was not unpleasant. "How is Joe?" he asked as his skin warmed to the crackling heat.

"You'll be pleased and happy. But Ben," she grabbed his arm when he turned to the stairs, "there is something you must know. His mind isn't all there. Somehow he got the notion. . .that I'm his mother. You might want to send the doctor out here tomorrow."

223

Ben pulled out of her grasp and ran up the stairs, hardly hearing a word after "you'll be pleased." Sure enough, Joe sat up in bed, his empty plate on the floor and sipping warm tea. "Joe!"

Joe smiled broadly but his expression disintegrated to near tears at the sight of his father's concern. "Pa, I'm sorry." The mug of tea trembled and spilt out of his hands, but neither of them noticed.

Ben pulled Joe into his arms. "You're all right, son, you're all right."

"I think so, Pa. I feel okay."

"Who did this to you? Do you remember?"

"The son. Bret. He shot at me but missed and I chased him. We fought, and he pulled a knife." He stopped as Ben stared at him, wide-eyed.

"The son? But Clete told me. . ." Ben laughed shortly. "And I believed him." Ben looked close at Joe's face. "How's your head? You took quite a bump in your fall."

Joe shrugged. "It feels funny sometimes, like everything I'm supposed to know isn't there. Ma says that I---."

"Ma?"

"Ma said. . ." Joe frowned, rubbing his head. "You mean you didn't get married again? She's not my ma?"

"Norma is… a very caring lady." Ben looked back at the door, hiding a frown. "She's very fond of you."

"You don't worry about me, Pa, with Ma here, you and Adam and Hoss can catch that Van Remus. I don't want to you fussing over me when there's work to do."

Ben mussed Joe's hair. "You make sure you don't make any more impetuous moves." He looked around the room. "I thought maybe

224

Adam would be sitting up with you. He must have worn himself out.
I'll go check on him."

"No, Pa, Adam's…" Joe covered his eyes. "Something's going on, Pa.
Adam got kinda upset. I can't remember what we were talking about."

Ben looked out the window over the yard. "He's left. Adam's gone."

"It's okay, Pa. He's gonna be fine. He made me bet on it, and I did."

"I'd bet on him too, son. I'm going down to talk to Hop Sing, if he's
awake. I'll be back, okay?"

Even though he knew better, Ben stopped to peer into Adam's room.
He took a deep breath and went downstairs. Things had gone from
bad to terribly bad.

CHAPTER 36

Hop Sing furiously chopped greens in the kitchen, muttering under his breath. Ben stood in the doorway watching the small servant, who was more a member of the family than any hired help. In back of him the clock chimed. It was past late – this whole house should be settled in for the night. Lately the sun and the moon had nothing to do with any of them.

Norma waited for him on the settee. He didn't blame her for Adam leaving but he didn't want to sit and talk, either. He hadn't expected Adam, his eldest, levelheaded son, to run out that way. But guilt had settled into the hole his logical mind vacated.

Hop Sing hadn't acknowledged his presence, so Ben cleared his throat. Hop Sing's chopping became more furious. Ben looked out the back door where he had a good view of the corral but Adam's sorrel wasn't there. "Hop Sing, are you and Miss Norma getting on all right?"

"Miss Norma, she mean lady!" He dumped the greens he'd been cutting in a bowl and pulled a side of pork off the block of ice. "She come here one more time, this be her!" He hacked it in half.

"Hop Sing, settle down." Ben put both hands on the short man's shoulders and turned him. Hop Sing glared up at him, the cleaver firm in his fist between them. Ben pried open his fingers and put it down. "Tell me what's bothering you."

"Mr. Cartlight know." Hop Sing broke away with incredible strength. "Not Hop Sing's fault!"

"Hop Sing, I know that everything you've ever done has always been in our best interest. You're not just our cook, you're one of us." Hop Sing threw another log in the cook stove, walked over to the water pump with an empty pitcher and pumped furiously. "Did Adam tell you where he was going? That's all that's important now, Hop Sing. Just finding him."

Felling of the Sons

"Want to stop him. Want him to stay. But he too smart for Hop Sing."

"What did he say? Try and remember it exactly, Hop Sing."

"He say you know. Him keep one velly big tree from being felled."

"Thank you, Hop Sing. That's what I figured." Ben went into the sitting room to poke the fire. "Blast it!" He could feel Norma's eyes on him, but he couldn't let her distract him from what he needed to do.

Ben didn't think he ride off but he didn't know what feeling that kind of guilt could do to a man. Adam's made mistakes before – they all have. For the innocent mistake of a boy to come back this way – what else could Adam do? But Ben couldn't just sit back and wait for his son to die doing the right thing. Now there was nothing stopping him from looking for both his sons. He grabbed his hat at the front door but stopped. They were cutting illegally on the north 40, but which section?

"Hop Sing!" He turned to see the Chinaman run out. "Did he say where in the north 40? Did he even have a clue? We had several camps set up. It could take all night to track them down, and half the day tomorrow. I need to know exactly where."

Hop Sing's pigtail bounced as he nodded. "He say, go to find Kudwa. Kudwa help to get Mr. Hoss."

"He's riding up into Paiute country? He'll never make it, Hop Sing!"

The Chinaman turned away, wiping his eyes. "I not want him to go, he strong he say but I see his face, he do long thing, light leason."

Ben put a hand on his shoulder but turned to stare at the front door. He could go out there in the dark, search all night and accomplish nothing except make his mind useless without sleep. And he could hardly split himself up, send one half to find Hoss, the other half after Adam. And Adam would not allow himself to be dragged home like a 10-year-old. Ben could end up doing more damage that way. Better to wait until the first light of morning, get some sleep and pray that wherever his boys were right now, they were also sleeping, and safe.

"What you do, Mr. Cartlight?"

"I don't know, Hop Sing." Ben sank his chin to his chest and pressed heavy hands against his temples.

"Mr. Ben like to think sons grown men."

"That's true." Ben shook his head, dizzy from sleeplessness.

"Maybe they do what they have to do."

"Why don't you go to bed? Joe doesn't need close watching anymore." Ben felt washed out, sick inside.

Hop Sing went back into the kitchen. Ben turned to see Norma by the fire, holding two snifters of brandy. "Come, join me, Ben."

He saw himself doing just that, relaxing, letting the brandy soothe him as he's needed after the past week. As he reached for the glass he saw his sons' rich red blood draining out of them into the earth where they lay dying. "No. I can't, my sons are out there." Ben got as far as the settee before his knees gave out and he collapsed, barely getting caught by the settee.

Norma ran to him and helped him sit. "Ben, be reasonable. You're exhausted. You can't go out looking for two vagabond sons in the middle of the night." She laid a cool hand on his forehead as he put his head back. "They've probably gone in two different directions and you'll end up going a third. Better to wait until morning and take a whole search party. You've got a lot of friends who will help, Ben."

"It could be too late by then. They could be---."

"I've heard you say you trust your sons' judgment. Trust them now."

Ben allowed his eyes to stay closed as Norma massaged his temples. When he finally pulled himself up in the settee he took the brandy she offered and swallowed the golden liquid. "I guess they may have found each other and are camped down for the night." He sighed, knowing that before another hour had passed he would have to leave.

He may be at the brink of exhaustion but the only way to sleep anymore was to collapse from lack of it.

A shy knock at the door made him jump. He shoved his glass at Norma and ran to answer it. Reeger stood in the opened doorway.

Ben knew him by his last name and as a miner from town but nothing more. "Something I can do for you?"

Reeger pushed his way inside. "Mite chilly out there tonight. Mind if I warm a bit?" He strode over to the fire and Norma stepped aside.

"I don't want to be rude, but I have to leave. State your business."

"Oh, Mr. Cartwright, you don't want to go out there right now. It ain't safe for ya."

"What do you mean?"

"It's Clete van Remus. He's bringing some real wicked vengeance down on ya, you'd best be looking for him in the daylight. And that ain't all. There's Indians out there, too, I saw 'em. They can see in the dark like panthers."

"Kudwa! That means Adam must be close by!" Ben grabbed his jacket. "Thanks, but I have to find my sons." Something about Reeger's stance made Ben suspicious. "Something else on your mind?"

"I suspect you might want to hear what I have to say. But you ain't gonna like it."

"Look, I don't have time! Speak your mind and be quick about it."

"Ben, he's obviously here to help." Norma poured Reeger a brandy and he accepted it gratefully. "And you're doing your best to scare him off."

Ben grunted. "I'm sorry, Mr. Reeger. Speak your mind. Please."

"Well, sir, I figure since Joe did me a kindness once, I owe it to ya to turn sides."

"Turn sides?"

"Van Remus had me spying on you and yours. Once he give me the feeling he had Joe killed, I decided I had enough."

Ben strode over to him, his need to leave forgotten. "Did he admit it? That *he* had Adam shot?"

"Yes sir. Hired to have it done."

"Right to you? He said it to your face?"
Reeger seemed taken aback. "That's it, Mr. Cartwright."

Ben grabbed his hand and shook hard. "You are going to ride to town with me and tell everything to the sheriff. Are you willing?"

"Not tonight I ain't."

"No, no, not tonight." Ben frowned, staring down at the fire.

"Van Remus says he'll kill me. I believe him, too."

"That's certainly possible. And you're finding it worth the risk?"
Reeger only shrugged. "Did he see you come here tonight?"

"See me?" Reeger snorted. "He sent me here. Wanted me to tell him what your next move will be. Don't know when he'll start getting suspicious about me though."

"Don't worry about that, we won't let him get to you." Ben tapped his fingers on the dining table. A softly feminine hand covered his, calming his fingers but not his wildly scattered thoughts.

"Ben, go to bed. You've had enough excitement for one night."

"Norma, this is important! This is the first break I've had since." He gave her a hug. "Norma, go up and check on Joe. Tell him I'll be up in a minute." He looked at Reeger. "With a guest."

"Little Joe? You mean he really ain't dead? Bret was saying all over town about Little Joe not being dead, but I got to thinking they couldn't be trusted no more."

"He and Adam are fine." Without warning a shudder passed through him. "Joe will be delighted to see you." He looked up at the stairs, under his breath adding, "I hope."

"Well, holy Sam Hill, that's good news. And Mr....Ben, between the two of us, we'll be able to keep van Remus from trying again, yessir."

Ben tried to convince himself that Adam was in the protection of his Indian friends and Hoss's guise as a Swede kept him safe. He was going to have to trust their judgment—at least until morning.

CHAPTER 37

Jim and Cookie stood apart from the others over the graves of Val and Chet. The drovers paid their respects following the makeshift ceremony and went to the chuck wagon for the coffee Cookie brewed. Jim looked up from the dirt where Val's body lay six feet under and around one more time for Butch.

Butch, Val's second, just up and disappeared. They didn't find him hurt and they didn't find his horse. Cookie said Butch may have gone for Mr. Cartwright but in Jim's eyes running off was running off. Jim knew Butch felt guilty about almost siding with those scruffers, but he wasn't the kind to pack and run.

There wasn't much left to call a cattle drive. They rounded up near half of what scattered and would probably find more. They would drive them on into Oregon as planned, Butch or no Butch. Jim had made that promise over Val's grave. Cartwright stands to lose plenty on this, but by driving in what they can they'll cut his losses anyhow. Maybe even make a little more on book count, though he'd have to catch a buyer on a sleepy day to get away with a book count after a stampeding. A cowherd carries a certain look once there's been a stampede, like ball lightning tugging at their tails, and this herd had shrunk considerably. Whatever they can get will be small enough comfort for a man who's already lost enough.

These drovers stand to lose as well, none of this being their doing. Cartwright may have to turn over more to appease them for next time. Maybe Cartwright would prefer they let the drive end here. But calling it quits in the middle of a drive wasn't Val's way – or Butch's.

Jim remembered Val raising that gun, and the horrible singular drop-to-the-ground look on men's faces. He's not sure he would've done any different, once Chet tried to move the direction of the herd. He could have tried to outdraw him, but Jim didn't think he ever saw Val pull his gun except to shoot a rattler or a beefer in misery. Whoever this Van Remus was, he sure didn't plan on someone like Val.

Felling of the Sons

Those two boys who rode in with Chet disappeared sometime last night after the bodies were found. Whether anything further will be tried against the herd Jim didn't know. And he didn't want to think about it.

Jim went to the wagon for a cup of almost hot coffee, sugared heavy. No one looked at him. No one spoke their mind. Just waited for the words to move them on. "I know we're tired. Beater than a squirrel with a canyon full of nuts. When Billy and Pete get back from beating brush, we'll cut our losses and head on with what we got."

"All day, boss?" Charlie was as close to Val as Butch was, heartache and exhaustion showing in his eyes.

"We'll break early, but we lost so much time we gotta move as far as we can from here." Jim pulled Charlie aside. "Be my second, Charlie. I didn't ask for this. But we've got to carry it off."

"We can manage. We've got less beeves anyhow. Indians in the arroyo are gonna get fat. I sure hate leaving Val behind." He looked over his shoulder toward the rising sun. "And Butch, wherever he is." Charlie went back for a quick refill of coffee and a smoke before they saddled up, and after a final look over his shoulder at Val's resting place, Jim joined them.

***

Hoss wasn't sure what woke him, or if he slept at all, with still about an hour left before dawn. That new boss made him feel as spooked as a fella about to get himself hitched. Joe's favorite expression filled him with melancholy. It's been so long since he'd seen his brother's face. He even looked forward to Joe's laugh when he tells him about the ox falling on him. His laugh could be dadburned embarrassing but could also make Hoss laugh like a maniac.

A rustling of pinecones cracking under someone's lumbering feet made him sit up. That gunman Carne was supposed to stay alert most of the night and then sleep during the morning. He didn't notice Hoss loosening the oxen or burning the gunpowder, which meant he wasn't very good at what he was hired for. But now Carne was up and probably aching for some breakfast.

This younger boss didn't introduce himself, playing his hand mighty close to his vest. But even a fellow working for Van Remus could be made friendly. Pa once told Hoss he could tame a mountain lion with a word and a handshake. He didn't want to test this belief on that half-crazed gunman, though.

"You might just want to lie back down, Swede." Carne stood with the gun pointed at Hoss's head, his mouth half-cocked in a grin, one eye squinted shut. His face reminded Hoss of tommy-knockers that crawled from the depths of the mines, like the stories Adam used to tease him about when they were young — gnome-like devils that dragged miners into the pits of hell.

Hoss laid back down. As Carne moved away Hoss counted the number of steps the gunman took, and a horse whinnied. Hoss slowly rose to his feet, flexed his hand and fisted it. He'd lost weight for sure, but figured he had enough strength to do what had to be done. With a quick glance to be sure the new boss hadn't stirred, Hoss got to his feet.

He used the trees, one at a time, to approach the horses. Every couple steps something snapped beneath his foot, but he only quickened his pace. Carne moved behind the horses and commenced with his relieving. In a couple very long-legged moves, Hoss was at the flustered man's side. Carne scrambled to fix his pants and pull out his gun at the same time. Hoss grabbed the hand going for the gun and bent it backward, hard, until the wrist snapped. Before Carne could cry out Hoss smashed his other fist across the back of the man's head.

Carne crumpled to the ground. Hoss whirled around with breath held. Generally, loggers in the high woods slept real fine, he knew from the times he felled trees himself, but that new boss concerned him. He threw Carne over his shoulder and moved quickly down a slope, headed to what would be obscurity for a felled gunman.

***

The moon sliced shy of full had almost crossed the sky when Kudwa gently shook Adam awake. Adam had dreamt of being trapped in the Ponderosa ranch house, unable to find a way out and the flames licked at him but he wasn't hot, he was cold, so cold. When he awoke, he saw the moon descending through the trees and at first thought the house had burnt down around him. Someone leaned over him but he couldn't focus on the face. "Pa?"

"Adam. Friend."

"Kudwa." He blinked hard to drag himself out of deep sleep. "Hoss. Help me up."

Kudwa helped Adam sit. Adam had slept out on the cold hard ground, unable to accept the lodge that was offered. "Adam Cartwright go gahnin. . .cannot demazai' rescue brother."

"Hoss could end up dead. . .deyaipe. . .if I don't get moving. Are you willing to help. . .demazai'?"

With darkness in his face reflecting the surrounding foothills, Kudwa looked off toward the mountains of Lake Tahoe. "I did not sleep well because of the rejection of help."

Adam understood the tone more than the words. "Kudwa, I apologize for rejecting your help. Please. Show me where you found those loggers. Are you willing?" Adam stood, feeling dizzy only for a moment. "Help me save the life of my brother and the trees."

Kudwa struggled with his English again. "Have been to Shoshone to gather more men. Adam, you say we Paiute cannot fight. I gather Shoshone and Washo. We are strong again. We will save your trees."

Adam nodded with a grin. "Friend, not only have you already forgiven me, but you have found a way to get the strength and numbers that are needed. All to help us."

"Adam Cartwright, your words are not clear."

Adam tried again with signing. "I am...honored to have you as. . .hainji. I have said no. . . gishaan . . . to your offer of demazai' and am now ashamed. . ." he struggled with the meaning of shame to the Paiutes, "am a nasundetehande. . .brother to you."

Kudwa finally raised his hand up to shake with Adam's. Their palms met, and then Kudwa grabbed Adam in a warm but gentle hug. "You will do this though you may die?"

Adam straightened and pulled away, his eyes and limbs steadied. "We will let the gods decide. Yours *and* mine. Are you ready to ride?"

Kudwa helped Adam to mount and one of the younger girls brought his horse to him. Council came to him, making him feel for the first time since the war as though he was a member of great standing. Kudwa spoke rapidly, talking of ultimately doing whatever they needed to do to keep any more trees from falling. Adam swore to them that he would take all blame for any violence.

"Lead the way, Kudwa. Together we will stop those loggers who destroy the trees."

CHAPTER 38

Hoss carried Carne's body from the camp far enough to be sure of obscurity. His feet slipped in the loose gritty sand as he worked down the edge of the cliff alongside the flume. Hoss slid again, clutching Carne tightly, until a section of level ground stopped his descent. Carne groaned when Hoss laid him on the incline, waking to the pain in his broken wrist. Hoss pulled out his gun and gave him a friendly tap on the back of his head to put him out again. He gagged the man and double-checked the wrist ropes. He will hurt like the devil kissed him when he comes to and finds his broken wrist bound. Hoss knew he could never leave the man down here for coyote bait, but untying him was low priority for now.

The flume shook as Hoss adjusted his footing and grabbed onto a wooden bracing. This was the first flume they built and needed some re-boarding. If a log were to come sailing down here, the flume would collapse right on top of Carne. He wouldn't worry about that though because he won't give them the chance. He climbed back up the slope.

Dawn was only a glance away but he couldn't sleep anymore even if he wanted to. He had mischief to make.

***

Kudwa pointed up the foothills to the place where he had shot the arrow at a logger. The climb took them over a particular heavy outcrop of rocks. They would have to walk.

"Think the two of us can get Hoss out of there?" Adam asked.

"We wait, Adam? Rest here?"

"Wait?" Adam shifted in the saddle. His teeth gritted as sweat beaded his forehead. "If we don't keep going, it could be too late for Hoss."

"Others meet us here. We will wait."

Adam looked up the hillside at the lightened sky of dawn's approach. Their talk found an easy rhythm, a combination of both languages. "If they were coming, they'd be here already."

Kudwa could not look at Adam. "You go back. I will wait for other Indians to come, we will save the trees and your brother."

"No." Adam urged his horse upward as far as he could before alighting to walk.

Kudwa sent a quick swift prayer to the heavens and followed.
***

Hoss found his appetite lacking as he stuffed himself with as much food as he could hold before the others stirred. He put a serious dent in their supply, anyway. His brothers would be proud—creating bad luck was as easy as ducking a ten-foot-high fence. He heard a logger stir and scrambled to his bedroll, flopped on his side and lay still, hoping his grumbling belly wouldn't give him away.
***

Claude crawled over to the fire, lifted the hemlock cover, and stoked it. There were a few sparks left that he encouraged into a flame by tossing more sticks on the fire. He grabbed the paper-wrapped bacon. The package was ripped open, nothing left but a few fat strands sticking to paper. "Hey! This was full of meat yesterday. Where'd it go?" He grabbed the gunnysack that had been full of sourdough biscuits and found only crumbs. "What the hell's going on here?!"

Bret turned on his side. "Who's making the ruckus? I'm trying to sleep."

"Where's that gunman?" Claude got to his feet. "Hey, Carne?"

Bret threw off his blanket and shivered as cold air crawled through him. "Why you bellyaching and not stoking the fire?"

Claude looked up at the stranger from his crouched position. "Who the hell are you? You weren't here last night."

"Sorry, got in after everyone was asleep. Name's Bret. I assist Van Remus in this operation."

"This is your land then?" Claude asked.

"Do I look like a thief?" Bret picked up the coffeepot sitting on the fire.

"I ain't looked at you close enough yet," Claude mumbled. "Why are you doing it then?"

"Doing what?" The pot handle burnt his hand as Bret poured a cup, going miserably well with the cramped feeling from a short night on the ground. His skin crawled with tiny wood creatures that had snuggled inside his clothes but he refused to give in to the itch.

"We got no business cutting in this section. You walk any direction and you can feel the ground sagging under your feet. See that tree standing right there? We hacked just to bleed it and now it's leaning sideways. And that's not the worst. Look up that way."

Bret listened intently, fascinated by the logger's assessment of the land.

"We keep hacking at the few mature trees and that'll be all it'll take to bring all these rocks tumbling on down. Van Remus wants us to blow the trunks right out of the ground. That's crazy. If we blast out those stumps, I'll be standing a lot higher than that gunpowder. Because everything below it's going to go."

"You talking about landsliding?"

"Hey, wait a minute." Claude stood. "Now that I think of it, I haven't seen any gunpowder around here. Maybe them stumps can stay where they is, no?"

"No gunpowder?" Bret leaped to his feet. "Clete had them pack a box."

Hoss yawned loudly and stretched, smacking his lips. "Donja keep the noise down to let a fella sleep?" He sat up. "You got the coffee, yah? I smell someting."

"Yeah, well, make your own. Something got in our food last night, coon or something. We ain't gonna have much to eat for a while."

"Not goot." Hoss shook his head sadly. "Logger need food to bring down da tree." He looked purposefully at Bret. "You still dere, skinny fellow? You got more gumption den I taut."

"Doesn't pay to be too quick to judge."

"Yah, yah, but I was tinking, dis land, maybe we find better place to cut, no? I hear what dis fella say---."

"You fellows don't know how to mind the affairs you're being paid for. Just do your work."

"First affair is getting da food," Hoss poked around. "I'm gonna take someting to dat poor fella whose leg come off." Hoss found a biscuit and stood. Bret, after eyeing him a moment, got up to follow.

Petey lie stretched out on the cold ground off his bedroll, shivering hard. Hoss put a hand on his forehead. Petey's face was chalk-like, his lips swollen and dry, and leaves and pine needles stuck in his hair indicated a restless night. Hoss shook his head. "No medicine. Tink he gonna die."

Bret pulled his gun. "Maybe we ought to put him out of his misery."

Hoss straightened and gently tilted Bret's gun barrel away from Petey's head. He handed Bret the biscuit. "I tink maybe I can make medicine. I learned once, from my mama. You give him water instead of bullet."

Bret munched on the biscuit meant for Petey as Hoss went off to search for plants. Behind them the other loggers roused themselves. Bret stood over Petey wondering about that big oaf, the Swede, off digging in the ground for roots. He seemed out of place here with these other timber rattlers. Even Claude's concern, with his talk about landsliding, was only for his own neck.

The loggers in waking complained about the lack of food. Coons? Someone named Carne? Or someone else? Bret thought maybe that Claude could have done it. He called for a Carne who didn't answer. Whoever made a mess of things here, Bret was certain old Ben Cartwright had a hand in it somehow.

"Hey, kid! Come here!" Bret went back to the campfire where McManus grabbed his arm and pulled him over to where the food should be. "I'd say you showed up just in time, mister. We can't work with no food in us. I'll tell you what we will do. We'll start hacking at the trees if you hightail it to the city and get us some grub without a single stall."

"Hey! Look at this." Louis, poking in the brush, came up with an axe with a broken edge.

"Looks like somebody's done all this deliberate," McManus said. As with a sudden thought he looked around. "Damnit, the oxen are gone!"

The loggers looked each other over.

"Got to be one of the new ones," Louis eyed Bob and Bart, who were pretty much minding their own business. "We was fine before they come."

"Hey," Claude said. "I'll bet it's that Swede."

McManus held up a hand. "Guess you better add some tools to that list when you go to town, Mr. Boss. Seems our friend Carne felt he wasn't getting enough out of this operation. He's missing." McManus lit up a roll. "I've half a mind to ditch this whole operation and look for other work. Been jinxed from the start." He blew out some smoke and turned to Louis. "Indian arrow came before them new loggers got here."

Bret looked over where the Swede forced something down Petey's throat. "That how he got hurt?"

"Indian attack! We was swarmed!" Adolf said, casting furtive eyes at the others.

"Indians?" Bret watched Hoss. "Think that accent is fake?"

Claude shrugged. "He's real close, that one is. If we're looking to cast some fingers, mine goes his way."

Bret looked hard at Claude. "Could be you got it in for him."

"Me? What would I got agin him?"

"Why you so quick to hang him?"

"I kin tell when a man's got something to hide. Been living with it all my life."

McManus picked up an ax and swung it hard into the nearest tree, making Bret jump. "Just get riding or this work will never be done. As it stands now, we'll be lucky to down one tree today and no stumps blown out either. Take that Swede with you. I don't need Claude going at him, and he's got no one to partner up with anyhow."

Bret went to Hoss kneeling next to Petey. "Doing any better?"

Hoss's hand was on Petey's forehead and slowly moved down Petey's face to shut his eyes. Bret stood again. Hoss's lips moved, his prayers soft.

"You know, this is probably the most anyone's ever cared about him. Come on." He pulled Hoss to his feet. "Let's get him buried. You and me got some riding to do.

CHAPTER 39

Ben rose before the sun and dressed in haste, which meant just pulling on his boots. No more putting off what needed to be done. The days have flown without his participation since Adam was shot, and Van Remus, the venomous snake, still slithered through his life. Time to loosen a poison mouse named Reeger, let him swallow whole and choke to death. Thanks to Reeger, he'll get Clete behind bars where he belonged – and that venomous son as well.

He lingered at Joe's bedside, watching his youngest sleep. Only time will tell if he recovers his mind fully. When he knocked on Hop Sing's door he received a quick "almost leady." Ben threw on a log on the fire and poked absently at the burning embers. He threw in a few handfuls of kindling and lit a match. He watched the small fire burn between his fingers before tossing it on the wood. If the house was cold due to the burnt-out room, he couldn't feel it – just the singular numbness that came with worry.

At least Norma agreed to stay on a little longer. Hop Sing looked drawn and tired, saddened that he didn't stop Hoss or Adam. Ben knew Hoss couldn't sit by waiting to be hit. And Adam, in shock, no longer thought at all, just acted to ease the guilt he accepted.

At footsteps on the stairs Ben looked up. Reeger, staring down, opened his mouth to speak, but Ben put a finger to his lips and waved the young miner down.

"Don't know how that Adam can sleep on such a hard mattress," Reeger said, rubbing his back as he reached the bottom step. "Plum drove me loco, turning every which way."

Ben grabbed his holster and gun from the middle drawer of the cabinet and checked it for bullets. "Ever since sleeping on the ground on his first cattle drive, says he prefers the ground to a bed. Leaves his window open a crack, even in winter."

"I know, I closed it."

243

"Come on, we got some hard riding."

"What?"

"We're going to town to talk to the sheriff."

Reeger turned to the fire and picked up the poker. "No, better bring him here." Old ash and soot rose up lazily as he poked at a log to encourage a new flame.

Ben pressed fisted hands to his hips. "Look, there's no time for this. I have to look for my sons, find Roy, I need you with me. We'll get this whole thing ended today!" Another two seconds' delay and he would be pleased to lay this Reeger flat and drag him to town unconscious.

Reeger turned back, warming his rear side as he faced the chill coming from his host. "If I get ambushed and kilt out there, will that help ya? Ain't I safer here?" He held up his hands in reflex but Ben didn't take more than a step toward him in threat before stopping.

Ben caught the vision of the long ride to Virginia City where plenty could go wrong, and Ben planned a cut through a corner of the north 40 on the way. "All right. I'll find Roy and bring him here. Just don't go anywhere." Ben paused. "I'll make it worth your while."

"Mr. Cartwright, if I'da wanted money, I'da asked for it last night."

Ben grunted, put his hat tight over his furled brow, and quietly left the house.

***

Hop Sing laid out a fine breakfast for Norma and Reeger – blueberry flapjacks, corn muffins, greasy bacon cooked crisp and plenty of well-scrambled eggs. Reeger thought maybe he already died and this was heaven. Hop Sing took a goodly helping up the stairs to Joe but there was more than plenty left for the two of them.

Norma drilled Reeger all through his fine breakfast on what he knew about Van Remus. Reeger wasn't sure he ever talked so much in his whole life, not while eating, anyway. He told her a couple times that talking while eating didn't seem proper in the company of a lady but she kept pushing more food at him. Finally he had to stop eating because the plates were empty. "Yeah, that Van Remus, you know, he's a smooth one. He told me about why he shot Adam, and I didn't mind helping, but when he admitted what he did to Joe---."

"Chew that one a little finer, would you, Reeger?"

Norma and Reeger turned. Joe, fully dressed, leaned on the rail halfway down the staircase for support.

As Norma hurried to Joe, Reeger slowly stood. "Huh?"

"That's Adam's chair you're sitting in." Joe shrugged of Norma's offer of help and finished taking the stairs. "You remember Adam, the one you didn't care got shot." Reeger looked back at the chair he sat on and scratched his head. "I hear you slept in his bed last night, too." "Something wrong, Joe?" Reeger wiped his hands on his pants.

"You were talking about Adam, my brother, a minute ago." Joe staggered slightly but straightened as much as he dared as he approached Reeger. "Tell me what you said, make it clear and simple."

"I said that once I heard you was hurt---."

"You agreed to work with Van Remus even after finding out he had Adam shot."

"Joe, the way Van Remus explained it---."

"Look, I don't care how he said it! You work for a man like that, you don't belong here."

"Joe." Norma took his arm. "Reeger is here to help."

"Ma, sometimes I don't think you know what's going on at all. Pa wouldn't marry a woman who didn't care about all of us." Shaky, Joe lowered himself into the settee. "I want you out of here, Reeger."

Norma bit her lip and turned to Reeger.

Reeger cleared his throat. He walked to the settee and faced Joe square. "I was telling. . .your ma. . . that things is different between you and me than between me and your brother."

Joe slowly drew himself up to stare into Reeger's eyes. "Anyone who does my brother wrong does wrong to all of us." Joe tightened his fists and caught Reeger off guard with a clip to his gut. Joe couldn't use much force but Reeger's gut was so full he doubled over anyway. "Now get out of here. Before I really lose my temper."

"Joe, he can't go out there!"

"Then take me back upstairs. My breath is closing up on me down here." Joe leaned against Norma. "I don't want to see you again, Reeger," he said as they climbed the stairs.

Reeger held his gut as he sat in the settee. There was no explaining to Little Joe in his present mood. Well, hell's fire, Joe took the whole story out of the situation. Never even let him get to the part about cutting out because of Joe being hurt. Joe can't expect everyone to feel about his older brothers the way he does.

When he heard the horse hooves in the yard, Reeger jumped to his feet. Maybe Ben came back for him. Reeger had the door open long enough to see it wasn't Ben. Somewhere above him he heard his name called.

He turned to close the door but the gun fired, the bullet faster than the door, catching Reeger sideways. He staggered backward, alarmed at first that he might be hit without realizing he was. He looked down at his shirt filling with blood and slipped to the floor.

Norma and Hop Sing were at Reeger's side when Joe joined them.

Joe shook him gently and patted his cheek. "Reeger? Reeger, listen to me. Is there anyone else?"

"Uh. Uh?"

Felling of the Sons

"Anyone else who knows what Van Remus said?" Reeger's eyes flickered but didn't open. "I'm sorry I didn't listen to you. Ma told me what happened. If there's anyone else. . .."

"Uh, no one." Reeger had nothing more to say.

Joe rubbed his mouth and laid Reeger's head back down. He stood gingerly, holding his side, and turned to pick up his holster and gun.

Hop Sing couldn't bring himself to look at Joe belting on the gun. "I bring him to bunkhouse, Joe?"

"Yeah. We'll need the sheriff out here before we…" he slouched visibly. After a moment's paused thought, he grabbed his hat.

Norma laid a firm hand on his arm. "Where do you think you're going, young man?"

"Look, I made a mistake. Now I gotta make it right."

"You can't go out there."

"I'll be careful. This time." He smiled and touched her cheek. "I'm sorry I yelled, Ma."

Hop Sing grabbed his arm. "Mr. Joe more stubborn than two other brothers and pen full of sows awtogether. But I not let you go. Mr. Cartlight must come home see one son still here."

"Hop Sing, you're not saying you've given up on my brothers, are you? They're going to be fine, and so am I. But we can't watch our backs the rest of our lives. As far as I know, I'm the only one who can get the son, because I'm the only one who knows him. "

Hop Sing cursed at the ceiling in Chinese before gesturing wildly at Joe. "Hop Sing tired of saying You Stay! And then you go. You, Mr. Joe, never can stop. Me know better."

"Why, Hop Sing," Joe winked at the Chinaman. "I do believe you care."

Hop Sing's eyes glistened. He shuffled back to the kitchen.

Norma grabbed Joe's arm. "Don't, Joe. Don't hurt your father this way."

Joe kissed her lightly on the cheek, took her hand off his arm, and walked out of the house.

***

"Clem, I stopped at Roy's house and he wasn't sick in bed and now you're saying he's not here either? What in the name of the Sierras is going on here?" Ben had ridden hard, found nothing of interest in the western half of the north forty, no sign of Roy at his house and his muscles stung from the efforts but Clem didn't even try to be cooperative.

"Sorry I can't tell ya more than I know. I think he's in trouble, though."

"We have to find him. I need his help and I need to go after my sons!"

Clem scratched his head. "Okay, Ben, but what you got to go after Adam and Hoss for?"

"Because they. . .because he…" Ben grunted in frustration. "Where could Roy be!?"

"Well, let's think here." Clem leaned back against the desk.

"Knowing Roy, he left to settle some kind of disturbance yesterday."

"That's it, Ben!" Clem said excitedly, jumping up.

"What's it?"

"Well, what you just said. I think we're on the right track."

"All right, Clem, what happened in town yesterday that Roy might have been mixed up in?"

"Well, there was that fight between you and---."

"Before that!"

"Say, that Van Remus had a terrible day yesterday, didn't he? His mine caving in, and now he's sealed off a section that's too dangerous, won't let anybody in, not even that Dutch fellow who's looking to fix things down below."

"The Dutchman's here?"

"Yup. Showed up this morning but Van Remus sent him packing back to California, says there's too much water anyhow. Can't imagine---."

"Van Remus sealed off a section, won't let anyone in? Since yesterday afternoon?"

"That's about right."

Ben needed Roy to get Reeger under protective custody and get his statement to get at Van Remus legally. That would free him to take every minute available to find his sons. He waited for his gut instinct to kick in. If only he knew, knew for sure that Hoss was safe as a Swedish logger and that Adam was in the company of the Paiutes.

Van Remus had something to do with Roy being missing. Roy found something out and Clete had to stop him. Roy was now either dead or hidden away, soon to be dead.

"What better place to hide a sheriff?" Ben burst out into the street and jumped on his horse.

"Who? What? Where? What are you talking about?" Clem watched Ben ride off up C Street. He was quite sprightly for a man his age. But Clem was not amused. It was looking like another one of those long days ahead of him.

CHAPTER 40

Juce rode fast and hard back to Virginia City, almost catching up to Ben though Ben had a good lead. The night ride to the ranch left him thirsty and with a nagging need for sleep. He remembered firing his gun but not at who. The cool clean feel of purposeful shoot was missing because he didn't know the target. He knew he'd just left the Cartwrights and wondered if maybe he killed the third son. The other two he heard were already dead. If that's what he'd done, he's in for a world of hurt. Time to get the hell out of Nevada.

***

Carne came to under the flume, a stinging like the bite of a snake running through his arm, with the snake's teeth still clinging to his wrist. He imagined himself back in Oregon with the woman's husband standing over him, getting ready to kick him again. She had been a good lay, though not always a willing one. When her husband came in all huffy like he owned her, Carne dodged two of his fists easily but caught the third on his jaw and went flat on his back. He would show that river monkey. Carne went for the gun at his side with the broken wrist tied to the flume. The flume shook, a piece of wood falling and clipping his brow. But Carne didn't feel it. He had passed out again.

***

When Clete finally dragged himself to the morning's coffee delivered by another of the cloth-footed gals, it had cooled from sitting outside the door. He checked his pocket watch, sure enough, mid-morning, and his head throbbed from last night's wine. With the mine shut down, there was no shift to check on.

Talk in town was he took too many chances in the Golden Cross, got too greedy, couldn't see the future past his nose, people thinking the town might collapse on top of him if he didn't shore up harder. He used to care about his operation but now the Ponderosa was within his grasp. Let the people fuss, it kept their meager lives semi-ambivalent.

He glanced into Bret's room. The bedclothes were untouched. Bret slept out under the stars? His son never had much liking for it.

250

Felling of the Sons

Perhaps his boy is out there taking care of those Cartwrights himself, one by one. And why shouldn't he? The Ponderosa was his legacy, after all. He took after his mother and Clete reminded the boy of it every chance he had.

Clete was about to set his mind to wondering what became of Juce when he heard heavy thudding footsteps outside his door. Juce looked like he'd been riding hard all night, his red eyes almost swollen shut. Clete jerked him inside. "Take care of loose ends, did you?"

Juce squinted wearily at Clete before falling into a winged chair. "Loose ends? Just what did I do for you last night?"

"Don't you know?"

"I had a bit too much whiskey to understand it all."

"But did you succeed?"

"I shot somebody down. But I still don't know who or why. And I don't know if'n I killed 'em like you wanted. What I'm asking now that I'm sober is, what the hell did I do for you?"

Clete reached into his jacket pocket. "If I wanted you to know, I would have told you last night. Hopefully, you cut off a loose end."

Juce laughed, a rusty sort of sound. "I'm cutting out. You keep your money," he said to Clete's hand inside the jacket pocket. "I only hope the fellow what took my bullet didn't die from it." As he met Clete's eyes he realized Clete wasn't pulling money out of his coat.

"I don't much like guns." Clete's hand shook a little. "But I don't figure I'll miss this close."

"You won't. . .can't. . .people will hear."

"Never trust a man who hires to kill."

Juce wiped his mouth with a hand, threw himself to the floor and reached for his gun, giving Clete the opportunity he wanted. His eyesight was just fine for shooting close up, and even though he never killed before, he hit the drunk center chest. Pulling a trigger was easy with the right incentive. As Juce's mouth worked in a death reflex, Clete figured he could kill just about anyone—as long as he caught 'em unawares.

***

Bret watched from on top his mount as Swede studied the ground.

"Any idea which way those oxen went?"

"Dem big animals stupid." Swede stood. "No trail dere. No can tink like oxen because dey stupid."

"You think the gunman was behind all this?"

"Dey say dis?" Swede mounted up. "I only know would be a man without anyting in his head to stay around after making trouble. He be fast and far away."

"You're probably right. Man would have to be pretty dumb." Bret looked out over the trail they were following, uneven and rocky, with the trees thinning just before a heavy slope where they'd have to alight and walk for a time. "Or so clever he'd never expect to be caught."

Swede let his horse get ahead of Bret's and looked back over his shoulder. "Dis dey could be too. Don't know we ever learn da truth." He reached the ridge of the slope and alighted. "I'll take the way down first, you see safe, and then you follow."

The Swede walked the slope, holding the horse off with one arm straight in back of him to keep the horse from running him down. Bret felt something phony about him, all right. Cartwright must have sent this man in to ruin the operation. But why this elaborate disguise? This Swede was no more immigrant Swede than Clete was.

With a few slips and stumbles, Swede reached the trail that would lead them back to the main road. The road had been cut through rock, making an even and easy walk for the horses as welcome to a Sierra rider as a summer rain in the desert.

"I wait, you come, yah?" Swede called up to him.

252

Felling of the Sons

"Sure Swede, be right down. This mean we're giving up on the oxen?"

"Hah!" Swede squinted up at Bret making the descent. "They're probably making themselves dizzy going in circles..." After a slight hesitation he continued, "Dey maybe wander back into camp by de time we done, yah?"

Bret lost his footing on a wrong step and fell backward, letting his horse finish going down ahead of him. He sat a moment to catch his breath, and finished taking the slope in a sitting position. He stood indignantly and wiped himself off.

"Yeah, I bet you're right about those oxen. If we pick up a couple saws and enough food for a week, we should have no problem getting enough trees hacked down in the next couple of days to make them Cartwrights plenty worried. I don't even care if we don't have oxen to pull them away. Clete isn't in this for the lumber anyhow."

Swede clenched and unclenched his fists. "Not for lumber?"

"Nope." Bret grinned widely at the Swede. "We don't go around claiming it but we're out to destroy Ben Cartwright, land, cattle *and* his family." Bret mounted again. "You know, this is enjoyable, a ride like this. Smelling fresh pines and mountain air, interesting company. I glad we got shut down for a day. I never chopped a single tree in my life. Believe it?"

"I come from family where we do everyting hard. Only way we get food."

"Ah, well, you must be an extra hard worker by the size of you. You don't always speak with an accent either. Why do you suppose that is?"

Swede only glanced at him and didn't answer. Bret grinned. Doggoned if he didn't just stumble across the middle Cartwright son.

***

Adam stared at the campfire he and Kudwa made for their salted pork fat. He took another sip of the berry juice Kudwa concocted and

253

winced at the sour taste that made his throat feel strange. He hadn't gotten more than a couple hours' sleep since leaving the ranch. Back at home he slept easy, even after the dreams started up. Here sleep met the horrified face of the woman he trampled and screams echoed through his head until he woke. Worst were the times when the screams didn't sound like him or the woman, but like Hoss or Joe – cows stampeding over his brothers. Only he could turn those cows away, by letting them trample over him.

Several times Kudwa came alongside him and straightened him up in the saddle or he would have tumbled. He had felt he was healing back in the comfort of the house. But here, riding a jarring horse, the horse he was so used to riding he should feel as good as lying still, brought up a hot stinging inside the wound that he didn't like. A couple of times when Kudwa wasn't looking he felt his shirt in back, thinking the wound had busted open, and then, angered by the worry, forced himself to sit straight again and think only about Hoss.

Kudwa threw more wood on the fire. "Berry good?"

Startled, Adam looked up. "For a second I thought you were Hop Sing." Kudwa only stared. "Sorry." He winced and got to his knees. "I've had enough. Let's get moving."

"You ate only one bite. Not good for healing."

Adam stood. "Don't worry about me, whatever you put in that juice helped some. What direction we going now?"

Kudwa didn't answer. He got down on his knees and lifted his arms to the sky. Quietly, using the voice deep in his throat, he chanted. Adam looked up at the sky and closed his eyes. He kept his own prayer short but intense. Still in his position Kudwa's chant turned into a song. Adam kicked the fire to spread it loose and watched as the flames died away. He wanted Kudwa with him, but he was too impatient to wait. After a quick scrutiny of the area, he came up with a direction.

***

At the Golden Cross Ben jumped off his horse and approached the guard. "I'd like to go down there." He felt queasy staring at the shaft opening.

254

"Sorry, Mr. Cartwright, sir. Mr. Van Remus has specific orders not to let anyone down who is not on his payroll."

Ben nodded and half turned, and then came back with a right fist into the man's face. He leaped down onto the ladder, in seconds ankle-deep in water, and felt his way along the damp crumbling walls. In the dark, holed up like a fish in a bucket, Ben couldn't tell which direction to move without worrying about bumping his forehead into an overhang, his hands in front of him to feel out the walls. There were no candles to light that he could find so he followed his sense of smell. One way of telling was by sniffing out the thickest air — that would be the area of the collapse. Finding a collapse didn't mean finding Roy – and he had precious little time to waste.

"Hey, you! Where you headed?"

Ben wheeled around. Two miners carrying candles approached him, grimy faces flickering in the flames. Ben didn't recognize them. "Just call me the Dutchman. I come here to help with your timbering problems. You see, no more rocks falling on your heads. That one upstairs, he's too stubborn to see things I do. So I knocked him down. You stubborn too?"

"Ah, that's right, Billy, I heard tell someone was going to be inspecting once Van Remus lets him in. You go ahead, mister. We sure ache to see an end to the mine cave-ins. You need any help?"

"Oh, no, no, you boys go on up. Only I need to take the danger, because I cannot come up vit theory mit-out the danger."

"Oh sure. Well, you holler, someone will be close by if you need it."

They moved off down the shaft and the light from their candles faded. Ben put his hand back on the wall to guide him and before realizing it, ran into a collapsed section. He could nearly hear his heartbeat echoing as he put his hands up and carefully pried some rock loose. He followed the wall along, moving slowly and carefully, every few steps pulling more rock loose.

Roy could be here, and he could also be dead. He wasn't young anymore. Roy didn't deserve to be a part of this, not this way.

"Roy?" Rocks were looser here. He put his hand up against it and felt a light movement of air. He winced when he smelled the sulfur air. "Roy!" He pulled out some more rock and sidestepped quickly as more rock tumbled down on him. He bent forward as the roof of the mine trembled, dust and rocks falling on him before subsiding again. He stopped to clear the dirt out of his eyes because of the pain, not because it helped him see well in this unholy darkness.

"Hey! Hey, you in there! Get on out, before this whole thing falls on your head!"

The yelling came from behind but Ben didn't stop digging, didn't give the dirt on his face any further attention. "It's Roy Coffee, he's trapped down here! Come on and give me a hand." Ben found a hole and stuck his arm through and the rocks fell easier. He threw rocks aside until he had enough space to crawl in. This wall was a deliberate trap, not caused by the cave-in but waiting for a cave-in to happen.

The rocks fell away beneath him, scraping him as he crawled through. His beige shirt wouldn't be wearable again, his vest probably beyond repair and he realized for certain how old he was. He wished he had a canteen, even in the dampness his throat bunched up from the thick, wet dust, his nerves trembling from the bad air. He crawled, thoroughly soaked, until his head butted a wall. He heard a groaning coming from the left. He crawled forward, reaching ahead with his hand until he touched something softer than the silver walls.

"Roy?" Ben shook his old friend's shoulder gently and finally Roy grunted. Ben was nose-to-nose with him and still couldn't see him. "Are you all right?" He felt Roy for ropes to untie, but there were none. Roy had been knocked out and left to languish until the mine collapsed on top of him.

"Ben. Nice of you to stop by." Roy coughed hoarsely.

"Don't talk, save your strength." He helped Roy stand. "Can you walk?"

"It's been a time. . .I think so."

Ben pulled him in the direction of the crawl space as the rocks over their heads trembled again.

"Hey! Hey down there! Did you say you found Roy Coffee?"

Had Clem followed them down? But before Ben could answer, something thudded in the ceiling over and ahead of them. Ben grabbed hold of Roy and fell back as whatever had moved above them started a tremendous rumbling and shaking and another wall of rock came tumbling down.

CHAPTER 41

With his chanting finished Kudwa rubbed his palms on the ground.
Adam had ridden on ahead, believing he knew where to find his
brother. Kudwa hoped his friend had enough wisdom to keep himself
low and wait for help. Kudwa had to wait for the others who were
coming. Only all of them together would be able to stop more trees
from falling. Kudwa kept his palms against the ground. He could feel
a trembling in the dirt that meant the ground had weakened. This land
had grown slanted, angled so deeply in places that only the roots of
the live and healthy trees held it together. Landsliding, Adam called
this trembling, when the ground falls from the top and takes
everything in its path down to the bottom, destroying land that would
take a long time to heal again. Kudwa could not picture this violent
destruction in his head – like trying to see the day the sun did not rise.

He checked that the campfire was out and led his horse to grazing.
Then he knelt again, eyes to the heavens, until Indian horses
surrounded him.

***

Arms wrapped around his head, Ben lay feeling trapped as the
explosive caving in of rock and soggy timber rumbled to silence. He
figured himself dead. This was the end of pain, of worry. Who would
save his boys now? No, Norma was right; he raised them. . .to take
care of themselves. Better just let them do that and let go of life. He
didn't want to, but there was no figuring on the Maker's plans. His
boys would miss him. . .if they survive, that is. . .they have to! He
tried to move but couldn't. No doubt then, he was dead, his spirit
slowly detaching from life. Joe. . .Joe still needed him. Joe was only a
boy and his mind wasn't all there. He thought Norma was his mother.
Ah, was that so bad? Joe never knew a mother.

"Ben."

And Hoss. . .so proud to be Cartwright, so unwilling to give up a
single tree on the Ponderosa or a single hair on a jackrabbit's head.
Ben realized he wouldn't have stopped him from going off into the

hills to stop those loggers. He would have sent someone with Hoss, but he wouldn't have stopped him.

"Ben, you hear me?"

Adam. The pain of telling the boy the truth hurt worse than any pile of rocks ever could. If only he had another chance, he'd tell his son . . . somehow convince him that this whole Van Remus mess was his fault, and not Adam's at all. Ben had considered himself guiltless over what happened to Van Remus and because of that, Adam took up the burden.

"Ben!"

Some kind of noise echoed through his cold still body, a shaking, maybe the cave-in wasn't over yet.

As Roy shook him Ben grunted, his eyes opening slowly. "Ben?"

Ben shook himself violently, feeling rocks and debris falling off him. "Yeah, I'm here." He shook his arms off and forced himself to sit up. His head throbbed and one ankle felt swollen.

"How are you doing?" Ben got to his knees and felt around for a way out, but in the frustrating dark his fingers touched nothing but rock.

"Ben, I ain't fit for this kind of activity. Think we're gonna die down here?"

"No. We'd be dead already. Let's see if the route ahead of us is open. I can't see a blasted thing, can you?"

"Nope."

"Crawl behind me." Ben moved ahead after brushing Roy's shoulder. Sure enough, no matter which way he crawled he hit more rock, a wall more solid than the one he dug through to get in. That wall had been a deliberate piling to hide a man. This wall was nature's doing, the earth rebelling against being tunneled into. Ben dug his fingers in and pulled some loose rock down, ducking as some rock from higher up fell on top of him.

Roy crawled up beside him. "Think we can make it out?"

"We have to. Are you all right? Can you dig?"

"My arms are awful sore, Ben, but it's either dig or pine away from want of clean air." Roy pulled out some rock and received a spraying of stone on his head. He ducked back. "Slowly though, Ben, or we'll be buried for sure."

Ben stood, reaching as high as he could. "Let's clear some of this loose stuff first. Then when we hit solid we can use our gun barrels."

They worked on silently except for coughing and grunting, pushing rock aside.

"Ben," Roy said, without slowing up, "that Van Remus is a bad'un all right. I guess I shouldn'ta played my hand so soon as I did but I figured on him not taking any more chances getting caught."

"Roy, sometimes there's no telling which way a man will go."

"How's Adam and Little Joe?"

"Adam's better, but now he's out looking for Hoss. . .how did you know about Joe?"

"I heard people talking. So it's true, he was kilt?"

"No, he was stabbed under the ribs but he'll be fine."

"And where's Hoss?"

"Can only think he went to stop the loggers from cutting trees on our land. Clem says he disguised himself as a Swede, like his Uncle Gunar."

"Say, I remember him. Clem knows you come down here?"

"Well, I think he realizes this is where I ended up. I'm afraid I bolted out of the office and might not have told him why."

"He ain't the brightest but we can count on him to figure it out. So what's this you said, you got trespassers on your land?" Roy cried out and shook his cramped hand before digging back at the rock.

Ben bit back his own pain time after time by thinking of his sons. He explained everything to Roy as they dug further, including his near-death revelation that he raised his sons so that he could trust their judgment. Roy nodded, grunting, sadly apologetic for getting Ben into this mess, and Ben responded with a laugh so that Roy would understand he had no regret for finding him first. Ben stopped sudden and put his head to the cool granite wall.

"Did you hear something?" Roy in the dark sensed Ben sudden motionlessness.

"I'm not sure." Ben pressed tight against the rock. "There's someone out there. Hey! Hey down here!" He pounded a fist against the solid wall, more out of frustration than the belief he would be heard.

Roy grabbed Ben's arm after a few faulty tries. "Better not, Ben. Could be Clem, but it could be Van Remus."

Ben stepped back as Roy leaned into the indent they'd made in the wall. "Hello, come help me out, will ya? I'm awful thirsty and there's no air."

"Oh, hey, that's a terrible shame, Mr. Sheriff. Too bad that cave-in didn't take care of you. Then you wouldn't have to suffer no more."

"Maybe you oughta poke a hole in this here wall and put a bullet to my head."

"We let you keep your gun, do it yourself."

"Can't. Ain't got the gumption fer it." Roy paused. "Can you stand yourself letting a fella suffer this way?"

"I got no trouble with---."

There was a scuffling and the sound of iron being pulled from leather. The gun connected against something with a solid thud and someone splashed down into the water.

"Roy? Ben? You in there?" Clem shouted, with excited shouts of rescue behind him.

"Yeah, it's us." Ben called back. "Dig us out of here!"

"Okay, just stand back."

                                    ***

Mac was hot and out of breath by the time he found Clete having a solitary lunch at the Dusty Brisket. Clete got Juce's body removed by telling Vince that Juce broke in, drunk as always, and tried to rob him. He found his appetite healthy but couldn't stomach the smell of the International's food. When Mac saw Clete, he stopped running and wiped his sweaty brow.

"Another cave-in at the Golden Cross, boss! Don't know what started it this time!" Mac plopped down in a chair opposite Clete.

Having already heard the cave-in horn sounding through town Clete chewed casually, the sausage not as easy to swallow as raw cow meat. "Not a bad concern, is it? There ain't no one down there right now."

Mac leaned forward. "They say the Dutchman's down there. Old Bill, the guard, took himself a nice clip to the jaw and two other fellows who was just checking came across this fellow, too."

"The Dutchman?" Clete put his silverware down and picked up his coffee. "What did he look like, they tell you?"

"Big, silver-haired. Dark eyebrows. They reckon he's down there lying dead in this new collapse and now the mines ain't never gonna be safe."

So old Ben figured out where he put the sheriff. Now it seems he's gone and bought the big one for himself. If that were true, then the game's over and he's won after all. He'll believe in heaven, too, when

262

he sees it. "Go on back and keep an eye on the situation for me. When they haul the bodies out, come give me a holler. I want to see them."

"But what if---."

"I don't want to know your problems, you heard me clear the first time. Now git! You're stinking up my meal." Clete's food tasted even better imagining Ben's dead carcass stretched out on the ground.

After his meal Clete strolled leisurely to his room to get the property claim papers. With old Ben dead, claiming the Ponderosa would not be as satisfying but it would be a whole lot simpler. And with his three boys homeless, they'll be a lot easier to kill besides. Can't leave them alive to come back after him. He and Bret deserved a little peace and quiet after all they'd been through.

CHAPTER 42

Joe rode Cochise slow to Virginia City though his impatience ran fast. His ribs were sore and he'd be no help if he fell off the horse in a dead faint. He wondered how Adam managed. Joe couldn't figure what to make of Adam killing that woman. Sure, as a kid Adam probably got himself in some dumb trouble, but why didn't he ever talk about it? He always lectured them about how they should talk things out.

A deep, painful breath escaped him as Joe pulled back the reins in front of Roy's office. He gritted his teeth and alighted. Cochise's reins dropped to the ground where he'd stay ground hitched. Inside the sheriff's office Joe found Clem with his feet up breathing into hot coffee. He was dirty and ragged, like he just wrestled in the street with some bandit. When Clem saw Joe a wide grin broke across his face. He got to his feet and put the coffee down, spilling some on his hand.

"God in heaven, Joe, good to see ya! When I heard you was dead I just about bawled." Clem grabbed his hand and pumped it. He dropped Joe's hand and leaned toward him. "Ah, let's keep that last part just between you and me, okay?"

Joe took the first opportunity to back away. "Sure, Clem. Where is Roy?"

"Roy? Ah, didn't you see him? He and your Pa went over to the doc's after the cave-in, and Roy says they were heading on out to the Ponderosa, to see about a witness."

"Don't know how I coulda missed them." Joe suddenly couldn't remember what trail he'd taken in to town.

"You're looking a might peaked. The doc could fix you up, too."

"Thanks, but I'm fine. I got something I gotta do."

"Well, maybe you do, but you just come back from the dead."

264

They both turned at the heavy boots clomping outside the sheriff's office and Van Remus burst in, red in the face and breathless. "Clem, where's that sheriff of yours?"

Clem stepped in front of Joe to hide the young Cartwright. "Roy has been rescued from your mine, and right now he and Mr. Cartwright are on their way to find a witness to some shameful attempts at murder."

"How'd they get out of that mine!? There was a cave-in. They should be dead right now!" Clete leaned against a chair, fighting for control. "I mean, they're awful lucky, when some of my workers were---."

"You wanted them dead, didn't you?" Joe stepped out from behind Clem. With an expression of physical stress from pulling his shoulders back, he attained the desired menacing effect.

Clete staggered backward against the door, pinching the bridge of his nose as he squeezed his eyes shut. When he looked back up at Joe and then Clem, the difference was startling. "You accusing me, boy? I warned Roy about going down there, warned him it wasn't safe. Now why Ben went down there is a different story. He had the express desire of causing my whole investment to collapse." He turned to Clem. "I want a warrant out on his arrest."

"How you gonna back up that story with Roy still alive?" Clem folded his arms and relaxed against Roy's desk.

Clete exhaled. "That sheriff a friend of the Cartwrights, isn't he? You think people can't be convinced what he'd do for friends? I've seen testimony like his shot down many times in court. Even a sheriff can be bought."

Joe pulled back a fist. "Why you low down dirty snake. You had my brother shot! You sent your son after me. If you think---."

"My son? Where'd you pick up a notion like that? My son died a long time ago. Are you referring to my associate? His methods may be a little crude, but he is perfectly harmless."

"Too bad he didn't kill me off, like you planned."

"Son, I don't expect you'd want to think poorly of your Pa. But what I got here might change your mind. Once upon a time your Pa kept me from claiming some very valuable land. This proves it." Clete pulled the property claim papers out of his jacket and handed them to Clem.

"What's he got there, Clem?" Joe peered over his arm. He could see several notations about boundaries he knew as well as his own name. "That legal?"

"Legal enough looking. But I ain't too familiar with the law. I mean, this kind of law."

"And now, since you don't think the fine Mr. Cartwright worthy of arrest, I expect I'll just have to present these to a court to take what is rightfully mine. The Ponderosa!" Clete chuckled as he turned away, an obscene sound Joe aimed for with his fist.

Before Clete could duck, Joe landed a fist to his jawbone, not a hard blow but Clete flew backward into the door and slumped down. He tried to shake it off and appeared ready to lurch back with a fist of his own but instead a good dosing of head misery gripped him. "AH! Damn you, boy. Didn't your pa ever teach. . .you respect for your. . ." He staggered to his feet and groped for the door like a blind man.

"Look at that, Clem, I think he might be having a seizure," Joe said, crossing his arms in front of his chest to still his aching ribs.

Clem walked over to Clete. "Yeah, well, I don't much like the thought of him dying in here." He opened the door and pushed Clete out into the street.

"About time, the place needed tidying up some." Joe stood next to Clem and watched as Clete fell to his knees with both hands pressed against his temples.

"What do you think he'll do with those papers, Joe?"

"I don't know." Joe frowned. "But I don't suspect he'll get that far with 'em right now. And I gotta find Bret. Any idea where the son of that snake might be holed up?"

"No, I don't reckon I do, but maybe ask around the Bucket of Blood. He's took to hanging out there quite frequent. Well, at least yesterday he was seen slugging them down right enough. Only take a clue from Van Remus there and don't ask for his son. Ask for Bret."

Joe tipped his hat at Clem and turned. Clem grabbed his arm, the sudden jerking motion making Joe wince. "I thought it was only Clete van Remus that you and your Pa was after."

"No, Clem, Bret's the one that gave me this." Joe pointed to his left side. "If you see him before I do, throw him in jail because I'm pressing charges."

Clem watched Joe walk out the door. "Will do, Joe. That I will do." He went out into the street to keep an eye on Joe's back, forcibly looking away, from the crowd gathered around the writhing villain in the street.

***

Clete flew into the street with great celebrity from Clem's shove, exaggerating the agony caused by his shameful fall until several people came over and offered their assistance. As they helped him down the street, his proud admonitions that he was fine were rightly ignored.

"Did you see what that deputy did?"

"What gave him the right to treat a dignified man like Mr. van Remus here that way?"

"We'll have to report him."

When the pain eased a bit, Clete blinked into the afternoon sunshine. "Please, please do. I'll. . .I'll press charges." The buildings moved past him somehow was his first thought, because he wasn't making any effort to go anywhere. "Where. . .are you taking me?"

"Why, to Dr. Jessup, of course."

"He'll fix you right up."

No one listened to Clete's pathetic attempts to deny he needed help. The last time he saw a doctor was shortly after he and Winnie were married. The headaches had just begun, small but nagging. The doctor told him to wear spectacles, and Clete went so far as to try a pair on. But Winnie laughed at him, saying he looked like a pumpkin in disguise, so he put them down and never touched a pair again.

At least they allowed him to brush himself off and walk into the doctor's house unassisted. Dr. Jessup, studying some reports, didn't look up. Finally, John waved Clete to a chair in his small study. Not much of an office for the only doctor in town, but then the city was young yet, with the feel of becoming something prominent, if Clete was any judge. Clete figured he was as good a judge of Virginia City as that Bill Stewart, who strutted around town as though he owned it, just because he was one of its first citizens.

The doctor put his report down and sighed. "Don't know if I'm up to it." He peered over his spectacles at Clete. "Why does a healthy-looking specimen such as you need a doctor?"

"I get these mind-busting headaches." The doctor stared at him, as if expecting more. Clete cleared his throat. "Ah, I am a businessman, and it. . .I'm looking for some medicine."

Jessup took his spectacles off and wiped them carefully, once looking at him through them as though checking to see if Clete was still there, and then got to his feet to look outside. Clete clamped his hands to the chair to keep from bolting. He didn't trust doctors but he never expected to have one refuse to treat him. The doctor finally turned from the door to stare at him, hands on hips. "You asking me for help? You've single-handedly kept me busier than I've seen in a month of cave-ins."

"That mean I've used up my quota of doctoring or something?"

Jessup sighed. "I can't just give out medicine. I have to check you over." He grabbed some tools off his desk and strode back. "Any idea when these headaches started?"

"Started?"

"Did you always have them?"

"No." Clete shook his head as a trembling hand slipped up to massage his temples. "Got 'em. . .just shortly after I was married." He looked up angrily. "Don't you start with those lambastes about marriage, doctor. My wife was a wonderful woman."

"I'm sure. How long has she been gone?"

"It's been. . .almost twenty years."

"And the headaches didn't go away?"

"No, I already told you."

"I see." Jessup took out his stethoscope. "Any other problems?" Clete shook his head and opened his shirt. "Rapid heartbeats? Hot breath, light headed?"

"It feels something like that during the headaches, you know."

Clete could feel Jessup's breath as he bent over him. Even his breath smelled sterile. Jessup straightened up after listening intently.

"Normal heart rate, no fluc---."

"It's not my heart, it's my head!" Clete wiped at his sweating forehead with his jacket sleeve. He squinted at the doctor's clock. "I have things to do, if you can't help..."

 Jessup nodded. "Could be a number of things, like anxiety. Unfinished business. Have you ever had your eyesight checked?"

Clete leaped to his feet. "I came for some simple headache pills. If you can't accommodate me, then I can send a rider off to Sacramento."

"Settle down. I thought you might be interested in a cure, rather than just a treatment. You know what they say about a man who cannot see clearly." Clete only returned the doctor's intent stare. Jessup walked with a slight limp to his cabinet. He pushed pills around for a moment, looking closely at one and then at another. Clete tried to see why the doctor was being so choosy, but the contents of his cabinet were a blur. Jessup finally settled on a bottle, after opening it and sniffing the contents.

"These ought to take care of it." He held the bottle out to Clete, who finished buttoning his shirt. "Use precaution with them. Only one at a time, and only when you feel the pain. And if you're interested in a cure, go back to San Francisco. For an eye doctor."

"Thanks, doc. Send the bill to the International." He grabbed the pills and ran out the door.

Clete dry-swallowed a pill as he strode to the livery to rent a mount. He climbed into the saddle and, as he sat high in the breeze, felt his mind sharpen. He saw himself squirming with a head misery in the street, those watching thinking him no better than a mule dog to be put to sleep. Bret was right — he's been weak all his life, too weak to win against a fortress of Cartwright men. Jolly shot just shy of his mark, Bret only nearly finished young Joe, and even Juce probably failed. And his cave-in on the sheriff failed. All his planning for nothing.

He felt the comforting crinkle of his papers in his jacket. He can still get his hands on the Ponderosa. And Ben, with his concerns over his sons, won't do a thing about it. He can have a judge serve eviction notices on Ben faster than Ben could blink.

He stopped outside the judge's house and stared incredulously. The judge had a notice tacked to his door: "Serving in Genoa for a week." A fit of rage rose through Clete, this time not accompanied by a head pain. Ben Cartwright even bought out the judge!

Roy will know these papers are real, friend or no friend. And Roy's gone with Ben to the Ponderosa. Time to pay that neighborly visit on his new home.

***

Felling of the Sons

Hoss got down to study the ground, although this plodding horse walked so slow he could see ants from up on his saddle. Bret leaned over his horse and pulled open Hoss's saddlebag. Hoss couldn't stop him. Since Hoss figured Bret was that son that Adam knew back in Sacramento, Bret might have figured out a few things about him, too.

"You see anything that looks like oxen tracks?"

"Nah, no ting dat I can see here. We just go on to Virginia City and buy new, yah?"

Bret got down off his horse and stood next to Hoss. "You know, this is rather dangerous territory. A few more steps north and the two of us would go tumbling right down the side of this cliff."

"Mr. Bret tink maybe he lost? I new boy to dis territory. I yust been going da way you say."

"Okay, I'll tell you why we're headed in this direction. There's a spot up ahead where I want to place a blast of gunpowder. Since you're the shooter, you can show me where to place it."

"You maybe blasting for silver mine too, yah?"

"Nope, even better. Didn't Clete tell you what you were hired for?" Bret walked his horse along the cliff and Hoss followed, nervously glancing downward where the cliff dropped off to a band of granite sand and rocks twenty feet below.

"He say we cut da wood."

"You are the shooter, aren't you?"

Hoss could think of no way around it. Bret saw the gunpowder. "Yah."

"Then you're the man for this job. See, we aren't logging here. We want a lot more than this land has to offer. Are you game?"

"Sure…yah. If da money is goot." Hoss felt like he was going in circles.

"We climb this ridge, straight up the side, with that load of gunpowder you're carrying. Tuck the whole mess of it up there and light it. KaaPow! Start a landslide. What do you think?"

Hoss stared up the fragile hillside. "But dis sound dangerous. How do we get away before the kabooming?"

"I wouldn't do this if I figured we'd get killed in the process."

"But. . .blasting is so tricky. Dere is no real way of knowing." He turned and found himself facing the barrel of Bret's rifle.

"Don't try to fool me."

"Yah, not good at fooling ya. The gunpowder, back at camp, I not like to see so close to campfire, so I tuck safely in bag. I not sure how to use. Maybe we just go to city, yah?"

"You know," Bret said, relaxing his grip on the gun, "I liked you, I really did. Watching you care for that logger, I thought, here was a fellow I could take as a friend. But not," his grip tightened on the trigger, "if you're going to play games with me."

Hoss swallowed hard. His eyes wandered nervously from the barrel of Bret's rifle to the gunpowder in his saddlebags. "I just. . .simple logger. Not much mind for playing games."

"So I figured," Bret continued, letting the barrel drop a little, "old Cartwright sent someone in to jinx the operation. You work for Cartwright, don't you?"

"I just dis fella hired for cutting da logs."

Bret laughed, pointing the barrel to the ground. "I am sorry, friend. I get suspicious sometimes. Nature of the territory, I guess." He started to walk again, pulling his horse.

Hoss caught his breath and followed. "If you feel dis is a bad---."

"This is the right thing. Maybe not in the eyes of the law, but in the eyes of justice." He nodded at Hoss. "Justice. I don't feel a speck of guilt over knifing that young Cartwright."

Visions of Joe's pale lifeless form in the woods flew through Hoss's mind, of hearing the doctor say he may never be the same again, and anger broke his fragile control. "You almost killed him!" With a solid fist he flattened Bret's jaw, knocking him to the ground.

Bret's rifle clattered to the ground. Hoss lunged for it but Bret rolled to the side, grabbing the gun. As Hoss advanced on him, Bret closed his eyes and pulled the trigger. Hoss took the bullet through the arm and staggered backward, catching himself before toppling off the edge of the cliff.

Hoss grabbed the barrel of the rifle before Bret could reload and tossed it aside. Bret backed up and grabbed the reins of Hoss's horse. He scrambled to his feet, keeping the horse between them.

"You keep your hands away from that saddlebag." Hoss spoke with the rage he had been holding inside. His arm felt shattered and the blood ran in a small river down his arm but anger made him lose all personal perspective. He pulled his gun with his good hand. "You thank your lucky stars I don't kill you right here."

"All right, all right." Bret took his hand off the saddlebag and held it up. He kept his other hand hidden down by his side.

Hoss kept his finger on trigger even though he pressed the hand tight against his bleeding wound. "You start walking. I'm taking you to the sheriff." He got ready to mount his horse but Bret suddenly whirled, stabbing a knife into the horse's upper thigh. The horse screamed and reared, knocking Hoss backward to the ground. He rolled, biting the scream of pain as his arm reacted to the stabs of pinecones. He couldn't stop as he rolled to the side of the cliff. He cried out as his bad arm crushed under him, and he blackened.

Before he knew it the edge of the cliff had let loose under him and he was falling.

**

Bret crawled to the edge and looked down. Cartwright was easy to spot in his red plaid shirt down at the bottom of the cliff. He felt a moment's surge of remorse, a foreign feeling that he shrugged off. Bret only did what he knew he had to do.

Clete, with his aching head and weak backbone, figured rightly enough that the land wouldn't weaken fast enough for natural landsliding. The Swede's bag of gunpowder should make up for it.

An unnatural landslide was better than none at all.

CHAPTER 43

Adam hadn't wanted to leave Kudwa behind. But Kudwa needed to wait for the Washo and Shoshone to come, and Kudwa would know which way to go. Adam let his eyes close as he gave the horse the trail. He was 12 again and a tribe of Indians was chasing him but why? He could remember them shouting, but he had known only enough about Indian language to be terrified. Now he counted on Indians for help. He had come in a circle, but much farther from the beginning than where he had started. Pa will understand. Even if he loses a son, he will eventually understand. He won't let Pa lose Hoss.

Why was that woman in the midst of the cattle? She looked like one of the cowboys trying to get the 50 heifers and 100 plus beeves into the spring branding pen and she held, no, she aimed a rifle into the herd. Not to kill a beefer. At someone. She was trampled because she was absorbed by hatred, because Pa and Sutter kept Van Remus from laying claim to land they wanted. She aimed her rifle at Pa.

Van Remus could have just taken the gold. Why did he want the land, too? Sutter's dream went the way of the gold rush. He has so little land left now, land he's fighting the U.S. government for the right to keep. Clete couldn't have held the land any better because very few of Sutter's squatter rights were recognized past the gold rush.

Maybe Sutter's goal was to keep all the gold to himself. No, that couldn't be right, because he's ended up with nothing, after all. Not the gold, the land or his 'empire.'

Maybe the Indians chasing Adam had been upset that Adam trampled on their land, land that Van Remus wanted to claim, land that Sutter claimed was his. Who did the land really belong to? Did his Pa and Sutter have the right to take it from the Indians, and keep it from Clete and his family?

Adam knew why the Indians had frightened him away. Because he realized even at that age that he was the trespasser, not them. He knew deep down that was why Inger died—because Pa had to pay the price for new land. Just like his ma had to die so that Pa would have a reason to go west in the first place. What remained was the last question—did Pa have the right to stop a man from claiming a discovery of gold?

Pa said to him once, the beauty of the land belonged to those who could see its true value, not those who could become money rich from it. Van Remus was uninterested in the beauty of the land, in preserving land quality, but in destroying it for greed.

Even with the noblest intention, Pa's denial to Clete wasn't justified. Some sort of compromise could have been found. And because of that — all this. Now Pa was close to losing all his dreams, as Sutter had.

Adam pulled his horse up short. He came to a fork in the trail. Somewhere off in the distance a rifle fired. He listened intently and as he did found a brief and distant memory of the stampede. But he shook it off, got his bearings and rode on, praying he wasn't already too late.

***

Joe figured he must have seemed a pitiful sort to Speavy, the barkeep at the Bucket of Blood. Without even being asked, Speavy offered up everything he thought Joe might need to know, including that Bret rode out of town last night and hasn't been back. That meant Bret was out where Adam and Hoss could take care of him. Joe felt disappointed but he needed sleep pretty bad. Those few hours he caught on the outskirts of town last night were long used up. He'd get his sleep and then he'd help his brothers, because no one knew better than him just how bad Bret could be.

***

Adam rode up the slopes. For a time he followed a rocky creek, staring intently at the ground and then urged his horse back up the slopes again. The rock was difficult for the horse to pick his hooves along so he kept it slow because a horse with a broken leg or even a split hoof would get him nowhere. He left the trail some ways back, keeping a feel on the direction the rifle shot originated from. The sound went in circles at first, echoing as it did off the Sierra foothills, but the last echo was the direction of the shot.

Was Hoss bleeding to death or already dead? "Hoss! Answer me!"

276

The slope took a sudden downward dive and he had to pull the excited horse back or go tumbling off the cliff. The horse pranced along the side as he looked down, trying to find a sign. He alighted and crouched down, noting the loosened ground and recent horse tracks.

Horses came up behind him. Adam gestured a greeting to Kudwa.

Kudwa sent most of his men up ahead to dispatch the logging camp, keeping two men with him. He jumped off his horse and knelt next to Adam, crouched on the edge of the cliff.

"Something happened here, Kudwa." Adam fought a sudden wave of dizziness.

"Adam! Look down!"

Adam used Kudwa's shoulder for support and peered further over the edge to where the red shirt was visible. "Hoss. Hoss!"

***

Ben and Roy solemnly considered the body of Reeger in the bunkhouse.

"Doesn't surprise me, Ben."

"This was it, Roy, proof that Van Remus tried to murder Adam and Joe. Can we throw him in jail suspecting he had Reeger killed to keep him quiet?"

"Umph. Mebbe. Don't know how long it'll take for Van Remus to get out with a good lawyer. Anyone coulda done this."

"We know better, Roy."

Roy itched his stubble absently. "Yup."

"Even getting him in jail for an hour might be enough time to get something else on him." Ben stared at the dead man. "I'm pressing charges, Roy."

When Ben turned to go inside, Roy grabbed his arm. "Ben, you go find your sons. I'll see to it he's thrown in jail." Ben jerked away and walked to the front door. "Because if you catch wind of him yourself I know you – and I'll be throwing you in jail for deliberate vengeful murder." Roy followed him inside. "I can't turn my back to it, Ben, much as I'd like to. So I'd think hard on it if I was you."

"I am thinking hard on it, Roy." Ben stepped inside the house. "If any of my sons die, I won't care who sees me kill him. Hop Sing!"

Norma came out of the kitchen, wiping her hands on her apron. "You'll have to forgive Hop Sing. He's up to his elbows in bread dough. I'm teaching him a new recipe." She paused. "It's relaxing."

Ben stared at the burned-out guest room, remembering his relief at finding Adam alive, a feeling he desperately needed right now. "Norma, we're riding into the hills. Pack some food, my boys will be hungry."

Norma shivered and poked at the subdued flames. "Going to look for them now, Ben?"

"Yes and we don't have much time!" he said, pulling her back to him. Her face went pale as her frightened eyes met his angry ones. "What is it? What's wrong? Is it Joe?" Ben ran for the stairs.

"Ben." Norma, clearly frightened, called him back. "Joe isn't up there. He's gone, too."

Ben froze, his hands on the railing. He smacked his palms loudly on wood. "I should have guessed. With his brothers out there, why would Little Joe just lie around?" His mouth set in an angry, helpless frown. He strode back to Norma. "How did he seem? All right?"

"He was really hurting over Reeger's death. Felt he was to blame."

"Those sons of yours, Ben, have an enormous sense of right. Got that from you, too, wouldn't you say?" Roy walked to the fire and tossed in a log. "A might chilly in here." He poked the fire and found a flame.

"Damnation! Norma, get us some food together. We can't delay any longer. Now all three of my sons are in danger." But he found no release for this feeling of helplessness. No matter what he does, where he goes, how will he ever find all three of them in time? Where to start? Which one to help first?

"I wish we could've saved Reeger, Ben," Roy said, sensing his pain.

"Roy," Halfway to the kitchen Norma turned back. "Reeger told me everything. Does that count? I mean, can I be the one to witness against Clete?"

Roy took off his hat and scratched his head. "I don't think hearing second hand holds much weight, Mrs. Jacobs, but I'll do some checking on that." He looked back at Ben, frozen in shock and fear. "Ben, your sons are grown men. They've all learned a trick or two, ain't they?"

"Yeah." Ben straightened, feeling nearly as much like he no longer existed as a breathing man ever could. "I've been telling myself that for a while now, Roy. When we were in the mine and it didn't seem I could do anything further, the thought was a comfort. It's not helping now. Let's move."

CHAPTER 44

Bret scurried up the hills with Hoss's gunpowder, stumbling as he ran, tripping over the rocks that fell away under his feet. He didn't have as much gunpowder as he would have liked. Bret didn't want to just destroy Ben, or a Cartwright, or a ranch. He hated the world, everyone, everything, and if he could, he would destroy everything if that meant he could have his mother back.

He set the bags of gunpowder, each big enough to pop a stump out of the ground, with rope wicks to take the flame. But a responsible logger didn't ignite them all at once, each in its own stump, at the top of the hill, where the trees had been stripped. Even though Clete had planned to fell all the trees before using the gunpowder, Bret knew unsteady trees when he saw them.

He heard voices from the camp close behind him. Those loggers wouldn't be doing much except drink coffee and may not be able to get out of the way. But Bret only cared about causing a bigger bang than he'd ever dreamed about, as he'd dreamed about every night since coming to this lousy peaked city. He even saw in his dreams how the water of Tahoe would fly up into the air and spread all over the desert of southern Nevada, making it a paradise, and that's where he'd go, because that's where Ma would be waiting. In paradise. The paradise she envisioned for them in Sacramento once, long ago.

"How can we build our own Garden of Eden if the land isn't ours?" she told him right before riding off to kill a Cartwright. Killing a Cartwright was the key.

He scurried along the top of the hill and planted the bags, each about three feet apart in stumps, under rocks, wherever an object big enough seemed to hold this side of the mountain together. He made each wick just a little shorter than the next and lit them, one by one, starting with the longest wick.

Felling of the Sons

"What's that?! Someone over there?" Sounded like McManus, although Bret didn't know any of them well enough and cared even less.

With the last wick lit Bret ran off above the blasting, far enough away to watch. McManus came into view, headed to where the last bag was set to blow, with goofy Adolf following.

And then the explosions began, one at a time yet close enough together to seem like one big blast, ripping off a long strip on the side of the hill, blowing rock and tree and massive amounts of ground upward. McManus and Adolf flew, too, their surprised voices drowned in the noise of the falling earth. This loosened ground with heavy rocks and fallen trees had nowhere else to go but down, rolling and picking up more and more material with momentum gained and gravity determined. A landslide—rolling debris of nature falling downward, picking up more ground as it went, trees and rocks dragging soil and brush as though part of the fare, all rolling down the hill and leaving the ground torn, stripped, and bare behind it.

That red shirt of Hoss's won't be visible for long.

After the explosions were complete and the ground rolling freely downward, Bret sat back, a boy saddened by the end of fireworks. The explosion didn't eat away the hate inside him. He ran off in the hills, found one of the horses running loose, leaped on and rode off as though running from the devil himself.

***

Claude and the others waited for McManus and Adolf to return but when the explosions went off, Claude immediately knew what they'd done. "Landslide!" he yelled. They all ran for their horses. Bart stopped dead when a rock slammed into his face, half buried by rolling debris. Bob and Louis couldn't catch their horses and kept on running.

***

The flume shuddered violently and fell in seams of shredded wood. Carne came to in the violence of the earth's shuddering just in time to see a large section of the flume falling down on top of him. His last thought was that a good lay wasn't worth getting beat up. Not one bit.

281

***

Clete rode into the Cartwright yard, seeing a house bigger than when he'd been here years before, much bigger to serve the needs of four men, but still only a log cabin, after all. He pulled out the papers. Not getting as much as these papers were worth. He looked up again at the burned-out section, and grinned. No, he was getting more.

He tied his horse at the hitching rail but felt a wash of fear run down him. Ben stood him off in town – he'll be stronger here. He pulled his pills out of his jacket and popped one. He had his own brand of courage. Raw, throbbing anger. Cartwright may think he owns this part of the country. Taking it away will pay Ben back for the part of the country Clete and his wife should have owned.

With his heels dug into the dry granite soil to sturdy himself, Clete stood firm in front of the house. "Cartwright!" The responding answer came from behind him as rumbles shook the ground. Clete looked up at the clear sky but saw no sign of a storm rolling in. A series of rumbles followed and Clete dropped to his knees, clutching the ground in a frightful attempt to hang on.

***

Hop Sing brought Ben bandages for the saddlebag as a precaution, and he and Roy were headed to the door when they heard the voice call, "Cartwright!"

Ben stopped Roy. "He's here." He stepped ahead of Roy when they felt the floor shaking under their feet. Behind them a water glass fell to the floor from the table. "What in the world?"

Ben and Roy ran out, followed by Hop Sing and Norma, all looking off in the direction of the low thundering noise until Roy saw Clete crouched in the dirt like a dog.

Roy pulled Clete to his feet. "What's going on, Van Remus, eh?"

Ben grabbed Clete by the throat, yanking him from Roy. "What was that noise, that shaking? Answer me! You have loggers out on my land, are they blasting stumps? What are you trying to do?"

"I don't know. I didn't give loggers those instructions."

Ben punched him in the face, knocking him to the ground. He charged at Clete as Clete tried to scramble away in the dirt.

Roy grabbed Ben's arms with Hop Sing's help. "Ben! Killing him ain't gonna help!"

"My sons are out there! He did this deliberately to kill them!"

"Use your energy wisely, Ben. Go out and find them," Norma said, stepping up between them.

Clete looked at Norma with a sudden sneer. "Well, if it isn't the third Mrs. Cartwright."

***

Joe was halfway up the hills to the ranch when the first explosion rocked the ground. His horse reared up but Joe bit back his pain and hung on. Cochise continued to dance as the ground shook beneath them. Joe wondered wildly who'd be blowing stumps out in the north forty. He thought to ride up there to stop whoever was being so stupid, but from what he could tell, as the ground continued to shake, this was more than just stump blowing.

He slid off the horse and tied Cochise to a pinion pine. Someone would be riding out of there heading back to Virginia City, and he was gonna catch 'em when they did. He sat to wait—and within moments was sound asleep, even as the ground continued to shake beneath him.

***

"Get the rope from my saddle, Kudwa."

"Adam, he cannot hold the rope."

"I'm going down." Adam jerked off his coat and removed his boots.

"No. I will go down."

"Kudwa, you can pull us up better than I can pull you. Now get the rope! And pull my horse over. We'll tie the rope to the saddle so you

283

can hang on to the horse. You're ah…" He gestured to the others watching, "friends can help when it's time to pull Hoss up." He swallowed hard. "He'll be awful heavy."

Kudwa handed Adam the open end of the rope and tied the other end to his horse's saddle. He watched with deep sadness as Adam tied the rope around his waist. "You take care, Adam." With solemn reverence he handed Adam his eagle feather.

"Hoss is the one who needs help now." Adam took the feather reverently, realizing its significance. "Keep the feather. If we get into trouble, use this exchange of the feather as your promise to help us out. I owe you a great deal, Kudwa."

Adam planted his bare feet into the side of the cliff and waved at Kudwa to lower the rope. In the seconds before the descent he felt an ominous weight hitting between his shoulders and for a moment the sky went black. With a jerk the rope started to lower. After a few feet down he looked up, squinting away the dirt that fell on his face. Kudwa watched him intently.

Halfway to Hoss the earth began trembling underneath his feet. Like firecrackers in the midst of a sudden, constant thunder, the sky was heavy with sound, loud enough to shake the ground around him. He could feel the rope pulling tight, pulling him up, away from Hoss.

"NO!" Adam let go of the rope and worked at the knot around his waist. With a jerk the rope dropped again as the ground continued its bizarre upheaval. The knot finally loosened enough to drop him through. Adam plunged to the ground, narrowly missing his brother. He couldn't move at first, the rope scraped his back and he landed hard on his gut. He caught his breath as he violently fought passing into the bliss of blackness. Finally he forced himself on his back and looked up the cliff, but couldn't see anything.

He crawled to Hoss and checked his vitals, relieved to find his heart strong. He couldn't find a mark on him except for his arm, badly shattered, probably shot at close range. There was an entrance wound but no exit, which meant the bullet had lodged in the bone. Hoss had a bad crack on the back of his skull, and heaven only knew what else, from the fall.

Adam looked up. "Kudwa!" He didn't have much voice but after a moment Kudwa looked down. "Throw down the rope!" Kudwa reappeared with the rope.

A slow, low rumbling started off somewhere above, off in the distance. The sky darkened. "Kudwa! Hurry!" The shaking worsened, a violent awakening of a malevolent monster, and the rumbling sound picked up in volume and speed. An earthquake – or a landslide. Adam saw Kudwa look behind him, down at them and behind him again. Kudwa yelled in distress but by that time the rumbling was so loud Adam couldn't hear a word.

The rope fell limp to the ground next to Hoss. Kudwa was gone.

Adam looked up just in time to throw himself on top of Hoss as the landslide of dirt, rocks and loosened trees crashed down on top of them.

***

Bret pushed the horse hard through the woods and when he reached a logging road pushed the horse even harder. As he reached the main road to Virginia City, he saw a pinto tied to a tree and a slumbering young man on the ground. Young Cartwright. Here he was with the perfect opportunity to kill but no gun. "Hey! Cartwright!" Bret waited until Joe looked up at him. "Your brother's dead. You're next!"

Joe recognized that grin. He got on his horse as Bret rode off toward Virginia City. This was between the two of them now.

***

"My third wife is dead. Norma is just a friend." But Norma was hardly safer as a friend. "Roy, get him behind bars."

Roy pulled out his gun and waved it over Clete. "Come on, get up, I'm taking you to town." Clete started to stand but Roy grabbed his coat in a fierceness he rarely showed. "Where are they?! Where are Ben's sons? What did you do with them!?"

Clete's teeth rattled as he tried to answer. "I don't know."

285

Ben grabbed Clete away from Roy and fisted him in the jaw. Clete stumbled backward onto the porch and held up his hands to ward off another blow.

"Please don't. I've got a bad head misery. Please."

Norma stepped toward them. "Ben, that's enough!"

"You tell me where my sons are or you're dead, with law as my witness." Ben grabbed Clete's arm and pulled him up.

"I can't. I came from town, they weren't there. I swear. Please, my head." Clete started to blubber. "Ben, why didn't you trust me? I could've been as quiet as a Mexican, too. You didn't even ask."

"Ask? You've proven your feeble character to me over and over."

Roy grabbed Ben's arm. "Ben, we've plum shook him enough, this ain't getting us nowheres. Leave him be now."

"Please, I have pills, in my saddle bag, I need to take. . .please." Roy went to his saddlebag and found the pills. "Ben, I'm sorry! My son's out there, too! I know how you feel."

Roy handed him his pills and picked up the papers strewn on the ground.

"How I feel!?" Ben threatened Clete again but Norma quickly stepped between them. "Two sons near death, the third out there in disguise trying to save our timber and you know how I feel?!!"

Clete swallowed his pill. "Who, the Swede? Your son?" As Ben stormed toward him, Clete held up his arms. "I swear, Ben, I don't know where your other two boys are. I thought they were here."

"That why you're here? To take another shot at them?"

Roy studied the papers before holding them out to Ben. "He's here to claim your land."

"What?"

286

"That's right." Clete found a modicum of pride and pulled away from Ben, straightening his suit. "I have come to take back what's rightfully mine. The Ponderosa. You stole land from me but I'm here to take it legal." He chuckled. "Ain't that a hell of a note?"

Ben stared off into the hills as though he hadn't heard Clete at all.

Roy held the papers out to Ben. "Ben, I think you ought to look at this."

"I have to find my sons."

"I agree with you, Ben. But in the meantime, he'll bring these papers to a judge---."

"None of that matters without my sons, Roy. All of this, the land, the cattle, the trees, even the sky and Lake Tahoe itself, I wanted for them. We have to find them." He ignored the papers Roy held.

"Does your lovely wife know what you did to my Winnie? How many women have you killed, Ben? One for each son?"

Ben grabbed his throat. "I'll kill you right now. Where you were logging?"

Roy pulled Ben away. "Ben, we got nothing legal to kill him over." Roy frowned. "And I kin hardly believe I just said that."

"Roy, look the other way."

"These papers appear legal. You kill him now, you'll lose everything."

"And my son will have it all," Clete said, beaming.

"Roy, those papers are phony, we both know that."

"Of course we do. But how's a judge gonna know it?" Roy watched sadly as Ben rubbed his temples. "Ben, you know how your sons feel about this land. They're out there right now, ain't they, trying to save

287

it? You can't save them and just let the land go. Now why don't we tie him up and leave him here while we look for your boys?"

"You can't do that!" Clete protested, gasping for breath. "You have no grounds for the accusation."

"Ain't I?"

Ben frowned, with a hand up at Roy. "Thanks, but you're right. We have to stay legal in this."

"Ben, I almost ended up dead myself. Now I know I don't have proof he was responsible. But I'm willing to bet my badge he was and we don't have the time for anything else. We tie him up, legal or illegal, so we can find your sons."

Ben nodded. "Hop Sing, get some rope. We'll keep him in the house till we get back. And make sure you watch him good and close. Norma, I'll send someone to bring you back to Virginia City as soon as I can. Please stay away from this one." He grabbed Clete by the collar. "And if just one of my boys die because of you, I'll. . ." Ben threw Clete backward in disgust and stared off into the hills as Hop Sing and Roy trussed Clete's arms behind him.

"Come on, Ben." Roy put a gentle hand on his shoulder. "Let's find those boys of yours."

CHAPTER 45

Kudwa kept a tight grip on the horses after the first rumbling but as the land rushed down he freed them, scrambled as far away as he could and then flattened. One of Kudwa's men flew off the cliff with a log imbedded in his gut, as the other narrowly escaped by flinging himself sideways and grabbing a huge jutting of rocky cliff. Kudwa lay with his head covered until the ground settled with a sigh of angry consternation. He shook off the residue of ground that had rolled over him and drew himself up to his knees, unsure what he would see. Flattened, distorted and ugly, landscape ripped and bare in one wide path leading down, the sky above him dull and gray. Just like his dream except that he had not been sucked down, his friend had.

Adam was at the bottom of a cliff, suffocated by the very land they had tried to save. He also lost a Shoshone friend. He knelt, staring down at the uprooted trees, rocks and granite dirt but could not see his friend and could not pray with nightmare wound so tight around his heart. For the trees they could not save, good men have died. Kudwa pulled the eagle feather out from his breeching. Eagles were brave guardians of the sky and now must guide Adam's spirit skyward. He leaned over the side of the cliff and, after a silent, emotion-filled prayer, let the eagle feather drift down.

***

Jessup re-read the new procedure notes he received that day by the Pony rider while eating his usual lunch of corned beef and cabbage at the International House. Three men, disheveled and wild-eyed, ran in looking for Clete van Remus.

Louis ran over to Jessup. "Ground purely shook! We were lucky we got out! If Van Remus thinks he can get us back in that jinxed Cartwright logging camp, he has another think coming."

"Yeah, we don't know if everyone got out behind us neither," Bob added. "We saw Indians! Maybe they're responsible for the ground shaking!"

"No, it was that Swede, he stole the gunpowder," Claude reminded them.

Jessup told them to go to his office and he'd check them over. He pushed his plate aside, no longer hungry. Ben mentioned trouble at one of his logging camps. Suddenly sure another of his sons needed doctoring, Jessup went back to his office, checked and dismissed the three loggers with a prescription of whiskey and bed, and packed his case with every precaution, including the notes he'd been reading from his colleague in Sacramento. Just in case.

He didn't want to use those notes. But reading a procedure beat sure and utter futility and a grave marked "the doctor didn't try hard enough." Too many people died because the doctor forgot he was supposed to be playing God.

***

"Would you like some more water?" Norma tiptoed closer to the little man who seemed older than his years and pale and weak as a kitten, all trussed up and tossed against Ben's desk like a sack of flour.

"Yes, please. You are so kind."

Norma reassured herself with a glance at the rifle propped against the dining table. She didn't know if she could use it, but she'd try. Even pale kittens could scratch.

Hop Sing met her at the door to the kitchen with a pitcher of icy well water and a glass. "Me listen for tlouble. You need me, you yell."

"I will, Hop Sing, I will." She watched as Clete with some dignity righted himself to sit more comfortably. "He's pretty subdued with his hands tied."

"He tlicky man. Hurt boys. Just lemember. And yell."

She nodded and poured some water, leaving the pitcher on the dining table. "Here you are." She helped Clete drink. "Are you feeling better?"

"I don't know, my head just. . .sometimes I think it might just burst on the spot. Could you take out one of these pills from my vest pocket and pop it in my mouth?"

Norma dug quickly, repulsed by this much closeness to him. "These?" She looked at the label but didn't recognize the medicinal print. She uncapped it and dumped a small white pill into her hand. With the reverent awe she felt for medical things she placed it inside his mouth carefully, without touching any part of him. After giving him more water she walked away from him and sat in the chair next to the fire.

"Do you really think Ben killed your wife?"

"No." When Norma looked relieved Clete chuckled. "He had his son do it. Yes, his eldest brat killed my wife, deliberately too, to keep us from claiming one simple acre of land on a river. Let me share something with you. Whatever Ben's had happen to him, he's had coming. If it were me causing him grief, believe me, I'd admit it. I wish I could take blame for his misery, but, dear lady, I am as meek as a lamb."

"I don't believe a word." She frowned and turned away. What did she know about Ben, really?

Clete struggled to sit up. "My dear, surely you are aware how love can blind a person to someone's true character. Sitting there before me, not blinded to my character, do I seem capable of everything he has accused me of?"

She looked into his eyes briefly before turning back to the fire to soothe a sudden chill. "Ummm." No one in town ever accused her of condemning anyone too quickly.

"Ahhh! I am getting a knot in my shoulder sitting like this."

"Oh no, don't try that with me. Ben wants you to stay tied. I wouldn't touch those ropes if you convinced me you are the Son of God."

"Ah. Well," he shrugged. "You will of course apologize when the truth is finally revealed, of course. Tell me, do you know how his other wives died?"

"Ummm, I never asked." She stood alone in the middle of the room, contemplating tell him she wasn't Ben's wife. She wondered if he even understood truth.

"Do you suppose you could find anything in the way of food? It is well past the hour I usually dine, and with these pills in me there's no telling how my empty stomach will react."

"Yes." She ran into the kitchen where Hop Sing packed food away on ice. "Hop Sing, do you know how Ben's wives died?"

***

After she left Clete climbed awkwardly to his feet and snuck over to the desk. He dug through drawers, standing backward and straining his neck to look over his shoulders, until his trussed hands finally found a scissors. With a slow shriek of fire in his neck, he strained to cut the rope. Ignoring the three feminine frames on the desk, he grabbed a glass paperweight and worked it from his palms toward his wrists until he forced his hands apart, relishing the rope burn on his wrists that felt real and tangible and under his control.

Hop Sing came out of the kitchen and grabbed the rifle when he didn't see Clete. He heard a noise coming from the desk and with his aim steady walked carefully until he saw the man struggling with his ropes. "You not move. I shoot."

Clete glanced over his shoulder, gripping the paperweight. "You can't shoot me."

Hop Sing's arms tensed as he squinted an eye. Clete dived sideways to the floor and hurled the paperweight upward, catching Hop Sing in the hip. Hop Sing fired.

Norma ran out of the kitchen. "Hop Sing! Did you kill him?"

"Don't know," Hop Sing limped a little closer to Clete. "Think I aimed away and hit floor."

Norma leaned over Clete, looking for blood.

Felling of the Sons

"Miss Norma, back!"

With the speed of a scorpion, Clete ripped a hand out of the loosened ropes and pulled the scissors from his back pocket. He grabbed Norma and pulled her close, holding the scissors against her throat. He noticed his wrist bleeding down his arm in an instant of chagrin and wiped his arm on Norma's dress. "Go on, Chinaman, put down the gun. Go on, or you'll get to see her blood as well." Hop Sing laid the rifle on the dining table. "No, put it here by me!"

Hop Sing, hesitant, picked up the rifle and did as instructed.

"How many shots left?" Hop Sing didn't answer. "Immigrants." He pushed it back at Hop Sing. "Load it." When Hop Sing hesitated, Clete's scissors sliced a bloody line on Norma's neck. "You know how much I want to kill a Cartwright wife?" Hop Sing loaded the gun. He handed the rifle back to Clete and held his arms out for Norma.

"Oh, no. She's mine now. See, I have to kill her. You tell Ben that."

"Please. She not Mrs. Cartlight, just a friend. Take me instead. I more clazy. I come after you if you leave with her." Hop Sing reached behind him, fumbling in the foyer desk drawer where Ben kept a spare gun.

"You're right. I can't leave you behind." With the butt of his rifle he slammed Hop Sing in the temple, and Hop Sing dropped to the floor. "Hope I killed you, you damn immigrant."

"Hop Sing!"

"Get out there." Clete threw open the door and pushed Norma out, leveling the gun at her. "Taking Ben's sons hasn't been satisfying enough. But when he finds your body beaten, battered and bloodied, then he'll know how I felt all those years."

Norma tried to run but Clete tackled her into the dirt, knocking her momentarily senseless. Before she could breathe again and untangle her legs from her skirt, Clete had pulled his horse up to her and grabbed her arm.

"You and I are gonna make a great team. For the next hour or so, anyway. Get on the horse or I'll drop you right here." He pulled the hammer back on the rifle.

"You can't." She bit back a sob and reached for the horn of the saddle. Feeling his hot breath on her neck as he reached down to help her up, she steeled herself with the thought of nothing to lose and hit him in the throat with her elbow, at the same time flinging herself to the ground.

The horse reared as she scrambled to get away but Clete caught his wind quickly. He lowered the rifle to her head.

He could barely croak at her but she could hear the cocking of the rifle's trigger. On her knees she kept scrambling away but she could never outrun his bullet, not if his aim was true.

"Drop lifle now!" Hop Sing bellowed from the front porch.

Clete raised it from Norma to Hop Sing and fired and Hop Sing fired in return. Norma threw her arms over her head, burying her nose in the dirt. She was afraid to look up again as Clete's rifle dropped at her feet and his horse rode off. She kept her face buried in the dirt and tears soaked the ground beneath her.

Hop Sing crouched next to her. "Miss Norma okay."

"Oh! Hop Sing! I thought he killed you."

He gently helped her to her feet. "But he get away."

"I'm sorry, it's all my fault. You took a bad hit, Hop Sing, are you okay?" She touched his head. "Come on, I'll fix you up."

"Hop Sing hard-headed."

"I always knew that. And I'm glad for it." Norma and Hop Sing helped each other back into the house, together casting a last sad and worried look behind them.

***

294

Felling of the Sons

Joe couldn't ride as fast or as hard as Bret but he knew where Bret headed. The trail he was sure he must have taken a thousand times didn't seem familiar. . .longer, harder as he traveled – and in places narrower, wavier. . .sort of blurry. . .

"Joe! What are you doing in town?"

Joe looked around. At first he thought he was dreaming. He could see the mineshafts at the edge of town and the buildings beyond, people walking and riding who usually mind their own affairs staring at him. Had he fallen asleep and let his horse carry him to Virginia City?

Dr. Jessup sat in his buggy waiting with mild consternation for an answer from an erstwhile patient.

"I got something to do." He half slid and half fell out of the saddle.

Jessup crouched next to Joe as he tried to stand again. "Joe, this is foolish, boy, let me help you in my buggy, I'll take you back to the Ponderosa, where you belong."

"Hey! Cartwright kid! Stand up and face me! You think I'm going to keep running from you?" Bret, holding the pose of a gunfighter, waited for Joe in the street. "I ain't done nothing."

Joe got to his knees, shrugging off Jessup's hands. "Your time is over, Van Remus. You just haven't owned up to it."

Jessup grabbed his arm. "Joe, you can't do this."

"Then who will?" Joe walked past Bret as though Bret wasn't there. Bret watched as Jessup followed behind Joe in the buggy.

Trail weary and dusted head to foot from a stampede, Butch rode into town to see a dramatic scene unfurling. He was looking for someone specific and at first ignored the youngest Cartwright's attempts to confront a young man. Joe puzzled over his appearance as though knowing that this is the last place Butch should be, but not knowing why he knew that.

Joe stopped across from the sheriff's office, feeling the strength return to his arms as he turned to face Bret. "All right, Van Remus, you want your fight here, ask for it again."

Bret regained his stance. "I'm not asking for nothing, I'm telling you. You leave me alone. I ain't done nothing."

"You got a short memory. I was there when you put the knife into me. Problem is you didn't make sure I was dead."

"You can't prove nothing."

"Joe, don't listen," Jessup said. "He knows you'll never outdraw him."

Joe ignored him. "Well," he said to Bret, squaring his shoulders. "You gonna go for it?"

Clem ran out of the sheriff's office. "Joe! Don't do this! I have a warrant for Bret's arrest, just like you told me."

***

Butch alighted and tied his horse to a railing, dusting off as he watched the fight in the street. He couldn't help but notice how poorly Joe seemed. Watching, Butch's fingers itched for the cold steel at his side, as they've itched since the stampede that killed his friend Val.

Bret turned on Clem. "Cartwrights own the town, deputy? You do everything they say?"

"Stay back, Clem." Joe's eyes never left Bret's face. "You gonna pull it or wait until I turn my back?"

"I gave you the chance to back off. Now I gotta defend my life. That's how I see it."

"Then you're blind." Joe grimaced and rubbed his eyes. His arms dropped suddenly, lifeless and trembling, to his side. He didn't appear able to pick up his head again.

Butch let his hand drift down to his gun. Joe must be trying to take care of his family's problems but at the risk of his own hide. He saw

Jessup riding his way and strode to meet him. "Has young Cartwright been injured? I've never seen the day he couldn't hold his own gun."

"He's about to get himself killed by that Van Remus. He's gone too far to be reasoned with, and is hurting too bad to come out ahead. Help out, would you?"

Butch's jaw clenched tight. The name Van Remus rang a mighty sour bell. He pulled his gun just as Bret drew against Joe.

CHAPTER 46

Down deep on the bottom of the cliff where the ground had plunged and continued to roll, two figures lay covered in displaced earth. The ground over them moved a little and then fiercely, as though awakening from a tormented sleep. Adam jerked violently to clear himself of heavy earth and gasped for air as his eyes blinked and teared and he coughed up dirt. Laying on top of Hoss he could feel his brother's warmth and breath. At least he had kept Hoss's face clear of dirt – at least he did that little. Adam grunted to slide sideways off Hoss, but his legs were so heavy with dirt and timber that he couldn't move them.

"Hoss, you need water. No telling how long we'll be here." He couldn't reach the canteen, no matter how hard he stretched. He put his head back. "Sorry, Hoss. Some rescue, huh?" What he could see of the land above him was stripped and ugly. They should have been crushed but Hoss landed in an almost indent against the side of the cliff, and the land for the most part continued on a downward slope. A lot of what came down missed them entirely.

Adam fought extreme sleepiness by lifting himself up on his elbows. "Hoss, come on, move, blink your eyes." He bit back a groan. At least, uncovered, someone should find them. "Hoss, back when we were kids, in Sacramento, Pa made a mistake. We all make mistakes. I want you to make sure he doesn't torment himself over this, you hear me? Hoss, you have to hear me." He tried raising himself up again but his legs wouldn't move. Something inside him screamed, a warm heat rushed into his head and he fell back against his brother.

***

Ben and Roy rode hard, driven by the idea that it could take hours to find anyone alive after the ground shaking that might have been a landslide. And finding Hoss didn't necessarily mean finding Adam or Joe. "Ben, look!"

Walking toward them at a rapid speed that made them appear comical were Kudwa and a companion. "Ben Cartwright?"

Felling of the Sons

"Kudwa! Do you know---?"

"We lead." They started walking back.

"Wait! Ride behind us on the horses, we'll move faster!"

***

Ben knelt at the side of the cliff near ground loose and unstable. Any wrong move could start a second landslide. And there at the bottom surrounded by dirt and fallen trees were two of his sons. The landslide hadn't killed them because by the looks of it they came to long enough to brush away the dirt. But could they still be alive? "Hoss! Adam! Can you hear me? Answer me!" The air that filled his nostrils with dirt was ominously silent. "Roy, get the rope."

Roy leaned over, looking down. "Ben, you're not gonna haul them up this way. Look at how loose this cliff is. And you don't know how bad they're hurt."

"Have you got any other suggestions?"

"No, but maybe the Indians have." Roy explained with sign to Kudwa what he figured they needed.

Kudwa spoke rapidly to Oshwabekona, who took off through the woods. He gestured to Ben a roundabout direction they would use to meet them down there, and started off.

Ben knelt down again, breathing against heavy chest pain. "Help me down there, Roy."

With one end of the rope secured to the horse, Ben tied the rope around his waist and started down, coughing as dirt splattered his face, eyes fogging with tears. He tried to analyze the odds of them both being all right but he wasn't a betting man. He dropped to his knees next to them and pulled the canteen from around his neck. He felt first Adam's head, and then Hoss's. Hoss was burning with fever but Adam was cool and dry. Ben dug out their legs, lifting the timber that had seemed too heavy but moved with effort just the same. He eased Adam to the ground the rest of the way off Hoss. After cleaning

299

them off as best he could he saw Hoss's injuries didn't appear too serious, although the wound to the arm would take some patching.

Ben could see no new injury on Adam. He grabbed Adam's hand and squeezed it tight. "Come on, Adam, hang in there, son." He eased water down Hoss's throat and wet a bandanna for his head.

Hoss's eyes fluttered. "Huh?"

"It's all right son, you're going to be fine." Ben smiled briefly. "Always knew you had a hard head. You're going to be fine." Ben finished tying the cloth around Hoss's arm to stop the bleeding and gave him water.

"Pa, sorry…had to. Reckon they got the best of me."

"Son, at this close range you could have been shot dead. Was it Bret?"

"Yeah," Hoss coughed. "Bret. A real prince." He struggled to move and saw his brother next to him. "Hey, Pa, what's Adam doing here?" He tried to sit up but Ben pushed him down.

"He came to help you, Hoss. Got stuck in the landslide the same way you did."

"But Pa, he shouldn'ta!"

Ben patted Hoss's hot head. "He'll be fine, son, don't you worry. We've got help coming to get you both out of here."
***

When Bret went for his gun Joe was nearly asleep. He snapped back into it and went for his own weapon hanging listless at his side, but in the same moment knew he couldn't outdraw a dead steer. Before Joe got his gun halfway out, he heard two shots and Bret cried out. Joe fell to his knees, the pain in his side telling him he'd been hit.

"Joe? You all right?" Butch leaned over him, his gun smelling of gunpowder.

Felling of the Sons

Joe recognized his pain and saw Bret running off. "Yeah. I gotta go after him." He kept his gun out as he dragged himself to his feet. "Thanks for your help but I can handle this."

"No, not that way. Go for the sheriff." Butch grabbed Joe's arm and held him back. "HOLD ON, VAN REMUS! YOU'RE NOT GOING NO PLACE!"

Bret kept running, heading for the Golden Cross.

"Look, you gave me a hand when I needed it and I'm grateful. I got to finish it."

"I don't know what all went on around here but he got to the cattle drive. Val's dead, Joe, just like your brother. I need to make sure this Van Remus pays."

"Val's dead? The cattle drive?" Joe rubbed his aching head. "All right. You go after his pa if you want, but you're better off going back to the herd."

"Joe, you didn't hear me. We weren't driving cattle anymore, we were driving scattle! Val's dead on accounta that Van Remus and half the herd is missing!" He noticed the dazed look on Joe's face and nodded. "Ah, I'll fill you in on it later, Joe, 'pers you got enough on your mind right now."

"Yeah." Joe staggered but righted himself again.

Butch grabbed his arm. "Who's got better odds, Joe, you or me? You don't want him to get another killing in, do ya?"

"He's trapped himself down in the mine. There's nothing more he can do." Joe looked over at Jessup. "Pa is going to need help out at the ranch. Adam went out to look for Hoss."

"I'm on my way." Jessup's hand slipped down to touch his bag. "Take care of him, Butch," Jessup whipped the buggy off out of town.

301

"If you want to help me, Butch," Joe straightened up with a swallowed gasp. "Find Clete van Remus. I'll meet you at the sheriff's with Bret."

***

Jessup hurried his buggy out of town, missing the stage coming in from Genoa. The clattering it made taking that last leg up the hill was enough to wake the dead in town, but Jessup had his own cluttered thoughts distracting him. The stage stopped at the Express office just as the last of Jessup's buggy could be seen taking the slope of Sun Mountain.

The stage driver jumped down and wiped the grit from his face with an equally gritty bandanna. He opened the door to help out two passengers, a distinguished looking elderly man, and a younger, friendly-faced fellow with a black bag. Paul Martin had read the despair in his friend Jessup's letter and closed his office up for a week. Things had been slow enough in Genoa and he left behind an able woman to tend to minor repairs. What Jessup indicated in his letter sounded too intriguing to pass up. He accepted his luggage from the driver and studied the streets until he saw Jessup's placard. No one answered his knock. One fellow stopped and indicated Jessup's path of departure just moments before. Martin sighed and walked over to the sheriff's office for better direction.

***

Kudwa emitted an eagle cry and waited. Before too many minutes passed, several Indians came through the woods. After hearing an abbreviated tale of what had happened, they quickly fashioned two travois using bark, grapevine, and mesquite brushing. With Kudwa in the lead, they made their way around torn earth and fallen debris to where Kudwa knew Ben needed help.

Ben waved them over and helped get his sons settled on the crude but effective litters. Their ability to fashion what was needed out of their surroundings so quickly reinforced Ben's desire to keep his land as natural as possible. "Okay, let's get them home."

As the sun traveled to the western half of the sky, Kudwa took Adam's cool unresponsive hand and chanted under his breath. Like

302

the medicine bag that had saved Adam's life the first time, Kudwa was doing his best to keep him alive again.

***

Jessup cursed the buggy for its slowness but he couldn't do much else to speed it along. He had to keep his nerves steady for the surgery he feared performing. He heard a rider coming and steered his buggy to the side of the trail.

Van Remus. The weasel's right arm was bleeding but Jessup wasn't about to offer his services. "Doctor! Say, I've got to thank you for those pills, they cleared up my head real fine."

"That wasn't my intent."

Clete cocked his head, sweating forehead wrinkling pensively. "What's that mean?"

"You've been torturing Ben Cartwright, trying to kill his sons. Against my better judgment I gave you medicine but that doesn't mean you deserved it." Jessup winced inwardly, knowing how that sounded. "Now get out of my way, so I can see if I can undo some of your miserable damage."
"You medicine men can't be trusted!" Clete clutched his chest. "Those pills, they were poisoned? You poisoned me!"

"Don't be foolish."

"I'll see to it you're hung along with Cartwright!" He took out the bottle of pills and threw them at Jessup. "Just you wait!"

"VAN REMUS! HOLD IT RIGHT WHERE YOU ARE!" Roy rode up behind him, pulling his gun. Clete spurred the horse off in a cloud of heavy granite. Roy fired once over his head as he pulled up alongside Jessup. "Was I seeing right? He got a bullet hole in 'em?"

"He was bleeding pretty good."

"If he hurt either of those folks at Ben's house, I'll kill him, legal or no." Roy shook his head. "Say, I was coming to town to get you, doc. You all right? He didn't hurt you none?"

303

"I'm fine. Joe sent me to see about Adam and Hoss."

"Joe in town? Say, that's good. We found his brothers and they need you bad. Tell Ben I've gone after Clete, wouldja? And I'll check on Joe for him, too." Roy nudged his horse on.

Jessup sat back with an exhausted sigh before moving on again as fast as he dared.

CHAPTER 47

Clete rode hard into town with the sheriff on his tail. The last few miles up Sun Mountain were slow going but the law couldn't handle the altitude any better, and Coffee, Clete figured, must still be suffering from his mine experience. And he felt dangerous, like a trapped cougar. He felt like the father his son would be proud of.

From his window of his suite Clete could see people gathering in front of the Lucky 7 Saloon, near the entrance of the Golden Cross. At the moment nothing mattered more than that he had been poisoned. "Bret!? Where are you, boy?" He collapsed into the wingback, trying to control the hot breath exploding from his lungs, sending barbs into his skull.

Everything he and Winnie ever wanted had been for Bret. Clete had the ideas and Winnie the courage to see them through, and the two of them would do anything for Bret. When Clete put the idea to kill Cartwright in Winnie's mind, nothing could stop her. She had figured, although Clete didn't agree, that they could get what they wanted out of Sutter with Cartwright dead. In a rush of guilt he insisted on doing the shooting himself but she made that damned point about his eyesight not being good enough. Winnie had determination and fortitude but she was too stupid to get out of the way of stampeding cows. He wasn't surprised to hear how she died, not really.

Sutter couldn't see that his golden valley paradise was bound to end. He lived in a delusional world, losing more than Clete ever had. And by then, Cartwright, up on his mountain, thought himself untouchable and unreachable, the only one not ruined by all of this. Clete wanted to even the score, nothing more. Was that too much to ask?

With his breathing calmed, Clete strapped his gun holster on, counting one notch for Juce and ready for another. The gun felt heavy and awkward over his dirty three-piece suit. The door of his safe opened on the first whirl of the clacking knob. With reverent awe he pulled out the case and a fresh copy of his claim papers. This was one child Ben didn't care about saving.

This, finally, will remove that vision of the Russians laughing at him, and knowing that Ben had told them something to make them laugh. Damn immigrants.

***

Joe, weaving slightly, faced the entrance to the Golden Cross. The miner guarding the entrance backed off when he saw the look on Joe's face. With a last deep breath of clean air, Joe descended. He slipped halfway down and fell into a puddle. He groaned and held his side before climbing to his feet again.

Candles flickered weakly and, as he walked further in, glowed with a small bluish flame. Bad air. He could wait for Bret to come up gasping. "Bret! You're trapped. Turn yourself in." Every breath birthed another stab of pain in his side.

"Think again, Cartwright!" a voice echoed from somewhere ahead of him. "One shot from my gun or yours and this whole mine will come toppling on our heads. You better get out while you can."

Joe hesitated. "You underestimate your timber, Bret. One gunshot won't do it."

"If you believe that, you're a fool." Bret sounded like he had flattened against a dead end.

"Tell the truth, Bret, what were you and your father after? What was that explosion out in the hills?" Joe walked hesitant with each step.

"That was my glory hour! Gunpowder set to go off all at the same time, ka-boom!"

Joe ducked when rock over him loosened and fell as the whole shaft seemed to shift. "Did you see Hoss out there?"

"Ah, yes, the second brother. Hoss. He called himself the Swede. He's buried — like you and me are gonna be."

Joe found Bret half lying in a small puddle of water, holding his hand out as though he didn't want to get blood on his clothes. His long dirty blonde hair half hung in his face. "Where's Hoss?"

306

"If I tell you, you'll go? You'll leave me here?"

Bret's suddenly small voice stirred memories of Joe's own childhood and the discovery of the deaths of mothers. Bret was just another version of himself. "Come out and we'll get you some help."

Bret leaned his head back against the silver streaked wall. "I'm going to sit here until Ma comes. She promised me paradise." He closed his eyes. "Ma always keeps her promise. If she had told me the hate didn't go away with revenge, I'da listened. I woulda, I swear."

Joe shook his head. "Talk to your pa, Bret. He can help you."

"I don't have a pa!" Bret started to laugh. "You kill him, okay? I know you want to."

Joe backed up a step. He placed his palm on the wood of the timbering next to him. "The mine is shifting. We better move back toward the center." The ceiling timber creaked above them and some of the soft rock fell. "Come on, it's gonna give!"

Bret pulled the knife. "Come for me and I'll kill you."

"All right. I'll...go get the deputy, he'll get you out." Joe backed up further as the section of timbering cracked and the ceiling collapsed. Amid screams, Joe threw himself forward, keeping barely ahead of the collapse. He kept throwing himself forward as more and more ceiling caved down around him. He reached the shaft incline and when he was halfway up realized that most of the screams were from above ground.

The Lucky 7's floor had given in and men were scrambling out on top of each other. The sides of the saloon fell into the mine like a house made of cards.

Joe crawled out of the Golden Cross mine and waved for someone to give him a hand.

***

Ben wrapped Norma's sprained arm in a sling as Hop Sing handed her some coffee. "I never meant for you to get hurt." He looked up at the bruise on Hop Sing's temple. "How are you feeling, Hop Sing?"

"Only hurt when I laugh."

"Nothing to laugh about yet." Ben heard the sound of a buggy and ran out, followed by Hop Sing.

"Ben! How are they?" Jessup handed the reins to Hop Sing and allowed Ben to help him down. "Hop Sing? What happened to you?"
"I on my feet. You help Mr. Adam and Mr. Hoss."

Dr. Jessup grabbed his bag and followed Ben inside.

"You made good time, John, I appreciate it." Ben led him to the stairs. "Hoss's right arm is almost shattered, we've got it bandaged to stop the bleeding and we've given him some of Joe's fever medicine. I tried to get the bullet but it pained him something fierce. Adam is lying so still, I fear for his life, John. He's been. . .bleeding from the mouth. I think. . .he might be in a…" Ben rubbed his eyes. "At sea we called it a…death stupor. He's got no color left, and his skin is cold." He leaned against the dining table, suddenly drained.

John's comforting hand on Ben's shoulder felt wholly inadequate. "I've never handled this kind of internal bleeding before but got instructions from Genoa." They stepped into Adam's dimly lit room. He took Adam's wrist and found the pulse in his neck after much difficulty. "Can Hop Sing assist me?"

"I can."

"Sorry, Ben, but in your present state you'll be too distracted." When Ben didn't move, John sighed and led Ben back out. "I'll be honest with you, Ben, it looks bad, really bad. There's practically no chance I'll pull him through. But without trying, he has even less hope. I'm sorry, Ben, I can't have you watching over my shoulder."

"John! You can't tell me---."

"I *am* telling you, Ben. You've been through hell, now go sit with Hoss and count your blessings that you'll come out with two of your sons still alive."

"I trusted their judgment." Ben pounded the wall in frustration. "Adam felt guilty and I couldn't talk it out of him!"

"He saved Hoss, didn't he?" John pulled equipment out, clearing a place on the table next to the bed. "Don't blame yourself."

Ben's hand absently pressed against his heart as he looked behind him at Hoss's room. "Joe."

"Joe's in town, Ben, he'll be all right."

"I'll bring him home." Ben couldn't pull his eyes from his still son being undressed for surgery.

"Hoss needs you more." Jessup washed his hands in the water Hop Sing brought. "Ben, go on!"

Allowing Ben a final look at the still form, Hop Sing closed the door.
***

Ben listened outside Adam's door as Jessup gave hurried orders to Hop Sing and called for Norma to lend her good hand. He wished something fierce to wake from this nightmare and never sleep again. If what Jessup said was true, he was never going to see Adam alive again. Two sons. He would only have two sons. "I'm so sorry, Liz." He sent a prayer to Adam's mother to watch over her son.

Hoss, awake, dazed and confused, seemed about to get out of bed. "Hoss, easy boy, you're going to be all right. Doctor Jessup will be in here soon to take care of that arm. A few stitches and you'll be good as new." He checked Hoss's bandaged and tightened the strap that stopped the bleeding.

"Pa? Where's Joe? He's supposed to be in bed, not me."

Ben hesitated. "Don't worry, he's fine. Good news, he woke up and his head is okay, too. You rest and you'll get to see him after Jessup fixes your arm."

Once he saw Hoss sleeping Ben ran quietly down the stairs and grabbed his hat and holster, but stopped himself. If he left, Hoss will have no one. And Adam, how could he leave a son who could be dead before he got back?

Ben walked to the fire and stoked it. Ever since this nightmare started he'd found himself torn by his desire to protect all three sons at once. He had been literally torn apart because there wasn't any way for him to choose. Clete knew how to destroy him, all right. Make him choose between his sons.

When he heard the quiet knock at the door, Ben thought he'd imagined it. By the second knock he threw the door open. A kind-looking stranger held a fist in the air to knock again and smiled awkwardly.

"Excuse me, are you Mr. Cartwright? Dr. Jessup here?"

"That's right, but I'm afraid he's busy." Ben couldn't take his eyes from the oversized black bag the man carried, nearly twice as big as Jessup's.

"I'm sorry if I'm too late. I'm Dr. Paul Martin. I received an express letter from Dr. Jessup about a new surgery procedure he wanted to try and I thought perhaps I could give him a hand."

Abruptly Ben grabbed Martin's arm and dragged him up the stairs. "You not only can give him a hand but if you've done the procedure before, you can take over for him."

"Well, I have had some success."

"In here, please." Ben took him to Adam's door. "I am so grateful to you." He opened the door a crack and Martin slipped inside, shutting the door behind him. Ben leaned with a heavy sigh against the door, waiting, listening. He hoped to hear a whoop, a holler for joy, but

310

heard nothing. Still, he felt a small renewed hope for his son, for all his sons.

As Ben checked on Hoss again, Dr. Jessup came into the room. "John! You're not helping him?"

"Ben, I don't know what lucky star you live under, but you should be thanking it right now. If anyone can bring Adam around, it's Dr. Martin. Now you and I can get to work on Hoss."

***

"Judge Whitaker! Judge! Open up, it's me, Clete Van Remus!" Clete pounded on the door, the one where the sign announced his absence. He felt a fire behind him, flames licking at his behind, his veins tightening with poison given him by the doctor's evil pills, pills he thought had helped the headaches.

Bret had all the answers but Clete never listened. Clete would never let anyone know that he had a son in town, but did that make Bret any less vulnerable? And they were good at it, too, oh yes, Clete and his *associate* Bret, and now even Bret believed it. "You're not my pa!"

"The judge is out for a week – didn't you see the sign?"

Clete slowly turned. Roy Coffee sat on his horse looking down at him. He turned back to the sign and ripped it down. "Think you own this town, don't you, Coffee!"

"Clete, I could have you hung where you stand. But I believe in due process of the law. Now if you don't want to have me drawing down on you, you back away from that door."

The door, before it could be backed away from, flew open and Judge Whitaker, in his sleeping cap and nightshirt, stepped out. "What in thunder is going on out here? Can't a man catch up on his sleeping after a miserable long coach ride? Roy, what's the meaning of this?"

"Sorry, Judge," Roy said as he respectfully alighted. "I tried to explain it to this fella here. I'll take him to the jail and straighten him out."

Clete held his papers out. "Judge, just take these papers and look at them at your leisure. I want you to be sure, in the morning, to call a hearing on the matter, and name Bret van Remus the estate guardianship, because I'll be dead by then."

"Eh?" The judge took the papers but glared at Roy.

"Sorry, Judge, there's been a little misunderstanding." Roy shifted on his feet, trying to look embarrassed instead of angry. "Let Van Remus keep his papers and I'll see to it personally that he apologizes—."

"Roy, confound it, I'll talk to you tomorrow!" And the door slammed shut again before Roy could get the papers back.

"Clete, you're under arrest." Roy took Clete's arm.

"On what grounds, sheriff?"

"On accounta disturbing a judge and letting him think I done it."

"You can do what you want to me, sir, but once the judge gets a good look at those papers, the Ponderosa will belong to Bret."

Roy kept a firm hand on Clete and their two horses, even though Clete had no inkling to escape. Outside the sheriff's office they both stopped briefly to watch a particular disturbance over at the Golden Cross. Men were crowding in to the Lucky 7 as others pointed at the entrance to the Golden Cross – there were too many, in Clete's mind, all crowding around one area of the city, for some reason.

Roy pointed. "Think I oughta go over there and get some of those men out of that saloon?"

"Do what you want. I'll be dead by morning anyhow."

"Who you trying to fool now?" Roy picked up his jail keys and pushed Clete toward a cell.

Clem ran inside the sheriff's office behind Roy.

"Your doctor poisoned me. Gave me medicine to that he knew would kill a man with a weak heart like me."

"Of all the confoundest, ridiculous, butt-headed---."

Clem put a hand on Roy's arm. "Sorry to hear you're dying, sir. But you might be the only one who can save your son. Last I saw, Little Joe chased him down into the Golden Cross."

Clete ran out into the street, followed close behind by Clem and Roy. The Lucky 7 Saloon built over his mine was crammed to the rafters with noisy rambunctious miners, all shouting out the latest gossip from the streets, including stories about the two who were holed up beneath them. And more thirsty men were pushing to get inside—no one noticing, or caring, as the saloon walls began to tremble.

"Roy!" Butch rode up to the sheriff's office. "I need to ask---."

"HEY!" Clete screamed, squinting at the saloon. "Don't all crowd in there at once. The floor is too unstable! Sheriff, get over there and establish some ORDER! My son is down there!"

The rumbling began under their feet and shook Clete and the lawmen to stumbling and falling into each other. Dust exploded up out of the mine in gusts that burst with each new section's collapse. Men poured out of the Lucky 7 Saloon, and Roy and Clem ran over to them, moving people away, holding down the panic, trying to rescue those caught in the floor as it caved under their feet. They pulled men out as voices cried for help, yelling for volunteers to help brace up walls that were already past rescue.

Butch walked over to the entrance of the mine, cautious of the ground under his feet. Two hands emerged from the shaft entrance. Joe pulled himself up and stared over at the Lucky 7 before passing out. Butch gently eased him out the rest of the way as the trembling continued beneath them.

Clete ran up to them and grabbed Joe from Butch. "Where's Bret?" he screamed. "What have you done with my son?"

"Bret. . .wouldn't come up."

"Where? Where did you leave him? Which tunnel?"

"Ahhh. Can't remember. Dead end. Right. . .and right. . .dead end."

Butch pushed Clete away. "Is he under the saloon, Joe?"

"NOOOOO!" Clete dived down the ladder.

Joe shook his head. "It's no good. He's dead."

CHAPTER 48

Lanterns lit up the sky around the collapsed Lucky 7 Saloon. Clete watched from the sheriff's office as they pulled bodies out—some still breathing, others not so lucky. One after another were brought out into the street, and in one prone form after another Clete did not see his son. After he lost Winnie he thought he would lose his mind but he didn't because of Bret. Bret was his life, his future. Bret owned the Ponderosa now. Bret couldn't be dead. If Ben's sons could live after every torturous act, so could Bret.

Clete ran to where the men were digging, working to get down into the Golden Cross through the hole in the floor of the Lucky 7. He pulled two men away and grabbed a shovel. "My son is buried alive!"

They had made some progress through the rock, but not enough. Clete could imagine Bret trapped under some timbering, enough wood holding the ceiling up over him, but he couldn't move, couldn't talk, maybe he was out cold, but he wasn't dead. Clete dug steadily, methodically, thinking only of finding his son safe. This was worse than losing a wife, because a wife had been a stranger who became a friend. His son had been in his arms and heart from the very beginning of his life and everything Bret did, everything he said, was because he was a part of his parents or because Clete and Winnie raised him.

After Winnie died, Clete taught him vengeance and they both forgot about how much they had just having each other. Now all that mattered was the two of them being together again to find the life Winnie wanted for them. Once they took control of the Ponderosa, they'd have everything she ever wanted for them.

"A hand. We got a hand over here!"

Clete dropped his shovel. As five men dug out another body he walked out in the street feeling the chill of night wind. He looked up at the sky but clouds covered the stars. He prayed as good as any man already. What more does God want? He heard the sounds behind him change from loud and hurried to slow and soft.

Two men brought the body out into the street and laid him at Clete's feet. Clete fell to his knees. Bret's face was smashed, barely recognizable. Gently, Clete stroked his hair. "I killed my son." Clete pulled his son's broken body close and tears streamed down his face. Clete took his last chance to hold his son, and his first.

***

While the rescue proceeded, Roy insisted Joe steal a couple hours sleep in one of the jail cells. Joe fell asleep instantly and woke restless. He needed to see Pa and his brothers. Roy explained that Hoss and Adam had been caught in the landslide and were taken home, and the doctor was with them. "You can't do anything there, boy. Stay here until you feel stronger."

Joe limped out of the cell despite Roy's persistence. "No, Roy. I got to get home."

"You'd not make it, the shape you're in. I'll bring you back in the morning."

"I don't want Pa worrying anymore."

"The doc told him that you're safe in town." But Roy saw his argument futile against Joe's determination. "I'll ride back with you." Roy followed Joe out on the walk.

"Roy, you can't. You're beater than me." Joe looked over where the commotion was dying out at the collapsed saloon.

"I got more gumption than you think, son. And I want to know how your brothers are doing myself." He pointed into the street. "Look over yonder."

They saw Clete holding his dead son in the middle of the street.

"Are you going to throw him in jail?"

"Depends, Joe. If I got something to throw him in jail for."

"Not tonight you don't."

316

At Joe's singular decision, Butch got to his feet behind them. "Yes, he does. I want him in jail for the death of Val Blessing."

"Butch, you can't mean that," Roy said. "Just because some of his men took over the drive and Val got caught in a stampede---."

"It's a plenty good reason, sheriff. Besides, they also admitted, practically, that he had Adam shot. Joe, can you forgive that?"

Joe looked down at the ground. "It ain't easy." When he looked back into the street, his expression had softened. "But he has no fight left. He's lost and he knows it."

Clete laid his son down gently and got to his feet.

Joe walked over to Clete. "I'm sorry about your son. I didn't want it to happen. I couldn't get him to come out with me, is all."

Clete drew himself up to a firm, strong stature. In the pale glow of the street lamps he appeared as though he could see perfectly clear for the first time in his life. "He's not my son. He's Winnie's son." At Joe's surprised expression, he nodded. "I couldn't make him proud of me." His hand slipped down to the gun hanging awkward on his hip.

Joe's hand rose as though to offer a handshake, but instead he turned away. Clete saw Butch talking in earnest to Roy. He looked back at Joe, walking toward his horse. He pulled his gun from his holster.

"Joe, watch out!" Roy yelled.

Joe threw himself to the ground as a bullet sailed wide off mark. He turned, rolling, and fired one back at Clete as Clete aimed again. He took Joe's bullet square in the chest. He dropped his gun, looked down at Bret and fell, landing on top of his son.

Joe slowly got to his feet. He watched as Roy and Butch leaned over Clete. Roy put two fingers on his neck.

"He's dead." Roy looked up. "You know, I never seen him wear a gun before today."

"Yeah," Butch said. "I got the feeling Van Remus didn't know where to aim." He scratched his head. "Is that possible?"

"I wouldn't have thought so." Roy took off his spectacles and looked at them thoughtfully.

"He wasn't trying to kill me." Joe stared at the gun in his hand. "He wanted to kill himself."

"Maybe." Roy put his glasses back on. "But maybe not. It was self-defense, Joe, don't go feeling bad." He patted Joe's shoulder. "Butch, help me get them over to the funeral parlor. He'll be pounding boxes into next year with all this new business. Joe," Roy called over his shoulder. "Go on into my office, I'll ride on back to the ranch with ya when we're done here."

Not even fifteen minutes later Roy returned, but Joe was gone.

***

Norma came down the stairs to see Ben strapping on his gun. "Ben, are you leaving?"

"My family isn't all here yet." He looked wistfully up the stairs. "Adam?"

"The doctor is finished."

Ben wanted to race up the stairs but held himself back. He couldn't find the words to ask. "I better see if I can find Joe."

Norma stopped him with a hand on his arm. "It's after nine. You haven't had a good night's sleep for days."

"How is he, Norma?"

"I think Dr. Martin would---." She saw Ben's eyebrows raise as he looked up the stairs.

Dr. Martin stopped halfway down the stairs. "Well, Mr. Cartwright, he survived the operation. That's the most important thing."

318

"Can I see him?"

"Not right now. I'm going to watch him the next couple hours." He went back up the stairs.

"Still alive." He threw his arms around Norma, mindful of her arm. "Still alive." He strode to the door. "I've got to find Joe."

"I want Joe found too, Ben. But surely Roy will---."

He touched her cheek gently. "You get some sleep. You've done far more than was ever expected of you."

"Please don't linger on it." Norma sensed Ben's thoughts as he looked back up the stairs. "Ben, Adam did what he had to do. He saved Hoss's life. If I hadn't seen his state of mind before he left here, I would have agreed that his leaving wasn't like him. But he had to go."

"I know." Ben headed for the front door. "But if he dies, I'll never live with myself." The door closed softly behind him.

A mile down the trail Ben saw three Indians on horses heading toward him. Even in the dark he could tell they pulled Cochise. The riders pulled up short and waited for Ben's approach. Kudwa held Joe, passed out against him.

Kudwa jumped down, still hanging on to Joe. "We looked at the trees. They will grow again. The land will become strong again. Found this one trying to come home."

Both spoke their own language but understanding between them didn't need words. Kudwa helped Ben mount with Joe.

"I am very grateful to you, Kudwa. And to your friends." Ben nodded at them. "It is late, please come and stay the night. I have warm beds in the bunkhouse. Please. You'll get plenty of good food."

"We are grateful to you, for love shared has the strength of tree roots," and Kudwa accepted the invitation to stay at the ranch and rest.

Ben got his third nomadic son settled for the night with Jessup's attention and found the Indians comfortable bunks. He sent Hop Sing out with food and plenty of water and told Kudwa that as soon as Adam awoke, Kudwa would be invited to see him.

When he went back in, Norma was in front of the fire holding a brandy for him. "Hold it right there a moment." He checked first on Hoss and Little Joe. Hoss was a little flushed but sleeping easier. Joe had ripped open his wound and was being tended by Dr. Jessup.

"He'll be fine, Ben, the bleeding is all on the outside," John nodded down at the boy. "Just totally exhausted. I have a feeling he'll have some story to tell us in the morning."

Ben nodded. "Can I see Adam now?"

"Dr. Martin is still with him. Why don't we both go in?" He followed Ben down the hall but grabbed Ben's arm before he could walk in. "Ben, I'm going to ask Dr. Martin to stay here in Virginia City. I'm heading back to Genoa, where I can set up a quieter practice."

"What are you trying to say, John?"

"I think the growing demands of Virginia City call for someone younger and more progressive, like Paul Martin. Help me talk him into it, Ben. He's needed here."

"You can both stay. There's enough demand for two doctors here."

When they walked in Ben saw Hop Sing, who faced the moon muted by clouds through the parting of trees out the window. As they approached the bed Ben could hear him praying under his breath. Dr. Martin sat on the side of Adam's bed, working some sort of fancy apparatus covering part of his son's face. In alarmed reflex Ben reached forward but John stopped him. The bag attached to the apparatus moved rhythmically, keeping time with Adam's chest.

"Paul knows what he's doing."

320

Felling of the Sons

With a trembling hand Ben stroked his son's arm. John patted Paul's shoulder and left the room. "What is that?" Ben asked Dr. Martin.

"We have to encourage his breathing. This device is connected to an air pump to help keep his lungs working." Dr. Martin took Adam's pulse again. "No change. If the pulse picks up even just a few beats more per minute, I think we can try letting him breathe on his own."

"When will we know?"

"He'll make it through the night or he won't. Go get some sleep, Ben. Hop Sing, you too. John and I have arranged to take turns sitting up."

"No. I'll stay. I have to tell him. . .there are some things we left unsaid." Ben pulled up a chair and sat as Paul continued working his apparatus. He took his son's hand but the words he wanted weren't there.

Norma poked her head in. "Do you mind, Ben? John said I could come in for a minute." Ben looked at Dr. Martin, who nodded. She walked to Ben's side and held out the brandy, smiling at Hop Sing as he left the room. Ben took the brandy and swallowed it quickly. "He looks better. It was scary," she sighed. "You did a real fine job, Dr. Martin."

"Only if he lives," Paul said.

"You've been through hell and back, Ben. I don't know how you're managing. But I can see where the boys get their constitution from."

"It's been a hard life, building the Ponderosa. We all feel a deep debt to the land, but little enough compared to how we feel for each other. If I had lost one of them, you'd see a much different man sitting here."

Norma rubbed his shoulder with her good hand. "Go on."

"It's hard when people see you a certain way, and you feel another. Sometimes, you just…" Quiet sobs racked his chest.

Norma stroked his shoulders until he calmed down. She took his hands and pulled him over to the window. "You need to pay some attention to yourself, Ben." She tiptoed to reach his lips. He held her there, feeling her heart, tasting his tears on her lips, for as long as she let him.

"Thank you, Norma. I do need to know that I have help."

"I'll always be here for you, Ben. You just have to ask." She limped to the door but Ben didn't answer. He stared at his once strong, now silent son half hidden in a mask and took his hand. She watched him another moment and left, shutting the door softly behind her.

Dr. Martin took Adam's pulse again, watching Ben as he squeezed Adam's hand. There was something very strong here, something he hadn't seen in quite some time. Chances were this boy would make it. There…the pulse quickened, just a little. He waited a full two minutes to see if it would drop again and removed the breathing pump from Adam's face, standing ready in case his move was premature.

Ben stood. "Doctor?"

Paul nodded. This was the best part of his job, where it seemed the patient might recover, after all.

CHAPTER 49

The sun rose on a new day behind dull gray clouds. A deep mist formed on Lake Tahoe and spread itself around tall Ponderosa pine. Hop Sing kept his mind from other matters by making the largest breakfast ever.

Norma brought a light gayness with her down the stairs. "Oh Hop Sing, breakfast smells divine! Is there anything I can help you with?"

"Miss Norma sit, have coffee. You earn special place at table today."

"Now Hop Sing, don't get too used to me. Today I get to go back and see if my home is still standing."

"Home? You leave here? But you are...Mr. Cartlight is---."

"No, I don't think Mr. Cartlight is at all." She smiled weakly. "I saw something last night, Hop Sing, up there in Adam's room, and I don't think I can compete."

The front door opened and Ben walked in, followed by Kudwa, Oshwabekona and Lutwena. Kudwa nodded at Hop Sing and stared at Norma as the other two looked up at the ceiling.

"Hop Sing, our guests are staying for breakfast. Make plenty of food, all right?"

"Yes, Mr. Cartlight."

"Wait, don't run off yet." He introduced Hop Sing and Norma to their house guests and explained how he found them bringing Joe home.

"PA!"

Ben ran to the edge of the stairs. Hoss and Joe stood on the landing, grinning at him. "What are you two doing out of bed?"

"You don't think you can keep a Cartwright down, do you?" Joe laughed.

"Now there will be no more talk like that, young man. You've had enough roaming for a while. And keep your voices down. You don't want to disturb your brother."

"Who, Adam?" Hoss said with a snort. "He's already awake and ornery as ever."

"He's what?!" Ben took the stairs two at a time. He patted Joe and Hoss on the back as they allowed him to walk into Adam's room ahead of them. John and Paul were both there, and John was checking Adam's heart.

Adam appeared groggy, but his color had returned, just a little, and he wore that familiar smirk. "Pa, where you been?" His voice was low and throaty. "Those sons of yours are tormenting me and me on my death bed yet."

"Your death bed, ha!" Hoss laughed. "St. Peter saw you coming and clanged them big pearly gate doors shut real fast!"

"Yeah, Adam, you should try smiling," Joe added. "It works better than that scowl of yours."

"Ha ha." Adam's eyes picked up just a bit of a spark.

Ben grinned widely as he listened to their banter. Hoss and Joe didn't know how close their brother had come, and Ben saw no reason to share it with them now.

"Say, Pa," Joe said, looking around the room. "Shouldn't Ma be in here, too? Not much of a family reunion without---." He saw the faces staring soberly back at him. "What'd I say?"

Hoss started to laugh.

Ben joined in, but only briefly. He knew what Norma had been through, and besides, laughing pained his eldest. "All right, now, Joe

324

has had a head injury, and his head isn't quite the granite of Hoss's. Joe, there's been a misunderstanding."

"You mean she's not…" Joe laughed until he stopped to hold his aching side. "Oh, well, having a ma was nice for a while anyhow."

"What," Adam coughed, squeezing his eyes shut. "What about Van Remus?"

"Oh boy, leave it to Adam to get serious," Hoss said, still laughing, until the look Ben shot him quieted him down.

Joe didn't find the topic amusing either.

Ben cleared his throat. "Joe, do you want to tell us what happened yesterday? Did you find Bret?"

"I found him, Pa." He covered his face as the memory ran fresh. "The Golden Cross caved in on Bret last night, taking the Lucky 7 with it. Clete, I think, went insane at the end, Pa. He shot at me but only meaning to get me to shoot back. They're both dead."

Ben looked down at Adam. He wanted them all to feel relieved. But the questions in Adam's eyes remained.

"All right, everyone out, Joe can finish what sounds like a very long story later," John said, noting the exchange between father and eldest son. He nodded at Dr. Martin. "Our patient has a long recovery ahead of him and we're delaying him."

"Joe," Adam whispered. "Glad you made it home."

Joe grinned, leaning on Hoss. "Hey, brother, you too, and with this big lug yet."

"Ha! If it wasn't for me, you two fellas would still be laying around the house."

The three brothers exchanged grins and Hoss and Joe led each other out of the room.

"John, Dr. Martin, Adam and I will never be able to thank you enough. Please, go down and help yourself to one of Hop Sing's special breakfasts."

"Sounds like an ideal plan to me," Paul patted Adam's leg before leaving the room.

"You're a fortunate man, Ben." John followed Dr. Martin out.

Ben gently brushed his backhand against Adam's forehead. Still so cool. "Adam, you've always been rational. To leave this house, you knew the risk---."

"Did you just do whatever Sutter told you? No matter what?"

Ben stared at his son's pale face, at the face he feared he would never see alive again. Leave it to his eldest to stick to the issue, no matter what. "I worked for Sutter, and yes, most of what he asked of me, I did. If you wonder why I went along with stopping Van Remus from having a piece of land, I went along out of respect for Sutter's judgment. He wanted to work with the Mexicans because the Mexicans lived more communally, which was Sutter's dream at New Helvetia. And we know what happened after Marshall's discovery."

"Was it right?"

"You don't remember much about our life there, or how beautiful the valley was. You've seen the way it's become since the gold rush. Sutter had a perfect community, a trading post, acres of farming land, everyone working together. He wanted to control it all. Now that may not sound right, but once he lost control, that pristine beauty disappeared. Sutter told me if he could have kept all the gold for himself he would have, but there was no way to buy every American off. I think he meant that as a joke."

"Why didn't Van Remus have a right to that parcel of land?"

Ben looked at his hands unclenching in his lap. "Van Remus knew Sutter and I talked about putting a sawmill there. He and Winnie knew we'd say no to their request. They were trouble from the start, Adam, unreasonable trouble."

"And the Americans found out about gold anyway." Adam seemed to gain strength as they talked, and for that reason Ben felt confidence in sharing what he never could before. Whatever helped Adam heal now was a good thing.

"I never thought I would say this aloud, Adam, but in the war of 1846, I had hoped for just a little while that the Mexicans would win. But Sutter had no regrets after the Americans won the war, and the situation at the fort actually improved for a while. Sutter tried to suppress what had been found at the sawmill race[13], tried to keep control of the land after Marshall found that gold, even tried to pan for gold himself but he wasn't good at it. He knew, I think, deep down that he had put himself in the middle of a very difficult situation."

"Did the war start over gold?"

Ben grimaced, remembering how they'd once discussed that possibility because the discovery of gold so soon after the war ended seemed too coincidental. "We'll never know that, Adam."

Adam coughed, his voice barely a whisper. "How did you keep from feeling guilty over what you did to Van Remus?"

Ben only shook his head. "He and his wife were always a miserable sort. They drove people out of the valley, killed Indians on little more than a whisper, and were in debt to Sutter for more that they could ever hope to repay. Still he let them stay. To this day I don't know why. We fought them – because they asked to be fought. Nothing more."

"Life is never that simple. But had they been honest people, all this could have ended differently."

"Winnie's death was not your fault."

---

[13] Dillon, 277-283. Also, in Sutter's own words: "I told the men that it would be necessary to keep the matter secret for five or six weeks, the time necessary to finish the construction of my sawmill, on which I had already spent $24,000." From *Sutter's Gold* by Blaise Cendrars, translated from the French by Henry Longan Stuart (New York: Harper & Brothers, 1926), 84.

"She was there to kill you. I saw her loading, thought she was you, at first." Noting Ben's surprise, Adam smiled briefly. "You never promised moving west would be easy."

Ben saw Kudwa standing in the doorway and waved him in. Kudwa said a few words in Paiute, and Adam's hand raised slightly. Kudwa reached Adam's side and put a feather in his hand. As Ben watched, they grasped each other's hand, the feather tight between them. Kudwa said something else low and slow, and Adam seemed to understand.

Ben left the room. They had more to talk about, but they had time. Kudwa deserved his time with Adam. What they shared together was also the result of what happened to a twelve-year-old boy — the good result.

When he got to the top step he froze suddenly, hand gripping the railing. Adam said, "I saw her loading." After they found the dead woman, just before Van Remus ran over to them, Sutter told Ben he thought he'd heard a gunshot, but then an Indian woman told him she'd found his son huddled behind the house sobbing, and all other matters were forgotten. Could the gunshot and not Adam's yelling have started the stampede? He and Adam had more talking to do, Ben thought with a small grin. A lot more.

Hoss and Joe were sitting at the breakfast table when Ben came down. The Indians were offered seats but instead took their plates and sat on the floor. "Where's John?" Ben asked as he sat next to Norma.

Joe looked down guiltily. "He asked me about the Lucky 7 Saloon collapsing into the mine and rode off back for town."

Dr. Martin dug in. "I'll tell you, I feel guilty sitting here eating this fine food, but this high Sierra air sure gives a body an appetite. I'm going to ride off as soon as I'm comfortable with Adam's progress to give John a hand. Sounds like he's needed one for days now."

"Some days are like that." Hoss stared at the food as though he couldn't remember how to eat.

Joe nodded at the Indians. "Pa, did you leave Kudwa up there?"

"He's good medicine." Ben noticed Norma staring down at her fork. Ben picked up his coffee cup. "I would like to propose a toast. To Norma. This house would not have stayed together without her."

"Oh, Ben," she looked up, flushing. "It's been my pleasure. To help you and your sons." She looked down again. "I think everyone should eat up before the food gets cold."

Hoss laughed until he noticed Joe trying to send Ben signals with his eyes to talk to Norma, and with a sheepish grin looked up at the ceiling, or everywhere but at Ben and Norma. Ben only cleared his throat and looked down at his plate.

"Well," Dr. Martin said, taking a sip of coffee. "I've got a patient I don't quite trust yet. But I'm sure it won't be long before I can leave him in very capable hands here." He noticed two Cartwright sons staring at their plates. "These two young men need to settle back into their beds, instead of sitting up and staring at food they don't have much appetite for. Joe and Hoss, upstairs with me."

Hoss pushed away from the food. "I kinda wondered why nothing smelled so good. I thought maybe Hop Sing lost his touch."

"You didn't get permission to be at this table, is why," Ben scolded.

Joe got to his feet. "Ma'am, even though you're not my real ma, I sure did enjoy knowing you that way, for a while." He winked at her and at Ben, and followed Dr. Martin and Hoss up the stairs.

"Ben, I didn't mean to make everyone uncomfortable."

"It's a good thing you did. As happy as I was to have my boys at the table, I don't want them out of bed a minute sooner than they should be. Not a second time, anyway."

Norma picked up her fork with a shaking hand.

"Norma," Ben stood and put his big warm hands on her shoulders. "I don't want you to think that because I don't need you here anymore, that. . .I don't need you here anymore. I would be pleased, and happy, if you'd agree to see me again."

"Ben, you don't have to---."

"Just a minute. Some people think I've got all I need up here on the Ponderosa." He picked up her hand and kissed it. "Now it's true that my boys mean the world to me. But even I can see beyond my sons to the real reason I married three different women."

Norma smiled up at him. "I'd love to see you again."

Hoss and Joe were listening at the top of the stairs. "What do you think, Joe? We gonna get ourselves a new ma?"

"I'll tell you what, Hoss," Joe said, yawning. "I did what I could, by calling her Ma. I'll let you and Adam worry about it now."

"Oh yeah, and I'll just bet you're gonna say you never really thought she was your ma, after that silly little bump you took to the head. Look at mine, look at this one here, and it don't bother me one bit."

"Oh yeah? Did you see what it did to your appetite? You'll be as little as me in no time! Littler! We'll call you Little Hoss!"

"Boys!" Ben hollered up the stairs. "You're recuperating!"

Their voices dwindled away. The two Indians got up and crept over to the table with their now empty plates, eyeing Ben. When he nodded, they sat gingerly in chairs and refilled their plates. Ben took Norma's arm and they walked to the door, where she stopped him.

"Ben? Being here made me realize how strong your wives must have been and how hard it was for you to lose them."

"Yes, they were strong." He looked up the stairs. "As are their sons."

She touched his cheek. "You're another reason for that."

Ben wrapped his arms around her to kiss her proper. He looked over his shoulder to see the Indians staring at them. "How about a little morning air?" Norma nodded as she caught her breath. Ben led her out to get their fill of each other in the crisp morning air.

Hop Sing came out with another plate of food in time to see them leave. When he saw the two Indians enjoying themselves heartily on his cuisine, he described all the wonderful things he prepared. The Indians listened as they ate, fascinated by the pride in his voice as he talked. After Hop Sing went back into the kitchen, they dug in again, making sure nothing went to waste.

Kudwa came down the stairs without the eagle feather. "We will go now, back to our land. We will tell our people that with our help, though some trees died, many more live." He grabbed a handful of biscuits and bacon and his companions followed him out the door.

When Hop Sing came back out, the dining room was empty and very messy. His grin broke out into wide laughter. He winced briefly and rubbed his bruised temple but laughed again, filling the house with his glee as he cleared the dishes away.

ABOUT THE AUTHOR

An avid tree fan, Bebow-Reinhard first loved Bonanza for its trees, and its horses. She was only six when the series started, but it quickly became her all-time favorite, and is delighted that this early western was in color, because that, and its storylines, means the show will never feel dated.

She earned a master's in history in 2006, at a time when she started penning her 2nd Bonanza novel, **Mystic Fire**, first published in 2009, and due to be released in 2nd edition later in 2017. She has since had three other novels published; **Dancing with Cannibals**, co-authored at published through KDP; **Adventures in Death & Romance: Vrykolakas Tales** by Solstice Shadows; and **Grimm's American Macabre,** by All Things that Matter Press, who is releasing another novel, **Saving Boone: Legend of a Half-White Son,** in 2017.

Like Bonanza, she loves to imbue real history tales with fictional characters, because we will never know all the people who peppered our history. Like David Dortort, she is dedicated to family; her master's thesis was on a great-uncle of her grandfather who was in the army from 1862 through 1884 and said "We didn't try hard to catch the Indians. We could see they were good people." She is proud to note that Bonanza, too, has this sensibility toward the native peoples, noting that they were good people. Her Grimm's collection is in honor of her own Grimm background, and is penned with the name Lizbeth Grimm.

With Bonanza's influence she had three children of her own, and is also a proud grandma.

You can find more on the author and her works, and the story of how she came to be an authorized Bonanza novelist, at www.grimmsetc.com where you'll also find her contact information, including free Bonanza offers.

Made in the USA
San Bernardino, CA
17 February 2018